Discover the

'A high level of reali[...]ck and fast. Like the father c[...]orsyth, Mariani has a knack [...]e fears and preoccupations of their time'

Shots Magazine

'The plot was thrilling . . . but what is all the more thrilling is the fantastic way Mariani moulds historical events into his story'

Guardian

'Scott Mariani is an ebook powerhouse'

The Bookseller

'Hums with energy and pace . . . If you like your conspiracies twisty, your action bone-jarring, and your heroes impossibly dashing, then look no further. The Ben Hope series is exactly what you need'

Mark Dawson

'Slick, serpentine, sharp, and very, very entertaining. If you've got a pulse, you'll love Scott Mariani; if you haven't, then maybe you crossed Ben Hope'

Simon Toyne

'Hits thrilling, suspenseful notes . . . a rollickingly good way to spend some time in an easy chair'

USA Today

'Mariani constructs the thriller with skill and intelligence, staging some good action scenes, and Hope is an appealing protagonist'

'If you haven't read any Mariani before but love fast-paced action with a historical reference, maybe this one won't be your last'

'A breathtaking ride through England and Europe'

'This is my first Scott Mariani book . . . and I totally loved it. It goes on at a good pace, and for me Ben Hope was brilliant, the ultimate decent good guy that you are rooting for'

'Scott Mariani writes fantastic thrillers. His series of Ben Hope books shows no sign of slowing down'

'A really excellent series of books, and would make a wonderful television series as well!'

'Scott Mariani seamlessly weaves the history and action together. His descriptive passages are highly visual, and no word is superfluous. The storyline flows from beginning to end; I couldn't put it down'

THE TUDOR DECEPTION

Scott Mariani is the author of the worldwide-acclaimed action-adventure thriller series featuring ex-SAS hero Ben Hope, which has sold millions of copies in Scott's native UK alone. His books have been described as 'James Bond meets Jason Bourne, with a historical twist'. The first Ben Hope book, *The Alchemist's Secret*, spent six straight weeks at #1 on Amazon's Kindle chart, and all the others have been *Sunday Times* bestsellers. Scott was born in Scotland, studied in Oxford and now lives and writes in a remote setting in rural west Wales. You can find out more about Scott and his work on his official website: www.scottmariani.com

By the same author:

Ben Hope series
The Alchemist's Secret
The Mozart Conspiracy
The Doomsday Prophecy
The Heretic's Treasure
The Shadow Project
The Lost Relic
The Sacred Sword
The Armada Legacy
The Nemesis Program
The Forgotten Holocaust
The Martyr's Curse
The Cassandra Sanction
Star of Africa
The Devil's Kingdom
The Babylon Idol
The Bach Manuscript
The Moscow Cipher
The Rebel's Revenge
Valley of Death
House of War
The Pretender's Gold
The Demon Club
The Pandemic Plot
The Crusader's Cross
The Silver Serpent
Graveyard of Empires
The White Knight

To find out more visit **www.scottmariani.com**

SCOTT MARIANI

THE

TUDOR
DECEPTION

Harper
North

HarperNorth
Windmill Green
Mount Street
Manchester M2 3NX

A division of
HarperCollins*Publishers*
1 London Bridge Street
London SE1 9GF

www.harpercollins.co.uk

HarperCollins*Publishers*
Macken House, 39/40 Mayor Street Upper
Dublin 1, D01 C9W8, Ireland

First published by HarperNorth in 2023

1 3 5 7 9 10 8 6 4 2

Copyright © Scott Mariani 2023

Scott Mariani asserts the moral right to
be identified as the author of this work

A catalogue record for this book
is available from the British Library

ISBN: 978-0-00-860112-6

Printed and bound in Great Britain by
CPI Group (UK) Ltd, Croydon

MIX
Paper | Supporting
responsible forestry
FSC
www.fsc.org
FSC™ C007454

This book is produced from independently certified FSC™ paper
to ensure responsible forest management.

For more information visit: www.harpercollins.co.uk/green

'Shall I be plain? I wish the bastards dead.
And I would have it suddenly performed.'
William Shakespeare, *Richard III*,
Act IV, Scene ii

'That which has always been accepted by everyone,
everywhere, is almost certain to be false.'
Paul Valéry, poet and philosopher

PROLOGUE

Co. Galway, Ireland
2005

While they'd been inside the pub a veil of clouds had drawn over to blot out the stars, and now a heavy downpour was lashing the pavements of the small fishing village. Aurora looked up at the sky, pulled a face and said, 'Ugh.'

'Doesn't look like it's about to let up any time soon,' Ben said, hunting for his car keys. 'We'll have to make a run for it.' The Interceptor was parked fifty yards down the rain-slicked street. He was glad he hadn't left the top down.

Aurora pointed at the keys in his hand. 'So are you going to let me drive back?' she asked, smiling at him. He couldn't tell if she was being serious, or just teasing. Her eyes flashed in the lights of the pub doorway. Inside, the band had started up another number, a rousing rendition of the old tune *Whiskey in the Jar*.

'Oh, I don't know about that,' he replied. Ben was liking Aurora much more than he'd been initially willing to admit to himself.

She giggled and nudged him with her elbow. 'You promised you'd let me have a go of your speed machine. And you've had too many pints of Guinness anyway.'

Maybe she had a point there. Even though he felt perfectly sober and it was extremely unlikely they'd encounter any Garda patrol cars in the few miles of quiet country lanes between here and Ben's remote house up the coast, it probably wasn't worth taking the risk of a drink-driving charge. Relenting, he handed her the keys and said with a show of reluctance, 'Fine, all right, then. You win.'

Aurora's smile widened to a beaming grin. 'Excellent. Come on. I'll race you to the car.'

The rain was coming down even harder. Just then, Ben realised that he'd left his jacket inside the pub, slung over the seat of the cosy little corner where they'd spent the evening. 'Shit. Hold on. Tell you what, you get the engine warmed up and I'll be there in a minute.'

Aurora nodded eagerly, pulled her own jacket up over her head and made a run for the car, moving with that long-limbed dancer's stride he was getting to know well, though they'd met only so recently. Ben hurried back inside the pub and pushed his way through the throng to their alcove. Up on the stage the band were belting out, '*I first produced me pistol and I then produced me rapier / saying "Stand and Deliver" for he were a bold deceiver . . .*'

Ben got back to their seats to find that another couple had occupied them – but his old brown leather jacket was still where he'd left it, unmolested. He grabbed it and pushed his way back towards the entrance. As he emerged from the doorway he could see Aurora down the street, unlocking the car door. The rain was lashing more heavily than ever, hitting the pavements with such force that the drops bounced on impact. So much for a beautiful May night. He shrugged on his jacket and went to go running down the street after her.

That was when Ben saw him again. The tall thin man with the thick glasses and the widow's peak. The same man he'd seen outside the Dublin hotel the day he'd gone to meet Mortimer. Watching him, or so it had seemed at the time.

Ben hadn't been sure of his instincts then, but he was sure now that seeing the same man again here tonight, right across the other side of Ireland in this tiny coastal village in County Galway, couldn't be any sort of coincidence. The guy had crossed to the other side of the street, walking from the direction of the car, hands in pockets, head ducked under the rain showing his high forehead and receding hairline. He was moving quickly, as though he was more than just in a hurry to get out of the wet.

Ben stared at him. This time it was the tall man who sensed he was being watched. He paused in his stride and glanced across the street, making eye contact for a brief moment. Then he looked away again and walked on, faster.

Ben called out, 'Hey, you. Stop.'

The tall man shot Ben another startled look. Then he took off like a hare.

Ben jumped down the steps of the pub entrance, hit the street running and went after him. The guy had about a thirty-yard start on him and he was light and fast on his feet. But Ben was faster, and he'd soon catch up. From behind him down the street, he heard the throaty eight-cylinder roar reverberate off the buildings as Aurora fired up the Jensen. She couldn't have noticed Ben emerge from the pub and go chasing after this total stranger.

Ben was almost on the guy now. Sprinting hard, pounding through puddles, ready for trouble. He expected the guy to resist him, and to fight back hard. He just didn't know why, or what the hell the tall man's interest in him was. But he'd soon find out.

Except he wouldn't.

Because at that moment, just as Ben's hand was reaching for the man's collar and he was about to grab a hold and pull him to the ground, the car blew up in a fiery eruption and a percussive blast that filled the street behind him.

Ben stopped running. He slithered to a halt on the wet pavement. Turned to gape at the explosion. The escaping figure of the man was completely forgotten.

He yelled 'AURORA!'

Chapter 1

One week earlier

Ben Hope sat alone on the barnacled flat slab of rock that jutted out over the pebbly beach. He liked to spend a lot of time here when he wasn't working, doing exactly what he was doing now, deep in thought as he smoked a Gauloise cigarette and gazed silently at the cold grey Atlantic waves rolling in.

He had just finished a twelve-mile run, which was two miles more than his usual daily routine, pounding up and down the long, deserted beach, over rocks and dunes and along the winding cliff paths high above the crashing surf. His legs were still on fire and his system was buzzing from the adrenaline and endorphins that flooded his body during hard exercise. Now at rest, he'd lit his sixth or seventh cigarette of the morning and uncapped the battered old flask he carried with him for a slug or two of whisky. Which soon turned into three or four, and on until the flask would be empty.

Staying in peak physical condition while recklessly abusing his body seemed like a strangely conflicted sort of lifestyle, he knew that. Winnie knew it, too, and worried for him. 'You'll wear yourself out, Ben,' she always warned, with that long-suffering look of a helpless observer watching someone they cared about slowly burning themselves to the ground.

He didn't give a shit about wearing himself out. Did. Not. Give. A. Shit. He said it to himself again, repeating it like a catechism.

Once more, everyone;
I
Do
Not
Give
A
Shit.

Winnie understood the darkness in him, knew what drove him. It was what had driven him for years, through the wild crazy days of his youth and then through all the years in the military and Special Forces, pushing him to the limit of his capabilities and sometimes threatening to tip over the edge.

She was the only person alive, apart from him, who had been there through all the worst times that had torn the family apart. Winnie was all too well aware that he'd never listen to her warnings. But she loved him like a mother, and so she still went on warning him anyway, and tolerated it with infinite calm and patience when he fought back against her.

Some days were darker than others, when his mood was low and memories haunted him. There was never any telling when they'd return.

Today was one of those darker days.

The flask was empty. Ben tossed the stub of his Gauloise into the surf, then reached for the crumpled blue pack and his Zippo lighter to fire up another. That was when his phone began to vibrate silently in his pocket. He fished it out. The call was from an unknown number.

'Who is this?'

The man's voice on the line sounded a little uncertain. Which could have been from the abrupt tone of Ben's reply, but it wasn't unusual for his clients to sound that way when they first made contact.

'Uh, ah, I trust I have the right number. Am I speaking to Mr Hope, Mr Benedict Hope?'

Ben said, 'And you are?'

'I'm sorry. My name is Mortimer, Hugh Mortimer. I got your contact from Jessica Hunter, on Jersey. Carl's mother. She's a friend of my ex-wife's. They play tennis together.'

Nearly all of Ben's clients came to him this way, by word of mouth. He didn't advertise his services, due to the delicate nature of what he did for a living. The Carl Hunter kidnapping episode was still fresh in his mind, even though it had taken place a year earlier and he'd been involved in several cases since, across Europe and beyond. When innocent and vulnerable young people went missing at the hands of ruthless, greedy criminals and the police were unable to get them back safely in one piece, that was when desperate families resorted to unconventional means of retrieving their loved ones. Ben was it.

In a warmer tone Ben said, 'Okay, Mr Mortimer, and what is it I can do for you?'

'Ah, uh, it's a matter I'm reluctant to discuss over the phone. Would it be possible to meet in person?'

Clients often said that. Again, it was in the nature of Ben's line of business that some things were too sensitive, too secret or too plain upsetting, to talk about by telephone.

'That might be possible,' Ben said.

'Jessica didn't tell me where you're based. I understand that you prefer to keep your location a secret. I live in York, but I'm happy to travel anywhere to meet you. It's very important.'

Mortimer was right about Ben's protecting his location on the west coast of Ireland. He didn't like clients coming to his private residence. When you helped people in a particular kind of need, and used the particular methodologies that Ben brought to the table, you needed to be very cautious about exposure.

'I can meet you in Dublin,' Ben said. 'You might be able to get a direct flight there from York.' Dublin was just a three-hour drive for Ben in his old but fast V8 Jensen Interceptor. He frequented the city now and then, and had a few favourite hangouts of the fairly rough and ready, spit-and-sawdust variety where the music was live and loud, the crowds were boisterous and raucous, the Guinness and the whiskey flowed freely and fistfights weren't unknown to break out for no apparent reason.

Mortimer sounded pleased. 'That's excellent. I happen to know Dublin quite well. What about the Merrion, say 1 p.m. tomorrow?'

The Merrion was a five-star luxury hotel right in the heart of the city. A far cry from those hangouts of Ben's. He said, 'I'll be there.'

'Thank you so much. I can't tell you what this means to me.'

When the call was over, Ben left his flat rock and headed up the steep shingle beach towards the lonely old house. His home stood alone not far from the shore, exposed to the battering of the coastal winds and frequent rain. The place was much too big for a single guy and the faithful old housekeeper who'd looked after the Hope family for many years and stayed loyal to him after everyone else was gone or dead.

Ben walked inside the large, empty kitchen and headed for the cupboard where he kept his stock of whisky bottles. Hearing the creak of the door behind him, he looked around and saw Winnie standing there.

In a life that had so often been precarious and unsettled, Winnie was that rarest rock of stability to Ben. She'd been there for as long as he could recall from his earliest childhood, and never seemed to change. In truth, he'd no idea how old she was – and he'd never have dared to ask. Likewise, there were things that Winnie would never ask him, such as the exact nature and purpose of those mysterious business trips he would often take, sometimes lasting weeks on end. As far as she was concerned his professional life was still vaguely connected to his time in the military, as a technical advisor or something in that line. She didn't really care, as long as he was safe and had plenty to occupy him, warding off all those unhealthy temptations that tended to dominate his life when he wasn't working.

'I got a call just now,' he said.

'Another job?' she asked with a smile. If he was away working, then he wasn't here wasting himself away boozing.

He nodded. 'Could be. I'll be heading off tomorrow morning. I can't say how long for.'

As he talked, he reached into the cupboard for his current bottle and a small funnel, and set about refilling his empty flask. Winnie's smile fell away as she watched him, knowing as well as he did that it wouldn't stay full for very long. He was ready to say to her, 'Spare me the lecture, Win,' but she didn't make any comment.

'I got a call today as well,' she said instead. 'From my youngest niece.'

Ben did vaguely recall something about a niece. Winnie had a younger sibling back in Hampshire, who unlike her sister had done the whole marriage-and-children thing and was a mother of four, now all grown up.

'Aurora, wasn't it?' he said, digging deep in his memory for the name. 'The actress?'

'Dancer,' Winnie corrected him, then added proudly, 'She studied at Elmhurst Ballet School and the English National. I haven't seen her in so long. Now she's got a holiday and wants to come and see her old auntie. I said I'd have to ask you first. See, this is her.'

Winnie magically produced a photo print as though she'd been keeping it hidden this whole time, and showed it to him. Ben looked and saw what looked like a professional publicity shot of a very slim, very attractive chestnut-haired young woman in her early twenties, smiling a beguiling smile for the camera. It was hard to imagine the beautiful aspiring ballerina could be any kind of blood relation to her stout, slab-sided and decidedly unfeminine aunt.

'Lovely, isn't she?' Winnie said. 'And so sweet and warm and funny. It would only be for a few days. It'd be good for you to spend some time with someone more your own age. And she's single, too.'

Someone his own age. There had to be a good ten or twelve years' gap between Ben and Aurora, but in her self-assumed role as his surrogate mother Winnie often carried on as though he was still a teenager. He wondered fleetingly about her covert motivation for showing him the photo, suspecting that she might be getting up to her matchmaking ploys again. It wouldn't be the first time that she'd made such a transparent attempt to hook him up with the opposite sex, in the belief that all his troubles would be automatically spirited away if only he had 'someone to love', in the proper and lasting romantic sense of the word. Winnie seemed to be under the impression that no woman on earth could possibly resist his charms. She also seemed persuaded that if only he could find the right girl he'd instantly settle down, put this strange solitary life behind him and become a completely new and other person. Domestic bliss, fireside and slippers and a pushchair in the hall. Yeah, he could really see that happening.

None of those thoughts were visible on Ben's face as he handed back the photo and returned to filling up his flask. 'She wants to come and stay a few days? You don't even have to ask, Win. This is as much your house as mine. There's six bedrooms in the place, might as well make use of them.'

'But what about this new job of yours?' Winnie said uncertainly. 'It'll be a shame if you're not here.'

'At least you'll have some company for a change,' he replied. 'Go ahead and call her.'

It all seemed innocuous enough at that moment, and he was genuinely pleased for Winnie that she had this opportunity to catch up with her niece again.

If he'd known what was coming, he would never have let it happen.

Chapter 2

At quarter to one the next afternoon, Ben parked his Interceptor down the bustling street from the hotel, flicked away the stub of one cigarette and immediately lit another. He'd skipped breakfast and he was hungry. Early that morning he'd received another call from his prospective client Hugh Mortimer, to tell him that he'd booked himself into room 21 at the Merrion and was about to board his flight to Dublin, due to arrive in plenty of time for their 1 p.m. appointment.

As Ben was walking up towards the hotel entrance, wondering what Mortimer would have to tell him, he felt the sixth-sense tingle that told him he was being watched. He paused in his stride and looked about him, and his gaze landed on the solitary figure of a man on the opposite side of the street. The guy was standing with his back to a shop front window, talking on a mobile phone. Tall and thin in a dark coat, late thirties or early forties, with a long lean face and a high receding hairline with a widow's peak. He wore a heavy pair of black-framed glasses with lenses so thick that even from this distance Ben could see his eyes magnified like a lemur's.

Ben's observational skills, already sharp when he'd joined up in the military, had been honed by his time in Special Forces to something preternatural. His acute sense for anything out of the ordinary was one of the things that had kept him alive through all those years with the SAS. Even he had to admit, however, that his instincts sometimes got the better of him, and could be deceptive, playing tricks. There was nothing wrong with being wary, but some men he'd known and served with had been made paranoid by their experiences.

As he watched, the tall thin man with the glasses ended his call, put his phone away and folded his lanky frame into a silver Ford Focus parked at the kerbside. The Ford's indicator flashed and the car filtered out into the traffic and disappeared up the street.

Ben mentally scolded himself for imagining things, forgot about the guy and walked the rest of the way to the hotel. Stepping inside the plush lobby he was met by a female staff member with plastered-on makeup who frowned at his cigarette as if it were a lit stick of dynamite and said primly, 'Sir, this is a no-smoking area.'

Here we go again, he thought. It had been a couple of years since Ireland had become the first country in the world uncivilised enough to ban smoking in all indoor spaces, and he still hadn't quite got used to the idea. He crushed out the half-finished Gauloise and dropped it into the empty wineglass she disdainfully held out for him. He gave her his sweetest smile and thanked her. No return smile was forthcoming. Some people.

He was still a few minutes early for his rendezvous. He walked over to the reception desk, told them he'd arranged to meet for lunch with the guest in room 21. The receptionist tapped computer keys, confirmed that Professor Mortimer had checked in and said she'd buzz up to his room to tell him.

'Please tell him I'll be in the bar,' Ben said, and headed across the lobby towards it. So his would-be client was *Professor* Mortimer. That was a first in his colourful but still relatively fledgling career as a freelance 'K&R crisis consultant', as he called himself. As he walked into the crowded bar and perched on a stool he was wondering what kind of professor the guy was. He was missing his cigarette. He comforted himself instead with a double shot of Tullamore eighteen-year-old Irish whiskey. Always more effective on an empty stomach. He'd have preferred scotch, but when in Dublin …

Ben hadn't been waiting long when a man in his late fifties or thereabouts walked into the bar. He was around Ben's height, just under six feet, and looked as if he might have been quite athletic in his younger days, before he got out of shape and the paunch appeared. He peered about as if looking for someone.

Ben's clients came in all shapes and sizes. This one looked every bit the portrait of the slightly eccentric academic, with unkempt greying hair, a well-worn tweed jacket with elbow patches and very shiny shoes. Slightly tatty, but with a certain aura of wealth about him. Ben caught his eye and slipped down from the bar stool to greet him as he came over.

They made their introductions and shook hands. Mortimer thanked him warmly for coming, and said that he'd taken the liberty of booking them a table for lunch. His manner was very polite and formal. They took a seat at the rear of the bar lounge, Ben sitting with his back to the corner where he could watch both the door and window. It was an old habit of his.

Mortimer thanked him again for agreeing to meet him, and repeated how important and urgent his situation was.

Before they could get into the details a waiter appeared with lunch menus and asked if they'd like something to drink. Ben said he'd have another Tullamore. Mortimer only wanted a glass of orange juice. The drinks quickly arrived. Ben noticed Mortimer eyeing the whiskey. Out of temptation or disapproval, who could say? They placed their order for lunch, a salad for Mortimer and a steak for Ben. The waiter left.

'Now, how can I help you?' Ben asked.

The lounge bar was filled with enough people and chatter to make their conversation private. Mortimer folded his hands on the table and got straight down to business. 'You find missing children.'

In fact, most people had no idea how many children and young people fell prey each year to the vicious and highly organised global trade that was the kidnap industry. More often than not, the victims had been targeted for their families' ability, or perceived ability, to pay heavy ransoms for their kids' return. That was the 'R' in 'K&R', and the sums that kidnappers routinely extorted out of their victims often ruined them completely, forcing them to sell their homes, cash in their life savings, anything to bring their loved ones home safely. But then even when the ransoms were paid in full, the stolen children were all too often never seen alive again.

Ben's freelance job since quitting the military had been to make sure that terrible fate never happened to them. His methodology for doing so drew heavily on his training and long experience with the most elite Special Forces regiment in the world. It was a simple system that he operated, and highly efficient. Kids came home. Their abductors mostly stayed where Ben found them, and ceased to be a problem for anyone.

Ben had dealt with a lot of desperate parents in this line of work and it didn't escape his notice that this Professor Mortimer didn't have the look of a man stricken with grief and worry over the disappearance of a loved one. Maybe he was just amazingly in control of his emotions.

'It's what I try to do,' he replied. 'Successfully, in little Carl Hunter's case.'

Mortimer pursed his lips thoughtfully. 'His mother can't say enough good things about you. And so, Mr Hope, I would like to employ your considerable skills to help me with my situation.'

'And your situation is what exactly?'

'It's rather a long story, but let me begin at the beginning. You see, I have been trying to trace the whereabouts, or perhaps I should say the fate, of two young children who disappeared. Two brothers to be precise, named Richard and Edward.'

Ben had one ear constantly to the ground in these matters, and if two British kids named Richard and Edward had been kidnapped any time recently, he'd have been reasonably sure to have heard about it.

'Okay, fill me in,' he said, making a mental note of that ominous-sounding word 'fate'. 'Are Richard and Edward your sons? Or related to you in some other way?' Sometimes the parents were so sick with anxiety that they'd get another family member to make the approach.

Mortimer pursed his lips again. 'Not exactly, no.'

Ben found the man's reticence a little curious. Normally you had to work hard to stop them blurting all their tortured story out in an uncontrollable torrent of emotion. He said, 'I understand that this is difficult. But for me to be able to help you, it's important to have the fullest picture possible. Why don't you start from the beginning. When were the boys taken, where and how? Are there any clues or indications as to who might have done this? Have the kidnappers made contact with the family? Is there a demand for ransom? What steps have the police already taken to locate them? Why come to me? As much detail as you can give me.'

Mortimer sighed. 'I'm not explaining myself too well, I'm afraid. This is admittedly perhaps a rather different situation from the cases you're normally called to deal with.'

'Different how?'

'Well to start with, you see, Richard and Edward weren't actually *abducted* as such. That is to say, in one sense, they were, in that they were removed from their home, by certain third parties who were not their parents. But the main issue is the question of whether or not they were murdered. At any rate that's the prevailing theory.'

'That they were murdered?'

Mortimer nodded. 'Yes, though I personally don't believe that they were. And I'm not the only one who feels that way.'

'So they weren't murdered?'

'It's unlikely. There's some very compelling evidence to the contrary.'

'I don't understand. Then are you saying you believe Richard and Edward are still alive?'

'Oh, no. They're dead, all right. That, I can guarantee.'

This conversation was getting more baffling by the second. The weirdest thing of all, it seemed to Ben, was that Mortimer didn't appear personally affected by any of it. He was talking about the apparent deaths of these two children like an abstract idea, as though quite detached from it emotionally.

'In any case,' Ben explained, 'whatever might or might not have happened to them, those kinds of investigations aren't what I do. I thought that was already clear to you.'

'Oh, perfectly clear,' Mortimer said. 'And yet under the circumstances it seemed to me that you were the perfect man for the job.'

'I don't see why. It's the police's job to investigate whether people have been murdered or not, and by whom. For what it's worth, they're generally pretty good at it.'

'The police,' Mortimer said, in a disparaging tone. 'I'm not certain they'd be able to help me very much.'

'So you haven't reported this to the authorities at all?'

'No. I'm afraid the details of the case would only baffle them. You see, the situation around which the whole thing revolves took place some time ago.'

Ben shook his head in confusion. 'How long ago?'

'Oh, quite a few years. To put an exact figure on it . . . let me think . . .'

Starting to get impatient, Ben said more abruptly, 'Let's cut to the chase, Professor Mortimer. What's this about?'

Mortimer leaned across the table and fixed him with an intense look. 'In a nutshell, it's about two young boys, aged twelve and nine, who disappeared in the year 1483.'

Ben rocked back in his chair and blinked a couple of times, in case he'd lost track of reality somehow, or slipped into a dream state in which he'd just heard Mortimer say that. He reached out and took a couple of tugs from his drink. No, he wasn't imagining it. He wasn't dreaming, either.

Not long after he'd got started in the kidnap rescue business, full of enthusiasm and drive, he'd travelled all the way to London to meet a prospective client who told him, with perfect sincerity, that his six children had been stolen by little green men who had whisked them away to the planet Mars in their spaceship. That meeting hadn't lasted very long.

And now it seemed to him that he'd been hooked in by another crazy person. He stared at Mortimer a while longer, then said, 'I'm sorry. You've just told me that these boys disappeared in 1483.'

'That's correct. At any rate, that's our best guess as far as the historical record shows.'

'1483 is more than five hundred years ago.'

Mortimer nodded. 'Five hundred and twenty-two years, to be exact. Which is the reason why, as I mentioned just now, the police wouldn't be able to offer a great deal of help in solving the case.'

Their food must be nearly ready by now and they were probably due to be called to their table any moment. Having gone without breakfast Ben had been looking forward to a steak lunch. But suddenly he wasn't feeling hungry any longer. He stood up.

'I don't think I can help you either. I'm afraid you'll have to hire someone else.'

'But why?' Mortimer burst out, as though genuinely surprised by Ben's reaction.

'Because I don't go hunting for ghosts,' Ben said. 'And because, frankly, I have better things to do than sit here listening to the ravings of a lunatic. Might I suggest,' he added, 'that the money you would have paid me for this job could be spent more usefully on the services of a good psychotherapist?'

'There's no need to get offensive,' Mortimer protested. 'Listen, I understand if my proposition sounds a little odd. But I haven't finished yet, so please, hear me out. It will all make perfect sense to you, if you'd just let me explain what I need from you. You see, I think I'm in some kind of—'

Ben cut him short. 'I think I've already heard enough.'

'Dear, oh dear. I seem to have messed this whole thing up completely, don't I? At least take my card,' Mortimer said, plucking it from his tweed jacket pocket. 'Then if you should change your mind . . .'

'I won't,' Ben said. But he accepted the card, just to shut the guy up and avoid making a public scene. He stuffed the card in his jeans pocket without looking at it.

'Goodbye, Professor. Have a safe flight home, and good luck. I hope you find what you're looking for.'

Chapter 3

The next day

Hugh Mortimer had returned home from Dublin with a mixture of emotions. During the flight back to England he'd been hopping mad with indignation at the way he'd been rejected and treated so rudely. How dare that man Hope accuse him of being mentally unbalanced! The arrogance of it! But by the time the plane had landed and the taxi was en route for his house near York, his mood had become more reflective, his anger had ebbed away and he'd begun to realise that perhaps this was all his own fault for not having explained himself properly. In fact he'd made a total hash of it from the start. In his eagerness he'd approached the whole thing badly, presented his case in a confused jumble that had given a totally wrong impression. Belinda had always complained that was exactly how he'd get when he was all worked up and intense about something. Which, apparently, was a lesson he had still failed to learn all these years later.

He'd barely managed to sleep a wink all night for turning it over and over in his mind. By morning his feelings of self-blame had only strengthened, and he could no longer fault the fellow for having reacted the way he had. And as he sat here now, gently rocking in his little boat, on this perfect, warm May afternoon with the sunlit lake waters glittering like diamonds all around him, he had to admit that he must have come across as rather eccentric, to say the least. Put it down to exuberance, perhaps, or to his inability to see things from the other person's point of view; but he could see clearly now what he *should* have said.

There were other things besides that Mortimer could beat himself up about. If it hadn't been for that damned drunken phone call he'd made to his old enemy, none of this would have happened. What had he been thinking, to swallow half a bottle of sherry and go and throw the cat among the pigeons like that?

Stupid, stupid, stupid.

The private six-acre carp fishing lake belonged to Hugh Mortimer's modest (in his opinion) but comfortable little country parkland estate half an hour's drive from the city. He'd lived here for many years, the last ten of those alone since Belinda had packed up and left him, but he still loved to take his little outboard boat across the water where he could contemplate and meditate. The lake was his haven, his main distraction from all the piled-up books and papers in his study where he spent so much of his time, and from the worries and concerns that had been preoccupying him more and more lately. Sometimes he brought his fishing rod with him – on a few occasions over the years he'd even managed to catch something – but mostly he'd just potter about on the lake for a few hours, enjoying the peace and listening to the birds. You could just about make out the half-timbered rear façade of the late-medieval house from here, peeking through the trees in the distance. It was a wonderful place to live.

Today, though, his private haven wasn't offering much in the way of respite from his anxiety. He'd been so sure, until yesterday, that he'd found someone who could help him with his situation. The disappointment was hard to bear, and even harder knowing that he only had himself to blame.

Quite apart from his usual personal failings, he knew that his worst mistake in this instance had been to not tell Ben Hope straight away about the threatening letters. Better still, he could have brought them along to show him, by way of proof that he wasn't making it up. He had a pretty good idea who'd sent them, too.

All would have been made clear, if only he'd been given the chance to explain himself properly. Then he was sure that Hope would have understood and agreed to help him. A man like that, with his experience and background, a world away from Mortimer's own sheltered existence, wouldn't be afraid of the risk.

Mortimer sat there gazing across the rippling lake and wondered what he should do next. Ought he to try again with Ben Hope, call him on the phone, apologise for the botched interview and explain the whole story? Or should he simply do what he should perhaps have done to begin with, and go to the police with the letters? That was what he'd been on the verge of doing in his desperation, when during a rare phone call to his ex-wife Belinda she'd completely by chance happened to mention her tennis friend. Jessica Hunter's amazing story about the man who'd rescued her son Carl had been like a ray of light. Believing that he'd found the solution to his problem he'd obtained Ben Hope's number from Jessica and contacted him the very same day.

Only to go and blow it all with his foolishness.

He was still wavering over his decision when he noticed a big ripple and some rising bubbles disturb the surface of the water, just a foot or two from the side of the boat. His first thought was that it must be a large fish. Some of the carp in the lake were real monsters, and there were pikes lurking there too. But it was highly unusual for them to come so close to the boat.

Then Mortimer saw a second ripple and more bubbles appear on the other side. He stared, realising it couldn't be any fish. What the hell was it?

Before he knew what was happening, the surface of the water each side of the boat suddenly exploded in a burst of white foam as two glistening black shapes erupted from below. Mortimer let out a sharp cry of terror. Their faces obscured by their scuba masks, the frogmen grabbed hold of the boat's gunwales and began violently rocking the hull from side to side. 'What are you doing?' he screamed at them. 'Stop it, you'll—'

Capsize the boat, he'd been about to say. But those last words never had time to come out, as Mortimer lost his balance and plunged scrabbling and wriggling over the side. He fell in with a splash and the shock of the cold water engulfed him, bubbles bursting from his mouth and the roar filling his ears. He'd been a strong swimmer in his youth, and had rowed for his university boat club. That had been a long time ago. As unfit and out of shape as he'd become in his middle age, the instincts hadn't completely deserted him. Mortimer kicked and struggled his way back to the surface and his head thrust free with a gasp.

But not for long. Because now the two frogmen had let go of the boat and were grabbing at his arms, plunging back underwater and dragging him down with them. He barely had time to snatch a breath before the water closed over his head and he was sinking into the murky depths with the divers' hands clasping him like iron.

That was when the second shock hit him with a chill much colder and more paralysing than the water. It was the realisation of what was happening to him. Of what these two men were doing to him.

They were going to drown him. Intentionally. Callously. Pitilessly. Hold him under until his lungs burst.

He was going to die. Here, today, now.

Hugh Mortimer fought them. He fought them with every shred of strength and energy in his body. Once upon a time, when he'd been an athletic young rower, he might have stood a decent chance of fending off a single attacker. But not two of them, and with the advantage of being able to breathe underwater. They held him in their pincer-like grips and dragged him down deeper. The water was filling his lungs now, and the streams of bubbles from his open mouth were becoming less. His muffled, gurgling screams of rage and fear were an incomprehensible roaring in his ears. His heart was exploding. His vision growing darker and dimmer. Still he kicked and struggled, but he was weakening fast and had only a few moments left.

The frogmen kept hold of their victim. Deeper, deeper, to where the sunlight could barely penetrate the murky water. The underside of the boat's hull was just a dim shape above them. Now the bubbles had stopped, and Hugh Mortimer was no longer thrashing against their grip. Moments later, when all the air had left his body, what remained of his life energy was gone too.

The divers had one more task to carry out before they could let the dead man sink to the bottom of the lake. The item they'd been ordered to obtain from him was attached to a slender chain he wore around his neck. One man held him while the other tore open his shirt collar, snapped the chain and carefully retained the small round metal item, which he slipped into a zippered pocket on the arm of his wetsuit. Then they let go of him and his body drifted limply downwards, arms and legs spreadeagled. The drowned man seemed to stare at his killers with a glassy expression of surprise and amazement that said, '*Why me? What did I do to deserve this?*'

Fact was, his murderers neither knew nor cared. They were simply two operatives following orders and getting nicely paid, and Professor Hugh Mortimer meant no more to them in death than he had in life. They kicked their flippers and swam back up towards the surface, leaving their victim to sink to the bottom. In a couple of days the putrefying gases inside his body would inflate him like a balloon and he'd bob up to the surface, if the police underwater search unit hadn't already dredged him up by then. As far as anyone was concerned, it would appear as though he'd just fallen out of the boat and been unable to save himself. No reason for anyone to regard his untimely passing as anything other than a tragic accident. Not that too many people in the world would have cause to miss this obscure retired academic whose historical research work would now never come to anything, nor cause any further trouble for anyone.

The frogmen swam to the far side of the lake, where their associates were waiting. The entire incident had been captured on a tripod-mounted video camera fitted with a powerful telephoto lens, to show the boss. He would be satisfied that the job had been carried out as quickly and discreetly as planned. The item they'd taken from the dead man would soon be in his possession.

The men quickly stripped off their scuba gear and bundled it into a holdall, pulling on jeans and sweatshirts in its place. The plain black van was parked a short distance away on a track through the trees. They and their associates climbed aboard. Someone lit a cigarette. Someone else made a joke. The driver started up the engine and the van rolled away up the track towards the road.

Bye bye, Professor Mortimer.

Chapter 4

Two days after Ben's unexpectedly early return from Dublin, an excited Winnie came hunting for him on the beach as he was finishing his run and about to light his post-exercise Gauloise. Her excitement was over the news that her niece Aurora had delivered on her promise of a visit, and was catching a flight over to the Republic this morning. For reasons that Ben didn't catch from Winnie's flow of details, she could only fly to Dublin and would be travelling to Galway by train; and since Winnie's little car was in the garage having its alternator replaced, would Ben be a sweetie pie and drive over there himself to pick her up from the station?

With no work assignments on his immediate horizon, he couldn't pretend that he had anything better to do, except sit on his rock drinking and smoking and gazing at the ocean. 'I'd be delighted,' he said. 'Are you coming too?' She replied that she needed to stay here, as she was planning on cooking up a feast for Aurora's arrival and wouldn't be able to tear herself away from the kitchen for a single moment all day. He knew the real reason was that she wouldn't set foot in his car, because the speed of his driving petrified her.

And so, late that morning he jumped into the Interceptor and roared off on his errand. The large, rambling home he shared with Winnie was situated in a remote and sparsely populated part of the Connemara coastline overlooking the western end of Galway Bay, near a place called Trá Mhór. It was about an hour's journey along the rugged R374 with its narrow stone bridges connecting the many little islands of the fragmented coastline, the Leitir Móir causeway and the spectacular views over the North Atlantic shoreline, then joining up with the R336 coast road that led all the way into Galway City. His route took him through some of Ireland's loveliest landscapes, passing by picturesque fishing villages and ports, ancient churches and great swathes of unspoilt countryside, all of it under a clear blue sky and the sunshine glimmering on the ocean.

He reached Galway station with time to spare for a cup of thin, vile-tasting railway coffee and was standing on the platform as the train rumbled in. He watched as the passengers disembarked, knowing who to look for from the photo he'd seen, but unprepared for the singular beauty of the young woman who was one of the last to step from the train. She was slim and finely-built, not tall, but she moved with all the grace and poise of a ballerina, drawing a good many admiring glances from men and women alike as she crossed the platform, carrying an elegant tweedy travel bag on a shoulder strap. He signalled to her, and she broke into a dazzling smile and quickened her step towards him.

'You must be Ben,' she said, putting out her hand.

'Your aunt sends her apologies, but she's slaving over a hot stove and couldn't get away.'

Aurora laughed. She had a nice laugh, rich and musical and infectious. He found himself grinning. Like a gentleman, he offered to carry her bag, and led her to the station car park.

Born in Hampshire and living in London these days, it was Aurora's first ever trip across the water to Ireland. 'I'd heard that it was nice, but this is something else,' she marvelled at the scenery as they headed back along the coast road, drystone walls flashing by. 'What I wouldn't give to be able to get away from London and live in a place like this. Now I know why they call it the Emerald Isle.'

'Suits me,' he replied. 'I wouldn't much fancy living in the big city either.'

'You're the lucky one. So it's just you and Auntie Winnie?'

'Just us. She's like family to me. We've known each other a long, long time and we rattle along pretty well. When I'm not doing my best to drive her nuts, that is.' As he spoke, he took a humpback bridge at just a shade under ninety miles an hour, then threw the Interceptor into a series of switchback bends like a racing driver.

'You certainly know these roads,' she observed with a smile.

'Sorry. Am I going too fast?'

'No, I love it,' she replied. 'This is a pretty amazing car. It's a real classic, isn't it?'

'I suppose it is,' he said. 'Made in 1975. It belonged to my father.'

'Wow. I wish my dad had a car like this he'd agree to let me have.'

'He didn't give it to me voluntarily,' Ben said. 'He's dead. Both my parents died quite young.'

She bit her lip, looking embarrassed. 'Of course. Auntie Winnie did tell me something about that, years ago. I'm sorry.'

'He loved the car too. Whenever he wasn't in court, he was either cleaning it or fiddling around with it or driving around the Cambridgeshire countryside. That's where I grew up.'

'In court? Was he in trouble a lot?'

'He was a judge,' Ben replied. 'Quite a senior one. Though I admit I didn't really pay attention to much of what he did, back then.'

'Winnie said you used to be in the army.'

'For a few years.'

'So you didn't follow in the family footsteps?'

Ben smiled. 'Not exactly, no.'

'I'm sure they'd have been proud, though.'

'I doubt that. But let's not talk about my family, okay?'

She nodded, sensing that it was a difficult subject for him even if she didn't understand why. 'What shall we talk about?'

'Tell me about you,' he said. 'Winnie says you're set to take the ballet world by storm and become an international superstar.'

Aurora threw back her head and let out another of those chiming laughs that it was impossible to hear without smiling. 'Oh, dear old Auntie Win. She does tend to exaggerate. I'm not exactly Margot Fonteyn.'

Ben drove and listened as she talked about her dancing career, her goals, her dreams, her disappointments. Ever since she'd been a little girl it had been her determined ambition to be a professional dancer and yes, she had managed to reach a certain level in that extremely tough and competitive world. The high point so far had been when she'd auditioned for the part of Juliet in a production at the Royal Ballet in Covent Garden.

'I'm impressed,' Ben said. Even though he knew nothing about ballet, that sounded like the dancer's equivalent of getting badged into 22 SAS. He knew from personal experience the kind of hell that young would-be recruits put themselves through to attain that life-changing goal.

'Didn't get it, though. Even though I tried. God knows I tried.'

'You'll get there,' he said. 'I'm sure of it.'

'Thanks for the words of encouragement. I'll keep plugging away, that's for sure. But there's so much competition out there, I only hope the big break comes my way before I get too old.'

'Old? You?'

'You'd be amazed. It's like trying to succeed as a tennis player, or a model. Most dancers' careers are all washed up by their mid to late thirties, so there's a limited time window if you want to make it.' Still, she explained, she worked hard every day, grasped every opportunity with both hands and trained twice a month at a studio run by a famous former ballerina who charged a fortune for her coaching services.

'You'll get there,' he repeated. 'I know you will.'

'Oh, you know,' she said philosophically. 'I've no illusions. Even if I never really hit the big time, I'd settle for opening my own ballet academy one day. To be able to pass on what I've learned to new generations of up-and-coming talent. That'd be a dream, too. Literally a dream,' she added with a laugh. 'It'd cost a fortune to set something like that up. Way out of my league.'

'Never say never,' Ben said.

The drive home seemed to take half the time, and he was almost sorry when they reached the house. But it was a joy to see Winnie so happy and animated. The rest of the day passed very pleasantly. Aurora raved about the house, the beach, the ocean views. The feast was no disappointment, either, as Winnie had excelled herself in the kitchen. Ben was a gracious host and took care of household duties so that the two of them could spend time catching up.

At breakfast the next morning, Winnie suggested that her niece might like to see something of the local area. Maybe Ben would show her around? Which again, being at a loose end these days and surprised at how much he looked forward to enjoying more of Aurora's company, he was happy to do. He'd long ago explored all the hidden little coves and bays, and knew the best walking trails and all the long, rocky beaches where you could wander for hours without meeting another soul.

They set off early, planning to make a whole day of it. He enchanted her with a visit to a lonely spot, far off the beaten track, where herds of wild Connemara ponies were often to be seen roaming over the hills and moorland. The horses were usually shy of humans and would bolt if approached, but to his amazement three of them came right up to Aurora and let her pet them, quite docile and completely trusting. 'They're wonderful,' she laughed, as bright-eyed with joy as a child. Further along the rugged coastline they went hiking along cliff trails where the seabirds wheeled and screeched and you could lean right into the wind and gaze across the heaving grey-blue North Atlantic with only a few small scattered islands between you and America.

'What's that one there?' she asked, pointing far out to sea.

'That's St Macdara's Island,' he explained. 'Nothing much there, except for the remains of a sixth-century monastery. Every summer people make a pilgrimage to the ruins, hold a mass and pray for the protection of fishing vessels from the sea. We could take a boat trip out there tomorrow, if you want.'

'I'd love that,' she said.

They had lunch at a harbour café in a coastal village. In the afternoon he took her to look at the rugged, mist-shrouded peak of Kill Mountain and they walked the Leitir Móir causeway that they'd driven over the previous day. The hours flew by faster than Ben could have imagined, and before he knew it the sun was beginning to dip over the ocean, painting the water with shimmering hues of red and gold. 'Winnie will be worried about us,' he said. 'And there'll be hell to pay if we're late for dinner.'

She squeezed his hand. 'I'm sorry to go back. I could stay here for ever.'

Chapter 5

'I could get used to this,' Aurora said later that night, lounging comfortably in the passenger seat as the Interceptor rocketed along the empty dark roads.

Winnie had cooked up another feast for their dinner that evening. Her culinary skills were geared more towards hearty traditional fare like roast beef and Yorkshire puddings than anything in the line of gourmet delicacies. It could be heavy going at times, but Ben was amazed at how Aurora could put it away and remain so slender. Perhaps her dancer's fitness routine, burning up five thousand calories a day, had something to do with it.

During dinner the conversation had drifted around to the topic of music. Ben's first passion in that department was for jazz, of the spiky, discordant and hard-to-listen-to modern variety. That wasn't so much to Aurora's taste. Nor to Winnie's, who when alone would often sing along to her favourite Max Bygraves records – which made it all the more surprising to Ben when she declared to her niece that 'You can't come to Ireland without hearing some proper Irish music.' To his certain knowledge, Winnie was no fan of that either. 'Ben,' she'd said, 'what about that pub in Roundstone? They have a lot of live gigs there, don't they?'

Roundstone was another village just down the coast. The pub Winnie had in mind was called O'Flanagan's, and it was famous for its often impromptu jam sessions with local musicians, some of which could get quite rowdy.

'Tonight?' he'd replied. 'I'm sure Aurora must be tired after all the walking we did today.'

'Not a bit,' Aurora had said, smiling across the dinner table. 'That sounds great.'

'Winnie?' Ben asked, out of mischief.

'Oh, Ben, I'd love to. But I think I'll get an early night. You two go and enjoy yourselves.'

Ben strongly suspected that he was being set up to spend more time alone with Aurora. She was crafty, that Winnie. Not that he was complaining. And so here they were, speeding through the darkness towards the village of Roundstone.

'You mean you could get used to Ireland?' he replied to Aurora's question.

'Everything,' she said dreamily. 'The kind of life you have here. The beauty of this place, the sea, a big fabulous house . . .'

'I'd hardly call that empty old pile fabulous.'

'Driving around these roads in this car . . .'

Ben replied with a shrug, 'It's just a mode of transportation.'

'I'd love to have a go.'

He looked at her. 'You can drive, can you?'

'Of course I can drive. I have a little Mazda in London.'

'This thing has a bit more oomph than you might be used to.'

'I can handle that,' she laughed. 'So will you let me drive it?'

'We'll see,' he said.

'That's no kind of answer. Will you?'

'Okay, I promise I'll let you drive it. How's that for an answer?'

'Perfectly acceptable,' she said, stretching out in the seat. 'And I'll take you up on it, Mr Ben Hope.'

That night's musical entertainment at O'Flanagan's was the usual combination of fiddles and guitars and banjos, together with a flute and a bodhrán. It was the kind of pub where it would be a sacrilege to drink anything other than Guinness, poured naturally with a perfect shamrock on top. The only problem with Guinness, Ben found, was that it went down too easily. He was getting started on his third pint by the time Aurora announced that she'd like to dance, and reached for his hand to drag him out onto the floor. He declined, rather than make a fool of himself, and so without missing a beat she skipped out alone from their little corner alcove to join the small crowd already dancing.

He turned to watch as she launched into an amazingly complex Irish step that was a long way from ballet but no less skilful, with her back as straight as a rifle barrel and her feet moving so fast and nimbly that they were a blur. Soon others were following her example, though nothing like as well. She was laughing and smiling, totally in her element. Ben couldn't stop watching her. Her whole body was one with the music, as fluid as water, seeming to pulse with the rhythms.

After twenty minutes without a break Aurora came back to her seat, beaming and not even slightly out of breath. 'I'd say that calls for another drink,' he said.

'Not for me,' she replied.

'For me, then.'

They talked more, having to raise their voices as the music got louder and more exuberant. He felt deeply relaxed and at ease in her company. There was something about this girl, he was thinking. Something he'd never bargained for. For the first time in a long while, he could feel the darkness lifting.

'Look at the time,' she said. 'Don't they ever close this place?'

'This is Ireland,' he told her. 'But still, I suppose we should get back. I'm supposed to be looking after you.'

'And doing a great job of it. I'm having the time of my life.'

'I'm happy that you are.'

It was raining as they stepped outside. Aurora looked up at the sky, pulled a face and said, 'Ugh.'

'Doesn't look like it's about to let up any time soon. We'll have to make a run for it.'

'So are you going to let me drive back?' she asked.

'Oh, I don't know about that,' he replied.

'You promised you'd let me have a go of your speed machine. And you've had too many pints of Guinness anyway.'

'Oh, all right, then. You win.' He handed over the car keys.

'Excellent. Come on. I'll race you to the car.'

Remembering that he'd left his jacket inside, he said, 'Shit. Hold on. Tell you what, you get the engine warmed up and I'll be there in a minute.'

When he came back outside a few moments later, Aurora had hurried down the street and was unlocking the car. Ben was about to follow her when he saw the guy again.

The same guy he'd seen outside the hotel the day he'd gone to meet Mortimer. He'd dismissed his suspicions at the time. But now they were back again, redoubled. The guy was walking quickly along the street, hands in pockets, head ducked under the rain.

From the pub doorway Ben called, 'Hey. You. Stop!'

The guy shot Ben a startled look. Then took off at a run.

Ben gave chase. He quickly started gaining on the guy. He was confident he could catch him easily enough, and get some answers. How could the man have known where Ben would be tonight? What the hell was he following him for?

The rain was coming down in sheets. Down the street from O'Flanagan's, Aurora fired up the Interceptor with a throaty roar.

And then it exploded.

Chapter 6

The fireball momentarily lit the dark rainy sky over Roundstone like a flash of lightning before roiling black smoke almost completely obscured the blazing wreck of the Interceptor. Ben turned and sprinted hard back down the street towards it with his heart in his mouth. The man running away from him was totally forgotten now, unimportant and soon to be long gone.

Ben had been in wars and experienced hard, bloody battle. He'd seen dozens of blown-up vehicles, both military and civilian, the result of combat damage or terror attacks. He'd been there to help drag the charred, mutilated bodies from the wreckage, sometimes still alive, sometimes not. Heard the screams of the dying, picked up the body parts littered at the side of the road.

When he'd left that world behind him, he'd never wanted to see anything like that again. Yet here it was, happening right in front of him. And for it to happen at this moment, to her, filled him with such paralysing horror that he was choked up and barely able to breathe.

He fought through the smoke and flames to reach the driver's side of the car. The Interceptor's soft top had been torn clear off, a crumpled mess of burning canvas on the ground. The door had burst wide open, ripped almost from its hinges, and the force of the blast had blown Aurora half

40

out of the driver's seat so that she was lying with her legs in the blazing footwell and the upper half of her body draped over the sill and lying in the gutter.

The heat of the fire scorched his flesh and singed his hair, the smoke stung his eyes and made him cough as he grabbed her arms and hauled her a safe distance away from the vehicle. He was afraid of a secondary explosion as the petrol tank ignited; and moments later it did, tearing the remains of the Interceptor in half and littering the street with blazing debris.

She wasn't moving and her head lolled limply as he laid her on the pavement. The lower legs of her jeans were on fire. He tore off his leather jacket and used it to beat out the flames. Called her name. No response. 'AURORA!' he yelled again. Nothing. Her body was inert. Her face was blackened and bloodied. Her eyes were closed.

His hands were shaking so badly that he could hardly check for a pulse. It was there, but reedy and weak. She was alive at least, if only just. 'AURORA!'

He thought he saw a flutter of her eyelids and the smallest movement of her head. 'You're going to be okay,' he said, over and over. Her eyes flickered open again, and her lips moved and she tried to speak, but all that came out was a murmur too soft for him to hear over the roar of the flames.

Then she was unconscious again. As he looked her over he could see her right leg was lying at an unnaturally twisted angle. He was no doctor, but all SAS troops received emergency training in case their unit medic copped it in combat. And he recognised an ugly compound fracture when he saw one. He touched her leg and felt the sickening ragged protrusion of bone through her flesh. Her blackened, singed trousers were soaked with blood. Much too much blood. He had to do something to stem the flow, or she could be dead in minutes. He unbuckled his belt and tore it off and wrapped it tightly around her thigh above the knee, putting as much pressure as he could on the ruptured blood vessels. His hands were red and slippery.

A crowd of pub-goers and passersby had gathered in the street outside O'Flanagan's. Ben could hear the cries of distress and horror-struck gasps behind him as he knelt there on the wet pavement beside Aurora, trying to stop her from bleeding to death. His phone was in his jacket, beside him on the pavement, but he didn't dare take his hands off the makeshift tourniquet. 'Someone call for help!' he yelled at the crowd. But he needn't have, because at least three of them were already on their phones.

Minutes passed, each one like an hour. The rain lashed down, dripping from Ben's hair and soaking his shirt and beating back the flames from the burning car. Aurora was drifting in and out of consciousness. He kept talking to her, hoping that the sound of his voice and the comfort of his presence might help to keep her from fading away. His fingers were numb with the pressure he was maintaining on the belt tourniquet, but he wouldn't let go for an instant until help arrived. He wasn't alone. A young woman who'd been inside O'Flanagan's stepped from the crowd to help, saying her name was Lisa and she was a nurse. She put Ben's jacket under Aurora's head and kept monitoring her pulse. 'She's doing fine,' she tried to reassure Ben, but it was clear she was deeply worried about the right leg.

Nobody asked Ben what had happened. Nobody talked about the bombed car. The people of Ireland had a collective history of these things happening. But for the moment all that mattered to anyone was the critically injured blast victim fighting for her life on the pavement.

The village was miles from the nearest police station or hospital, and it seemed like an eternity before the first sound of sirens became audible in the distance. 'Thank God,' Lisa murmured. Until then the remaining rain-sodden crowd had been standing almost silent, apart from the sobs of one woman and the softly repeated prayers of another.

And then the flashing blue lights appeared through the smoke and the rain, as the ambulance and fire engine and police vehicles came racing at last to the scene. Someone in the crowd called excitedly, 'Here they are!' and an angry man's voice rasped, 'What the fuck kept them so long?' Ben barely even noticed their arrival, and the paramedics had to tear him physically away from Aurora. By that point she'd passed out again and been unresponsive for the last eight minutes. 'We've got her,' they told him, and it took all his willpower to stand back and let them take over.

He backed away and sat on the steps of a recessed doorway, out of the rain. He felt suddenly drained and exhausted, his whole body trembling and his knees weak. Someone from the crowd put a dry blanket over his shoulders and someone else brought him a glass of whiskey from the pub, which he accepted gratefully and knocked back in one gulp. Lisa, the nurse, asked him anxiously if he was okay, but he barely replied and just mumbled his thanks for her help.

The crowd was beginning to disperse as the street filled with emergency services personnel. In the swirl of red and blue lights the paramedics raised Aurora onto a gurney and loaded her into the ambulance. Ben wanted to ride to hospital with her, but after a few questions they refused to let him unless he was a relative. He managed to find out that they were taking her to University Hospital in Galway. With no transport any longer, he'd have to make his own way.

By this time the fire crew had finished putting out the last of the flames from the burnt-out Interceptor, now just a black and smoking ruin ready for the bomb squad specialists to move in and search for secondary devices and booby traps before the wreck would be taken away to a police pound for full forensic examination. The smoke drifted like an acrid fog and the gutters were choked with charred debris. The cops had shown up in force, blocking the street with several patrol cars and vans with their GARDA livery, accompanied by two more unmarked and armoured BMW X5 SUVs belonging to the Garda's Emergency Response Unit.

Something like a car bombing would be bound to draw out the cowboys, as Ben had anticipated. The ERU guys were strutting importantly about the scene, kitted out in full paramilitary gear with visors and tactical vests and carrying Uzi submachine guns. Maybe they'd rushed out here in the hopes that they'd get to shoot someone, just like in the good old days when the irregular warfare of the Troubles had often spilled over south of the Irish border. They looked sour and disappointed that they wouldn't have a lot to do that night. More officers were evacuating the O'Flanagan's clientele and local residents from the cordoned-off scene, as though they expected more bombs to start going off at any moment.

For the moment at least, Ben seemed to have been forgotten. In the midst of all the chaos and noise and mayhem and flashing blue lights, he retreated to a quieter spot and took out his phone. The call to Winnie, telling her what had happened, was one of the hardest he'd had to make in his life. Her cry of pure grief when he broke the news was more than he could bear to hear. Her sister's reaction would be even more distraught.

After the initial emotion Winnie was able to talk, sounding subdued and stupefied like a person in shock. 'I'm coming,' she kept repeating. 'I'll get a taxi.' He told her the name of the hospital Aurora was being taken to, and said he'd see her there.

But something told him he was going to be delayed getting there. As he was winding up his phone call to Winnie, two plain-clothes cops with grim faces had singled him out through the mayhem and were heading his way.

Chapter 7

One of the plain-clothes guys was burly and broad and a shade taller than Ben at around six-one or -two. His companion was one of those short, wiry little guys that made Ben think of a Jack Russell terrier.

They held out their police IDs as they stepped up to him. 'I'm Detective Inspector Gallagher and this is Detective Sergeant Nolan,' said the big one, scowling like a bear chewing on something prickly and foul-tasting. He pointed back at the burnt-out wreck of the car. 'That yours?'

'Was,' Ben replied.

'So you're Major Benjamin Hope?' said the Jack Russell. The Interceptor's rear registration plate was still intact and legible. They'd wasted no time tracing the owner's identity, which would quickly have led them to Ben's UK Ministry of Defence records – or, at any rate, the parts of his military history that were available to their relatively low clearance level. When soldiers left the 22 SAS regiment, whether through retirement or death in action, they instantly reverted back to their official military unit. Their Special Forces role was a closely-guarded secret. Even wives and kids were forbidden to talk about it. Some didn't even know that Hubby or Daddy was in the 'Sass'. And these cops wouldn't be privy to the more sensitive areas of Ben's past, either.

'I'm not a major any more,' Ben replied. 'Just Mr Hope. And it's not Benjamin. It's Benedict.'

'Okay, *Mr* Hope,' said Gallagher, putting sarcastic emphasis on the 'Mr'. 'Then you'd better come with us. We've got some questions.'

'I'll bet you do,' Ben replied. 'So do I.' Though his questions weren't for them.

They walked him past the wreck of the Interceptor to an unmarked patrol car parked further along the street. The Uzi-toting ERU goons eyed him suspiciously as he passed by. He ignored them.

The Jack Russell held open the back door for Ben, and he got in. Gallagher sat up front next to the driver. The car dipped under his weight. The Jack Russell, Nolan, got in the back beside Ben. He smelled of cheap aftershave.

'Let's go,' Gallagher told the driver, and they took off.

From the village of Roundstone, they soon rejoined the same route that Ben had followed to pick Aurora up from Galway station the day before. Nobody spoke as the car sped through the night. Not until Ben pulled a Gauloise from the crumpled pack in his jacket pocket, clanged open his old Zippo lighter and fired up the cigarette. He leaned back in the car seat, drawing the smoke in deep.

'Hey,' snapped Nolan. 'You're not supposed to smoke.'

'What are you, a doctor?' Ben said.

'In the car. You can't smoke in the car.'

'Then you'll just have to throw me out, won't you?' Ben said. 'Fine by me. I never asked for a lift from you.'

There was no reply. Ben went on smoking, trying to settle his nerves and blot out the vision of the blast that kept filling his head. As the adrenaline-fuelled horror of the moment began to subside it was replaced by the kind of numbness that he'd so often experienced in the immediate aftermath of a battle. The three cops in the car with him seemed to barely exist.

Nobody spoke again until the car had reached Galway, cut across the city and pulled up around the back of the Garda Regional and Divisional Headquarters. The building's many windows glowed in the darkness. The rain had stopped. They led him from the car to a small rear entrance, and through the usual labyrinth of bare-walled corridors that were identical to the inside of every large police station or administrative HQ Ben had ever been in. Gallagher and Nolan were joined by another detective who didn't introduce himself. Ben already knew where they were taking him.

The interview room was painted the same dull institutional greyish colour as the corridors. Inside, it was the usual routine. A plain laminated table with nothing on it except some audio recording equipment, four plastic chairs, no windows, and no inner handle on the door. They ushered him to a chair. The unnamed officer sat next to him at one side of the table, and Nolan and Gallagher sat opposite. Gallagher leaned heavily forward, staring at him with dead fish eyes.

'No coffee?' Ben asked.

'Perhaps later,' Nolan said.

'What about an ashtray?'

'Don't even think about it.'

'Just so you know,' Gallagher said, 'this conversation is being recorded.'

Ben didn't care. 'Will this take long? I'd like to go and find out how my friend is doing.'

'Friend, is it?' Gallagher said, expressionlessly.

'Just a friend. Her name's Aurora.'

'Aurora what?'

'I don't know her last name,' Ben said truthfully.

'Let's talk about what you do know,' Gallagher said.

'That won't take long. I know nothing,' Ben said.

Nolan raised an eyebrow. 'But you are aware that your car blew up with your friend in it?' he asked sardonically.

'I noticed,' Ben said, fixing him with a look that made the cop glance away.

'So you're saying you have no idea what caused this incident?'

'At least half a pound of something like RDX high explosive, with a crude detonator perhaps connected to the ignition wires in a hurry using crocodile clips,' Ben said. 'Or remotely activated by a mobile phone. I'm sure your bomb guys will figure out what kind of system was used. As for why it was there and who put it there, on that score your guess is as good as mine.'

'You seem to know a lot about car bombs,' said the unnamed detective.

Ben shrugged. 'No secret that I was in the military. We were known to blow stuff up now and then.'

'It's your army background we're interested in,' Gallagher said. 'There hasn't been a car bombing in the Republic since the nineties, and not a single one ever in this region. Now here we are all of a sudden, and it just so happens that the target vehicle belonged to a former British officer who served in Ireland.'

'Been doing your homework,' Ben said. What the police had uncovered was only a fragment of the truth: while still a regular rank and file soldier he'd done his stint in Northern Ireland like many of his peers, but his real involvement in that theatre of war hadn't taken place until much later, when he'd been an active participant in the long, dirty and ultimately inconclusive conflict between the IRA and UK Special Forces.

Gallagher shrugged. 'All I'm saying is, strikes me as more than just a coincidence, wouldn't you agree?'

'Here's the thing,' Nolan said. 'There are still a lot of active Provos and groups of dissident Republicans on both sides of the border, some unforgiving types of men with an axe to grind, who might well be looking to settle old scores. But they'd be focusing their attentions on particular individuals, not just anybody. A higher level operative, someone who really pissed them off, caused them a lot of damage. Maybe took out some of their mates and relations.'

'We think you might be one of those particular individuals,' Gallagher said.

'I see,' Ben said, looking at him. 'And how do you work that out?'

'There's a big hole in the middle of your military record. Plenty of information concerning your first three years in the army, when you were starting out. Looks like you did very well for yourself. Then no operational details at all for more than a decade, until they spit you out the other end with a final rank of major. That doesn't just happen. Kind of makes us wonder what you were doing all that time. There's usually only one reason for that level of secrecy.'

Ben could see where they were leading with this. It was guesswork, but fairly educated guesswork. And in essence the theory they were pushing was plausible enough. In a lot of ways it seemed to be the most obvious conclusion. Their line of thinking also explained the tangible degree of antagonism in their attitude towards him. He was no ordinary civilian victim of a violent attack. As far as they were concerned, his presence here in their country was nothing but a trouble magnet. A red rag to a bull, almost as if by choosing to live here he was deliberately goading old enemies to come out of the woodwork and stir things up.

'Fair enough,' he admitted. 'If you had the clearance you'd see I served those years with 22 SAS. And yes, I was deployed in Ireland for some of that time. More than that, I couldn't tell you even if I wanted to.'

'Above our pay grade,' Gallagher said.

Nolan grinned a mirthless grin. 'Just like we thought. An SAS major, eh?'

'You boys certainly made a big dent in the Provos' operations,' Gallagher said. 'And that's an understatement. Made a lot of enemies, too. The kind of enemies I wouldn't want to have, that's for sure.'

'And now you think someone's worked out who I am, or who I was, and that's why my friend got blown up tonight.'

Gallagher spread his hands. 'Bad luck for her. Could be they hit the wrong target by mistake. Or maybe it was meant as a warning to you.'

Ben said nothing.

'We'd be interested in some names,' said the third detective, who was yet to give his own, and wasn't saying much in general. Ben wondered if he was something more than a normal police officer, something in counter-terrorism. The Garda's National Crime and Security Intelligence Service was the nearest thing Ireland had to a spy agency. He went on,

'Identities of potential suspects in this incident, men you might have reason to suppose still harbour a grudge from back in the day and could potentially be behind this, even if they didn't plant the bomb themselves. You're not that long out of the regiment, after all. And these fellas don't forget.'

'I've been living here for some time,' Ben said. 'If the people you're talking about could have found me, they'd have done it by now. If they haven't, it's because I cover my tracks.'

'Maybe you do,' Gallagher said. 'Or maybe you're not as smart as you'd like to think you are. So how about we take a trip down memory lane, just in case we might be able to catch the bastard who blew up that poor wee girl?'

Ben was silent for a few moments. Then he said, 'Ronan Quaid. He was one of SAS's prime targets we never accounted for.'

'Top of our list, too,' the unnamed officer said. 'Until we crossed him off. Stomach cancer, eleven months ago.'

'Then there was Dominic O'Doherty,' Ben said. 'He and Quaid were implicated together in the Ashford security van raid in '98. Two years before that, he shot one of your Garda detectives to death in the course of a botched post office robbery in County Limerick.'

'That detective's name was Jerry McCabe,' growled Gallagher. 'I knew the man, worked with him, counted him as a friend. Sure I'd have liked to get my hands on his killer. But our Dominic got himself banged up in a Vietnamese prison in 2002 for trying to smuggle four kilos of heroin into the country. Cheated us out of the chance of putting him away ourselves. My consolation is, he won't be having a very good time there, and he won't be getting out in a hurry.'

'That's all I can give you,' Ben said. 'Most of the others were either taken out by us, or are spending the rest of their lives behind bars here or in England. Aside from Quaid and O'Doherty, I'm out of ideas.'

'Are you sure?' Gallagher said, looking piercingly at him.

'Pretty sure,' Ben replied.

'Not quite the level of cooperation we were hoping for, Major Hope,' said the unnamed detective who Ben was now certain was an intelligence agent. 'I'd have thought you might be a bit more forthcoming, under the circumstances.'

Ben had never met an intelligence agent he liked, and he was beginning to like this guy even less. 'My friend has been hurt,' he said, containing his rising anger. 'How badly, I don't know, because I'm sitting here wasting time instead of being at the hospital where I ought to be. If this has happened as revenge for something in my past, don't you think I'd be interested in helping put away the piece of shit responsible? And if I found him first, there'd be nothing left for you to lock up.'

'We don't care too much for that kind of vigilante talk,' Gallagher said. 'Do we, boys?'

'No, we don't, Inspector,' said Nolan.

The cops weren't giving up that easily. They kept him there for the best part of another hour, hunting and probing in their typical way, sneakily cajoling one minute and attempting to intimidate the next, for whatever else he might be able to offer in the way of clues. He could have told them about the tall guy with the widow's peak and the glasses. Could have given them an exact account of the man's mystery appearance in two separate locations, and a physical description so detailed that an identikit likeness would look like a photograph. But he'd already decided to hold that back.

He had his reasons for staying silent. The main one was that no matter what, he was certain they'd stick to their theory like glue, and that he wasn't buying it. God knew he'd been mixed up in some nasty stuff in Ireland back in the day. He'd done things, carried out orders, that he hadn't always agreed with. A lot of lives had been destroyed, both directly and indirectly, and a lot of bitter enmity had been stirred up that would never go away. Ben lived with that knowledge, just as he lived with all those other bad memories, and he had long faced up to the fact that that ugly part of his past might possibly catch up with him sooner or later.

Not this time, though. This time, he sensed it was something else. Something totally different.

Because if the tall guy with the widow's peak and the glasses was an old IRA enemy looking for revenge or a hitter sent by the likes of Ronan Quaid or Dominic O'Doherty, what had he been doing outside the Merrion in Dublin the day Ben had gone to see Hugh Mortimer? Why not simply target Ben at home, plant a bomb there or else just shoot him in the time-honoured tradition, instead of going to such unnecessary lengths as to track him all the way across to the other side of Ireland? How could they have known about his arranged rendezvous at the hotel? At that point Ben had only talked to Mortimer on his mobile phone, which was a prepaid-for-cash burner job registered neither in his real name nor in any of the various aliases he used in his K and R work: in short, it was untraceable and unhackable. None of this made sense, unless there was some strange connection to Mortimer himself.

But what? Ben had no idea, as yet. And he saw no reason why the cops needed to be included in his search for answers. As always, he'd be working alone on this one.

Chapter 8

At last, late in the evening, they had to let him go. Gallagher looked even more sour after the unproductive session than he had on the way here. Towards the end of the interview he'd offered Ben police protection, but Ben hadn't wanted it. 'Your funeral,' Gallagher said.

'Why do you live here?' Nolan asked as they walked him back along the drab corridors. 'You're English.'

'Half Irish,' Ben said. 'But that's not the reason I came back to live in Ireland after the army. I just so happen to like it here.'

'For the peace and quiet, eh?' Gallagher grunted.

'Until tonight, that's how it was,' Ben said.

'Maybe it's time to get out.'

'When I decide it's time, it's time,' Ben said. 'Right now, the only place I'm going is University Hospital.'

Nolan drove him there, in the same unmarked car. 'Hope she's going to be all right,' Nolan said as he dropped him off outside the hospital.

'Thanks, Sergeant,' Ben replied. 'Nice to know maybe you are human after all.' Nolan grunted and drove off.

Ben hurried into the brightly-lit reception lobby. At this time of night, the place was pretty quiet with no more than a few admin staff and medical personnel bustling about. Ahead of him was the main desk, and to his right was an open-plan waiting area. His heart gave a lurch as he spotted Winnie sitting there. She was hunched in her seat, staring at the floor, too preoccupied with her own thoughts to have noticed him arriving. Her downturned face looked pale and grim and she looked twenty years older. He was dreading how she might respond to him, or what she was going to tell him.

'I got here as fast as I could,' he said, hurrying over to her. 'Police kept me talking. Have you been here long?'

'A while,' she replied. There was no anger in her reddened eyes, barely any emotion left after crying out all the tears she had, only exhaustion and total defeat as she stood up and hugged him tight. She was a good ten inches shorter than he was, and he had to bend down to hold her.

'How is she?' He was almost too afraid to ask.

'Sit down, Ben,' Winnie answered in a flat tone. She patted the seat next to hers. Just the same way she'd done years ago when she told him of his mother's death. Then after that, when his father had gone too.

He sat, holding his breath. His blood had turned from the pulsing heat of anxiety to ice cold. 'Is she dead?'

Winnie shook her head. 'She's not dead, Ben. But it's not good.'

Aurora had been rushed into the operating theatre on arrival, and she'd still been there when Winnie arrived by taxi. Shortly after that, a doctor had come looking for her with a situation report.

'She's out of critical condition,' Winnie told him. 'They say the burns and the other injuries most likely will heal almost as good as new, in time. She's a strong and healthy girl, always was. But . . . the leg . . .'

'What about it?' he asked anxiously. His stomach muscles were knotted like oak, heart was thudding in his throat and he could feel the colour draining from his face.

'They did all they could to save it, Ben. But . . .' She sniffed. 'But it was no use. They had to take it off below the knee.'

Ben sank his head into his hands. 'Oh, Christ.'

That first acute wave of shock was just the beginning as the full impact of it slowly sank in. All he could see was the blood and the flames and that awful twisted shattered leg with the ragged spike of bone jutting from the flesh. All he could think about was Aurora's pain and suffering. And that was just the beginning, too, because in that instant when she'd turned the key and the world exploded around her, her life had irreparably changed forever. Now the thing she loved the most of all, the goal she'd pursued since childhood with every ounce of determination and passion and verve and energy her soul possessed, was gone, obliterated, literally blown away. Nobody could have known that those happy, carefree few minutes on the dance floor at O'Flanagan's had been the last time she'd ever get up on her feet, letting the music flow through her, doing the thing that came most naturally.

Aurora would never dance again. To extinguish that spirit in someone like her was almost like killing her. Like a bullet to the head. Perhaps it was even worse.

At last Winnie broke the silence by saying, 'I called Helena. She's on her way. They're all coming over.'

Helena was Winnie's younger sister. Aurora had told Ben all about her, what a wonderful and supportive mother she'd been not just to herself but to all of her siblings, Justin, Dominic and Melanie. Ben didn't need to ask how the family had taken the news. It was going to be a bad few days and it wouldn't get any better over the coming weeks, months or years.

'They'll be welcome to stay at the house for as long as they need,' Ben said. 'At least we can offer them that. I'll lease a car or a minibus that they can use to travel back and forth.'

Winnie nodded sadly. 'That's good of you, Ben. We're all going to need all the support we can give each other, to help her get through this.'

'I don't think I'm going to be around, Win,' he said, feeling terrible for saying it. 'I don't think I can face seeing them.'

'Where will you be? Where are you going?'

'I can't say. But I've got to follow this through. And I can't do that by sitting on the beach waiting for something to happen.'

'She needs you.'

'She'll have her family around her. They've been there for twenty-four years and given her nothing but love and happiness. Me, she's known for all of two days. Look what I've managed to do for her in that time. Needs me, does she? Yeah, like she needed to lose her leg.'

'You can't blame yourself for this, Ben,' Winnie said.

He looked at her, feeling a sharp blaze of anger inside. 'Can't I? She was with me when it happened. She wouldn't have been in danger, if I hadn't put her into that situation.'

'But you couldn't have known what was going to happen, any more than I did,' Winnie said, fresh tears rolling down her face. 'Could you?'

He shook his head. But he couldn't just exonerate himself. It was still down to him, whether he'd known or not.

'She'll be sleeping now, poor thing,' Winnie said, dabbing the tears away with a tissue. 'I wonder if she even knows what's happened to her.'

'What else did the doctors say?' he asked.

'That they'd come back later and keep me updated on how she's doing.'

'Then we'll just have to wait.'

Ben and Winnie sat for a very long time without speaking, each lost in their own thoughts. Ben's were driving him wild. After a couple of hours, unable to stand it any longer, he got up and started pacing restlessly up and down the waiting room. He was interrupted by the arrival of a female doctor, come to deliver the promised update report. She was about his age, fair-haired and elfin, and looked even more exhausted and careworn than he felt. Her name tag said DR K MOORE. Before she could get a word out, Ben had marched up to her and collared her with a snappish 'Well, how is she?' whose tone he instantly regretted.

'As well as can be expected, under the circumstances. She's lost a lot of blood and a severe trauma like this is a shock to the system. What on earth happened? The police have only told us the basics.'

'I can't tell you more than they have,' Ben said.

Dr Moore frowned. 'Nothing like this has ever happened here before. I'm so sorry. But if it's any consolation, the damage could have been a lot worse.' She explained that, the car being a soft top, the explosion must have theoretically generated far less pressure than there would have been inside a solid bodyshell. Otherwise, the trauma would almost certainly have been much more severe, and very probably fatal. Just Dr Moore's hypothesis. This was her first experience of treating a bomb blast victim.

'She's fortunate to be alive, but she's going to have a long healing journey ahead, both physically and mentally. In due course we can talk about options regarding prosthetic limbs. It's amazing what they can do these days.'

Ben knew that already. A couple of former comrades of his were now going around on artificial limbs, one thanks to a long-range sniper's bullet in Afghanistan and the other from stepping on a Russian-made landmine in Africa. A lot had changed since the days of wooden peg-legs. Thanks to the wonders of modern medical technology they'd got a lot of their mobility back, and some kind of life. But they weren't dancing the tango, let alone leaping about like Nijinsky. It was little consolation.

'That's all in the future,' Dr Moore said. 'For the moment, we'll do everything we can to get her through this.'

'I truly appreciate what you're doing for her. I'm sorry if I sounded impatient before.'

She gave a weak smile. 'It's all right. You're under a lot of stress too. Are you her husband?'

'We're not related.'

'Ah. Then you must be Major Hope. The owner of the car.'

Those cops did love to blab, didn't they? 'I'm retired,' he said. 'This is Aurora's aunt. The rest of her family are on their way.'

'That's good. She's going to need all the emotional support she can get. Loss of a limb is a devastatingly traumatic experience. Some patients handle it better than others, but even so, recovery from such a major life-changing event is going to be a long haul.'

Ben said nothing.

Winnie asked, 'When can we see her?'

Dr Moore shook her head. 'Not until morning, at the very soonest. She's peaceful now. Do you have somewhere to stay locally? Is there a contact number where we can reach you?'

'I'll be right here,' Ben said.

They thanked the doctor again, and then they were alone once more in the waiting room as she hurried back off to her duties.

'Win, there's no reason for you to hang around here all night. Let me see if I can book you into a hotel, all right?'

But he should have known what Winnie's response would be. 'For heaven's sake, Ben. If you're staying here, what makes you think for one moment that wild horses could drag me from this spot? I'm not going anywhere, and don't you try to make me.'

It was past three in the morning by now. Ben fetched them coffee and something to eat from a vending machine, though neither of them had much appetite. He longed for a Gauloise, but he'd have to go outside for that and didn't want to leave her on her own. They tried to make themselves comfortable for the long sleepless night ahead. Winnie was looking pensive, as though something else was troubling her mind and she didn't know whether to speak out or not.

Finally she said, 'I keep asking myself why something like this would happen. I can't understand. Is it possible that someone your father sent down—?'

'Is out of jail after all these years and came back for revenge?' He'd already considered that possibility, and dismissed it.

'I'd say that's a long shot, Winnie. His biggest criminal case was the guy who bludgeoned his wife to death and then killed himself in prison. Anyhow, that was decades ago.'

'Then it must have had something to do with your army days.'

'That's what the police think, too. But I don't believe it did.'

'But it's the only other reason that makes sense. Why else would anyone have—'

'Tried to kill me?' he finished for her. If only she knew how many people still tried to kill him all the time, in his line of work.

'Explain it to me,' she said. 'You know more than you're letting on. I can see it in your face, Ben. That day you went to Dublin. Did that have something to do with this?'

'Maybe,' he said.

Her eyes were filling again. 'I've always been afraid something like this would happen. And now it has, we can't stay here any more. It's not safe for you.'

'To hell with me,' Ben said. 'Who cares?'

She looked as though she wanted to slap him. 'Don't you dare talk like that, Benedict Hope, after all we've been through. *I* care, that's who.'

He felt sorry for what he'd said. 'Nobody knows where we are. I've made sure of that.'

'Then how did they find you? If they tried it once, they'll try it again. Oh, Ben, whatever this is about, whatever you're involved with in these trips away from home that you never want to talk about, you have to stop. You're the only one left of the Hope family. I loved them all so much. I couldn't stand to lose you as well.'

He shook his head. 'I can't stop doing what I do, Win. Don't force me to explain why.'

'Then at least tell me who could have done this.'

'I don't know yet,' he replied. It was all he could say to her, because it was the truth.

But he did know one thing, with absolute certainty and a resolve that had hardened like forged steel inside his heart. That he was going to devote himself, from this moment onwards, to figuring out who had hurt Aurora. That he was going to track them down.

He was going to find them.

He was going to punish them.

And then he was going to send them all to hell.

Chapter 9

He'd spent the night wide awake and not looking forward to what he'd have to do early next morning. Now that time had come, he was looking forward to it even less. In his day he'd faced hard, violent men determined to end his life with guns and blades. Held the line in the face of withering enemy fire. Pushed himself beyond the limits of physical endurance. But all that seemed easy compared to finding the right words to say to a young woman who'd had her whole future snatched away, just because she'd happened to be with him.

Ben knew that Winnie would want to see her niece, too, but Winnie had somehow managed to fall fast asleep in the uncomfortable waiting area chair and he didn't like to wake her. Besides, he preferred to see Aurora alone. Her family would be arriving any moment now. He didn't have a lot of time.

'It's not visiting hours yet,' the nurse told him in the corridor outside the private room. 'Technically I shouldn't let you in.'

'Please. If she's awake I need to see her. One minute, not a second more. Then you can kick me out, okay?'

Call it charm, or the powers of persuasion, or just the look of raw desperation that must have been visible in his eyes; the nurse relented and showed him in to see the patient.

Aurora was sitting up under a crisp white sheet with her head propped by pillows. Where it wasn't masked by the livid bruise on one cheek and the dressing that covered the burn injury on the other, her face was very pale. Her hair was covered by a surgical cap. There was a drip on a stand next to her bed. She looked smaller and thinner and completely washed out, but she was perfectly lucid and even managed a small, weak smile as he uncertainly approached the side of the bed. He willed himself not to look at the empty, flat place where the lower half of her right leg should have been.

All night long trying to think of the things to say, and now he was here he couldn't find the words.

'I don't know what to tell you,' he said.

'You don't have to say anything, Ben,' she replied quietly. 'It's just good to see you.'

He felt the hard lump that had been in his chest move up to his throat. 'How you can say that, after—'

'This?' She glanced down the bed at the place he didn't dare look at. 'It's only a scratch. It'll grow back.'

Humour, at a time like this. Ballet dancers were strong, all right. He'd never seen such fortitude in a person before, and it made him feel about an inch tall.

'I'm so, so sorry.'

'It happened,' she replied. 'There's nothing more to say, nothing more anyone can do. Except just get on with life. Start looking for a new career. Nobody's going to come and see a one-legged ballerina trip the light fantastic, are they?'

He said nothing. Felt nothing. No rage at this moment. Just utter emptiness.

'Come and sit by me,' she said softly.

He sat there silent for a moment, looking at her and wondering how she could be so composed after all she'd been through. They must have her on about fifteen kinds of antibiotics and pain medications, enough to wipe out most people's memory and turn them into a zombie.

'Do you remember much?' he asked her.

'I remember everything. It was a memorable evening.'

'Please don't say that.'

'I got to dance. One last time. If this is how it has to be, I couldn't have asked for more.'

'Is there anything I can do?' he asked her. 'Anything at all?'

She managed another smile. 'You mean, other than make me whole again?'

'Other than that.'

'I'll tell you one thing you can do for me,' she said.

'Name it.'

'Lean closer.'

He leaned closer, until her lips were just inches from his ear. Very softly, in little more than a whisper, she said, 'Look after yourself, Ben. I don't think anyone went to the trouble of blowing up a car for my sake. Promise me you'll be safe.'

He tried to find a reply, but couldn't. Just then, the nurse appeared in the doorway, eyeing him and pointing at the clock on the wall. Looked like his time was up.

'I have to go,' he said. 'Your aunt's downstairs. She can't wait to see you. And your mother, brothers and sister will be here soon.'

Aurora gave a tiny nod and closed her eyes.

'It's going to be okay,' he said. Right now he couldn't see how that could possibly be. But it seemed to comfort her a little, so he said it again. 'It's going to be okay.'

Then he left her lying there, with the strangest and most powerful sense of reluctance combined with relief that he'd ever felt.

The anger didn't come back right away. Not until he'd walked a whole thirty steps from her room. Then it came surging back through him, like a blue acetylene fire that burned even hotter for his guilt and made him clench his fists and jaw as he walked faster and faster down the corridor.

On his way towards the lobby he spotted the elfin doctor he'd met last night. She didn't look as though she'd had a lot more sleep than he had. 'Dr Moore, could I have a word?'

'Of course.'

He told her that he had to go off on an unavoidable trip for a while, but that when he returned he wanted an appointment with the top private prosthetic limbs expert in the business. No expense would be spared in obtaining the best for Aurora.

'I've already been searching online,' she said. 'There's a Dr Waters of the Waters and Mallory Clinic in London. The work they do is the absolute cutting edge.'

'Then I'll want to talk to Dr Waters,' Ben said. 'Can you set it up?'

'I'll call his office. Leave it with me.'

'Thanks. And I don't want Aurora or the family to know we talked about any of this for the moment, okay?'

'Strictly between you and me, Mr Hope.' she said with a smile. 'Did I get the name right this time?'

'Just Ben,' he said, and put out his hand.

'And I'm Kathleen.'

'Thank you again for all you did for her, Kathleen. I'm truly grateful.'

Make me whole again, Aurora had said. Ben couldn't give her back the leg she was born with. But he'd make damn sure she would walk again. And dance again, too, if such a thing was possible.

Winnie wasn't in the waiting area any longer, because Aurora's family had arrived and she was greeting them outside. It was an emotional scene that he watched through the window. He didn't have the heart to join them, so he slipped away unnoticed through another exit and went off in search of a taxi stand.

An hour later he was back at the house. The place felt oddly empty and lifeless without Winnie's presence there. He headed for the kitchen first, stuck a coffee percolator on the stove, and then went down to the basement where the laundry room was, containing big industrial machines that he'd bought in a military surplus auction. It wasn't all missiles and rockets in the army.

In spite of all Winnie's mothering efforts he'd always insisted on taking care of his own washing, and he reckoned had his domestic arrangements pretty well organised. He didn't own more than a minimum of clothes for his needs. Dirty stuff went in one large wicker basket and clean stuff went into another, before being carried up to his little garret bedroom at the top of the house. He grabbed the basket full of dirty clothes and upended the whole lot on the floor. Among them was the crumpled pair of black jeans he'd been wearing the day of his rendezvous with Hugh Mortimer in Dublin. Never bothering to empty pockets until stuff was just about to go into the machine was one of his slovenlier old habits that the years of military discipline had failed to iron out of him. From the jeans pockets he fished out the usual accumulated rubbish – among it a wine cork, a car park ticket, a crumpled banknote and some loose change, an interesting striated pebble he'd found on the beach, a spent 9mm cartridge case that still smelled faintly of burnt

68

Hodgdon HS-6 nitro powder, and the business card that Mortimer had pressed into his hands as he'd been cutting their meeting short. He'd barely glanced at it then, but examined it with much more interest now.

It was a simple, old-fashioned unadorned calling card with 'Professor Hugh K. Mortimer' printed in fancy script across the centre and an English home address and telephone number in a smaller, plainer font beneath. The landline number had the local area prefix 01904, for North Yorkshire.

He carried Mortimer's card back to the kitchen, where by now the percolator was bubbling on the stove. He made himself a mug of coffee, no milk, no sugar, the way he always took it. Then sat at the kitchen table with his mug in front of him, massaged his temples with his fingers to help ease away the headache that was boring through his skull, lit a Gauloise, pulled out his phone and dialled the number.

After a few rings a man's voice came on the line. Ben thought it didn't sound quite like the voice of the man he'd met. Younger, lower-pitched. And edgy, anxious and tense.

'Professor Mortimer?'

'No, this is Lance Mortimer. Hugh's brother. Who's this?'

Ben ignored the question. 'Is it possible to speak to him?'

There was a sound on the line like a gasp, someone catching their breath. It wasn't a normal sound and it instantly told Ben that something was wrong.

'No, it's not possible,' said Lance Mortimer. 'I only wish it were.'

'Is he away?' Ben asked.

'That's not the reason you can't talk to him. Nobody can. My brother is dead.'

Chapter 10

Lance Mortimer's strange tone of voice had prepared Ben for bad news. In a grimly predictable way, this new turn of events fitted the picture perfectly.

'There was an accident,' Lance Mortimer said. 'Two days ago.'

Two days ago was the day before yesterday. The day before the bombing. Ben asked, 'A car accident?'

'No. It happened while he was out in his boat. He . . . he fell in the lake near his home, and drowned.'

'My condolences,' Ben said. 'This comes as such a terrible shock.'

Lance Mortimer thanked him. After a pause he added, 'I'm here at the house trying to sort out his things. There's no other immediate family, you see. Hugh was divorced a long time ago and they never had kids. Are you . . . were you a friend of his? I'm sorry, I didn't catch your name.'

Like a chess player thinking two or three moves in advance, Ben's mind was speeding ahead and working out his best strategy. 'Harris,' he replied. 'Paul Harris.' He could prove that if necessary, because it was one of the fake identities he used on his international business travels, and he'd had a full set of papers in that name made up for him by a master forger in Paris called Thierry Chevrolet. 'I was a student of his,' he added. Another lightning-fast strategic decision.

Unlike a 'Dr' who could be anyone with a PhD, the title of Professor generally had to belong to some kind of teacher. And teachers had students. Ben had been one of those once upon a time, before in a strange twist of fate he'd quit his Oxford Theology course to run off and join the army.

'History? At York?' Lance Mortimer asked. 'Must have been a while ago. My brother took early retirement.'

Ben was building up a profile here. Hugh Mortimer had been a former history professor at York University. Now he was a deceased former history professor. Most likely a murdered one.

'We hadn't been in touch for some time,' Ben said. 'This is awful. What on earth happened?'

There was a long sigh on the line. 'Nobody really knows. A dog walker came across the body washed up on the bank. The boat was found in the lake, half full of water. It looks as if it must have just capsized, or he lost his balance and fell in.'

Ben was thinking that people didn't generally just fall out of boats, and especially not on a smooth, tranquil lake. He said nothing.

Lance must have read the meaning behind Ben's silence. 'I know what people will say. That he was drunk, or that he did it on purpose. The police were asking the same questions. But it turns out there was zero alcohol in his blood. And Hugh wasn't suicidal. He had plans.'

'I'm sure he wasn't,' Ben said.

'What makes it so strange is that he's fished on that lake for years and years. He was an experienced boatsman. And he was a good swimmer, too . . . or at any rate he used to be. I suppose that was a long time ago.' Lance paused. 'It's terrible. I still can't quite believe it's not some kind of weird dream. I had to identify the body, you know,' he added, sounding maudlin. 'It was horrible. Seeing him lying there like that. All puffed up and pale and swollen from being in the water.'

Ben said nothing. He knew from experience what drowned corpses looked like.

'He looked so different.' For a moment it was as though Lance was talking to nobody in particular, just speaking his thoughts out loud. 'Something else was different about him, too. Something . . . *missing*. I can't put my finger on it.' He sighed. 'Anyway, there it is,' he said, back in the present moment again. 'Poor old Hugh. I suppose it comes to us all in the end, one way or another.'

Ben asked about the funeral arrangements, repeated his condolences and got off the line as quickly as decently possible. He took a slurp of his coffee, leaned back in his chair and sat there smoking and thinking for a long while about the chronology of events.

Someone had followed him to his rendezvous with Hugh Mortimer. Someone with prior knowledge of their meeting, or who was under orders from another person who did. Soon afterwards, Hugh Mortimer had become the victim of a surprise boating accident. And then the very next day, the same unidentified individual who'd shadowed Ben in Dublin had been hanging around the scene of the car bombing intended to take him out as well.

Coincidences?

Ben finished his coffee and his cigarette, then changed into a pair of old army shorts and a T-shirt and went for a run on the beach. Only a five-miler, but he drove himself twice as hard, channelling his pent-up anger into every pounding stride. By the time he returned to the house and headed for the shower a light rain had started falling, his muscles were pumped and tingling but the anger was still there undiminished, just as fresh and raw as before.

He knew where he needed to go from here. In his bedroom he grabbed the battered green canvas military haversack that was the only luggage he ever carried on his travels. Stuffed a few essentials into it: one change of clothes, real and fake ID papers in the names of two of his aliases, Paul Harris and Mike Palmer, a wad of cash from his safe, some extra cigarettes, his whisky flask. Then he headed back downstairs and called a taxi, a local guy named Pat whom he knew and often depended on. Pat also happened to have a cousin, Seán, who ran a small car and van rental business in the nearby Connemara town of Clifden. Just the person to provide the necessary transport for Winnie and Aurora's family back and forth to the hospital.

While he was waiting for the taxi to arrive he brewed up another pot of strong black coffee and threw together a couple of sandwiches using the cold remains of Winnie's roast. He lit another Gauloise, locked up the house and stood outside watching the sea until his ride turned up.

The taxi carried him back along the same familiar route to Galway City. His first port of call wasn't to the Divisional Police HQ but the smaller, older Garda station on Mill Street, in another part of town. Ben happened to know that was the location of the fenced yard where stolen, suspicious or impounded vehicles were kept. It was also where the Garda would have taken what was left of his Interceptor, and from where it was unlikely to be released for a while. He doubted that the cops would have even begun their forensic examination yet.

Compared to some of the facilities he'd been required to infiltrate with the SAS, and even to a lot of kidnappers' dens and safehouses, the police station was a pretty low-security affair. An automated pole barrier gate was watched by a couple of cameras on masts, but the rest of the compound was encircled only by a low iron fence, painted a fetching shade of institutional blue.

Ben had Pat drop him off at a nearby shopping mall, with instructions to hang around nearby for thirty minutes before he'd be needed again. In a low-end men's clothing store Ben bought a nondescript black hoodie. Not his usual mode of dress, but they had their uses. In the changing room he stuffed his leather jacket into his bag and put the hoodie on in its place; then with the hood pulled down low over his face and changing his gait to the loping stride of a younger and more laddish sort of individual he walked back along Mill Street, to a blind spot along the station perimeter that wasn't overlooked by any of its windows. He loitered for a few moments to light a cigarette and wait for a woman with a pram to pass by, then glanced left and right to check nobody was looking and quickly hopped the blue iron fence.

Once inside the compound, he threaded his way between the buildings, keeping to the camera blind spots – of which there were plenty – and unseen by the few staff members and uniformed cops wandering about. Any terrorist worth his salt who might have fancied blowing this whole place to shit with everyone inside would have had such an easy task. Luckily for the Galway Garda, the thought had obviously never occurred to them.

It took Ben under ninety seconds to reach the area of the facility he was interested in. Right at the back of the car pound, up near the far end wall next to a prefabricated workshop building, the once familiar, now distorted shape of his old Jensen Interceptor sat unnaturally low on a trailer covered with a tarp. The only personnel member in sight was an old guy supposedly on guard duty, sitting in a Portakabin and bent over his *Racing Post*. Ben watched him for a few moments. He wasn't moving or turning the pages. Maybe he was asleep. It must be an exciting job.

Ben slipped past the Portakabin like a ghost, reached the tarp-covered trailer and ducked out of sight behind the vehicle next to it. He lifted the corner of the tarp and made a low whistle at the state of his car. It had looked pretty comprehensively wrecked under the streetlights and flashing blues of the emergency vehicles, but in the cold light of day the blackened, twisted remains of the burned-out bodyshell were a sad sight. Dr Kathleen Moore had been right when she'd said Aurora had been very fortunate to get out of it without sustaining far worse damage.

Still, Ben wasn't here to dwell on what had happened. He'd formed a possible theory on how the bomber could have been able to follow the Interceptor along the deserted coastal roads from Trá Mhór to Roundstone, in darkness, without being spotted. Now he wanted to see if his hunch was right.

After just a couple of minutes' search of the wrecked car he found the item that confirmed his instincts. Judging by what was left of it after the effects of the initial bomb blast and secondary fuel tank explosion, the GPS tracking device wasn't completely state of the art – but it wasn't the kind of amateurish gadget you could have obtained from a high street Tandy electronics store either. It looked to Ben like a custom-made job, which would pretty much thwart any attempt to trace where it had been bought, and by whom. It had been magnetically clamped to the inside of the Interceptor's right rear wheel arch, a straightforward matter of bending down and pushing it into place. Any pedestrian passerby on a busy street pausing to crouch next to a parked car on the pretext of retying a loose shoelace could do it quickly and unobtrusively.

Ben was certain that it was the tall man with the glasses and the widow's peak, or an accomplice, who had put it there while the Interceptor was parked down the street from the Merrion in Dublin. The meeting with Mortimer, even though cut short, would have afforded them more than enough time to carry out such a simple operation. And of course Ben had completely fallen for the trick – why would he have had any cause for suspicion, at the time?

And so his would-be killers had been following his movements around his sleepy corner of rural Ireland from that moment onwards, looking for their perfect opportunity to plant the bomb. A classic convertible with a canvas roof and none of the security gadgets fitted to modern cars was an easy vehicle to reach inside and stick some kind of explosive device under the dashboard console. More than likely another custom-made item, designed to detonate when it sensed the electrical surge from the ignition system on starting.

Ben hadn't learned a great deal from his reconnaissance mission, but it was a start. And it confirmed his understanding that he was dealing with some fairly clever opponents. Opponents who could very easily have contrived a way to capsize Hugh Mortimer's boat and drown him in his Yorkshire lake.

He sneaked out of the Garda station the same way he'd come, and disappeared back down Mill Street. He dumped the black hoodie in an alleyway wheelie bin and changed back into his leather jacket, then called Pat again.

Next stop, Galway Airport.

Chapter 11

At the same moment that Ben was calling Pat the taxi driver, another phone conversation was taking place. On one end of the line was a very angry man speaking from his large and luxurious home more than 460 miles to the east of Ben's current location, in England, not far from the Scottish border.

On the other end of the line, this side of the Irish Sea, was the tall man with the thick glasses and the widow's peak whom Ben had last seen running away from the scene of the car bomb attack in Roundstone. The tall man was saying little as his employer yelled at him over the phone.

'It would have been bad enough if you'd just let him lay eyes on you the one time. But oh no, you bloody idiot, you let him see you twice! He must have spotted you in Dublin, or how else would he have been able to recognise you the second time in Galway? Do you think he's stupid? I told you what we're dealing with here!'

'I—,' the man with the glasses began to protest, but he didn't get very far. And in any case it wouldn't have been a good idea to argue with this employer.

'Shut up. Do not speak. In other words, you managed to single-handedly bugger up the whole carefully laid plan. Not only did you fail to eliminate your target, but if it hadn't been for your sloppiness the Irish police would have put this incident down to a simple IRA reprisal attack. One dead ex-officer, clear motive, obvious modus operandi, case closed. And a few people in Ireland wouldn't have been unhappy to see their idea of justice being served, either. What do I get instead for my money? Some silly bitch minus a leg and what was supposed to have been a dead man still very much alive and now on the warpath. Which is very, very far from being an ideal state of affairs. Do you understand? *Now* you're allowed to speak. And you'd better say the right thing.'

The man with the glasses and the widow's peak swallowed back his pride and said in a low voice, 'I apologise for the error, sir. It won't happen again.'

'Good. That's what I want to hear. So moving forward, let's see if we can't rescue this situation, shall we? At this point, we have to assume that Hope's suspicions have been alerted about the connection between the attack and his meeting with Mortimer. That's the reason he called the house, and gave Mortimer's brother a false name. It was only thanks to our voice recognition software that we flagged it was him. So I anticipate that his next move will be to travel to England and start sniffing around for more information, and you're going to go after him. He may use the alias "Paul Harris", or possibly another that we don't know about yet. Given his present occupation and past training it makes sense for him to have several. Either way, it's imperative that we get to him before he discovers too much.'

The man with the glasses and the widow's peak asked, 'What about the brother?'

'I don't regard that buffoon as a threat to us, not at this stage,' his employer replied. 'He may have some vague knowledge of Hugh Mortimer's research activities, but none with regard to where they were leading, or any of his specific plans. Besides, we can't afford to attract more suspicion by eliminating the second brother as well. It's Hope we're after. And you'd better make sure that he doesn't slip through our fingers again.'

'He won't.'

'Then get on with it. You know what to do.'

Chapter 12

By mid-afternoon Ben was stepping off the plane onto English soil at Leeds–Bradford Airport. He'd called Winnie before boarding his flight, to confirm to her that he was going away again, perhaps for a while, and to say that Pat's cousin Seán was going to be bringing her a mini-van to use for her and Aurora's family to use to travel back and forth to the hospital over the next few days. Winnie thanked him, but there was so much more he wished he could have done.

As he left the terminal he had more vehicle hire business to deal with. The guy at the Hertz desk was young and balding with a bad case of nerdiness. Ben told him he wanted the highest-performance car they had available, and after a quick search of the inventory the guy picked out a last year's model BMW M3 saloon. Seeing Ben's dubious frown he said, 'If speed is what you want, you won't be disappointed. Of course, the real beast of the Beemers is the Alpina – now those are *fast*. Hand-built with all kinds of special performance upgrades and a massive increase in power. But we don't have any.'

Ben hadn't heard of an Alpina and wasn't that interested. He said, 'Okay, I'll take the M3.' Partly out of habit and partly out of caution he filled out the hire agreement paperwork in the name Paul Harris, grabbed the key, and minutes later he was blasting from the airport towards York. The car was quick and responsive, for sure, but it felt overly sanitised and mannered after the raw, brawny rolling thunder of his old Interceptor. And it was just too damned *German*. Ben didn't think he'd ever be able to love a BMW.

It was a warm and sunny afternoon and the Yorkshire countryside was beautiful, as vividly green and grandly rugged in places as southern Ireland. But he wasn't here to admire the scenery. He pushed the car hard and fast, wilfully abusing the rental company's no-smoking policy and pumping out a wild, chaotic Miles Davis live performance on a jazz station at full volume as he chewed up the miles from the airport to the city. The BMW came with its own sat nav, but his army experience had taught him to prefer the fail-safe, no-tech navigation option of a paper map to GPS. His route bypassed the city and led through some pretty stone-built villages before he arrived at the home of the late Professor Hugh Mortimer.

Set in its own extensive and private grounds surrounded by trees and a stone wall with a tall gateway, the dead man's residence had been a fairly impressive rambling old pile of a place. It was more than just a house and a little less than a mansion, but not by much. The original building with its timbered walls looked as if it dated back to the sixteenth or seventeenth century, and had been added to in a rather slapdash way over time, with jutting wings and a clock tower, complex gabled roofs sloping in all directions and leaded windows framed by red and green ivy. Like its late owner, the house and gardens had an aura of tatty eccentricity about them. As the car crunched slowly up the long driveway flanked by straggly overgrown rhododendrons and buddleias he caught a glimpse through the trees of the lake in the background, sparking in the sunshine.

Ben pulled up and got out of the car. He had travelled to the place with the intention of getting inside and poking around to see what he might find in the way of clues. Mortimer had been divorced and childless, so there wouldn't be a grieving wife or kids to get in his way. But as he approached the house he saw he wasn't the only visitor that afternoon. The dinky little Triumph Spitfire two-seater parked near the steps of the pillared entrance had its keys in the ignition and a leather golf bag jammed into the passenger footwell. Whoever had arrived in the Spitfire had entered the house leaving the front door slightly ajar.

Ben's first instinct was to make himself scarce and come back later when nobody was around. But then his curiosity got the better of him and he changed his mind. Climbing the front steps he peered through the crack in the door and gently pushed it wider. He called out, 'Hello?'

No response.

The inside of the house smelled of wax polish and old leather. It was an impressive entrance hall. Hugh Mortimer's passion for all things historical was immediately obvious from the artfully arranged displays of ancient weapons – halberds, flails, swords and daggers – that decorated the dark-panelled walls, and the two armoured knights standing guard either side of the passage that led deeper into the house. A broad staircase led upward from the hallway, and to the left and right were two sets of double doors. Ben tried each in turn. The room to the left was a music room, with a large antique grand piano by one bay window, a harp by another and a whole collection of old stringed instruments lining the walls. Ben was no expert when it came to early music and couldn't tell a lute from a mandolin, let alone a citole or a dulcimer, but they were all obviously period examples and probably highly valuable. It seemed that the late professor had been quite an enthusiast.

The room to the right was a comfortable sitting room with chunky, well-worn leather armchairs and a tall fireplace, lots of books and no TV. On a grandiose mahogany sideboard stood a collection of silver trophies. Ben paused to read the engraved inscriptions on their bases. They all dated from the sixties, and had all been won in traditional archery competitions back during Mortimer's Cambridge days. Above the sideboard hung a framed black and white photo that showed a group of young men in a field, posing with their tall bows, jutting out their chests and trying to look as manly and dangerous as possible. In the background of the photograph stood a row of straw-boss archery targets. The caption below it read CAMBRIDGE UNIVERSITY LONGBOW CHAMPIONSHIP, 1965. Peering more closely, Ben spotted a very young Hugh Mortimer at the front and centre of the photo. He was almost unrecognisable with a mop of curly black hair, a proud grin and his weapon in his hand. Perhaps the very same weapon as the one hanging from mounts on the wall above the picture, Ben thought.

He moved on. The passage from the hallway led down to a kitchen, a sunlit dining room with a long walnut table in the centre and Renaissance art on the walls, a scullery, utility room and cloakroom. No sign in any of them of the owner of the Triumph Spitfire and the golf clubs.

Ben headed for the stairs and moved quietly up to the first floor. There was a galleried landing overlooking the hallway below, and off it several glossily varnished doors with heavy brass knobs. The first one he tried was a bedroom, with a big four-poster bed and a broad window with a view of the rear garden and the lake beyond. The second was a study.

And it was there that Ben found the mystery visitor.

The study was pretty much what one might have expected of a man like Hugh Mortimer, and it was clear this had been the room in which he'd spent most of his time. Not just its many bookcases and shelves but also just about every horizontal surface was piled high with books, periodicals, folders and papers. At one end, in the light from the draped double window, stood a desk with its drawers pulled open and much of their contents seemingly scattered over its top, adding to the clutter.

And standing by the desk, half turned away from the door, was a man Ben had never seen before but who bore a striking resemblance to the late professor. He was perhaps fifteen years younger, with less grey in his hair and none of the look of the batty academic. Instead of an elbow-patched tweed jacket he wore the kind of garishly patterned cardigan that only a chap of the golfing persuasion could have considered stylish, and a white linen baker boy flat cap. The cap went well with the Triumph Spitfire, in a self-consciously dashing kind of way that might have been convincing to its owner in the mirror, but to Ben's eye simply said 'poser'. He had little doubt that he was looking at Hugh's younger brother, Lance Mortimer.

But Lance Mortimer was looking at something else, something he'd apparently found in a desk drawer as he went through his brother's things, and which had grabbed his attention so completely that he hadn't noticed Ben in the doorway. What Lance was staring at with a look of horror was a sheet of paper that fluttered in his right hand, while in his left hand he clutched a second. From where he stood, Ben couldn't make out what was on the sheets. They could have been personal letters, or official documents, bills, tax demands, or anything at all. But whatever their content was, it obviously had shocked Lance Mortimer to the core, and judging by his expression he must only just have come across them moments before Ben appeared.

Ben decided it was time to announce his presence, and he cleared his throat. Lance Mortimer went as rigid as if someone had discharged a shotgun in the room and wheeled around to face the doorway, still clutching the two sheets of paper. He took a step back and gaped at Ben, half indignant and half terrified.

'Who the hell are you?'

Chapter 13

Ben stepped into the room, spreading out his open hands in a friend gesture. 'I'm sorry if I alarmed you,' he said. 'And please forgive the intrusion. My name's Harris. Paul Harris. You must be Professor Mortimer's brother. We spoke on the phone.'

Lance Mortimer's face, white with shock only instants earlier, now began to turn to the colour of a beetroot. He blinked a couple of times, started to say something and then remembered the sheets of paper he was holding. He moved back towards the desk and quickly shoved them in the drawer and rammed it shut. 'Oh . . . y-yes,' he stammered, 'I remember now. You studied with Hugh. I . . . excuse me, I didn't recall that we'd arranged to meet.'

'We hadn't,' Ben replied. 'But I was passing through the area, and I thought I should come and pay my respects. I didn't know if anyone would be here. Just to see the old place again, you know?' He looked around the room as if he'd been there a thousand times before. 'Brings back so many memories. Poor Professor Mortimer.'

'How did you get in the house?' Lance asked, still flushed.

'The front door was open,' Ben said. 'You shouldn't do that, you know. Can't be too careful these days. Left your keys in the ignition, as well.'

Lance was having a hard time taking his eyes off the closed desk drawer and he obviously was only half-listening. 'I . . . well, anyway, thank you for your kind words. So you studied history at York with Hugh, did you?'

'The best tutor I ever had,' Ben replied. He was taking a risk by winging it like this, though he doubted that Lance was really interested enough in him to start asking too many hard questions.

Like Lance, Ben was more concerned with the papers in the desk. What were they, and why had he been so quick to whisk them out of sight like that? Ben went on, 'It's thanks to your brother that I developed a passion for the subject. That's what I was calling about, you see. I've been working on a research project of my own and I wanted to pick my old professor's brains about something.'

'Research project, eh?' Lance snorted. 'It isn't about those two bloody princes again, is it?'

That wasn't the kind of hard question Ben had been worried about, but it threw him nonetheless. He managed not to let his hesitation show as he replied, 'No, it's not about the princes.'

Whoever the hell *they* were, he thought to himself. *What princes?*

'Thank goodness for small mercies,' Lance said sourly. 'I'm amazed he'd want to talk to you about anything else. He was forever banging on about them, and the sodding Ricardians. I swear, sometimes I used to think that if he ever mentioned them again to me, I'd strangle the living daylights out of him.' Catching himself, he suddenly turned pale again, his shoulders sagged in defeat and he swallowed hard. 'Oh

God, what a bloody awful thing to say,' he sighed. 'Christ. I could do with a drink. You want one as well?'

Maybe old Lance wasn't such a bad sort after all.

'I won't say no,' Ben replied. It was the only sincere thing he'd said so far.

'Sit yourself down then, seeing as you're here,' Lance said, waving to an armchair. He skulked over to a cabinet built into a bookcase, and as someone who just happened to know his brother had kept a stash of booze in there, he pulled out a bottle and a couple of glasses. Ben heart fell a little when he saw it was pale sherry. The sickly sweet concoction tasted to him like cough mixture. Lance poured out two hearty measures, carried them over with the bottle stuck underneath his arm, handed Ben his and sat in the mismatched leather armchair opposite. 'Cheers,' he muttered, and drained his glass in one gulp. 'Needed that,' he said, reaching for the bottle and topping it up again to the brim.

Ben raised his own glass, still full. 'To Hugh.'

'To Hugh,' Lance said, and knocked back another gulp. He certainly was drinking it as though he needed it. Ben wondered how much of that was due to his grief, and how much to the discovery of those papers in the desk. It had clearly shaken him up.

'This must have come as a terrible shock,' Ben said. Watching him closely, trying to gauge his thoughts from his body language. 'A death in the family is bad enough, but when it's so sudden and unexpected—'

Lance nodded sadly, beginning to sink lower into his chair as the sherry relaxed him. 'Though I don't mind telling you – and perhaps you already know this – my brother and

I, we weren't really that close. There was quite an age gap between us.'

'I do remember he mentioned that part,' Ben said, playing along.

'Our mother passed away many years ago, as he might also have told you. And poor Father suffered from premature dementia, so Hugh sort of took it upon himself to protect his little brother.' He paused, drank some more sherry, then said bitterly, 'Since you knew him, you must have found out first-hand how cranky and downright unpleasant he could be. He never approved of how I wanted to live my life. Wanted me to become an academic like him. I was a bright kid – okay, maybe not as brilliant as he was – but sports were more my thing. He made no secret of his disgust – it's not too strong a word – when I went off and trained to be a golf professional. Then I went to live in the States for quite a while. Florida.'

Lance was one of those types who needed to talk when he was stressed out. Ben let him.

'After I came back to Blighty to take up the pro job at the local course in York I only lived half an hour away down the road from here, but we didn't see one another all that often. Last time we spoke he said some awful things to me, about wasting my life on a mindless game knocking little balls into little holes. I said, "Look who's talking, spending all these years on all this dusty forgotten old history crap nobody gives a shit about." We had quite an argument. Hadn't seen each other since.'

Lance reached for the bottle again, topped himself up and offered it to Ben. Ben shook his head. He'd barely touched a drop compared to Lance's several glassfuls.

'But he was my brother,' Lance said, shaking his head sadly. 'And if now it turns out something terrible has happened to him . . .'

Ben thought that was an odd thing to say. 'I thought something terrible had.'

Lance knocked back his sherry, poured yet another. Working his way quickly through the bottle. He looked tormented, as if something was eating him. He kept glancing back towards the desk. Something was definitely up with those papers.

'Oh, he drowned all right,' Lance agreed, with a wild look at Ben. 'But what if it was no accident?'

Ben narrowed his eyes. 'You're losing me there. You told me on the phone that it was. Why the change of story?'

'Because I've just found something that puts rather a different light on it,' Lance blurted out. 'Here, let me show you.' Filled with sudden energy and the urgent desire to share his discovery now that his inhibitions had been loosened by the sherry, he put down his glass, sprang over to the desk and yanked open the drawer. He grabbed the two sheets of paper that he'd been so quick to hide earlier, along with a third, and brought them over to show Ben.

'See? I told you what I told you on the phone, because that's what I believed at the time. But look at these. What's anyone supposed to make of them? Eh? Eh? You explain it to me, because I can't bloody understand it.'

Ben took the papers and laid them on his knee, studying each one carefully.

He might have known.

They weren't bills, or official documents. Nor were they personal letters, in the usual sense. They were the old-fashioned kind of anonymous threatening notes, made from odd bits of newspaper headline stuck together on a blank piece of paper. Some kidnappers still used these for demanding ransom from victims' families.

But these weren't ransom demands. One said simply, **BACK OFF. YOU KNOW WHAT WE'RE TALKING ABOUT**. Another was a little more explanatory: **KEEP YOUR NOSE OUT OF WHAT DOESN'T CONCERN YOU**. And the third said, **YOU HAVE BEEN WARNED**.

Lance stood re-reading them over Ben's shoulder with his arms folded and a scowl on his face. 'What the hell was my idiot brother mixed up with?'

'And you say you found these just by chance?' Ben asked.

'Yes! Like I told you, it was just now, moments before you arrived. I'd finished with clients for the day, and I came over here to get on with sorting through all this mountain of stuff that's going to take me weeks and weeks because it's just me on my own, you know, with nobody to help as usual, and there they were in the drawer. They were in a plain brown envelope, right on top of all his other papers. I thought it was something legal or financial. But this! I can't believe it. What can it mean?'

Ben sniffed one of the notes. The stuck-on letters still smelled faintly of newsprint ink and glue. These had been done quite recently. 'I think it's fairly self-evident, don't you? Someone was threatening your brother.'

Lance started pacing up and down in agitation. 'And whatever it was about, they got him so stressed out and terrified that he jumped in the lake. It's the only way this makes sense. He was trapped. He needed a way out.'

Ben was thinking that there were other ways that it made much more sense. Lance couldn't see the obvious. Maybe he couldn't bring himself to see it.

'But *why*?' Lance exclaimed, throwing up his arms. 'What possible reason would anyone have for threatening Hugh? He wasn't into anything dodgy or criminal. I can't believe there was anything that remotely interesting about his life. He had nothing to do with women, never really cared much about them to begin with. Same goes for money. He wouldn't have touched gambling, or drugs. His only vice was this stuff here' – pointing at the now almost empty sherry bottle – 'and even then he'd only take a small glass once in a while. He was just this fuddy-duddy dry old stick of a retired academic who lived his life buried in books and dusty journals, obsessed with solving some forgotten historical mystery nobody else in the world gives a toss about.'

What Lance was saying suddenly made an idea flash through Ben's mind like a bolt of lightning.

A historical mystery. It took him back to the things Hugh Mortimer had been talking about in Dublin. The disappearance of a pair of children, young brothers, more than five hundred years ago. It had been right under his nose and he hadn't made the connection until this moment.

Ben said, 'You told me he was always banging on about the two princes. What princes are you talking about?'

Chapter 14

Lance Mortimer stopped pacing and stared incredulously at Ben. 'I thought you said you were a historian. How can you have studied with my brother Hugh and not know about this stuff?'

'History's a big subject,' Ben replied.

'Not for my brother Hugh, it wasn't. Forget the rest – as far as he was concerned, the only events of any consequence that ever took place in the entire universe happened in the courts of medieval England. His world began with the Plantagenets and ended with the Tudors. He was a nut. Even learned to play the bloody lute so that he could immerse himself deeper in their way of life. I'm surprised he didn't dig a moat around the house and ride about on a horse, saying "methinks" and "forsooth".'

'Sounds as if you know a bit about it yourself,' Ben said.

'How could I escape it, with a brother like that? I was force-fed this bollocks for years. But I thought everyone knew about the princes in the Tower. The story of Richard the Third? You know, like, as in Shakespeare?'

'Forgive my ignorance,' Ben said. 'I was never much of a Shakespeare fan.' He wasn't big on the historical kings of England, either. The only one he remembered from school was an earlier Richard, the famous Lionheart. And then only because that king had been vaguely mixed up in the legend of Robin Hood, which had captured Ben's imagination as a boy.

'Good for you. Who cares anyway?' Lance replied, waving it all away impatiently. 'It's just one of those nasty little episodes from bygone times that some people seem to get all worked up about, as though they had any relevance today. I'm sick of hearing about it.'

But Ben wanted to know more. 'These princes, were they brothers? Two young boys who disappeared?' It was all connecting together in his mind with Hugh Mortimer's bizarre missing persons case, though he still couldn't understand what it was about.

'Yeah, something like that,' Lance replied dismissively.

'And their names were Richard and Edward?'

'All coming back now, is it?'

'Tell me the rest,' Ben said.

'Why? What does it matter? Some bastard was threatening Hugh and might have been the reason he drowned, and I have to go through all this shit again? Christ, you might not be much of a historian but you're not any less crazy than he was.'

'Humour me,' Ben said. 'Sit down and let's finish the bottle. Not like you've anything better to do, is it?'

Lance reluctantly threw himself back into the armchair and poured the last of the sherry into his glass. 'Well, it's a long story and frankly I can't be bothered trying to remember it now, but it seems that these two brats were a threat to the king at the time. Usual story, all about clinging on to power. That's all these people were interested in. So he banged them up inside some dank hole in the Tower of London, where they couldn't cause him any trouble. Hence "the princes in the Tower". Get it?'

Ben was quickly finding out just how big the gaps were in his knowledge of British history. 'I get it. And the king in question was Richard the Third?'

'Yeah, yeah,' Lance replied disinterestedly. 'Another one. Everybody seems to have been called Richard in those days. He was the last of the Plantagenet kings that had been running things in England for centuries. The deformed one. Only thing that sets him apart from the other lot. Apart from being a sadistic child murderer, that is.'

Ben wondered what the hell he was talking about. 'Deformed?'

Lance had to smile. 'Oh, Hugh would go bananas if you used that word. Better still, if you said "King Quasimodo" he'd throw an absolute fit. He couldn't stand any mention of Shakespeare either, because of how his beloved King Richard was portrayed in the play as a villain and a creepy sicko. And so I used to memorise lines from it that I could quote at him, or else I'd tell a load of hunchback jokes, just to wind him up. Like the one about the hunchback and the guy with the club foot. Ever hear that one? He'd be climbing the walls.'

Ben hadn't heard that one, and he wasn't in the mood to hear it now. 'And so this king, he was threatened by these two kids? Why?'

He'd come to Mortimer's house to search for clues. Now here he was, drinking nasty sherry and getting a History 101 class with a half-inebriated golf pro in a silly hat. The joys of detective work.

'Because,' Lance replied wearily, as if he didn't want to spend another instant of his life on this tired subject, 'there's a theory that he'd grabbed the throne illegitimately, though don't ask me how, and that they had a claim to it.'

'So he locked them up.'

'To begin with. But then it seems that wasn't enough for him, because he was paranoid that someone might spring the brats from prison and use one or the other as a figurehead to mount a rebellion against him. They were always rebelling against each other in those days. So to protect his own position and prevent that from happening, he sent a couple of his knights round to nobble them in their beds. Wasn't until centuries later that someone dug up their skeletons deep inside the Tower. Poor little buggers. What a way to go.'

Ben cast his mind back to his meeting with the late professor, and remembered him expressing his doubts on the theory that the boys had been murdered. *And I'm not the only one who feels that way*, Mortimer had added cryptically. Ben was starting to wish he'd given him a chance to say more, before cutting him off the way he had. Had he been too quick to dismiss him? Maybe. But there was no use regretting it now. All he could do was try and understand what the hell was really going on here.

'And that was the end of the princes in the Tower,' Lance went on. 'Or so the story goes. Could've been worse, I suppose. The bloodthirsty slimebag could've ordered them to be hung, drawn and quartered. They were a right vicious lot, those Plantagenets. Not that Tudors were exactly all sweetness and light, slicing heads off left, right and centre. But at least old King Henry the Eighth didn't go around murdering children. That's the absolute pits.' Lance drained the last few drops of his sherry, and gave a loud belch. 'Anyhow, who gives a shit? None of it matters now.'

'Apparently it mattered a great deal to your brother.'

Lance let out a loud snort of derision. 'You bet your arse it did. More than his own family. Why do you think Belinda buggered off and left him? She couldn't stand it any more. As he got older he was getting more and more loopy. Like getting mixed up with that weird fringe historical society, little more than a cult if you ask me.'

'Are these the "Ricardians" you mentioned before?'

'That's them,' Lance replied, rolling his eyes. 'The so-called Richard III Society. The fan club. They're not even real historians, most of them. Nothing but a gang of amateur misfits who for some bizarre reason have a bee in their bonnet about wanting to exonerate some psychopathic hunchback from five centuries ago. Freud would have a field day.'

'So these Society people don't believe the princes were murdered, either?'

'"Believe",' Lance grunted. 'That's the key word. It's no more than a belief system they have. Like a religion. I reckon they're just a bunch of folk with nothing better to do than sit around a pub table raking over the same sad old story. I told Hugh over and over again that he was wasting his time with the whole nonsense.'

Lance was getting redder in the face and his voice was growing louder as he warmed to his theme. Ben could see this had clearly been a big sore point between these two brothers, each of whom seemed to have some fairly strong ideas about how the other should live his life.

'That's why none of it matters any more,' Lance went on emphatically. 'And I refuse to waste any more time talking or even thinking about it. Because it's absolutely not possible that all this princes in the Tower garbage could have anything whatsoever to do with these threatening letters. Still less with anything suspicious about my brother's drowning and whatever else is going on.' He let out another of his explosive snorts. 'I mean, come on. Seriously? Give me a break.'

Maybe Lance was right. Maybe this whole thing was a crazy waste of time. Then again, his brother hadn't thought so.

Ben asked, 'Then what? People don't make threats for no reason.'

'No, and there's got to be something else going on here. But the police will get to the bottom of it. Don't you worry about that. I just so happen to have some pretty well-placed connections in that department.' Lance tapped the side of his nose with a knowing look, and seemed to be inviting Ben to ask what those connections were. Ben said nothing, so Lance went on, 'One of my golf clients is the Deputy Chief Constable of North Yorkshire Police.'

'You've called him?'

'I can go one better than that,' Lance said importantly, shaking his head. 'Because I also happen to know that my pal the Deputy Chief Constable is at the Fulford Road station in York this afternoon. I'm going to drive over there right now and personally show him these letters. He doesn't mess around, my pal. He'll be straight over here with a squad of officers. Then we'll soon find out what's what.'

'I'm sure you will.' Ben looked at his watch and stood up. 'Then I'd better not hold you up a moment longer. I'll be on my way.'

'Here, take this,' Lance said, digging out a business card and pressing it into Ben's hand.

Ben looked blankly at it. 'What for?'

'In case you hear something more,' Lance replied. 'Or maybe someone you know in the area might want golf lessons.'

Ben seriously doubted that. 'Best of luck, Lance. It was nice meeting you.'

He left Mortimer's brother in the study gathering up the letters in their plain brown envelope and headed back to his car. But rather than drive back the way he'd come, towards the village, he turned down a leafy, shady narrow country lane that took him around the side of the house. He parked the BMW where a stand of oak trees screened it from sight of the Mortimer residence, grabbed his bag and left the car, climbed the wall and dropped down behind the bushes inside the grounds.

The overgrown garden provided enough cover for a whole SAS troop as he stalked quickly and silently back towards the house. He reached the sprawling rhododendron at the edge of the driveway just in time to spot Lance emerge from the house and hurry across to his little Spitfire, clutching the brown envelope with the threatening letters inside. Lance tucked the envelope into a pouch of his golf bag, fired up the sports car, slewed it around dramatically with a spray of gravel and sped up the driveway past where Ben was hiding.

Ben waited until the sound of the Spitfire had faded away to silence before he stepped out of the bushes and returned to the house.

Chapter 15

Ben Hope was someone with an extremely sharp eye for details, a talent that had saved his skin many times. He was also pretty good at breaking into houses, whether or not they contained kidnappers to be taken out and victims to be rescued. It was thanks to that sharp eye of his that, during his quick tour of the downstairs earlier, he'd noticed the broken catch on one of the utility room windows.

That was where he headed now, skirting around the outside of the house to the rear. He was pleased though unsurprised by the lack of security cameras, Hugh Mortimer not being the kind of man who would deface a fine historic home with such vulgar modern additions. Glancing up at one of the windows of the study where he and Lance had been talking minutes earlier, Ben saw that the ivy grew thick all along that side wall of the house. A little beyond the rear gardens, the gently rippling waters of the lake sparkled through the trees.

Ben paused, looking at the house and then back towards the lake and thinking about how much time he had to poke around the place before the police might turn up. York was only a few miles away, and in that zippy little sports car of his Lance wouldn't take too long to get there. No telling whether the cops would even take his newfound evidence seriously enough to mount a rapid response. But if those golfing connections with the top brass paid off, this place could soon be swarming with officers searching for more evidence of a possible crime. Ben reckoned on a safe time margin of about forty minutes. Before he began his search of the inside, he decided he'd go and take a look at the spot where the professor had drowned.

Turning away from the house he headed down the long, sloping and unmown back lawn, and at the bottom of the garden found a bark chip path that led him through the trees to the lakeside. It reminded him of the way he could walk down from his own house in Ireland and be at the water's edge in moments. But at this or any time of the year, Mortimer's lake was a lot more tranquil than the pounding waves of the Atlantic shoreline. As Ben waded through the long grass by the bank he looked across the smooth, empty water and wondered again what had happened to Hugh Mortimer. A procession of ducks was tracking across the lake nearby. Over among the yellow reeds by the far shore he could see a pair of swans gliding, pausing now and then to dabble under the surface. The sky over him was perfectly blue and the sun was warm. It was a lovely and peaceful spot, the last place on earth where anyone could have imagined a man could meet with a sudden, violent end. Then again, if Ben had learned anything, it was that sudden violent ends could pretty much happen anywhere, at any time.

A little way further along the bank he spotted a small outboard motor boat that had been pulled up from the water and was lying half-hidden in the long grass. *Hugh's boat*, he was thinking as he walked over to it. The grass was partly trampled flat around the boat from when the forensic pathology team had examined it in the aftermath of the drowning. Once the coroner's verdict had come in as accidental death, the cops would have lost interest and the boat would have just lain here abandoned.

Ben circled it, thinking about how an experienced boatman like Hugh Mortimer could just have fallen out of it by accident. From the depth of the hull and the high sides of its gunwales, that seemed even less likely to him now. Assuming some kind of foul play was involved, Ben could imagine how a scuba diver could appeared out of nowhere – or maybe two divers, one to each side of the boat – and grabbed hold of the edges of the hull, rocking it back and forth with enough force to tip someone out into the water. He had no way of knowing for sure. But that was how he would have planned it, in the shoes of an assassin.

Just then, the two swans on the far side of the lake suddenly burst out of the reeds as if something had startled them, and took off with strong beats of their long white wings. He watched them fly in an elegant twin curve over the water and then come skimming gracefully down to land further from the shore. He wasn't going to learn any more here. He turned away from the boat and started walking back towards the house.

Back at the utility room window with the broken catch, it took him less than thirty seconds to get inside. He still had a comfortable amount of time to hunt around for anything else he might be able to find. He moved quickly back through the house towards the entrance hall, between the knights in armour, reached the stairs and trotted up them to the galleried landing and the study. He went straight to the desk where Lance had found the threatening letters, hoping he might find more of the same that Lance had missed. He spent some time carefully rooting through the remaining drawers opening every envelope and sifting through every sheaf of papers, but none of the drawers contained anything of interest. He pulled them out to check for items hidden in the recesses of the desk behind them, or taped to their undersides. Zero.

Aware of the sand slipping through the hourglass, he kept on hunting. But there wasn't much. In Ben's experience of this kind of clandestine detective work, people's diaries often revealed a lot of useful information, as well as the old-fashioned kind of address books of those who still used them. Hugh Mortimer seemed to have had neither, and the few forthcoming events he had lined up were scribbled on a medieval-themed calendar that hung on the wall near the desk. Of those, leaving aside the dentist's appointment in two weeks' time and a house insurance bill to be paid by the end of the week after that, the sole entry that caught Ben's fleeting curiosity was pencilled in under the abbreviated heading 'R3 SOC'. It didn't mean a great deal to him until after he'd moved away from the calendar and come across the stack of periodicals jammed into a bookcase. They were the quarterly publications of the Richard III Society, the historical group that Lance had been lambasting earlier.

It seemed to Ben that not many so-called fringe cults would have been capable of publishing such a well-produced glossy journal, filled with illustrations and detailed academic articles written by actual historians, but what did he know? Mortimer had underscored single lines and entire passages here and there. A few of the articles were heavily annotated down their margins, and on some of the inside covers were numbers, dates, names, and various other arcane scribblings, all in the same tiny, barely decipherable chicken-scratch handwriting.

Returning to the calendar and understanding now what 'R3 SOC' was short for, he noted the date and time of what could only be the next Society meeting. By coincidence their next get-together was coming up very soon, only the following evening. There was no location mentioned, but Ben intended to find it and be there.

His search hadn't been as fruitful as he might have wished for, and it had taken longer than expected to sift through so much clutter. He suddenly realised that his self-imposed time window had almost closed. Moments later, he heard the sound of tyres crunching on the gravel outside. He cursed softly under his breath. The study was a long room with two windows, one overlooking the front of the house and the other on the ivied side-wall. He stepped quickly over to the window to see Lance Mortimer's Spitfire rolling up the driveway with two police cars in tow, one marked and the other a plain navy saloon.

It seemed that Lance's golf club connections had paid off after all. You could call 999 to report a massacre in progress at an old folks' home and not get a response this fast. Peering from the window, Ben watched the cars pull up in front of the house. Lance was all pumped up and excited and still wearing that damn silly hat as he jumped out of his Spitfire. Three uniformed cops emerged from the patrol car, while from the unmarked Ford stepped a burly middle-aged guy in a dark suit, whom Ben took to be Lance's high-up golfing client buddy. The younger, gingery-haired homunculus who accompanied him had the look of a Detective Sergeant. Guys like these didn't need uniforms. They virtually had the words POLICE OFFICER stamped across their sweaty foreheads.

Ben was pretty sure that Lance would bring the cops straight upstairs to the room where he'd come across the letters. That meant it was time for Ben to make his exit. It also meant he wouldn't be leaving through the front door, or even the back. He quickly wiped down the surfaces he'd touched, stuffed the journals into his bag, waited until Lance and the cops were out of sight inside the house, then hurried over to the side window, pushed it open, slung the bag over his shoulder and climbed out.

It was a long way to the ground, with no ladder and not so much as a drainpipe to hold on to, but the ivy was strong and it held Ben's weight as he scrambled down the side of the house. He jumped the last eight feet, landed quietly and sprinted across the garden to the cover of the trees. It took him under a minute to skirt around the perimeter to the place where he'd scaled the wall. Moments after that, he was back in his car and taking off, unseen and unfollowed.

Or so he thought.

On the far side of the lake, the leader of the observation team who had been watching the house through their high-powered binoculars reached for his radio to update his base command.

'Blue Leader, checking in.'

'Report, Blue Leader.'

'Mortimer's brother just turned up at the house with five cops. Reason unknown.'

A pause. 'What about Hope?'

'Target exited the property through a first-floor side window and made his escape from the grounds, ten seconds ago.'

It was their second radio contact with base in the last forty minutes. The first had been to report that their target was down at the lake, checking out the boat. 'We thought we might have a problem with some birds that got startled when they came near us, but he didn't get suspicious. Green light to enter and neutralise?'

'Negative, Blue Leader,' the reply had come back. 'It's too close to the scene. Stand by and report back the moment anything happens.'

Which instruction the team had duly carried out. Now the radio call from base said, 'Copy that. Is the new tracking device secured to his vehicle?'

'Affirmative. We're locked on and receiving. Target is heading south.'

'Stay on his tail, maintaining safe distance,' base replied. 'See where he goes and wait until it's a good time and place. Then move in and kill him.'

The watchers had their orders. But what they didn't know was that they themselves were being watched.

Chapter 16

Ben headed south from the Mortimer residence, back towards York city, planning his next move as he drove. In his bag on the passenger seat was a wealth of material that he would now have to plough through. It might lead him somewhere useful, or it might equally turn out to be a blind alley. There was only one way to find out whether or not he had any viable leads.

That wasn't something he'd be able to do sitting in his car, or a café somewhere. He would need room to spread out and organise himself, which meant he was going to have to find a base to work in. Somewhere he could hunker down in private, bury himself in his task and bide his time until the Ricardians' meeting tomorrow evening, location still to be determined.

In the heart of the historic old city he found a cosy little inn that had a room available, and off-road parking monitored by surveillance cameras to cut down on the chances of anyone planting a bomb in his car. The building was old and pleasingly traditional, with a lot of exposed beams everywhere, creaky, uneven floors and not a right angle in the place. A friendly, frizzy-haired overweight girl called Trish showed him up the narrow winding stairs to his accommodation on the first floor, which was much nicer than he needed, being someone who'd put up in all manner of ratholes in his time. The room was small and simple with two single beds, a tiny ensuite shower room, and a little window alcove with a table and chair where he could spread out his papers and spend all the time he needed studying them. The bar and restaurant directly below his room served local beers and decent, unpretentious food of the pie-and-chips variety.

It was better than perfect. Unless his research led him to discover something amazing in the meantime, there would be nowhere else he'd need to go until tomorrow night's meeting.

Somehow, Ben doubted he was going to find anything amazing, though you never knew. He wasn't particularly looking forward to trawling through pages and pages of dry-as-dust academic research. He'd already had his fill of that kind of stuff, years earlier in his previous life as a Theology student at Oxford. He sometimes found it hard to believe he was the same person who'd done those things.

He got himself a mug of strong filter coffee from the bar, no milk, no sugar, and then closed himself in his comfortable bolt-hole, pulled the chair up to the desk, jerked open the ancient sash window, lit a Gauloise and got down to the business of poring over the journals from Mortimer's study. They were a collection of various editions of the *Richard III Society Bulletin*, their quarterly magazine, spanning several years. Each edition was laid out the same way with an editorial piece at the front, letters from members, events news and a section for book reviews, while the bulk of the text was feature articles on various historical topics related to the king and the period of his reign.

Ben started with the most recent journal, published just a couple of months ago. Its glossy cover depicted a late sixteenth-century portrait of Richard, by an unknown artist. He gazed at the face: it was long and thin and rather mean-looking, with a lined brow under a shapeless cloth hat and a tight-lipped expression that could have been a pinched sardonic smile. The king had had seriously bad hair, a long dark mop that looked like a Cocker spaniel's ears protruding from under the hat. But then, maybe everyone had looked like that in those days. Moving on from the cover, Ben leafed through some articles: one on Richard's Scottish military campaign in 1482, before he was king; one about the Florentine ruler Lorenzo de' Medici who had been a contemporary of Richard's; and one about some new research claiming to show that medieval warhorses hadn't been quite the hulking great chargers they were portrayed as in movies. Ben was a little disappointed to read that, but he couldn't say he was learning much so far of any value to his investigation.

Quickly becoming disenchanted with the articles he flicked through the pages until he came to a Community News section towards the back, and that was where he found something more interesting. He hadn't realised until now that the 'cult' had so many branches and groups across Britain, in the USA and as far afield as Australia. There were news snippets from the Bristol branch, Merseyside and Worcestershire, and an announcement of a change of meeting place for the Northern Ireland group. But the one that attracted Ben's focus concerned the York branch. They had a quarter-page news item to themselves, with a group photo taken at their regular meeting venue, the White Boar pub.

Bingo. Ben made a note of the name. At last he'd learned something of practical use. He wondered if their choice of pub had to do with the Ricardian emblem of the boar he'd noticed pictured here and there throughout the pages of the bulletin, a fearsome creature with great curling tusks. The group photograph showed the regional group's chairman receiving one of those oversized cheques used for publicity shots, made out to the Richard III Society York Branch to the tune of three hundred pounds. Pretty small money, but judging by all the delighted faces of the assembled members, it wasn't every day their little group received that much of a donation. Standing in the centre of the shot, clasping one end of the cheque and beaming as though it were worth millions, the chairman was a short guy around his late forties or early fifties, with a protruding round belly and a greying beard. He had on a leather Barmah hat, well-scuffed and tilted at a jaunty angle, and a sleeveless tactical-style vest jacket like outdoorsy types and fishermen wore. In the small printed caption below, his name was given as Tony Kitson.

Not all the faces in the picture were unfamiliar to Ben. Standing in the back row of the assembled group, sporting a cheesy grin and a crooked tie along with the same elbow-patched tweed jacket Ben had seen before, was Hugh Mortimer.

Seeing him again brought a flood of other images to Ben's mind, just as vivid as the photo in front of him. He saw Aurora running through the rain towards the parked Interceptor. Saw the man with the glasses and the widow's peak hurrying away from the scene. Saw the bright flash of the explosion and the flames that engulfed the car with Aurora inside it. Saw her lying in her hospital bed with a flat patch under the sheet where her leg ought to have been. He closed his eyes. Sighed. Then reopened them and returned to the bulletin. Nothing here yet to explain murders and car bombings. No obvious clues pointing in the direction of possible perpetrator. Just a bunch of articles and pictures of dead people from history, old buildings and tapestries. Something about this whole thing felt weirdly off to Ben. People were getting hurt and killed, and here he was reading up on the activities of an amateur historical society. Either he was following the wrong lead entirely, or there was a lot more to this princes-in-the-Tower mystery than met the eye. Sure, people argued about stuff from history. But to kill or maim each other over it – that was taking things to a whole other level.

And yet Ben's instinct was telling him to persevere. The more he reflected on his meeting with Mortimer, the more he was convinced that it had been the things the man had left *un*said that were most significant. By Mortimer's own admission, he hadn't explained himself very well. He'd been asking for a chance to clarify what he was talking about when Ben had cut him off short.

Now it was clear Mortimer had known he was in danger. Had he been intending to tell Ben about the threatening letters? Had he been about to mention them, if Ben hadn't dismissed him as a crank and walked out of the meeting?

That was a possibility that haunted Ben's mind. At the time he'd formed the impression that Mortimer wanted him to go on some crackpot mission searching for two missing boys from five hundred years ago, but in fact Mortimer had never asked him for that. All he'd said was 'I've been searching for them and I need your help'. Maybe if Ben had been more patient, Mortimer would have explained what he really needed from him, about his fear that something bad might happen to him if he didn't have someone skilled and used to danger watching his back.

What if that was what Mortimer had really been asking for, Ben's protection? Ben might not have taken the case, but at least he'd have been able to recommend one of the many good ex-SAS men he knew who specialised in that kind of work.

Then Mortimer might still be alive now. And maybe nothing bad would have happened to Aurora. Maybe.

Ben said out loud, 'Shit.' His coffee was cold, and tasted bitter anyway. He uncapped his whisky flask, took a slurp, ran his hands down his face and then refocused his mind on his work. Setting the more recent journal aside, he went back to the ones on which Mortimer had scribbled little notes and doodles in some of the margins. Maybe there'd be more to learn here.

But if there was, it wasn't jumping out at him.

It took him quite a while to work out that not all of the pencilled notes had any bearing on the text of the articles in whose margins they were scrawled. After a lot of wasted effort trying to cross-reference the two, Ben could only conclude that Mortimer, in his scatty professorial manner, had simply grabbed the nearest and most convenient scrap of paper on which to scribble his random thoughts and ideas as they came to him, for want of a handy notebook or jotter. There were eight references to something or someone called 'PW', which Mortimer had obviously considered important enough to underscore or circle with question marks and exclamation marks, sometimes so heavily that his pencil point had almost torn through the page. Four of the 'PW' notes appeared together with a different date in the 1480s or 90s. One said simply 'PW 1497', and it wasn't clear to Ben whether or not it was related to the article next to it, which had devoted a couple of paragraphs in passing to the subject of King James IV of Scotland. Three more were accompanied by a cryptic reference to some unknown book or scholarly article: 'Arthurson p. 42', 'c.f Pollard, 1913, pp 101–107' and 'see Brit Lib Journal vol.18, no.1 (Spring 1992)', all of which were totally obscure to Ben without anything to check them against.

Aside from the meaningless and frustrating 'PW' references, Mortimer had scribbled a few other, more recognisable, names that Ben was able to find in the pages of the bulletins, like Margaret, Duchess of Burgundy, and King Henry VII. Which seemed to confirm that Mortimer's notes were all somehow connected to the history of the time. But it was a small relief, as none of these other references offered any kind of clearer understanding, let alone answered the questions that were swirling around his mind. Trying to piece together a coherent picture out of this heap of historical detail was like trying to drink out of a fire hose or drive blind through a snowstorm. After two hours of concentrated effort, Ben's head was spinning.

The only non-historical note from Mortimer was one that Ben found scratched in jerky ballpoint pen on the back of the second most recent bulletin. It said 'R. Berg new add', and below it was an address in the Principality of Liechtenstein, with an overseas phone number that was only barely readable. Given the way that the professor seemed to use whatever odd bits of paper he could lay his hands on to scribble on, this 'R. Berg' – presumably a person – could be anybody at all, and might be totally unconnected with all this other stuff. There was only one way to find out. Ben tried the number, but got only an international dial tone with no way of leaving a message.

It hadn't been a very fruitful research session. After another hour of racking his brains and searching for enlightenment in the pages of the bulletins, Ben finally took a much-longed-for break. Feeling too frazzled even to smoke another cigarette, he stretched out on the single bed nearest the window and closed his eyes again, but he couldn't shut out the vision of all those meaningless words and numbers, names and places floating about like dots of static on a TV screen.

He was beginning to think that there just wasn't enough to go on. And now a new anxiety started creeping into his mind. What if Tony Kitson and the other York Ricardians decided to cancel tomorrow night's meeting, coming so soon after the death of one of their prominent members? That thought was enough to make him spring up from the bed and reach for his phone and a general Society contact number from the back of one of the bulletins. The number rang and rang, but again nobody was answering.

Darkness was beginning to fall outside his window. Realising suddenly that he'd barely eaten a scrap all day, the hunger hit him and he grabbed his jacket, locked up the room and headed downstairs.

The inn was a lively and popular place, filling up with punters for the evening, and the buzz of conversation and even the high-pitched warbling of Mariah Carey's latest hit blaring from the jukebox were a welcome relief from the hours of brain torture. He quickly knocked down a pint of local ale at the bar while chatting with the amiable Trish, who was in a flirtatious mood and full of questions about where he was from and what he did. Ordering a sixteen-ounce grilled ribeye steak and chips from the bar menu, Ben graciously escaped to a single corner table at the back of the bar lounge, lit up a Gauloise and worked on a second pint of ale while his meal was being cooked. When it arrived, his steak was thick and juicy with just the right touch of pink, and the home-made chips were perfectly crispy and fluffy in the middle. He ate slowly, taking his time and getting started on a third pint as the inn filled up more and more and he was surrounded with chatter and laughter. The beer and the ambiance were working on him. He hadn't felt this relaxed since his last dinner with Winnie and Aurora at home in Ireland. He had a sense that it wouldn't last. But he intended to enjoy the moment as best he could while it did.

Meanwhile, the watchers who had tracked him unnoticed from the Mortimer residence that afternoon were paying close attention to their target's every movement. Two of them were perched on stools by the bar, to all appearances just ordinary members of the public, and another pair were occupying a table in the lounge just a few metres away from where he sat quietly eating. The two attractive young girls with them were paid escorts who were being generously recompensed for their time and had no idea of the purpose of the job.

The problem for the watchers was that, as far as movements went, the target was making very few of them. Their orders were to wait for an opportune time to take him out and dispose of the body. But as long as he remained here in such a busy public space, that opportunity wasn't forthcoming.

One of the watchers by the bar took out a flip phone and called base to give a situation report. The fat, cheery barmaid had disappeared into the kitchen for a moment with another customer's food order.

'Where is he now?' base asked.

'Right now he's eating steak and chips and drinking a beer,' the watcher replied in a low voice, inaudible to anyone else over the music. 'Afterwards he'll probably go back up to his room. We can deal with him then.'

'That's a negative, Blue Leader. I repeat, discretion is your top priority and will be observed at all costs. Is that understood?'

'Understood.'

'Stay on him. He can't remain put for ever.'

The watchers at the bar slowly finished their drinks and ordered another two half pints of non-alcoholic lager. They went on observing their target as instructed, with no idea that everything they were doing was being carefully noted by the slim, elegant Middle Eastern gentleman in the dark jacket who had wandered nonchalantly into the bar a few minutes earlier, politely and in perfect English ordered a Coke and a packet of crisps and taken a seat in an alcove by the fireplace.

From that position the gentleman in the dark jacket could casually observe the four-man surveillance team as well as their unsuspecting target. He was fully briefed on the identity and background of the man called Ben Hope whom the watchers were tracking. Thanks to his employer's great wealth of contacts and resources, he also had detailed information on the identities and backgrounds of the watchers themselves.

After a few more minutes, having seen enough to make his report, the man in the dark jacket got up and left, with a courteous nod and a smile to the young woman behind the bar. The watchers paid no attention to him as all their concentration was focused on their target, now close to finishing his meal.

The man exited the inn and strolled unhurriedly across the street to the parked black Mercedes with tinted windows, where three of his associates were waiting in silence. The other three were sitting in a black mini-van at the other end of the street, in radio contact with the Mercedes.

The man in the dark jacket got into the car's front passenger seat. He didn't speak to his associates. The two in the back seat had their compact submachine guns, the stubby Kurz version of the Heckler & Koch MP-5 as issued to their national military, across their laps. They were hard and fearless men, experienced combatants and ready for action, even though at this moment their team was deployed in a purely scouting role with instructions to monitor from a distance and report back. Still, they knew enough about the outfit they were dealing with to know that if things kicked off for whatever reason, the situation would escalate quickly and violently.

The man in the dark jacket took out his phone and made the call to his faraway employer.

'This is Farouk. They are still watching him.'

Chapter 17

Whatever the watchers might have been told, their target did remain put. But not for ever. After his evening meal was finished Ben took his time over a fourth ale, then paid his dues at the bar and returned straight to his room, locking himself in. He didn't look again at the historical bulletins that night.

Awake early the next morning, he did two hundred press-ups on the floor by the bed, followed without a break by a hundred sit-ups, until the muscles in his chest, shoulders and abdomen were burning and tingling. Then he took a cool two-minute shower in his little ensuite bathroom. When he was dried off and dressed again, he lit the first Gauloise of the day and then picked up his phone to retry the number for the Richard III Society.

Getting through this time, he spoke to a nice lady to whom he introduced himself as Paul Harris, a former student of the late Hugh Mortimer. He was interested in joining the Society, he explained, and was calling to enquire if tonight's York branch meeting was still going ahead? If so, he was interested in attending. Expressing her own sadness at the professor's untimely demise, the nice lady said she'd find out for him, and took his number. A few minutes later she called back to say that yes, as far as she knew, tonight's meeting was going ahead from eight until ten o'clock as planned. She hadn't been able to talk to Mr Kitson, the branch chairman; would Mr Harris like to have his number? Mr Harris said thank you, he didn't think that would be necessary.

With the SAS you learned to become very good at waiting for things to happen, especially as the majority of military operations they were deployed to were stood down without a shot fired after days or even weeks of painstaking preparations and stakeouts. Ben had spent extended periods holed up in some pretty dire places, barely moving, existing on very little, completely blended into the landscape. By contrast, a day resting up in a comfortable room with everything he needed and a bar and restaurant immediately below him was a cushy number. At 9.15 he went downstairs, ate a breakfast of eggs, bacon, sausages and beans, drank a mug of the bitter coffee, then headed back up to the room and spent the next hour perusing the articles in the bulletins. Next he tried redialling the phone number in Liechtenstein in the hope of speaking to the mysterious 'Berg', whoever he or she might be. But like yesterday's attempt, all he got was an endless dial tone and no messaging service.

He skipped lunch, because he was burning up so few calories sitting around doing little, and spent the afternoon mostly resting and thinking in the privacy of his room. Come evening, he grabbed his things, locked up the room once again and headed quickly to the off-street car park to jump in the BMW and go speeding off across York.

The evening was pleasant and warm. After stopping at a newsagent's en route to buy a motoring magazine, Ben found the White Boar pub quite easily, not far from the castle in the heart of old historic York. The city was full of venerable and ancient buildings and the pub was no exception with its half-timbered black and white façade, looking as though it must date back to the sixteenth century: a little after Richard III's time but still very respectable. The picture on the sign outside bore some resemblance to the Ricardian white boar, tusks and all. There was a car parking area in front, and beyond that a fine ivied wooden archway framed by ancient gnarly trees led through to a small courtyard, off which what had certainly once been a coach house or mews adjoining the side of the main building had more recently been converted into a relatively modern extension tastefully incorporated into the historical architecture.

Warm golden light spilled from the pub's windows and plenty of movement could be seen within. The place seemed to be doing a brisk trade. From where Ben sat in his parked BMW across the street, he could hear the sound of music and voices. Some cars had already gathered in the courtyard area and more were steadily arriving, while small groups and families were turning up on foot. Ben lit a Gauloise and watched from his driver's window, wondering if any of the people he could see were there for the Society's meeting.

Then one person turned up who certainly was. Ben spotted the short, portly figure ambling down the darkening street, limping slightly and walking with a stick as though he suffered from a hip problem. Over his shoulder hung a bulging leather satchel on a strap. Apart from the stick and the satchel Tony Kitson was sporting the exact same outdoorsy kind of garb he'd been wearing in the photo in the bulletin. The battered broad-brimmed hat was poised at an identical angle. Maybe he'd been sleeping in the same clothes and never taken the hat off since the day the picture was taken.

As Ben watched, Tony Kitson limped up to the main entrance of the White Boar and disappeared inside. It was 7.51 p.m., with the meeting due to start in a few minutes. Ben grabbed his new motoring magazine, rolled it up into a cylinder and stuck it into the side pocket of his jacket. Then he got out of the Beemer and crossed the street to the White Boar's little parking area. He walked between the stationary cars, stepped aside to let a new arrival park and passed under the wooden arch into the courtyard at the rear. The open space doubled as a summertime beer garden, with some benches and picnic tables. Two of them were still vacant, and he sat pretending to make a phone call on his mobile while facing the windows of the coach house, which gave him a good view of the interior of the pub. The coach house had alcove seats and restaurant tables but seemed to be mostly empty with the majority of customers crowding together in the main lounge bar. He could see the bearded, hatted Tony Kitson meeting up with a group of eight or nine fellow members, a mix of male and female, variously older and younger but nobody much under fortyish. There were a lot of long faces, some hugs and handshakes were exchanged and it was clear from this distance that a good deal of emotion was being expressed over the recent death of Hugh Mortimer.

Still talking to nobody on the phone, he kept watching as the group filtered towards the back of the coach house, away from the crowd, and gathered round the largest of the round tables. It took them a couple of minutes to get drinks and organise themselves, by which time another half-dozen members had arrived.

With the meeting about to start, Ben ended his feigned phone call and headed inside the pub. The decor was all period-style wood panelling and beams, rather like his inn but probably a little more authentic. And unlike his inn, they stocked a decent selection of single malt whiskies, so Ben ordered a double shot of twelve-year-old Laphroaig and carried his drink over to a leather-upholstered alcove near the back of the bar lounge where he could be within sight and earshot of the Ricardians' gathering. He spread out in his alcove, sipped his drink and opened his magazine, to all outward appearances getting deeply immersed in motoring classified ads while his mind was completely focused on the activity a few yards away.

The punters in the main lounge were an active lot and making quite a bit of noise, but the Ricardians had the coach house almost completely to themselves and it was a much quieter space. Tony Kitson had hung his stick over the back-rest of his chair, opened up his satchel and taken out a pile of Society literature that was being distributed around the table. He'd also produced from his bag a large framed picture of Hugh Mortimer, which he had placed in the centre, handling it with almost reverential care as though it were a religious icon. Someone had brought him a pint of dark ale in a dimpled glass. He cleared his throat, raised a hand to signal for silence and the murmur of conversation around the meeting table fell to a hush.

Tony Kitson thanked them all for coming. 'I see we have some new members this month, which is fantastic. Welcome aboard, Jim, Sally and Pete. Very sadly, though, this York branch meeting is also the first in a long time where we haven't had the pleasure of seeing our dear old friend Hugh Mortimer, who as you all know is no longer with us.'

There were some mournful murmurs and bowed heads around the table. One of the women dabbed at her eyes with a tissue. Kitson said, 'I know a lot of us would have wanted to cancel tonight's meet, in light of this tragic event. But I'm glad that we decided to come in spite of everything, to raise a glass in honour of our fallen comrade. It's what he would have wanted us to do.' He held up his pint. 'And so, a toast. Hugh, we thank you for the tireless work you did to support and promote our group. We thank you for the gift of your historical scholarship and erudition, second to none. But most of all we thank you for sharing the warmth and joy of your friendship through all the years we were privileged to know you. The world just isn't the same without you. Cheers, me old buddy.'

It was a moving elegy, and there were some more tears flowing among the members by the time he'd finished. Everyone raised their glasses and chorused, 'To Hugh.'

Ben wondered from Kitson's use of 'fallen comrade' whether he was ex-military, possibly invalided out of the armed forces some time back, hence the stick. He went on idly leafing the pages of his motoring magazine as the meeting continued. It was hard for him to follow everything that was being said, but it was all basically the sort of history talk that was to be expected. It appeared that some kind of discussions were underway at York City Council concerning the restoration of a fifteenth-century church that had some association with their favourite King Richard. They covered that topic in some detail before moving on to the matter of suggested new formats for the Society bulletin and an upcoming election of Society officers.

None of which was either scintillating or particularly instructive, from Ben's point of view, and midway through it he decided it was worth risking a break from it to go and get himself another whisky and a packet of bacon fries.

Returning to his alcove a few moments later, it didn't seem as though he'd missed anything critical. By the time he'd finished the packet the meeting had more or less dissolved into general conversation. At about 9.50, ten minutes before the end, Ben slipped away and went back to his BMW.

He wasn't worried that the content of the meeting had been of no use to him. That wasn't why he was here.

He had the faces of the group members embedded in his memory. Sitting in the car watching the pub entrance he counted them off one at a time as they left. Some got into their cars and drove off into the night. Some left on foot, in ones and twos. Some had obviously hung around for another drink, but Ben was happy to wait until closing time if necessary. He wasn't going anywhere.

Tony Kitson was the last of the group to leave. Ben watched him emerge from the doorway and set off on foot in the direction from which he'd come, hobbling on the bad hip, his bag over his shoulder.

Ben got out of the car, crossed the street at an angle and followed him at a fast stride, soon catching up. When he was ten yards behind him he called out, 'Mr Kitson? Tony Kitson? Could I have a word, please?'

Kitson froze at the mention of his name. He looked around and stared at Ben in the glow of a streetlight, and obviously didn't like what he was seeing, because he quickly turned away and kept walking, faster than before, the gammy leg swinging out wider with each hurried step and the exaggerated limp making him sway from side to side like a listing ship, his stick tap-tap-tapping on the pavement.

'Mr Kitson, it's about Hugh Mortimer. Please, I'd like to talk to you.'

That didn't seem to reassure Kitson either. He was hurrying as fast as he could go, in danger of tripping over his own feet. There was an Indian takeaway joint ahead, with the narrow, dark mouth of an alleyway entrance just the other side of it. Kitson stumbled past the takeaway joint and darted out of sight into the shadows of the alley, in so much of a jittery rush that he dropped his bag. Ben swore under his breath and quickened his pace after him.

By the time he reached the corner and gave chase down the alley, Kitson was gone. Ben hesitated, letting his eyes get used to the darkness. All he could see among the shadows was the restaurant's row of large plastic wheelie bins and metal dustbins lined up along the wall to his left. A dim light was shining through the frosted window of the restaurant kitchen and cooking smells emanated from a whirring ventilator shaft above it. He could hear the sound of voices from inside, speaking rapid-fire Bengali. It was hard to see where the alley led, if anywhere. Perhaps right between the buildings to a street on the other side, where Kitson could have made his escape. Or he could have slipped through some unseen doorway and be hiding there. Ben ventured deeper into the dark alley, angry with himself for letting the guy get away from him so easily.

He turned suddenly as a sound from behind him caught his ear and he sensed a movement in the shadows. It wasn't an alleyway rat. A burly shape lunged at him out of the darkness and something long and thin and metallic that gleamed dully in the light from the restaurant kitchen flashed towards him, slicing the air with a hiss.

Ben instinctively dodged the arc of whatever it was and stepped back, lowering himself into a bent-knee fighting crouch. The burly shape came at him again, and now he could see the outline of the broad-brimmed hat silhouetted in the light of the restaurant window. The glittering steel whooshed through the air towards Ben and he had to jump back once more to avoid it.

'Get away from me,' rasped the same voice he'd heard addressing the meeting at the White Boar. 'Get away from me or I'll poke a hole in your guts! You hear me, you bastard?'

Tony Kitson was more visible now as he lurched closer, into the pool of light. He wasn't as steady on his feet without his cane. But he hadn't lost it. It was still there, except it had suddenly taken on a different form. The slim three-foot blade in his right hand was pointing at Ben's belly. In his left hand was the wooden shaft that had come away like a scabbard to unsheath the weapon deceptively hidden inside.

A sword stick. The defensive choice of nineteenth-century gentlemen looking to protect themselves from footpads and cutthroats who might be inclined to accost them in a dark alleyway. The weapon was made more for stabbing than for cutting. Not very sharp-edged, but potentially very deadly indeed. As many a villain had found out the hard way, back in olden times. And the way that Tony Kitson was brandishing his left Ben in no doubt that he was ready to make good on his promise. The point came lancing Ben's way again, forcing him to retreat. Then again, and again, darting at him like a spear with enough force to skewer him right through. For a man with a hip disability, Kitson was attacking with surprising speed and determination.

He was no fool, either. Ben understood now that Kitson's flight hadn't been meant as an escape. It was a lure, intended to draw his pursuer into the privacy of the alleyway where no witnesses could see what happened next. Kitson was fully prepared to leave him dead on the ground if need be. But he was no homicidal maniac. He was someone who was clearly very afraid for his life and prepared to defend it at all costs.

Just what was he was so scared of? That was the question Ben wanted to answer. But right now wasn't the time to be asking, because he needed to focus all his concentration on not getting himself perforated.

They circled one another in the darkness. Ben was trying to manoeuvre around close enough to the restaurant's metal bins to be able to grab one of their lids by its handle and use it as a shield. But Kitson could see his play, and wasn't having any of it. The next strike came at Ben with lethal ferocity, and if he hadn't dodged it as quickly as he did, it would have been his liver on the receiving end.

Enough.

As Kitson came lunging at him one more time and the blade speared point-first towards his belly, Ben saw his chance, stepped nimbly to one side, let the weapon thrust past his body and delivered a sharp, stunning downward blow with the ridge of his hand to the nerve centre in the man's right wrist that was intended to temporarily disable his grip. There was a cry of pain as the shock exploded up Kitson's right arm. At the same instant, Ben grabbed the blade and twisted it easily out of the man's numbed fist. Then he delivered a stamping kick to Kitson's upper right thigh that sent him sprawling backwards against the wheelie bins and dumped him solidly on the ground.

Ben stood over the fallen man with the captured sword stick in his hands. He hadn't wanted to hurt the guy. Just to put him decisively out of action so that he might be able to talk some sense into him.

Kitson didn't know that yet. Lying on his back breathing hard and looking up at Ben with hatred in his eyes he grunted, 'Go on then, you sodding scumbag. If you're going to kill me now, then you'd better get on with it.'

Ben said, 'Tony, if I'd wanted to kill you, you wouldn't even have seen me coming.'

'Then what do you want with me?'

'You and I need to have a conversation.'

Chapter 18

Tony Kitson stared at Ben, the fear and hatred in his eyes giving way to a look of total confusion mingled with pain. 'Who the hell are you?'

'I'm the guy your friend Hugh Mortimer tried to hire to solve a problem he had,' Ben replied. 'He came to me because he believed he was in danger and needed help. I didn't make a good job of that. Now people are getting hurt and I'm here to find out who's doing it.'

'Then you definitely haven't come to kill me.' Still not fully convinced.

'Not unless you really piss me off,' Ben said. 'I'd sooner sit down with you and talk. I have a lot of blanks I need to fill, and I think you might be able to help with that.'

'And if I don't feel like talking?'

'Then you just missed your best chance of catching whoever murdered your friend.'

Kitson stared at Ben for a few moments longer, as though trying to decide whether or not to trust him. Then he breathed a sigh of relief that made him appear to deflate like a balloon. 'Christ. I really thought you were one of them.'

'You mean one of the people who killed Hugh?'

'I know someone did,' Kitson said. 'I just don't know who, or why.'

130

Ben nodded. 'Then maybe you and I can figure it out together. Let's go.'

'Go where?'

'Your place.' Ben reached out a hand. Kitson took it, and Ben helped him to his feet. 'That's a handy little accessory you have there,' he said, giving him back the sword stick.

Kitson carefully replaced the blade in its shaft, clicking a little retaining catch built into its handle ferrule, and it was an ordinary-looking walking cane again. He shrugged. 'It's illegal, but who cares? You never know when you might need to look after yourself.'

'I'm sorry if I hurt you.'

'Took a lot worse tumbles than that in the Royal Marines,' Kitson replied, dusting himself off. 'Like the one that buggered me up for good.'

'Parachute training?' Ben asked. Not all Marines went in for it, but for those that did, the training was no less intensive and risky than what he'd gone through himself.

'You guessed it. One bad landing, and that was it. End of my service days.'

'Jumping out of aeroplanes can be an iffy business,' Ben said. 'I've jumped out of a few myself.'

'Paras?'

'Special Air Service.'

'Huh. Might have known I was tangling with one of you lot. You've got the look. All those blokes are the same.'

'Not me,' Ben said. 'Do you have a car?'

Kitson shook his head. 'Still got the old Landy but I had to give up driving it because of my hip. Doesn't get any better. These days I use the bus. But if we don't hurry we'll miss the last one going out that way. It's right out in the sticks.'

'I'll drive you. Come on.'

They retrieved Kitson's fallen bag at the mouth of the alleyway. As they headed back towards the car, the older man limping a little more stiffly than before, he explained to Ben that he lived a few miles from York, not far from the small town of Pocklington, the gateway to the Yorkshire Wolds. 'Just me and the cat,' he said. 'The Missus walked out on me a long time back.'

It took a little effort to wedge Kitson into the BMW's sporty passenger seat. Ben sped out of York and they were soon winding up into a rural region of low hills and sweeping moonlit valleys, now and then a farm or a lonely greystone church. On the way, Kitson talked about his conviction that foul play had been involved in Hugh Mortimer's drowning. 'He was being threatened, you know. Told me not to tell anyone. Then after it happened, I went to the police about it but they didn't want to know. Where was the evidence? Why didn't Hugh report it himself? Basically they brushed me off as a bit of a nutter.'

The cops might be taking it a lot more seriously now that Lance had shown them the letters, Ben thought. Not that they'd be any more likely to learn anything useful. He asked, 'Didn't he give any indication of who might be threatening him?'

'He wouldn't say. Keeping his cards close to his chest, as always. But I'm pretty sure it had to do with the research he was doing. What else could it be? That was his whole life.'

'His history research? Richard and the princes?'

Kitson nodded. 'Sounds barking mad, doesn't it. How could events that happened all those centuries ago lead to a man's murder? But I can't see any other explanation. He must've stumbled on something really big.' He looked at Ben. 'How much do you know about what Hugh was researching?'

'Only what his brother told me.'

'Lance. Huh.'

'You know him?'

'I only met the prat once. Once was enough.'

Ben asked, 'So tell me. How does a guy like you, an ex-Marine, get involved with all this history stuff? Forgive me for saying so, but it seems like an unlikely kind of fit.'

'I never paid much attention at school,' Kitson said. 'Thought all my lessons were a load of boring old shit, and history most of all. Kings and queens and dates and all that – I mean, give me a break. Then I left the place as soon as I could, signed up for the forces and never gave any of it another moment's thought for years and years. Until one day, long after my accident, and not long after Suzy left, I was sat drowning my sorrows in the White Boar and it just so happened that there was a Society meeting on that night. Well, I ended up getting talking to them, and that's when I first met Hugh. He made me understand.'

'Understand what?'

'That it's not about names and dates and things that took place long ago. It's about real people. And in the case of Richard, it's about the principle of standing up for a bloke who's been treated like garbage, had his name and reputation dragged through the mud and spat on by everyone for centuries. And I realised, Christ, if they can do it to a king, they can do it to anyone. They can do it to the little guy, guys like you and me. And so that's what got me hooked on learning everything

I could. It's not so much about history as it is about trying to set the record straight, righting an injustice.'

'What was the injustice?'

Kitson gave him a knowing look. 'You'll see.'

Some twelve or thirteen miles to the east of York, they passed by the small rural town of Pocklington and soon after that came to the even smaller village of Barmby Moor. Kitson had made his home in a remote valley half a mile from the village, on a twisty narrow road with empty countryside all around and out of sight of his nearest neighbour. He was lucky to have a bus route passing anywhere near the place at all.

Ben parked the car and helped Kitson out. The solitary cottage was enclosed by a low drystone wall, and had a lean-to outbuilding with a tatty old Land Rover looking sad and neglected outside. The house's exterior had seen better days too, but inside it was as well cared for as it could be by a mildly-disabled single man existing on an army pension. A tiny, narrow front hallway led to a bedroom to one side and through a rustic wood-slat door to a living-room on the other. In cottagey style the doorway was low enough that Ben had to bend his head slightly to avoid braining himself on the jamb, while the shorter Kitson could walk straight under.

The main room was a well-lived-in space, comfortable and homely. A pair of threadbare armchairs stood facing one another either side of a well-used inglenook wood-burning stove, in the glow of a side lamp. A couple of stuffed and mounted animal heads, one a fox with its fangs bared in a snarl and the other a red stag with an impressive ten-point crown of antlers, peered glassily down from the walls. Historical books and papers crammed several shelves and bookcases – if not quite to the chaotic extent of Hugh Mortimer's study, they nonetheless gave the impression of Kitson being a widely-read self-educated scholar. Ben recognised the framed art print above the fireplace as the same medieval battle scene he'd seen in one of the Ricardian journals. A large ginger moggy uncurled itself from its resting place on the sofa, eyed him resentfully and slunk off to hide.

Kitson hung his leather hat over one spiky antler of the stuffed stag's head and hooked his stick over the other. 'Did you shoot that?' Ben asked, pointing at the taxidermy.

Kitson shook his head. 'Me? Nah, bought both of these as a job lot in an antique shop in York. I haven't shot a gun since I left the military.' He took the framed photo of Hugh Mortimer from his bag and set it on the mantelpiece, gazing wistfully at it for a moment before he turned towards Ben and said, 'I'll put the kettle on for a cuppa. Unless you'd like something stronger? There's some scotch left, if you don't mind drinking it out of a mug. We don't stand on ceremony here.'

'No problem for me,' Ben said.

'Watch out for Marmalade, by the way,' Kitson said. 'He doesn't like people too much. Tends to bite strangers.'

'I'll try not to get mauled. Thanks for the warning.'

Kitson limped over to a sideboard, grabbed the whisky bottle and sloshed generous helpings into a pair of chipped, tea-stained mugs. He handed the one to Ben that said BIG BOSS MAN and flopped heavily into one of the armchairs clutching the one with the picture of a classic Series One Land Rover. 'Where do we begin?' he asked Ben.

'At the beginning,' Ben said. 'If we're going to figure this out, you need to tell me everything you know about Hugh's research and this whole bloody business of Richard and the princes in the Tower.'

'All of it?'

'Every damn detail. I need to get as full a picture as I can.'

Kitson took a slurp from his mug. 'All right then. Better buckle up. It's a long and crazy story.'

Chapter 19

'If all you know about this is what Lance could have told you,' Kitson began, 'then you know about as much as most people do about the story of Richard and the princes. Which is to say, bugger all, and I'm going to have to get back to basics.'

'I'm all ears.'

'Right. So the official version goes like this: wicked nasty horrible King Richard III, a twisted hunchbacked child-murdering piece of shit, locked his poor little nephews in the Tower of London, aged just twelve and nine, because their royal blood made them a threat to his ambition for power. They were the sons of Richard's brother, who had been king before him but died young. The elder of the two boys was lined up to become king after his dad, but their evil uncle wasn't having any of that. Grabbing the throne on his brother's death, he kept the poor little kids in prison until such time as he had them smothered to death, to make sure they'd never be a problem. Probably the most famous, or infamous, unresolved murder cases in British history. Sound about right?'

'That's more or less the way Lance told it,' Ben replied.

'And it's pretty much the way it's taught in schools, history lectures, books. There's only one problem with it. It's a pile of total and utter bollocks.'

'I had a feeling you were going to say that.'

'The all-time worst ever case of slander is what it is,' Kitson said indignantly. He was already getting heated up to his theme and Ben sensed there was a lot more to come. 'Nothing but lies and deception. A load of trumped-up accusations made against the most unfairly maligned man in history, who can't defend himself and has had almost nobody to stand up for him all these years. It gets my goat, I can tell you. And the person we have to thank for this paragon of factual accuracy is none other than a certain fairly well-known dramatist called William Shakespeare.'

'I would've thought Shakespeare just told the story based on what happened,' Ben said. 'Didn't he?'

'Ha! That's a laugh. You want to know what really happened? I'll tell you what happened.' Kitson waved his whisky mug in the direction of the medieval battle scene over the fireplace. 'August 1485, the Battle of Bosworth Field. Where Richard III finally met his death in combat, marking the end of the Plantagenet line of English kings and queens going all the way back to 1154, and the start of the royal Tudor dynasty that would hold the throne until the death of Elizabeth I in 1603. Richard's slayer was a relatively minor Welsh nobleman called Henry Tudor, who proclaimed himself the new king, Henry VII, right there on the battle-field. Later in the Tudor line came the next Henry, Henry VIII of beheaded wives fame, and a few years after that his daughter Elizabeth became queen. Okay? I'm skimming, because I want to bring us up to the time of Shakespeare, our beloved "Bard", who was writing his plays during Elizabeth's reign.'

'Okay,' Ben said. He wasn't sensing too much love for Shakespeare in Kitson's account.

Kitson went on, 'Now, people don't generally think of "the Bard" as a political player. But it's easy to understand why

Shakespeare needed to keep in with the royal regime of the time. One reason was that, around this time, the Puritans were raising their ugly head again, being a bunch of killjoys as usual and wanting to prevent anyone from enjoying plays, music, any form of entertainment. Whereas Queen Liz loved music and the theatre, and she was opposed to the idea of banning them. Definitely someone a professional playwright like Shakespeare would have wanted to keep in with. Besides which, generally speaking, you just didn't want to go against the Tudors, seeing as they had this terrible habit of lopping the heads off anyone they took against.'

'I can see the logic of that.'

'So for political reasons old Willy was happy to come up with a play, his *Richard III*, that portrayed the last Plantagenet king as a grotesque, deformed, sadistic monster who lusted after power and murdered his own nephews. Audiences were shocked by it, and they were meant to be.' Kitson shook his head. 'What's really incredible is that, to this day, most historians still base their view of Richard on the totally fictitious version of events partially cooked up by a playwright's imagination. Just because it's "the Bard", like he's some kind of sacred bloody cow of literature, you're not even allowed to question it. It became the gold standard. Case closed, end of story. And what people fail to realise now is that the whole thing was just pro-Tudor propaganda.'

Ben said, 'Then what you're implying is that Richard didn't order the boys' deaths at all.'

'I'm not implying it,' Kitson replied, reaching for the bottle to top up their mugs. 'I'm stating it as a fact. Because why would he have done that?'

'I have no idea,' Ben said.

Kitson smiled at the look of confusion on Ben's face. 'Don't worry, you're not alone. But it's really not that complicated. You see, the boys' father was Edward IV, who'd been heavily involved in the Wars of the Roses, but managed to reign peacefully over England since then. Now flash forward to 1483, when the king suddenly and unexpectedly pops his clogs at the tender age of forty, leaving the elder of his two sons next in line for the throne. In accordance with the late king's will, his brother Richard is appointed Protector of the Realm to look after the kingdom until the young king can be crowned. After which, considering that he was just a kid, he'd need someone to guide and advise him on matters of state. That would have been his uncle's job, too. With me so far?'

Ben asked, 'So the two boys were called Edward and Richard, like their father and uncle?'

'Yeah, there are too many Edwards and Richards in this story, I know. You often wonder why they couldn't have called them something different, but that's how it is. Anyhow, that's when the two young princes, little Edward who was soon to become the new king and his younger brother Richard, were brought to the Tower to live.'

'Why the Tower?'

'Because,' Kitson explained, 'the Tower of London was the formal residence of kings and queens, where royals traditionally lived in luxury and splendour before their coronation. Forget what you think you know about the "Bloody Tower" and all those images in your head about dark dungeons and torture instruments. It only got its horrible reputation later on, thanks to the Tudors, once they got into their full brutal swing.'

'Then the boys weren't banged up in prison by their uncle.'

'Absolutely not. There was nothing remotely sinister or unusual about them being taken into the Tower. And their uncle wasn't even dreaming of the throne at that stage. As far as he or anyone else were concerned, the next king was going to be young Edward, following straight on from his father and becoming Edward V.'

'This is a bit different from the story I heard before.'

'You betcha it is,' Kitson said. 'In every way you can imagine. Take Uncle Richard himself, for a start. All through his brother's reign he'd been a strong and chivalrous warrior, fighting and winning battles since he was nineteen years old. Pretty hard to imagine Shakespeare's crippled hunchback being able to straighten himself out enough to strap on a suit of armour, let alone ride a warhorse for miles at the head of your army and get stuck into a ferocious bloody battle at the end of it. Some of those scraps went on for days on end without a break. You'd have to be pretty damn fit, carrying at least sixty pounds of steel armour on your back and swinging a sodding great broadsword around non-stop without your arm dropping off. A lot fitter than some of the numpties we call soldiers in this day and age. They'd shit their pants and run for the hills if they had to face combat like that. But I suppose that a brave warrior knight wouldn't have fitted with the image Shakespeare wanted to give his character.'

'So what happened next?'

'As Protector of the Realm, Richard gave detailed orders for the boy's coronation, which was set for 22nd June of that year, 1483, and he also had letters of summons sent out to the forty squires who would be made Knights of the Bath in honour of the occasion. Sound like a guy frothing at the mouth to seize power for himself? Meanwhile young Prince Edward entered the Tower in May 1483, and his little brother joined him there shortly afterwards, in early June. At the last sighting of them together, the two boys were enjoying themselves practising archery in the gardens. But then something happened that changed both their lives for ever.'

Chapter 20

'In mid-June of that year, 1483,' Tony Kitson went on, 'just days before the coronation of the new boy king, disaster struck. Out of the blue came an official statement declaring that Edward IV's marriage to the boys' mother, Elizabeth Woodville, was invalid. The reason was that, as had been discovered, throughout their marriage the king had been subject to an existing pre-contract with another woman, Lady Eleanor Talbot.'

'He was engaged to someone else?' Ben said.

'Yup. One witness, the Bishop of Bath and Wells, went a step further and claimed that Edward had actually married Eleanor Talbot in secret, making him a full-blown bigamist. But even if the bishop's claim hadn't been true, in those days an engagement was considered as binding as a marriage itself. Whichever way you cut it, this revelation spelled disaster for the princes, whose birth was suddenly declared illegitimate, by law. Needless to say, they couldn't be heirs to the throne any longer. And so, overnight, the elder boy Edward's future as king was down the toilet.'

'Leaving the way open for their uncle to step in.'

'By default, just because he was now next in line. The clergy, the nobles and the common people needed someone to fill the empty throne, and they came to Richard and petitioned him to accept the job. He didn't much want it, but he had no choice. That's how he became king.'

'Lance was pretty clear that he'd forced his way to the throne.'

'Well, Lance doesn't know shit, and I'd say the same about any historian who claims likewise. Those are the real historical facts. But go and look it up and what will you read? Time and time again, the same old lies. "When he died in 1483, Edward IV was succeeded by his son Edward V, but Edward IV's brother Richard III soon seized the throne"!' Kitson was getting himself all worked up again. 'Absolute utter bollocks! It makes it sound as though he deposed a crowned king, in a coup d'état or something. When in actual fact he didn't "seize the throne", because the throne was empty. There was nobody to depose, only some poor kid who must have been pretty gutted when they came to him and said, "Sorry, son, looks like you won't get to be king after all." And the country needed a ruler. Of course, there are some Richard-haters who like to twist it that he'd somehow engineered this whole situation so that he could become king instead of his young nephew. But that's a ridiculous stretch of the imagination and there's not a shred of evidence to back it up.'

Ben thought for a moment, trying to focus on the strands of the story that mattered most to him and his situation. He still couldn't make much sense of it all, as far as Mortimer's death and the bombing were concerned. But maybe if he kept on pushing, things would come clearer. After a pause he said, 'Seems to me that if the boys were illegitimate and were no longer princes, the whole child-murder narrative falls apart. He's supposed to have killed them because they were a threat to him.'

Kitson nodded in agreement. 'But now they couldn't possibly be a threat any longer, because neither of them could ever be a contender for the throne. Exactly. Now you understand why Richard III hadn't the slightest reason to wish his young nephews any harm. He wouldn't have dreamed of such a thing, in any case. He'd been very cut up by their father's death, and he swore a public oath to honour and protect his children. That's exactly what he did after becoming king.'

'And yet everybody today apparently believes the opposite,' Ben said.

'Yeah, and like I told you, it's largely thanks to good old William Shakespeare a hundred years later, who lifted ideas from various pro-Tudor sources and blew it up into the fictional story that we all know and love. Back in the late fifteenth century, the thought that Richard might have done anything so cruel and terrible never occurred to anyone. Not even to his worst enemies.'

'You sound very sure about that.'

Kitson nodded. 'You want proof? There's plenty. Flash forward a couple of years to 1485 and the Battle of Bosworth Field. The last great battle of the Wars of the Roses and the conflict that finally gave the Tudors what they'd wanted for so long. After fighting so many battles in the past, Bosworth Field was where Richard came unstuck. He'd been heading a cavalry charge of armoured knights against the forces of Henry Tudor when he found himself cut off from his troops and surrounded by enemy foot soldiers, got pulled off his horse and hacked to death, and that was the end of him. The victors paraded his body in the streets of Leicester, stripped naked and tied to a horse.' Kitson pulled a disgusted frown. 'It was no way to treat a king. But it seems that his successor, the new Tudor monarch Henry VII, had already decided from the outset that he would take every opportunity to discredit, dishonour and generally piss all over the reputation of his dead enemy.'

'As you do.'

'Right. So what Henry Tudor did next, virtually his first action as the new king of England, was to publicly announce something called a Bill of Attainder. That's an act of legislature formally declaring a person, or persons, guilty of some serious crime. Basically, it was a list of all the accusations of heinous wrongdoing that he could possibly bring against his predecessor, as a way for the victor to claim the moral high ground over the man he'd just slaughtered, and so gain public favour. The Bill of Attainder was intended to paint Richard as thoroughly evil and nasty and corrupt in any way Henry could think up. It accused him of cruelty and tyranny and double-dealing, and a whole raft of other charges. But guess what it didn't even mention?'

'The princes?'

'Correct. Not a peep about Richard's having harmed a hair on their heads. Doesn't that strike you as a little bit strange? Given that Henry was determined to show his conquered enemy in the worst light possible? Wouldn't that have been the perfect opportunity to show what a monster Richard had been? Even in those brutal times, people would have been *appalled* at the idea of their king having had two little boys' lives snuffed out like that. Bad enough to have harmed an innocent child, but these were royal, his own flesh and blood, and that mattered a lot to the people. Also, wouldn't Henry have wanted to produce the bodies of these poor children, to stir up even more scandal? Yet he never tried to look for them. Why? Because it had never entered anyone's mind that the princes had been murdered.'

Ben reflected on that for a moment. 'Hold on, though. Lance Mortimer told me that their remains had been found in the Tower. Maybe the reason Henry didn't mention it was just that he didn't know yet that they were dead?'

'Forget what that idiot Lance told you,' Kitson grunted. 'First off, we've already established that Richard had no motive for the crime. Second, you have a total lack of any physical evidence of a crime even being committed. There *were* no bodies. Sure, if you visit the Tower of London today you'll see a little plaque on the wall claiming to mark the spot where the dead princes were found. That refers to a discovery made in 1674, of some human bones that were dug up from the bottom of an old staircase deep inside the Tower. They were *assumed* to be the remains of the two boys.'

'You're saying they weren't?'

'Show me someone who can prove that they were. To begin with, the bones were in such bad shape that nobody could even determine whether they were male or female. And this was a long time before DNA testing might have shown up anything conclusive. The fact is, all kinds of human remains have been dug up from the Tower. The damn thing was built by William the Conqueror, you know? It's been there a hell of a long time and we can suppose that plenty of people must have died there over the ages. But in any case, we don't need to rely on a *lack* of evidence that they died there. We have a lot of positive proof that they didn't.'

'Such as?'

'The boys' mother, to begin with. It's known that Elizabeth Woodville stayed on good terms with Richard the whole time he was king. Don't you think maybe, just maybe, she'd have had a bit of a problem with the bloke who'd murdered her two sons in cold blood?'

'If she knew the truth.'

'I thought you'd say that. But it takes us back to the same problem of no motive,' Kitson said. 'Okay, I can see we're not ready to let Richard off the hook just yet. Fine. Then how do you account for the other siblings? What about Elizabeth of York, the boys' elder sister? And what about the son of Richard's brother George, Edward of Warwick, who lived out his uncle's reign peacefully as a member of the royal household at Sandal Castle?'

'Another bloody Edward,' Ben groaned.

'Never mind what they were called,' Kitson said impatiently. 'The point is that if Richard had felt, against all logic, that he needed to knock off the first two siblings to protect his throne, then why not kill the whole lot of them while he was at it? The others were no less of a threat to his ambitions, if you go along with the mainstream narrative. As a matter of fact they were a bigger threat than the two boys, because nobody had declared them illegitimate. It's all very well to speculate and play Devil's advocate. But *none* of the accepted story makes sense. None.'

Ben could see he was on the losing side of the argument here, in the face of overwhelming evidence and the force of Tony Kitson's unshakeable moral conviction. He put up his hands in submission and said, 'Okay, okay, I get it. You win. But if the princes were still alive, then where were they? I'm guessing, not in the Tower any more.'

'No, Richard would have had them removed from the Tower as soon as the news broke about their illegitimacy,'

Kitson replied. 'That's only logical, given that they were only there pending the elder boy's ascension to the throne, which was now cancelled. Where they went from there is still a matter of debate, but *we* think that Richard sent them to live on one of his estates in the north of England for a while, and from there across the Channel to stay with their aunt, his sister, the Duchess of Burgundy. That was where they lived for some time, until it's thought that the elder boy, Edward, died of a fever. We don't know much about his illness.'

'And what about the other boy? Young Richard?'

'We'll come back to him in a minute,' Kitson said. 'First, I need to tell you about another strange twist that happened soon after Henry became king.'

'As though there weren't enough strange twists already.'

'I told you this was a crazy story, didn't I?' Kitson said. 'And it's just about to get even crazier.'

Chapter 21

'Here's the twist,' said Tony Kitson. 'Are you ready?'

'I'm not going anywhere,' Ben said. 'Not until I understand what the hell this is about.'

'Now, you remember what I said before about Edward IV's, shall we say, *irregular* prior marital arrangements that made his marriage to the princes' mother legally null and void? What happened next throws all that situation back into chaos yet again.'

'It does?'

'Because in 1486, soon after taking up the throne, Henry Tudor decided he needed a queen. And guess who was the lucky lady he set his sights on? None other than the fair and beautiful young Elizabeth of York.'

'The sister of the two princes?' Ben said, surprised.

'*Ex*-princes. But that was all about to change. Since of course, Elizabeth's birth had been rendered illegitimate along with her brothers' three years earlier, when the whole scandal broke. And obviously, having been declared a bastard child of an invalid marriage, she couldn't be a queen. Unless . . .'

'Unless?'

'For his next magic trick, Henry decided to overturn the original ruling, so that the children of Elizabeth Woodville and Edward IV could be re-legitimised.'

'Just like that?'

'Pretty much. Which of course, being the monarch with virtually omnipotent authority, he had the power to do. But I'm sure you can see the implications of him doing that. Whether or not he could see them, or even gave two hoots about it, that's another matter.'

Ben said, 'If the boys' sister was made legitimate again, then they would have to be as well.'

'Absolutely,' Kitson replied. 'Which created all kinds of weird and wonderful legal repercussions. One of which is to have undermined Richard III's reign as king, but of course that no longer mattered because he was dead and gone. What *did* matter was that by this reversal of the ruling, Henry was in effect making the two boys back into potential threats against him. Because now they were real princes again. And they were both next in line from their father Edward IV, which technically meant that Henry needed to step down right away and let the real king take over in his place.'

'It's madness,' Ben said.

'Especially when you consider how weak his own claim to the throne was. Henry had never been much more than a minor noble himself, with only a shaky royal connection through the female side. Whereas Richard III and his brother were full-blooded Plantagenets, born from a long line of kings. Hence the boys were much more kingly material than Henry Tudor had ever been. Now, for whatever reason, whether he'd done it out of sheer stupidity, delusional self-importance, or was just carried away by his lust to marry Elizabeth, he'd gone and given them back their prior status. It was an incredible mistake to make.'

'Except that they weren't in the picture any longer,' Ben said. 'And the elder brother had died anyway.'

'True. But with the death of his older brother, young Richard, now thirteen and living possibly in Burgundy, became the heir apparent. With a suddenly cast-iron claim to the throne since his birth had been redeclared legitimate, ironically by the same guy to whom he was now a renewed threat. Is this making your head spin yet?'

Ben was finding it impossible not to get drawn into the story as it grew ever more convoluted and bizarre. 'If the younger Richard was a threat to Henry's crown,' he said, thinking hard, 'then surely the other kids were too? Like Edward, George's son, who you mentioned before. He was always legitimate, and directly connected to the Plantagenet bloodline.'

'You're right,' Kitson said. 'And Henry VII wasn't the sort of ruler who'd idly allow threats like that to stand against him. He did eventually have George's son Edward imprisoned and executed. Kind of rich that it's the innocent man, Richard III, who ends up with the reputation of a killer, don't you think?'

'But what about young Prince Richard?'

'Aha,' Kitson said, smiling and holding up a finger. 'Did the young Plantagenet heir to the throne return to England to claim what was rightfully his? There's the billion-dollar question. And that's where the tale takes yet another twist that's weirder and crazier than ever. Because just a few years later, a new player was about to enter the scene. His name was Perkin Warbeck.'

Ben's mind flashed back to the mysterious 'PW' initials he'd found in Hugh Mortimer's notes, and he realised that they must have been referring to this Perkin Warbeck character. 'Okay, so who was he?'

'Warbeck appeared out of the blue claiming to be none other than Richard, the younger of the two princes of Tower fame, and declaring himself as a pretender and rival to Henry's throne. His claim was supported by the Irish, who were always looking to supplant English kings by whatever means they could, and also by the French, who weren't any less keen on the idea of deposing Henry VII. Remember that King Henry, as a lower nobleman who'd only grabbed the throne by conquest, had a far weaker claim to it than a genuine member of the Plantagenet bloodline. If this Warbeck bloke really could prove he was who he said he was, then Henry was going to find himself in a real bind.'

'How did Henry respond?'

'The only way he could, which was to pull out all the stops to block Perkin Warbeck's claim. It wouldn't have been the first time he needed to fend off a challenge to his throne. There were a lot of false claims being made. A little while earlier, there had been the case of a young kid called Lambert Simnel, who was also touted as being the older of the princes. But that doesn't stand up, as he was only ten years old and the numbers didn't compute at all. Simnel ended up getting a job in the royal kitchens. Kind of nutty, but there's a lot about this part of history that's nutty.'

'What about Warbeck – was he a fake too?'

'Henry certainly needed to prove he was. To do that, he turned to his powerful and efficient spy network, in the hopes that they could dig up evidence to discredit him. But for all their efforts they were never able to come up with a single shred of evidence as to who this "Perkin Warbeck" really was, if not the real prince. There were no written records of the man. Nobody seemed to have ever heard of him before. He just didn't seem to exist.'

'As if he'd just made up the name,' Ben said, thinking of his own phony identities like Paul Harris and Mike Palmer.

'We believe, and Hugh believed, that that's exactly what he did. Which would mean that "Perkin Warbeck" was very likely the real deal. There's a ton of evidence to support that idea. Even his choice of an alias speaks volumes. In case you wondered how anyone could have come up with the unusual name "Warbeck", it turns out to be a play on words by someone who knew Flemish as well as French. The name was originally spelled "Wesbecque", from the Flemish "wezen", meaning "to be" or "to be real", and "weze" meaning "orphan". Might explain why Henry's secret police weren't able to dig up any dirt on him, don't you think? If "Perkin Warbeck" was a made-up identity?'

'It might,' Ben said.

'But you don't have to be a linguist to see right through the official narrative. If Perkin was just another opportunist bullshitter, then how come he didn't pretend to be the elder prince, Edward? That would have been the obvious choice, given that Edward had been the heir apparent. There would have been no way for an outsider to know that Edward was actually dead. And also, if Perkin was a faker, why would Henry VII have been so upset about him that he went to war against France over the whole affair, the French being Perkin's main supporters? It was a rushed campaign, starting in late autumn, definitely not the best time of year to deploy large numbers of troops across the English Channel. Hardly something you'd do unless you had a very compelling reason.

Henry did. He was scared, and he had every reason to be. His hold on the throne was looking shakier by the day.'

'What happened?'

Kitson shrugged. 'If Perkin had been successful, it'd totally have changed the face of English history. Instead it all lapsed into the usual political wheeling, dealing and backstabbing. In the end the French and the English made a deal, so that the French king, Charles, would get to become ruler of the Duchy of Brittany, in return for giving up his support of the pretender. So poor old Perkin found himself betrayed and left out in the cold. Soon after, in late 1497, he got caught and brought back to London.'

'I suppose Henry wouldn't have wasted any time getting rid of him.'

'You'd have thought so. But, strangely, Henry not only spared Perkin's life but gave him a lot of freedom, letting him live at court as his guest. He's said to have often referred to him as "Richard", too, which kind of says a lot, although maybe he was just teasing. Perkin was technically a prisoner, under house arrest, living at court with his wife Catherine Gordon, a young Scottish noblewoman who was a cousin of King James of Scotland. Perkin had met and fallen in love with her a couple of years earlier, when he was still travelling around Ireland and Scotland trying to convince people of his royal identity. Which she and her aristocratic family must have been convinced by, or else why would they have consented to her marrying him? More proof that he was who he said he was. How likely do you think it is that some ordinary bloke would be able to pass himself off convincingly as a noble?'

'I know I couldn't,' Ben said.

'Nor me, and that's for sure. But it would have been even harder back then. Commoners had absolutely no education at all in those days, and hardly anyone except the nobility and the clergy could even read and write. Nobody born and bred outside those circles would have had a hope in hell of being able to bluff their way through it, like by talking in a posh accent and knowing what fork or spoon to use at the table, stuff like that. Noble kids were taught the social graces while they were still in nappies. They learned Latin and often other languages too. The boys were schooled in riding, fencing and the art of chivalry. Comportment and dance, diplomacy, courtly etiquette, music – something Perkin was especially good at, by all accounts. The list goes on. It'd have taken him years to learn how to fake all those skills, if he could even find anyone to teach him. It's just not feasible. Yet Lady Catherine's family seem to have been taken in, and were pretty fond of their new son-in-law. Her father was the Earl of Huntly, who owned huge great amounts of land in Scotland, and he made a present to the young couple of a big estate there. As for King Henry, he was obviously concerned about Perkin's possible royal legitimacy, too, because he wouldn't allow the couple to sleep together and therefore produce any heirs. But you know how it is. They managed to have a secret child, nonetheless.'

Ben wasn't sure where this was going, and he was beginning to worry about getting off track. 'I'm sure this is all very interesting to a historian, but—'

Kitson waved him off. 'You said you wanted all the details, didn't you? Anyway, I'm just getting to the important bit about Perkin. Because it wasn't too long before he finally pissed off King Henry one time too many.'

'How did he do that?'

'He kept escaping and causing trouble. Which for the Ricardians is really yet more proof that Perkin wasn't just some chancer trying his luck and pretending to be someone he wasn't. Imagine, you're this opportunistic young guy, a fraud, a con artist, who came up from nowhere and decided to have a crack at becoming king. It didn't quite pay off, but it's worked out pretty well for you. Now you're living in security and comfort – okay, you're a prisoner, but a prisoner in a seriously gilded cage, with everything you could ask for and a standard of living that would have seemed like a dream to an ordinary citizen. You've married the beautiful girl with lots of money, you're in love, and her family think highly enough of you to gift you land and property. You've come a long way. What on earth would possess you to throw that all down the toilet?'

'He wasn't pretending,' Ben said.

Kitson jabbed a triumphant finger at him. 'Right. Exactly. If you were the real deal, maybe you'd feel you were destined for better things. You might not be willing to settle for a compromised, protected life under house arrest. Maybe you'd resent being the prisoner of the man who slaughtered your uncle on the battlefield and treated his body with total disrespect, then went on to besmirch his name by calling him a tyrant and a villain. Maybe you'd be thinking, "Right, you bastard, I'm going to raise an army, knock you off your throne and take back what's rightfully mine." And you might even be willing to risk all the good things you had, even losing your beloved wife, for a shot at the title.'

'Makes sense,' Ben said.

'And makes none at all otherwise. So off he went, managing to slip away from court without arousing Henry's suspicions that he was up to his old tricks again. Perkin had lost a lot of his earlier supporters, and his Scottish connections didn't pay off either, after King James mounted a failed attack on England on his behalf. But he found support in Cornwall, where the locals were upset over Henry's high taxes and were already organising themselves to march against London. Perkin saw his chance, rallied together a little army of about three thousand men and marched them from Bodmin to Exeter with the intention of starting a full-scale rebellion. But his army soon dwindled, the campaign lost momentum and he was taken prisoner again.'

Their whisky mugs were empty. Kitson divided the last dregs of the bottle between them. The big ginger moggy must have softened its attitude towards Ben, because it had finally emerged from its hiding place behind the sofa and hopped up to drape itself over Kitson's lap and hang there bonelessly, snoring.

'I can't imagine Henry was going to go easy on him again this time,' Ben said.

'No, by now he'd had it with Perkin's shenanigans, and finally ordered for him to get the chop. But the way that happened is interesting too. If he'd been just anybody, you would think they could just have dragged him off to the gallows and strung him up without a second thought. In actual fact Henry seems to have been a bit reluctant to kill him, the same way that Queen Elizabeth I wasn't too happy about executing Mary of Scotland later on, and only did it as a last resort.'

'Even though Henry and Elizabeth were both bloodthirsty Tudors,' Ben said.

Kitson chuckled. 'Maybe so, but they still had certain standards to observe. You see, there was this moral code they abided by in those times, called the "Great Chain of Being". It was all about the natural hierarchy of men and the idea that members of the royal bloodline were so far above the status of the common folk, second only to God, that you couldn't just go around giving them the chop willy-nilly. It wasn't the done thing, except of course on the battlefield where anything goes. Henry's reluctance to kill Perkin Warbeck suggests even more strongly that he knew he was a genuine royal. But he was causing too much trouble and he had to go. They made him confess under torture that he really was just a pretender and a nobody who'd been born in Flanders, the son of a boatman. Which is exactly what the *Encyclopaedia Britannica* entry on Warbeck still says to this day, stating he was a fraud and an impostor. Basically, mainstream historical scholarship has done the same kind of hatchet job on Perkin as it has on his uncle. And of course, the trumped-up confession spelled the end for Perkin. It gave Henry the free hand he needed, so he could carry on as if he wasn't really executing a royal at all, but a mere commoner, which made him fair game.'

'Nice,' Ben said.

'So that was the end of Perkin Warbeck, hanged as a traitor on November twenty-third, 1499. But here's where the next big twist in the tale comes in. Remember I mentioned the secret child?'

Chapter 22

Ben said, 'From when Perkin and Catherine managed to sneak off together. I remember.'

'It was a son,' Kitson replied. 'And of course the identity of a secret child needed to be protected by another false name. He's believed to have been called Richard Perkins. Yes, another Richard.'

'They must have kept him well hidden.'

'Nobody really knows much about that period of his life,' Kitson admitted. 'We know that Catherine stayed at court for a while after the execution, and from that time the history books refer to her as Lady Catherine Huntly. She wasn't a prisoner of the king's any longer. Henry was really quite generous towards her, which might have something to do with the rumour going round at the time that he was in love with her. Maybe he was. Or maybe he just had a guilty conscience, after what he'd done to her husband. She married several times afterwards. Her third husband, who she married in 1517, was a Welshman called Sir Matthew Craddock, Steward of Gower.'

'That's a relief, someone not called Richard or Edward.'

'Catherine moved to Wales to live with him,' said Kitson, 'and it's thought that her son Richard lived there too. What happened to the kid after that is obscure. He grew up, got married, had kids of his own. And now we come to the

160

kicker. Because Hugh had reason to think that he was a direct descendant of Richard Perkins – and, by extension, of Warbeck himself.'

That came as a surprise to Ben. He raised his eyebrows. 'Hang on a minute. What are you saying, that Hugh Mortimer believed he was related to the Plantagenets?'

'And his brother Lance too, if you can believe that daft prat has even a tiny squirt of royal blood in his veins.'

Ben thought about it for a moment, and decided he wasn't buying it. 'Doesn't that seem a bit too much of a coincidence? An expert on the princes in the Tower just so happens to discover he's related to one of them?'

Kitson said, 'No, it happened the other way around. Hugh became aware of his ancestry years and years ago, in his student days. He'd always been interested in the history of medieval Britain, but he told me that what really started the ball rolling was a box of very old, very rare coins that he inherited from his great-great grandfather, along with a collection of fifteenth-century letters and documents and some other artefacts from that time.'

'Coins,' Ben said.

'Not just any old coins. These had been minted in the Duchy of Burgundy for none other than Perkin Warbeck. Again, you wonder why they'd have gone to the trouble, if he hadn't been the real thing. And there were other items in the collection that were connected with the history of Warbeck and the princes. Hugh became fascinated with that area of history. It was what started him on his whole Ricardian journey. He spent most of his life on it.'

'What other items?' Ben asked, still sceptical. 'How did they prove he was related to Perkin Warbeck?'

'I don't know,' Kitson replied. 'He never really said much about them. It was all a bit vague. I think he didn't want to say too much, until he could be totally sure.'

It sounded to Ben as though something must have happened more recently to cement Hugh's belief in his royal family tree, rather than just a vague conviction he'd held for years. 'When did Hugh tell you this about himself?' he asked Kitson.

'Not long ago. Just a couple of months. I'd known something was up for a while. He had a look in his eyes.'

'A look.'

'Like a sparkle. Like he was excited about something and bursting to tell someone, but holding back.'

'And how long had he had this sparkle?'

'I don't know, really. Maybe a month before that. Hard to say.'

Ben felt a wave of frustration rising up, and swallowed it back down. 'When he made this . . . what would you call it, this *revelation* to you, you didn't ask for more detail? I mean, it's not every day someone tells you they're related to the Plantagenet kings of England, is it?'

'Hugh wasn't someone you could press too hard. If I'd started badgering him for more, he'd only have pulled his head into his shell like a tortoise. He was like that. He might even have regretted telling me as much as he did.'

'Did you believe him?'

Kitson held up his hands in a helpless gesture. 'What can I tell you? I was pretty stunned, when he told me. And coming from anyone else, I might have thought it was a load of twaddle. But Hugh Mortimer was the most meticulous researcher I've ever known. He did history the way a microbiologist does science, always looking into every detail, never a stone unturned. Unlike some so-called academics I could mention, he was totally objective, and he'd never settle for repeating the same old debunked crap that too many people still keep on trundling out. Hugh wasn't one for making idle claims, and he'd rather say nothing at all if his ideas weren't fully backed up. So if he believed he belonged to the Plantagenet line, I'll stick my neck out and say that yes, I believe it too.'

Whether it was true or not, something told Ben that this strange new turn in the story was bringing him a step closer to understanding what had happened to Hugh Mortimer. When people started tracking down their famous and wealthy historical ancestors, there was always the chance it could lead to trouble if those claims were disputed by a rival contender. Ben thought back to the threatening letters, warning Mortimer to back off and keep his nose out.

'Okay, so he didn't tell you much in the way of specific detail,' he said to Kitson. 'But did he give you any hints about what might have been involved? Was there any mention of money, anything like that?'

'Nothing like that,' Kitson replied, shaking his head. 'Nothing he told me about, anyhow.'

'Is there anyone else in the group apart from you who he might have spoken to about this, might have said more to?'

Kitson reflected, then shook his head. 'I don't think so. I mean, everybody gets on well together. We're a good team. But me and Hugh were special mates, you know? If he was going to say more, I reckon I'd have been the first person he'd told.'

'And that's it?'

Kitson shrugged. 'Yep. That's it.'

Until now, Ben's new ex-Marine acquaintance had been a fast-flowing river of information. Now it seemed to be suddenly running dry, just when they were getting to the crux of the matter. 'We could be close to cracking this, Tony. All we need now is some idea who might have been unhappy about this possible ancestral claim of his. If indeed he had any intention of making one. Who was he going to go to, and what did he expect to gain from it?'

'I've told you everything I know,' Kitson said earnestly. 'Like I said to you, he was such a careful man. Cagey, even, sometimes. He'd have been worried about committing himself by saying too much, just in case he was wrong. As for making some kind of formal claim, I really have no idea what he was planning, if anything. I'm sorry I can't tell you more.'

'All right,' Ben said. 'You've told me a lot already. Don't beat yourself up.'

Kitson fell quiet for a moment, sunken in thought. Then his face brightened as he seemed to remember something. 'But now I think about it, there is one person he might have told more to.'

'Who?'

'He mentioned something about speaking with another historian about his research. How he wanted to compare notes with this other person, to verify his findings. Yes, yes, that's it. I think that'd be the reason, if he hadn't made any kind of formal claim yet. He'd have wanted to be absolutely sure he was right. That would be typical of Hugh.'

'Do you know the name of this person he was in contact with? Is it another member of the Richard III Society?'

Kitson's face moved as the wheels of his memory turned. 'No, I don't think so. I'm sure it wasn't anyone in the UK, either. I seem to recall he said something about another country. But which one? Ah, shit. If only I could remember. It was in Europe. I definitely know it was somewhere in Europe.'

'So the person we'd be looking for is somewhere in Europe,' Ben said. 'That's great, Tony. Narrows it down nicely.'

Kitson pushed the cat off his knee, lurched out of his armchair, then grabbed his stick from the deer's antler on the wall and started limping up and down the small room, visibly racking his brains. Then he suddenly froze and stared at Ben. 'Liecht . . . liecht . . .'

'Liechtenstein?'

'That's it! No wonder I couldn't remember the bloody name, if I couldn't even pronounce it. Liechtenstein.'

'Was the historian he talked to called Berg? B – E – R – G, first initial R?'

'Never told me the name.'

'Are you sure?'

'I don't have bleeding dementia,' Kitson said irritably.

'I'm glad to hear it.'

So now Ben knew that this R. Berg from the address in Mortimer's mess of notes was a historian, and someone who might well be able to provide a lot more useful information. If only two people in the world were in on Hugh Mortimer's secret and one of them was this Berg in Liechtenstein, the other one would be the killer.

Ben was thinking about what his next move would have to be when he heard a strange sound from across the room. He looked round. The ginger moggy had jumped back up onto Kitson's empty chair and was standing up on all fours staring fixedly at the cottage window, as if threatened by something outside. His back was arched, his ears were down flat and his fur was spiked up like the bristles on a hedgehog. Another low, strangled growl came yowling from his throat.

Kitson said, 'Marmalade? What is it, puss?'

And that was when it happened.

Chapter 23

There had been no lights outside the window, no noises or warning signs of anyone's approach. Whoever was out there had stalked up to Kitson's home silently and stealthily. They'd moved into position, and now they struck.

Just instants after the cat alerted them to the presence of an intruder, a sudden violent juddering crash seemed to shake the cottage as the front door was smashed in. A heart-beat later came the trample of heavy footsteps filling the entrance hallway, racing towards the living-room door.

Ben was already on his feet and leaping across the room, but the door burst open before he could get to it. He skidded to a halt as the shape of a large, heavy man appeared in the low doorway. He was several inches taller than Ben, at about six-four, and he had to stoop low to pass under the edge of the jamb. He was dressed from top to bottom in black. Black combat boots, black gloves. His whole face apart from his mouth and eyes was covered by a black ski mask. But what Ben was looking at was the short pump-action shotgun the man was clenching in his fists, the butt tight against his hip, the stubby black pipe of the barrel pointing straight into the room and ready to blast anything inside that lived.

What happened next all took place within the space of only seconds. Tony Kitson let out a yell of anger, surged out of his chair and toppled to the floor. The cat shot across the room. Ben whirled backwards, snatched the whisky bottle and hurled it end-over-end like a stick grenade at the gunman's head. It went high, shattered against the top of the door frame and showered him with broken glass. The shotgun in the man's hands went off like a bomb exploding. But the impact of the breaking bottle had put him off his aim and the blast of buckshot hit the picture over the fireplace, blowing its frame into spinning pieces of wood and bringing it down from the wall in a cloud of plaster dust. Recovering fast from the surprise the man worked the pump on the weapon for a second shot, this time directed right at Ben.

Fast, but he'd have needed to be faster if he wanted to hit his mark. Before the cocking cycle was finished and the round was in the chamber, Ben had already grabbed the first improvised weapon that came to hand and was flying into the attack. In the down and dirty philosophy of combat of which he was a master, you learned to make use of whatever defensive objects were available, even if they were the stuffed remains of a ruminant herbivore. He tore the stag's head down from the wall, held it by its wooden mount and jammed the spiky antlers with brutal force into the face behind the black ski mask.

There was a high-pitched scream of agony and the man went staggering back through the doorway, blinded and pouring blood from under his mask and letting the shotgun slip out of his gloved hands. Ben caught a glimpse of two more men in the hallway behind him, guns pointing his way but unable to shoot because of their large, wide colleague blocking their field of fire. Like in a military or police raid team, the guy with the shotgun had been designated the point man, going in first and equipped to blow out door locks or hinges with a blast of a twelve-gauge. The rest of the team backing him up would normally be armed with bullet-firing small arms like pistols or carbines. Ben's sharp eye picked out the all too familiar lines of an AR-15, telling him that was the case here too. It also told him that whoever had sent these men had access to serious resources. Even hardcore criminal gangs in Britain had a hard time getting hold of fully-automatic military weapons.

But this wasn't the time to wonder about the whos, the whys and how they had found him here. He knew he had to act now, or he and Kitson would both be dead men within the next minute.

Ben booted the injured, howling big guy the rest of the way back into the entrance hall and crashed the living-room door shut. There was no lock or bolt on the door, so he snatched a wooden chair and jammed it at an angle with the top of the backrest wedged under the handle. That wouldn't hold the attackers at bay for very long. He darted away from the door and kept his head low as the expected bullets ripped through the wood with a rattle of full-auto gunfire, spraying splinters into the room and destroying cups and plates on a dresser behind him.

He snatched up the fallen shotgun. A Mossberg Persuader, the combat variation with an eighteen-inch barrel, flat black Parkerised finish, tactical sling. He worked the action the rest of the way, finishing the job the big guy had started. The weapon's tube magazine held five cartridges. Each one containing nine round lead pellets of 0.33 inches in diameter, so that if they all slammed into your body at once it was the equivalent of being shot with nine .32-calibre handguns simultaneously. A massive shock to the system that would put the biggest, toughest opponent straight down, effectively and permanently, without too much argument.

Ben levelled the weapon at the door where the bullets had punched through and let off a blast. The hard-recoiling shotgun jumped like a live thing in his hands and the noise was huge in the small room. Somewhere behind the deafening boom and the ringing it set up in his ears, he heard the yowl of another casualty from the front hallway. That might deter them from their assault on the living-room. But Ben knew the attackers wouldn't be ready to give up just yet.

Ben turned to Kitson. His face was rigid with shock and his eyes were fixed on Ben, his mouth open but too stunned to utter a sound. His hat and stick had fallen to the floor. Ben ignored the hat, scooped up the stick and tossed it to him. 'We need to get out of here, right now.'

'But where to? They're all around the cottage.'

Ben had no time to reply before the power suddenly died, plunging the room into darkness. Almost in the same moment, a gun blast from outside blew in the living-room window; simultaneously there was another juddering, splintering crash from the other side of the house.

Kitson's hand was a faint blur in the pitch blackness as he pointed across the room at another door. 'Back hallway!' Ben could just make out the door's pale rectangular shape. He raced to get to it before it could burst open, racking the Mossberg's pump as he went.

This time he made it. Wrenching the door open he saw the shapes of the two men who'd forced their way inside the hall, silhouetted by the light of the open doorway behind them. He fired without aiming and the nearest silhouette let out a cry and crumpled to the floor. The other returned fire with a pistol, its reports small and muffled after the deafening blast of the shotgun, then retreated back to the smashed rear door before Ben could get off another shot.

By his count a couple of the attackers were down and at least one more injured. But they'd keep coming, because there were still several more armed and determined men out there. What would their next move be? Any moment now, he anticipated that a petrol bomb or grenade might come through either door or the living-room window. Which would complicate their situation quite considerably.

Ben had three rounds left in his weapon. Three rounds weren't enough to repel any kind of force of men. Glancing out of the window, his vision adjusting to the darkness by now, he saw more running black shapes flit past as the remaining attackers regrouped for a fresh assault. Then he heard the roar of a fast-approaching vehicle and blinked as dazzling headlights appeared over the brow of the hill, speeding towards the cottage. The lights swept across the broken window and he stepped quickly back before he could be seen. In their glare he caught a glimpse of two of the men half-carrying, half-dragging their injured associate, the big guy who'd received a faceful of stag antlers. Ben guessed that the one he'd shot through the living-room door was still lying in the hallway, dead or dying.

The vehicle coming down the road was a plain white commercial van. It screeched to a halt just short of the cottage, and the men quickly loaded the injured guy into its open tailgate. At the same time, a rattle of gunfire and the flicker of bright muzzle flash told Ben that they were pumping rounds into his car. That was bound to make the rental company happy.

Keeping back among the dark shadows of the room, he levelled his weapon and went to shoot, but the shapes of the men were moving about too fast in the darkness and the van's dazzling lights made it hard for him to pick out his targets. He couldn't afford to waste ammunition on wild shots. He stood and watched helplessly as they blew out the tyres and windows of the BMW and peppered its bodywork full of holes. So much for a quick getaway.

'Does that old Land Rover still go?' he asked Kitson.

'No battery in it,' came the reply from the darkness.

Which limited their options still further. Making a stand here in the cottage wasn't viable, either. They were going to have to try and get out on foot. All they'd have to do was slip past the unknown remaining number of attackers still circling the property. But there was no way of exiting either the front or back doors, with both certainly well covered.

Ben thought about the roof. Sometimes, if you couldn't leave a place by the doors or windows, you could make your escape vertically. He'd had to resort to those extremes a couple of times in the past. But never with a semi-disabled man in tow. And there was no way he was leaving Kitson alone here.

Kitson must have been reading his thoughts. 'Coal bunker,' he said in a hissing whisper.

'Where?'

'Trapdoor in the kitchen floor. That way.' Pointing. 'Bunker's sunk into the ground like a basement. There's a chute leading up to the outside.'

'Any other way into the kitchen?'

'Only a small window above the sink. Doubt they'll try to climb through there.'

'What about the access through the coal chute?'

'Bolted from the inside. Hasn't been opened in years.'

Ben thought about it. Reaching the kitchen would mean having to cross the breached rear hallway, which was taking a hell of a risk. An awful lot could go wrong. What if the attackers were already inside the kitchen? What if the chute access doors couldn't be opened? He didn't like it. But there seemed to be no other way out of here. And only one possible outcome if they didn't go for it. Any moment, now that the attackers had finished extracting their injured and immobilising Ben's vehicle, they'd be refocusing their attentions on the cottage and the endgame would all be over all too quickly.

'On three,' Ben said. 'Ready?'

'I'm ready,' Kitson said.

'One, two, three, *go.*'

Ben led the way across the room to the rear hallway door, weapon in one hand and gripping Kitson's arm with the other. He burst through the door, finger on the trigger and prepared to blast anything that moved in the hall. But there was nothing there except for the broken back door hanging off its hinges and the inert shape of a dead man lying silhouetted on the floor tiles, a dark blood pool gleaming faintly in the moonlight shining in from the breached doorway. Ben yanked Kitson across the empty passage and they reached the door beyond it, leading to the kitchen.

Nobody seemed to be lurking in wait for them there. Faint light shone in through the little window over the sink. Ben took out his Zippo lighter, thumbed the flint striker and waved the flickering orange flame around him to get his bearings. The kitchen was small and basic and smelt of boiled vegetables and cat food.

'Trapdoor,' Ben hissed, and in the dim light of the flame Kitson pointed down at a dark square in the floor, two feet by two. But first, Ben needed to secure the doorway. Spotting a mop propped in the corner he grabbed it and wedged the long wooden shaft against the door and under the handle to stop it from turning. Then he turned back towards the trapdoor, shining his lighter for a closer look. The lid was held down by a bolt recessed into the floor and had a metal ring to lift it open with. The bolt was stiff and encrusted with old grease and grime. He kicked it free, grabbed the metal ring and heaved the lid open.

A musty smell of damp, ancient coal dust and mildew wafted up from the black hole below. Ben shone his flame down into the grimy red-brick bunker. Kitson had been right about it being small. A little cottage like this had only ever needed a minimal cellar space to store its coal. There was barely enough room for two people to squeeze in. But they were committed now, with no other choice.

A short, rickety wooden ladder led down from the trap-door. Ben went first. Nobody had been down here in a long, long time. Cobwebs brushed his face and stuck to his hair. He reached the bottom and reached up a hand to help Kitson down after him. Kitson had difficulty getting down the ladder. Ben pulled the trapdoor lid down shut over them. The head-room was too limited to stand up fully.

'That's the chute,' Kitson panted, motioning towards a mass of dusty cobwebs that covered the wall. Ben clawed them away with his fingers and there, set into the brickwork, was the ancient, rust-pitted metal hatch through which the coalmen of old used to unload their truck. Or maybe their horse-drawn cart, back when this thing had last been in use.

Like the trapdoor it was secured with an iron bolt, unopened in so many decades that it was rusted solid.

'They're in,' Kitson's voice rasped in his ear. The sound of heavy steps rang through the floorboards above them as the attackers surged inside the cottage and started searching from room to room. It wouldn't be long before they discovered the wedged kitchen door and smashed their way through.

Ben hated to risk drawing attention by making noise, but the rusted bolt was going to need some persuasion to open. 'Hold this,' he said to Kitson, giving him the lighter. It was getting hot to hold and Ben was worried about the flame giving out. By the dull orange flicker he reversed the shotgun in both hands and hammered the end of the butt against the bolt.

Nothing. Some little flakes of rust fell away but the bolt handle itself didn't budge. If a century's worth of corrosion had fused the metal completely, they were going to have problems getting out of here. Ben dared to hit it again, harder. The blow produced a loud clang but nothing more.

'We're in trouble,' Kitson muttered. The thump of footsteps seemed to be right above them now. How long before the men figured out where their targets were hiding?

It was hot and stifling inside the bunker. Ben could feel the sweat running down his face and sticking his shirt to his back. He thought, *fuck it*. And whacked the butt of the shotgun with all his strength against the bolt handle. The crash of the impact reverberated horribly inside the bunker and he was certain that it must have been heard all through the cottage. At the same instant, the flame of the lighter guttered and died.

'Oh, shit,' Kitson said.

Ben's heart was thudding as he felt for the bolt handle. Then with a flash of relief, he found that the last hammering blow had loosened it enough to wiggle with his fingers.

'Hurry,' Kitson said. 'Come on! They're going to find us!' Ben made no reply. He gritted his teeth and worked the loosened bolt back and forth, feeling the grind of rough metal against metal. It moved half an inch further and stopped. He pushed against it with all the strength in his fingers and it started moving again. And then it suddenly gave, and he felt a sharp stab of pain as some jagged rusty edge gashed his hand. But that didn't matter, because as he pushed against the hatch it creaked open and a waft of fresh air cooled his face.

Ben peered out of the coal chute. He was at face level with the uneven flagstone path that ran around the end wall of the cottage, and the scrappy area of garden between the building and the perimeter wall. Looking up and scanning from side to side he couldn't see any of the men, just the glow of van headlights. To his left, beyond the drystone garden wall, ran the road. To his right was a small lane perpendicular to it, little more than twin tyre tracks in the dirt with long grass growing up along the middle. About twenty yards down the lane, off to the left, he could see a dilapidated farm gate leading to what appeared to be open meadow land. And some forty or fifty yards across the meadow was a dense stand of trees where a forest must once have been.

That was where Ben knew he and Kitson had to go, if they were to have any chance of getting out of here alive. But could they reach it without being spotted?

Chapter 24

Before they could escape across to the trees, first they were going to have to scramble out of the coal chute. That wouldn't have been a problem for one younger, fitter and far more agile man on his own. But for Tony Kitson it was going to pose a challenge.

'I don't think I can make it,' he muttered. 'You go on your own. Leave me here. I'll only hold you up.'

'Don't talk crap, Tony. We're going.' Ben looped the shotgun's sling over his neck and shoulder. Reaching up out of the hole, he got a purchase on the rough metal frame around the hatch and heaved himself up from the bunker to ground level outside.

He could still hear movement and voices from inside the cottage but nobody was lurking around the exterior, at least not yet. All it would take was one of them stepping around the side of the house and this escape attempt would be over before it began. Ben crouched by the hatch and held his hands out for Kitson. The man was boggling up at him as though he was being asked to climb Everest.

'Throw me your stick,' Ben said sharply, and Kitson passed it up to him. 'Now give me your hands.'

Ben braced himself, gripped the man's wrists and heaved him up with all his strength as Kitson grunted and panted and scrabbled for a foothold with his one good leg. It was a struggle, but after a few seconds of extreme effort he was out and on his knees outside, wheezing as though he was going to expire at any moment. Ben yanked him to his feet, gave him back his stick and kept a tight grip on his arm as together they ran for the drystone perimeter wall.

Ben hopped lightly over it onto the road. 'Quick. Quick!' Kitson somehow managed to pile over after him. They headed through the darkness for the narrow dirt lane that ran by the side of the cottage, Kitson hobbling badly and puffing like a steam train. Ben was afraid he was going to collapse, and kept urging him along. 'Keep moving. Go, go.'

Glancing back towards the cottage, Ben could see torch beams sweeping about in the windows. One of the lights was shining behind the smaller window above the kitchen sink. They were in. Not long now before they discovered the trapdoor in the floor and figured out where their targets had disappeared to.

A little further up the lane, Ben and Kitson made it to the farm gate. A cool breeze was blowing, inky black clouds rolling across the face of the moon making the night so dark that they could barely see three feet in front of them. But that worked to their advantage, too. Ben groped about for the gate latch, found it and raised it; but the chink of a chain told him that the gate was locked up.

'We'll have to climb it,' he whispered to Kitson. 'I'll give you a leg up.'

'I feel like I'm back on the sodding Royal Marines assault course,' Kitson wheezed.

'You're doing well, Tony. We'll make it.'

They reached the other side of the gate and Ben urged him across the meadow, in the direction of the trees. The ground was uneven and full of ruts and rocks, and Kitson was finding it such hard going that his hip kept giving way under him every couple of steps and Ben virtually had to carry him. The man's breath was coming in short gasps. He would have been an awesomely fit fighter once upon a time, but too many years of inactivity had turned him into a heart attack waiting to happen.

Moments later, the dull red-orange glow of flames became visible in the cottage windows. Kitson saw it and let out a cry of dismay. 'No! They're burning my house!'

Probably with the intention of burning them along with it, Ben thought. He said, 'There's nothing we can do, Tony. Keep moving.' The stand of trees seemed an impossibly long way away, and their progress towards it was painfully slow. If they could just reach it, they could take refuge under cover and take a moment to try to work out where to go from there. Kitson pointed. 'There's a farm the other side of that hill. Jim and Sandy. I know them well. They'll help us.'

Ben wondered how the hell Jim and Sandy could do that, unless they possessed their own armoury of weapons and the kind of outlaw attitude that would preclude them from wanting to call the police. The powers of law enforcement were the last thing Ben needed landing on him right now. But he knew all too well that it was almost certain some of Kitson's neighbours must have heard the gunfire. While countryside dwellers were pretty much used to hearing the occasional shot and even welcomed it, when hunters were going after foxes, the attack on the cottage would have sounded like a serious incident going on and someone was bound to sound the alarm. Not just the cops but the fire brigade too, when the blazing cottage started to light up the night. The flames in the windows were becoming brighter as the fire began to spread and intensify. There was an acrid burning smell in the air.

'Jesus, I bloody hope Marmalade got out,' Kitson panted. The things people think about at these moments, Ben reflected. 'Marmalade will be fine,' he reassured him.

'All my things. That's a whole lifetime in that place. The bastards!'

Ben and Kitson were more than halfway to the trees by now. It seemed as if they might manage to slip away into the night unnoticed. But then that hope vanished as a hoarse yell came from the direction of the cottage and Ben turned to see figures of men appear outside it with torches. 'They're onto us. Go, go!'

Moments later, things got worse as a diesel engine snorted into life and the blaze of headlamps from behind the cottage lit up the night like a search beam. Then the van appeared and came roaring towards the entrance to the dirt lane.

'Shit! They're coming!' Kitson tried to run faster but his leg wouldn't let him. He stumbled in a rut and fell, gasping. Ben picked him up and forced him on. It was hopeless. The van lights had picked them out and were washing them in a brilliant white glare like two rabbits in a hunter's lamp. There was no getting away now.

A few more stumbling steps over the rough ground, and Kitson fell again. 'I'm sorry! I can't make it!'

But Ben would not leave him on his own. Whatever was coming, they'd face it together like soldiers. Now the van came speeding along the lane and headed for the farm gate without slowing down. It smashed right through, sending bits flying and ripping the chain and padlock from the gatepost. One headlight went dark, the other still pointing at Ben and Kitson as they tried to make the trees. The van's rasping engine note was rising and falling as the driver pushed it hard across the uneven meadow, slithering and pattering in the dirt as the tyres scrambled for grip, battering over the rocks and boulders. The dark shape of a man appeared from the passenger window, leaning out with a weapon in his hands. A burst of muzzle flash and the report of a gunshot, and dirt flew up two feet to Ben's left.

Almost there. The trees were just a few yards away. At least they might provide some protective cover from the gunfire. Ben yanked Kitson along behind him and they reached the trees just as the van was bearing down on them. He shoved Kitson down behind a thick trunk and took shelter behind another. 'Don't move!'

Just a few feet behind them, the van veered away to the right of the trees and came bouncing and lurching past where the two men were crouching. Another burst of fire rattled from the passenger window and bullets ripped a length of bark away. Ben raised the Mossberg, but with only two rounds left he didn't fire for fear of using up his last remaining ammo. The van roared by.

There was no way of knowing how many men might be inside. If they all jumped out at once and came on shooting, he wouldn't have the firepower to resist them. It flanked the trees in a full circle, still bumping and lurching wildly over the ruts. Then suddenly there was a grinding crash and it came to such a violent stop that its rear wheels lifted clear of the ground. With his visibility halved by the broken headlight the driver had piled straight into a huge boulder half-hidden in one of the ruts. His engine stalled and there was silence for a few moments; then came the whine of the starter motor and the engine rasped back into life, followed by the crunch of the gears as the driver slammed the van into reverse and hit the gas, trying to back away from the boulder. But all that happened was that the wheels spun uselessly, spraying dirt upwards in twin arcs. In his panic all the driver could do was rev harder, digging the van in deeper.

When you were outnumbered several to one and trying to hold an indefensible position, sometimes the best means of defence was to attack. And now that his enemy was suddenly in a much weaker position, it was Ben's intention to exploit it.

Chapter 25

Ben darted out from behind his tree, pointed the Mossberg at the windscreen where the driver's head would be, and pulled the trigger. The gun boomed and smacked his shoulder with its recoil and the screen blew into an opaque crumpled mess of cracks. The engine cut out again and the second headlight went dark, plunging the meadow and the trees back into the blackness of night.

Ben couldn't tell if the driver had done it on purpose or whether his shotgun blast had destroyed the electrics. The van sat there, still and silent, a dark shape silhouetted by the growing blaze of the cottage in the background. For an instant or two it seemed as if everyone inside was dead.

But the fight wasn't over yet. Next thing, the doors flew open and the figures of men jumped out and took cover behind their vehicle. They might have been counting how many rounds were left in the gun Ben had taken from their colleague, or they might not – but either way they couldn't afford to assume he was running out of ammo and they weren't going to take any chances.

The other thing the enemy must be worried about, Ben knew, was the possibility of the emergency services suddenly showing up. The prospect of this whole area filling up with police cars wasn't just a concern for him: the attackers wanted to avoid it just as much as he did. They almost certainly hadn't expected the job to take any longer than three minutes before they were done, dusted and out of here. And now he could use that extra element of stress to put pressure on them.

He slipped back behind his tree, moved quietly to another, crouched low to the ground and waited. Absolute silence, just the ringing in his ears from the gunfire. In the background the fire was turning into a beacon that would soon be visible for miles. Blazing embers were spiralling up like fireflies in the night sky. Each passing second was an agony. He counted off a full sixty of them. Then another sixty. He could almost taste the men's impatience to finish their job and get out of here.

He was right. Because just moments later, they made their move. Two of them broke away from the van and ran towards the trees, making a pincer movement to try to attack from both sides at once, in the hope that they could overwhelm him. They didn't want to use their torches, for fear of drawing his fire. A sensible strategy on their part, and one that he'd often employed himself in the past. But again, that was something he could use against them. Because if they weren't easily marking their positions in the darkness, that also meant they couldn't easily see one another.

A level playing field. And Ben Hope was the master of the darkness. Night had always been his element. He was the predator now, and they were his prey.

Tony Kitson was still where Ben had left him, hunkered down low, staying motionless and well concealed in the undergrowth behind his tree with his stick lying next to him. Ben was there in two fast steps. He snatched up the stick, pressed the little catch in the handle ferrule to release the hidden blade, and slipped it smoothly out. On a moonlit night the long, pointed tongue of steel might have made a telltale glitter. Under the cover of the clouds, it was as invisible as the unseen hunter who was about to deploy it to its full lethal effect.

Ben stepped silently around the base of a tree, flitted to the next and stopped, barely breathing, absolutely undetectable, just a few short feet from the nearest of the two men. The man was standing very still, weapon trained, certainly believing he couldn't be seen as he scanned the darkness for any kind of movement he could open fire at. Ben moved up behind him like a shadow, clamped an iron hand over his mouth and ran his torso through with the sword stick. He held the man tightly until his death convulsions had passed and the body went limp in his arms. He relieved the standing corpse of its weapon, then let it slump quietly to the ground.

Ben could tell from its shape and feel that his new firearm was an AR-15 automatic rifle. And from its weight he could estimate to a few grams how many rounds were left in its magazine: no more than twelve, no fewer than eleven. The second prowling among the trees a few yards away. Ben would have preferred to take him out swiftly and silently with the sword, but any moment now the man was about to stumble on Tony Kitson's hiding place, and he might start blasting into the shadows and hit him just by luck.

Ben planted the tip of the sword stick blade in the soft, spongy ground. Lowered himself down among the bushes, centred the dark silhouette of his creeping enemy in his rifle sights and fired. The rifle's loud crack split the darkness. The silhouetted figure folded and went down.

Two for two. But now Ben had revealed his position. More gunfire was directed his way, bullets flying past his ears, clipping leaves off the trees around him and thunking into solid wood. Ben fired back. A burst to the right, a burst to the left, in a short but fierce exchange. He saw another dark figure crumple to the ground, and then another; and then his rifle had shot itself empty and he let it drop and without hesitation grabbed the shotgun again. Two rounds left in the tube.

He broke away from his position and stalked to another spot among the trees. The enemy fire had slackened almost to zero now and he was fairly sure that there were only one or two, at most, left alive. Their mission had fallen apart. Several casualties down the line, their target was still very much in the game. Now the last men standing would be starting to panic.

As it turned out, there was only one. As the black clouds overhead scudded away from the face of the moon, Ben saw him make a break for the driver's door. Something gleamed as he ran, a glint of moonlight reflected in the lenses of the glasses that the man was wearing awkwardly under his ski mask. Ben fired at the fast-moving figure, but his shot just punched a colander of holes into the van's bodywork. The running man made it to the driver's door and ripped it open, jumped behind the wheel and restarted the engine. But the van was still stuck in the dirt, and the spinning wheels couldn't get any traction. The man gave up trying, leaped back out and disappeared behind the side of the vehicle.

Ben wanted to shoot, but this was his last round and he couldn't waste it. He emerged from the trees and started stalking towards the van. As he got closer he heard the sound of its rear doors opening, followed by two fast shots that resonated loudly inside the rear cargo space. Ben couldn't understand why the guy was directing fire inside the vehicle.

But he had no more time to think about it as the man reappeared for a brief instant and sprayed the darkness with a last wild burst that made Ben throw himself to the ground for cover. Then the man took off at a sprint.

Ben fired off his last round at the fleeing figure. He thought he saw the man stumble as if he'd been winged by the shot, but then he regained his stride and kept running. Ben swore, threw down the empty shotgun and went to give chase.

That was when he heard the low, agonised groan from the bushes and realised it was coming from Tony Kitson. He was in trouble.

Ben hesitated, torn between choices. Should he run back to check Kitson, or should he go after his escaping enemy? He could see the tall, thin dark shape sprinting away across the meadow, heading roughly in the direction of Jim and Sandy's farm. If he went after him, it would be the second time in a matter of days that he'd given chase to a tall, thin man with glasses hurrying away from the scene of a deadly assault. His gut told him that this was the very same man he'd already encountered twice in Ireland. The car bomber. He'd have dearly loved to get his hands on him.

But then Kitson let out another tortured moan and called out in a croaking voice, 'Help me, I'm hit!' He sounded bad. Really bad.

There was no choice. Ben turned his back on the disappearing figure and went to him.

He wasn't expecting to find anything good. What he did find was worse. That last burst of fire before the man with the glasses had made his escape had cut a swathe through the trees and one of the bullets had found its way to where Kitson was lying low. He'd been hit in the belly, but as bad as that was, it wasn't the most serious part of the damage. The bullet had penetrated his abdomen and from the amount of blood that was pouring out of him and soaking into his clothes, almost black in the moonlight, Ben was certain that it must have hit his liver.

A person might be able to survive this, if they didn't bleed to death. But not without immediate surgical intervention. And Tony Kitson knew enough about combat injuries to be fully aware of that fact. 'I'm done,' he gasped. 'Oh Christ, it hurts.'

On the battlefield, someone could at least have dosed the dying man with a syrette or two of morphine. But Ben couldn't even offer him that. All he could do was talk to him, tell him that help was on its way, try to make his last moments as comfortable as possible and wait for the inevitable to take its course. Which was only a matter of two or three minutes, but it seemed to Ben like hours before Kitson finally went still and his pulse stopped. Ben passed a bloody hand over the poor man's eyes to close them. 'I'm sorry, Tony.'

The man with the glasses was long gone by now, and there was no point in even trying to go after him. Ben walked over to the van. Two dead bodies lay beside it and another was slumped in the passenger seat. There was a long steel Maglite torch on the dashboard. Ben took it and shone it into the rear. He wasn't surprised to see another corpse back there, that of a big burly fellow with some severe facial trauma. What Ben had done to him back at the cottage wouldn't have killed him, but the two rifle bullets that the guy with the glasses had pumped into his chest before running away had certainly done the trick.

To execute your own man in cold blood to prevent him from being captured alive and made to talk – that was some pretty brutal treatment, but Ben wouldn't have expected anything less of someone capable of blowing off an innocent young woman's leg with an explosive device.

By his count nine men had come for him, one had managed to escape and the rest were now so much litter to be disposed of. First, Ben was going to have to get the van out of the rut into which it had deeply dug itself. SAS military Land Rovers carried heavy-duty recovery tracks for wedging under wheels trapped in sand, mud or snow. In the absence of any such equipment, he was going to have to improvise. And he was going to have to move fast, before the police and fire brigade turned up.

The two dead bodies lying conveniently close to the van would serve his purpose fine. The van was front wheel drive, so he dragged each body over in turn and jammed it as tightly as he could up behind each front tyre. Just one of the many uses you could put a dead scumbag's body to in a time of need. Then he climbed into the driver's seat, restarted the engine, engaged reverse and gently eased off the clutch at low revs. He felt the tyres bite down against the firm bodies and get traction, and revved a little harder. The van rocked and gyrated as the tyres spun, found a purchase, spun again; then with a bounce and a lurch the van was free of the rut.

Ben reversed the van around in a bumpy semicircle, left the motor idling and jumped out. The two dead guys were a little chewed up from being used as wheel tracks but they didn't seem to mind. He dragged them up to the back of the van and loaded them aboard next to the big fellow. Then he did the same with the one in the passenger seat. Next it was the turn of the two he'd killed over by the trees. Ben grabbed each one in turn by the ankles and hauled them over the rough ground to add them to the growing pile of bodies in the back of the van. Once that was done he gathered up all the fallen weapons and dumped those in the rear as well.

Last came Tony Kitson. With a sigh, Ben walked back to the spot where he'd died. He crouched by the body, hefted his dead weight up over his shoulder, carried him over to the front of the van and managed to load him into the passenger seat.

Ben couldn't leave Tony without his stick. He retrieved that as well, and placed it across his knee.

Too much time had gone by, and he was worried that the emergency services would be arriving any moment. He drove the well-laden van back across the rutted meadow and through the ruins of the gate. By now the fire had completely consumed the cottage. Ben drove around the back of the blazing building, put the van in neutral and jumped out, letting it roll under its own momentum into the flames.

The rental BMW was in a sad way, with all four tyres shot out, bullet holes punched all over the bodywork and not a single window intact. But in a tribute to German engineering, the damn thing managed to splutter into life at the first press of the starter button. And not a moment too soon, because the wail of sirens could be heard growing steadily louder in the distance and he could see a glow of blue lights over the brow of the hill.

It was time to get out of here.

Chapter 26

The limping, smoking car managed to carry Ben nearly four miles through the night before the ominous knocking sound coming from under the bonnet turned into a death rattle and he was forced to pull over to the side of the lonely, empty country road.

It looked as though he'd be continuing on foot from here, for a while anyway. He was glad now that he'd had the foresight to rent the car in the name of Paul Harris. Mr Harris would no doubt be permanently blacklisted by the rental firm for destroying their property, but at least nobody would ever trace it to him personally.

Ben used the edge of a coin to unscrew the BMW's registration plates and put them in his bag, for future use. Before he abandoned the car, a thought came to him and he carried out a quick exploratory search under the wheel arches. And sure enough, under the rear driver-side arch – the same one where he'd found the suspicious item attached to his Interceptor – was another GPS tracking device.

Unbelievable. So that was how the bad guys had followed him to Tony Kitson's cottage. He shook his head in amazement at his own stupidity for not having checked it sooner, and tried to think when the device could have been planted there. It must have been in the hotel car park in York, or outside the White Boar pub, or at Mortimer's place before that. Whichever it was, they'd done this to him twice now.

There wouldn't be a third time.

He set off on foot along the dark country lanes, keeping an eye out for a farm or cottage where he might be able to steal alternative transport. Vehicle theft behind enemy lines was an age-old speciality of the SAS, and he'd been quite adept at it back in the day. After a couple of miles he came to a stone bridge over a river, and made his way down the grassy bank to the water's edge to clean himself up. Killing people up close and personal and hauling carcasses around was gory work, and he couldn't return to civilisation looking like something out of a slaughterhouse. He stripped off his clothes and washed away the blood, then did what he could to clean the russet stains off his shirt and trousers. The result was satisfactory enough, as long as he wasn't contemplating attending any respectable social events in the near future.

He walked on for another two hours, during which time the only vehicle he encountered on the quiet road was a truck that rumbled by ignoring his outstretched thumb. Finally, deep in the night, he found what he'd been looking for earlier, a rough little farm at the bottom of a muddy track where there were various tractors, trailers and vehicles sitting around the yard. Nobody was around and the farm-house windows were all in darkness. Farms were good places to steal from in his experience, unless there were dogs around. This one didn't have any. What it did have was a hard-used, unloved and scabby Toyota Hilux pickup truck with some farm implements on the flatbed and its key in the ignition. Ben removed the implements, eased off the handbrake, slipped it into neutral and rolled it a safe distance down the track from the house before he jumped behind the wheel, fired up the engine and sped off into the night.

A few miles down the road he swapped the Toyota's plates for those of the Beemer, to cut down the chances of getting nabbed with a stolen vehicle. In the event, he didn't see a single police car all the way to York. He grabbed a couple of hours' sleep in a quiet layby, then headed into the city just as the first stores were opening. His first stop was to buy a new pair of black jeans, an olive-green T-shirt and a blue denim shirt to replace the clothes that still, in the light of day, looked as though they belonged to a busy serial killer. He stuffed the soiled things into a rubbish bin. The old brown leather jacket had cleaned up fine and he was too attached to it to get rid of it.

From there he returned to his room at the inn, where he took a fast shower and gathered up Hugh Mortimer's Ricardian periodicals before heading downstairs to settle up his bill and check out. He wasn't in the mood for Trish's bubbly, inquisitive chatter, and left quickly. Breakfast was a plate of bacon and eggs at a greasy-spoon café down the road. While he wolfed his food and washed down the high-cholesterol mess with a mug of coffee he checked back through the scribbled notes in the Society bulletins and found the name and address of Mortimer's Liechtenstein historian contact, R. Berg.

Whoever they might be, that was going to be Ben's next port of call. There were still a lot of unanswered questions and loose ends needing to be tied up. With any luck, the mysterious Berg could help him put the rest of the pieces together. Switching identities from Paul Harris to Mike Palmer he phone-booked an early afternoon flight from

Leeds–Bradford to Zurich, which was the nearest he could get to his new destination by air. The train journey from York to the airport would take a couple of hours. As for the banged-up Toyota Hilux, it had served its purpose. In a backstreet far from the prying eyes of surveillance cameras, Ben replaced the pickup's original plates. He left a polite thank-you note to the owner and three hundred and fifty pounds in cash in the glove box, then called the police anonymously to let them know where the stolen vehicle could be found. Not all car thieves had to be inconsiderate bastards. Then he called a taxi firm to hurry him to the railway station.

At 1.45 that afternoon the lone traveller by the name of Mike Palmer was boarding the KLM Royal Dutch Airlines flight to Switzerland. Three hours and 626 miles later, Mr Palmer morphed back into his alter ego, Benedict Hope, and walked into the Sixt luxury and premium auto rental office at Zurich Airport. It wasn't a desire for comfort and opulence that had made him pick that one. He had a seventy-mile road trip ahead of him and he had no particular interest in savouring the misty mountain views and dreamy lake vistas along the way.

'*Ich hätte gerne das schnellste Auto, dass Sie haben*,' he said to the young guy at the desk, who might have been a German-speaking clone of the one in the Hertz office at Leeds–Bradford. Ben's own German wasn't good enough to pass for a native, but perfectly fluent.

'The fastest we have?' the guy replied, raising an eyebrow. 'Now, let me see . . .'

And twenty minutes later, Ben was about to find out the real difference between a run-of-the-mill BMW production saloon and a hand-built B5 eight-cylinder BMW Alpina. Namely, five hundred horsepower under the bonnet, blistering acceleration from zero to sixty in four seconds and a top speed of something very close to two hundred miles per hour.

Maybe he could learn to love Beemers after all.

The Principality of Liechtenstein was one of the world's smallest micro-nations, about twice the size of Galway City, sandwiched in a tiny niche among the Alps between Switzerland and Austria. All Ben really knew about the place was that being a tax haven for billionaires, it attracted just about as many rich folks as Monte Carlo. He wondered if Hugh Mortimer's contact, Berg, was one of those. Then again, if he was that wealthy, in the same way rich people had staff to cook and clean and do everything except wipe their arses for them, maybe he could have employed someone to answer his telephone. Ben had tried the number twice back in England while waiting to board his flight, and again on landing at Zurich, to no avail. It was frustrating. Now he was pinning all his hopes on being able to catch the guy at home in person.

The address he had for Berg was located in the town of Schaan, just five minutes' drive north of the capital, Vaduz. What should have been at least a ninety-minute to two-hour drive across Switzerland had been shaved down to just over one hour, thanks to the scorching performance of the Alpina. Ben was beginning to think he might buy one of these one day.

It was early evening by the time he arrived in Schaan. The light was just beginning to fade and the sun was slowly sinking over the forested mountains that loomed over the town. Schaan was a mix of new and old architecture, quaint traditional houses with shutters and balconies sharing space with gleaming white modern apartment buildings on peaceful streets that were low on traffic and high on typical Swiss-style cleanliness. The kind of place where the local authorities would see you clapped in irons for dropping so much as a sweet wrapper on the pavement, and that probably imposed the death sentence for anyone found loitering with a can of spray paint.

Ben soon found the address he was looking for. Berg's home was an attractive traditional townhouse, white with blue shutters, in a pretty little street on the northern edge of Schaan. He parked the Alpina down the street and walked up to the house. And that was when he discovered the reason why its occupant hadn't been answering his landline phone.

Chapter 27

The sign in the downstairs window said KOPPENSTEINER IMMOBILIEN A.G., with an office address in Vaduz, and underneath in larger print EIGENTUM ZU VERMIETEN. *Property to let.* Which meant that the townhouse hadn't belonged to Berg at all, because he'd only been renting it and now must have moved elsewhere.

Damn.

Ben walked slowly back to the car, lit a Gauloise and leaned against the Alpina's warm, ticking front wing, gazing at the vacant house and thinking hard. He refused to accept that he'd been foolish enough to come all this way for nothing. A couple of passersby he took to be local residents came down the street as he watched, and he smiled politely, wished them *guten Abend* and asked if they knew the man who lived here. Neither of them was able to help. 'I'm sorry, I have only lived here for a couple of weeks' was the first reply. 'I'm not from this area' was the second.

Ben was considering what to do next and wondering whether he should start knocking on doors when he spotted someone else appearing round the street corner and making their way slowly in his direction: a fat, asthmatic old man with an equally geriatric dog that was waddling along with its tongue hanging out and having to stop to lift its leg on every tree and lamppost. Now these two must be local, Ben thought. Neither the old man nor his canine companion looked to be in a state to walk more than a couple of hundred yards without needing medical assistance. Putting his polite smile back on he intercepted the pair as they reached Berg's former home.

'Sorry to bother you, sir, but do you happen to live nearby?'

The old man and the dog both looked at Ben with the same empty expression. Then the old man slowly pointed back at the street corner, nodded and replied, '*Ja*, we live just up the street, Caspar and I. Are you looking for directions, young man?'

'Not exactly. I came to visit my friend who lives in this house, but it seems he's moved on. I wondered if you might know him, in which case you might have an idea where he went.'

The old man gazed at Berg's door and seemed to need to think carefully about it. 'I've seen him a couple of times. Tall fellow, about your height but thin, like a scarecrow. Never spoke to him, though.'

Another blank, Ben thought. It had been worth trying, though.

The old man wheezed, seemed about to cough something up, then swallowed it with a grimace. 'Gone off has he, did you say?'

'Looks that way,' Ben said.

'That's no good, is it? Not much of a friend, to go off and not tell you where he's going.'

'Nope,' Ben said, starting to wish he hadn't approached this guy. Next he was going to get the life story, and probably the dog's too.

The old man started wheezing again. Maybe he had hairballs from living with Caspar. Finally he managed to clear his throat, then waved a gnarly finger towards the house and said, 'Tell you what, though, young man.'

'What?'

'Funny thing, it is. You're not the first person to ask me about the fellow who lived in that house.'

'I'm not?'

'No. Couple of days ago, I think it was. Yes, that's right. Because we'd just been watching Caspar's favourite show on TV, and that's on a Monday, and it's Wednesday now.'

'Who was asking?'

'Well, I'm trying to tell you, if only you'd stop interrupting me,' the old man replied irritably. 'We were on our walk, Caspar and me, and there was another car parked here where yours is. Red car. Audi or a Mercedes, now I don't remember. But I remember the two men. Never seen them before. Came up to me like you did just now, except not so friendly, I thought. Didn't like the look of them much. Caspar didn't like the look of them either. Did you, Caspar?'

Caspar didn't seem to remember much about the incident. He squatted on the pavement and started slurping noisily at his nether parts.

'And these two men were asking questions about Herr Berg?'

'That his name, is it? I didn't know. Like I said, never spoke to the fellow. But yes, they said they were friends of his too and wanted to know where he'd gone. Must have a lot of friends, this Berg of yours.' The old man frowned. 'Berg, is that what you called him? They had a different name for him, now I recall.'

Ben asked, 'What was the name?'

'Oh, I couldn't tell you. At my age you forget things. It sounded a bit like Berg. But it was different. More to it.

Bergmann? No, that's not it. Bergenthal? I think that might have been it, but I'm not sure.'

'Berg's just the nickname I use for him,' Ben explained. 'So what happened then?'

The old man spread his arms. 'Nothing. I told them what I told you, that I didn't know anything about this Berg or Bergenheimer or Bergenstein or whatever he's called, and then they got back in their car and went speeding off. Not very friendly. Very rude.'

'Well, I'm grateful for your help,' Ben said. 'You've been very kind.'

'My pleasure,' the old man said. 'Goodbye now. I hope you find your friend. Oh Caspar, look what you've done.' He swiped the fresh dog turd into the gutter with his foot, and went ambling on tugging at Caspar's leash and muttering to himself.

So Berg wasn't Berg, Ben wasn't the only one searching for him, and the two men in the red car seemed to know more about the man than Ben did. That was interesting, though it wasn't very comforting.

Ben decided that his next port of call should be the Koppensteiner estate agency office in nearby Vaduz. He jumped in the car, and less than ten minutes later he'd located the offices in the town's Äulestrasse, but they were now closed for the evening. Ben swore. He'd have no choice but to wait until morning, and hope like hell that the competition hadn't beaten him to it by then.

Not far from the Koppensteiner offices, on Mareestrasse, he found the Park Hotel Sonnenhof and opted to set up base camp there for the night – if 'base camp' was quite the term for a high-class establishment featuring a gourmet restaurant and a private park with views of the mountains and nearby vineyards, the Rhine Valley and Vaduz Castle, where Liechtenstein's royal family had their official residence. All they could offer him was what they called a 'superior' double room, complete with a giant bathroom, a private balcony and the biggest bed he'd ever seen. It was a little more luxury than Ben either needed or was used to, but he decided it was only one night and he'd just have to endure it.

His first act was to flout the no smoking rules and light up a Gauloise while raiding the mini-bar for whisky. His second was to take a lingering hot shower in his movie-star bathroom, after which he called room service and ordered up a bottle of Liechtenstein Pinot Noir and a dish of Tiroler Gröstl, a local speciality that consisted of pan-fried meat and potatoes with lots of butter and onions, just a poshed-up version of corned beef hash as far as Ben could see. He hadn't had a bite since York, and ate greedily. He polished off the bottle of Pinot outside on his balcony along with a couple more cigarettes, watching the stars twinkle over Vaduz Castle and wondering what tomorrow would bring.

Then he undressed and crept into the huge, soft bed and tried not to dream about cars blowing up, murder by drowning, Tony Kitson bleeding to death or two strange men driving around in a red car with a head start on him, who might very well be in the process of derailing his whole plan and leaving him with precious few available options.

He was up again at dawn, went for a run in the grounds and swam forty lengths of the hotel pool before a light breakfast of coffee and ribel. After checking out, he gave the

Alpina a thorough examination for anything that shouldn't be there. It seemed that nobody had sneaked into the hotel car park to plant any suspicious tracking or explosive devices, but after being caught out twice already he didn't think he could be blamed for being paranoid.

At exactly one minute to nine, as planned, he was outside the door of the Koppensteiner property agency in Äulestrasse. A small dark-haired office manager called Fräulein Stumpf introduced him to her associate, Werner Gattermayr. 'This gentleman, Herr Palmer, is interested in renting the villa in Schaan. Do you think you could show him around the place this morning? Right away?' Ben thought that Werner Gattermayr seemed strangely preoccupied and a little reluctant, but Fräulein Stumpf had a steely eye and an authoritative manner that her colleague was unable to resist, and he agreed.

'Can I ask whether anyone else has expressed an interest in the property?' Ben enquired.

'No, not since it became vacant,' Fräulein Stumpf said. 'You're the first.'

'So you haven't had a couple of men in a red car turning up here asking about it.'

'In a red car?' she replied, bemused by the question. 'Er, no. Not at all.'

Gattermayr led the way in his Audi Quattro, and Ben followed in the Alpina. They arrived at the villa and the estate agent unlocked the door and ushered Ben through the spacious entrance hall and into an adjacent living-room. Ben noticed that the man seemed even more preoccupied than before. He wondered whether it had something to do with the two men, and whether his boss had been telling the truth.

'As you can see,' Gattermayr said, 'it's fully furnished. Unfortunately the previous tenant, Herr Bergenroth, left in something of a hurry without providing any notice.'

So 'Berg' had been Mortimer's shorthand for the name Bergenroth. Ben said casually, 'Well, it's not an issue for me.'

'It's a little inconvenient for our agency, though,' Gattermayr went on, 'as it's our policy to redecorate rental properties before letting them out again. I'm afraid one of the bedrooms is still full of a lot of personal items Herr Bergenroth left behind. He didn't give us any forwarding address and I don't even know if he'll be coming back to collect them. We might have to dump it all. It's very aggravating and I do apologise.'

Twice while he was talking, Gattermayr glanced at his watch, and he kept biting his lip. He was obviously uptight about something more than just the troubles with the former tenant.

'No need to apologise,' Ben said. 'But tell me, why did the bloke leave in such a hurry?' So as not to sound as if he was probing for information he added, 'Is there something I should know about the place, like spirits or poltergeists?'

Gattermayr laughed nervously. 'No, no, nothing like that.' He glanced at his watch again.

'Sounds like a bit of a character, this tenant of yours,' Ben said, smiling.

'I think he's some kind of historian,' Gattermayr replied distractedly. 'But I'm not sure what he does exactly. An academic or a teacher, perhaps, except he seems to move around rather a lot. He wasn't here for very long. I don't know. Anyway, we'll soon have the place all freshened up. Decorators are coming in tomorrow and the new phone line

is scheduled to be installed in a few minutes, at nine-thirty.'
As though the mention of a phone had prompted him, he
took out his mobile to check it, frowned and tutted unhap-
pily to himself.

'Is something the matter, Herr Gattermayr?'

The agent flushed deep crimson with embarrassment.
'Please forgive my rudeness. It's just that I can't get phone
reception in this building and . . . well, to cut a long story
short, my wife's expecting our first baby at any moment. She
called me while I was on the way to work this morning to
say it was coming and her sister Anna was driving her to
the hospital in Triesen. I was about to mention it Fräulein
Stumpf and ask if I could have the morning off, but . . .'

'But then I turned up and your boss is a hard lady
to refuse,' Ben said. 'I get it. We've all worked for people
like that.'

'I'm hoping I can get away after this,' Gattermayr said
apologetically.

Ben felt for the guy. Besides which, a thought had come
to him. 'Listen, you go outside where you can get reception
and make your call. Give me exactly five minutes to look
around the house and I'll soon tell you if I want to take
it. Okay?'

Gattermayr thanked him profusely and hurried outside
with his phone in his hand. Alone in the house, Ben headed
straight up the stairs for the spare bedroom where Bergenroth
had apparently left a lot of his stuff behind. The clock was
ticking and he didn't have a lot of time, but with any luck
he might find some clue as to what might have prompted
him to leave in such a hurry. Better still, some indication of

where he'd gone from here. It was a gamble, but Ben had been lucky before.

Bergenroth's abandoned possessions seemed to consist mainly of books and clothes that the estate agents had piled into cardboard boxes and garbage bags in their attempt to clear the place up. Ben emptied a few of them over the floor and sifted through their contents. There were some folders stuffed with paperwork, which seemed tantalisingly promising at first. But while a sheaf of personal correspondence between him and Mortimer revealing the identity of the killers would have been nice to find, all the folders contained were miscellaneous goods receipts and official stuff to do with car leasing, tax and a bank loan Bergenroth had taken out three years ago and was paying off in instalments. Nothing of relevance to Ben. Maybe the two men in the red car had broken in without leaving a trace, and taken away the important stuff.

Three minutes of his precious time had ebbed away. From the window he could see Werner Gattermayr pacing in the street outside, talking on his mobile. It seemed as if Ben's luck had failed him on this occasion. What else could he do? Revert back to his plan of going door to door talking to the other neighbours?

He muttered, 'Shit.'

In the next moment, just as he was ready to give up the search, the landline phone started ringing downstairs.

Chapter 28

It was 9.28 a.m., just two minutes before the existing phone line was due to be switched over to the new. Ben hesitated, then thought *fuck it* and on an impulse ran down the stairs to where the phone sat on its little alcove table, hard-wired into the wall fixture. Before it could stop ringing he snatched the old-fashioned receiver from its cradle. '*Ja*? Hallo?'

'Rudi?' It was a woman's voice on the line, and she sounded tremendously excited and relieved to talk to him. 'It's me, Ingrid,' she gushed in German. 'Where have you been? I've been calling and calling! I didn't know what to think.'

'I'm sorry,' Ben said. 'If you're looking for Rudi Bergenroth, I'm afraid you've missed him.' Thinking on his feet, he added, 'This is his cousin, Stefan.'

'Oh.' Ingrid sounded crestfallen. 'I thought you were him. Your voice sounds a little the same. Or maybe I just wanted you to be,' she said bitterly, after a pause. 'Do you know where he is?'

'No,' Ben replied truthfully, 'I have no idea.'

'Huh. Then he left, did he. Just like that, without a word. No goodbye, nothing.' Ingrid's voice sounded tight. Then she broke down and started crying. 'I mean, I've always known he was a bit of a rolling stone. But to just disappear without even telling me – I thought he loved me!'

Rudi Bergenroth, the heartbreaker. 'I'm afraid my cousin was always that way inclined,' Ben said. 'He moves around a lot.'

She replied, sniffing, 'Oh, I knew that. I had no illusions. Are you trying to find him, too?'

'As a matter of fact I am,' Ben said. 'There's an important family matter I needed to talk to him about. But the house is vacated and he didn't leave a forwarding address.'

'I'm just so devastated,' Ingrid said. 'I wish I knew where he'd gone.'

'Maybe you could help me find him.'

'Or you could help me,' she replied. 'I'm desperate to speak with him, even if it's just to say goodbye properly. To hear his voice one last time.' She started crying again. Poor Ingrid really had it badly.

Ben glanced at the time. Almost nine-thirty. The phone line could be cut off at any moment. Werner Gattermayr was still pacing and talking in the street outside. 'Ingrid, do you live nearby?' Ben asked. 'Because if you do, I was thinking maybe we could meet and talk. Perhaps you and I might be able to figure out where he went, between us.'

Ingrid clearly wasn't the most streetwise of ladies, to fall for what could easily have been a lure by a total stranger. But in her moment of weakness she replied, '*Oh, das wäre doch wunderbar!* That would be wonderful! I live in Eschen. It's maybe ten or fifteen minutes' drive from there and I'm here at home all day today. Why don't you come over?'

Ingrid gave her address, and Ben finished jotting it down on the back of his hand just as the phone went dead. He hurried downstairs and outside, to find that the estate agent had finished his own phone call. The anxiety had melted from Gattermayr's face and he looked radiant with joy as he greeted Ben with a beaming smile. 'I was just talking with Anna. Leni gave birth to a beautiful little baby girl! I wish I could have been there. But I'm so happy!' He laughed out loud. 'I'm going straight over to see them and I don't care what Fräulein Stumpf says.'

'That's fabulous,' Ben said. 'Congratulations. And to hell with Fräulein Stumpf.'

'I really have to rush. Have you decided about the house?'

'It's a very nice house,' Ben said. 'But I think I'll have to pass. It's a little on the small side for me and my fourteen children. See you, Werner. Thanks for the tour, and give my regards to Leni.'

He left the property agent standing there goggling at him, jumped in the Alpina and took off with a roar towards the nearby municipality of Eschen, just four miles to the north of Schaan. The handy thing about such a tiny country was that the travelling distances between towns were compressed to almost nothing. Five minutes later, he was entering Eschen and following the street directions Ingrid had given him.

The directions led him up a winding road to an imposing, expensive-looking villa on a hill overlooking the picturesque town. A sleek white Jaguar roadster was parked in front of the house, and fine manicured gardens stretched away to the rear. He could hear the buzz of lawnmowers in the distance. He was walking towards the front door when it opened and a peroxide blonde of about fifty appeared in the doorway. She was shoehorned into a little white dress and the ice tinkled in the glass she was holding in one red-nailed hand. Vodka cocktails, at 9.40 a.m. Some people liked to get started early. Ben put it down to her emotional state. She seemed to have got over the worst of it, but her eyes were red and she was a little unsteady on her high heels.

'Ingrid, I presume?'

'And you must be Stefan,' she said, looking him up and down.

'Stefan Nachtnebel. It's a pleasure to meet you.'

'I'm sorry I was upset before. What must you think of me?'

'Not at all,' he smiled. 'I can only apologise for the shoddy way my cousin has treated you. It's unforgivable.'

She blinked her long lashes, and for a horrible moment Ben thought she was going to start crying again. 'I do love him, you know. More than I probably should.'

'He doesn't deserve you,' Ben said.

She ushered him into the airy villa. Everything in it was white, including the miniature poodle that appeared out of nowhere and nipped him on the ankle. 'Do excuse Mitzi,' Ingrid said. 'She gets overexcited. Would you like a drink?'

It was rare for him to turn down the offer, but even he liked to wait until the sun was a little higher in the sky. 'I'd have a coffee, if you're making any.'

Ingrid led him into a vast white kitchen and he perched on a stool at the white marble breakfast bar. She plucked a tissue from a box, dabbed her eyes and then set about making the coffee. Gold bangles on her wrists jingled as she worked. Looking around him, Ben noticed a half-empty bottle of Iordanov vodka, another of tonic, and a cut lime on a chopping board on the kitchen counter. Next to the vodka stood a small framed photograph of a smiling, happy-looking Ingrid pictured with a taller, leaner man of around fifty-five or so. He had a long, rather wolflike face and a grizzled little goatee beard, and was wearing little round blue-tinted glasses. They were standing with their arms around one another, beside a traditional stone farmhouse that could have been Scottish or Irish, or maybe Cornish. A slate sign over the door said BEAUVOIR HOUSE, and in the background were green hills and blue ocean. Ben peered curiously at the man in the photo. So this must be the great Rudi Bergenroth, he thought.

'Rudi never mentioned a cousin called Stefan,' Ingrid said from across the kitchen as she bustled about preparing coffee. 'Do you live abroad? Your accent is a little unusual.'

'I'm from Düsseldorf but I've been living in England for some years,' Ben replied. 'I'm almost like a native now. I never would have thought you could lose your first language, but there it is. Now people take me for a foreigner in my own country.'

'I know some English. Only a little. But Rudi speaks it very well. I've heard him talking on the phone.'

'That might have been to me,' Ben said. 'He uses me to practise on.'

'I'm sure it might have been. His history friend, too. Professor someone.'

'Professor Mortimer?'

She nodded. 'Yes, that's right. Do you know him?'

'We only met once,' Ben said.

'How do you take your coffee, Stefan?'

'Just as it comes, thanks,' he said. 'No milk or sugar.'

When the machine had finished spurting out the dark, rich-smelling brew Ingrid came over with a dainty china cup and saucer and sat beside him at the breakfast bar to resume working on her cocktail. He reckoned she'd probably start on another after this. 'Oh dear,' she muttered. 'My head's feeling a little muzzy this morning. Where was I?'

'We were talking about Rudi's friend, the history professor. I understand they're quite close.'

Ingrid obviously hadn't been told about Hugh Mortimer's demise. 'Oh yes. Rudi's deeply into his history. It's what he does when he's not doing his crypto . . . crypto . . .'

'Cryptography? Cryptology?'

She sipped her drink. 'Or whatever it's called. You know, like cracking codes and stuff.'

Interesting, Ben thought. 'What has Rudi told you about that?'

'Oh, nothing he shouldn't have told me. I understand it's all quite secretive and important work. All I know is that he deciphers old documents and things.'

Interesting, indeed. 'That's right,' Ben said. 'That's what he does.'

'It's a talent that must run in the family, seemingly. He told me all about his famous ancestor from centuries ago – I think his name was Gustav, Gustav Bergenroth – who was a code breaker too. How he'd deciphered all these secret letters from Ferdinand and Isabella and other kings and queens of Europe, way back in history. It's really fascinating. I think that's what Rudi was talking about with his professor friend, but I'm not sure. My English isn't really that good.'

'You're right,' Ben said. 'It is fascinating.' Suddenly a whole new dimension had opened up in the intrigue with Mortimer and his mysterious associate. Why codes? What could these two historians have been working on together?

Ingrid asked him, 'Are you into that kind of thing too? Belonging to such a clever family.'

'Me? No, I wouldn't have the patience or the discipline. Not everyone is as brilliant as Rudi.'

She looked sadly down at her hands and murmured. 'He really is.' Then brightening up a little she asked, 'So what do you do, Stefan?'

'I work in advertising,' he replied. 'Nothing very exciting, I'm afraid. So tell me, Ingrid, when did you two meet?'

'About nine months ago,' she replied with a sigh. 'Soon after he arrived here, I think.' She gave a bitter little laugh. 'I don't even know where he lived before that, only that he was born in Austria. Just goes to show. How well do you ever know anybody?'

Her absence of knowledge about her lover boy's past history or current movements wasn't boding too well for their chances of figuring out where he might have gone, Ben was thinking. But he had to keep hoping, and pressing for more information. He asked, 'You were going out together all this time?'

'Yes, when he wasn't involved with his work. It's been wonderful. We even went on holiday together, last September. He took me to see his dream island. That's where that was taken,' she added, glancing tenderly at the framed photo. 'Outside the lovely big farmhouse we stayed in. I'll never forget it, for as long as I live.'

'His dream island?'

'It's a place called Sark, off the south coast of England. Do you know it?'

'I've never been there,' Ben said. 'But Rudi might have mentioned it to me once or twice, now I think about it.'

She smiled wistfully at the memory. 'Oh, it's just magical. So romantic, so beautiful. There are no motor vehicles allowed on the island, only horses and bicycles, and hardly anyone lives there so it's very peaceful and private. I found it completely enchanting. Rudi often told me that he'd like to retire there some day. It's really his kind of place.'

'Maybe he will,' Ben said.

Ingrid's smile suddenly vanished and her eyes filled with tears again. She rubbed at them, smudging her mascara. 'This morning, when you picked up the phone my heart skipped a beat, thinking it was him. I know it's stupid of me to get so worked up. I suppose I knew deep down that it wouldn't last for ever between us. But I can't help the way I feel. I go round there sometimes, during the day, even at night, and keep expecting to see him. Thinking like a fool that he might have come back. Who am I kidding?' She knocked back the rest of her drink and then sank her face into her hands, sobbing gently.

Ben was silent for a moment, thinking. Even though he'd done everything possible to cover his tracks coming here, whoever was behind all this might still be just one step behind. Rudi Bergenroth must have known it too. That was the reason he'd gone AWOL and left his lady love in the lurch. And it bothered Ben that this poor woman could be putting herself in danger by showing up at the house in Schaan. Enough innocent people had already been hurt in this. He touched her arm and said softly, 'Ingrid—'

She sniffed and looked tearfully up at him. 'Yes?'

'I really hate to tell you this, but I think you should know that it's not the first time my cousin has done a bunk.'

Ingrid stared at him. 'What on earth do you mean?'

'It's delicate,' he replied, frowning. 'You see, Rudi has . . . well, I'm afraid he has a gambling problem. A bad one. A full-blown addiction, in fact.'

She gasped. 'He never showed any sign of anything like that!'

'Well, he wouldn't have. He's very good at hiding it from people, because he's really quite ashamed of his habit. And he's worked hard to put it all behind him. He promises never to do it again, and I think he really means it. But his gambling urges are stronger than he can control. Cards, horses, roulette, you name it. Once the temptation gets a grip, you can't stop him. It's really a mental illness.'

'*Aber das ist ganz schrecklich!* It's just awful!'

'You've no idea what a torment it is to him,' Ben replied. 'But unfortunately, it's often landed him in a good deal of hot water. Up until now the family have always been very willing to bail him out, but I'm concerned that one day he might get himself in so deep that we'll be powerless to help.'

Ingrid was reeling with shock. 'I can't believe I'm hearing this. It doesn't sound at all like the Rudi I know!'

'I'm afraid it's true,' he said, looking at her earnestly. 'It's the reason I came to Liechtenstein to look for him. Because I – we, the family – have reason to think that he might be up to his old ways again. And the way he's run off like this, I'm extremely concerned that he could really be in trouble again.'

'I have money,' she protested. 'Plenty of money. I could have helped him, if only he'd told me!'

'We're talking about some very large sums indeed,' Ben said. 'And more seriously, the kind of people he runs up these debts with aren't the sort you can easily just pay off and walk away from. Which is why you need to promise me that you won't go around to the house any more. If it's like last time, some really unsavoury characters might come looking for him and I wouldn't like you to be there when they turned up. These animals are capable of anything.'

'*Mein Gott!* But . . . but what about you?'

'Don't you worry about me. I can look after myself. Now, if you promise to stay away from that house, then in return

I'll promise you that if I find Rudi, I'll make damn sure he calls you. Do you think you can do that for me?'

She wiped her eyes and nodded. 'If you think it's for the best. Yes, yes, I promise! I'll never go near the place again, I swear. Oh, please let him be all right!'

'And there's one more thing I'd like you to promise me, Ingrid.'

'What, Stefan? Anything you ask.'

He pointed at her empty glass, then at the vodka bottle on the counter. 'That you'll lay off the hard stuff for break-fast,' he said. 'It's not worth wrecking yourself over, and giving in to temptation is never a solution. Look what it's done to Rudi, after all.' The new Saint Benedict, paragon of temperance and clean living.

She sighed. 'You're right. I'm such a fool. What am I doing to myself?'

'Good. Now you sit there while I make us another coffee. And then I'll be on my way.'

'To look for Rudi?'

He nodded. 'Yes, to look for Rudi.' And thanks to Rudi's poor, heartbroken, abandoned girlfriend, Ben had a feeling he might know where to find him.

Twenty minutes later, Ben left a more sober, collected and infinitely grateful Ingrid behind him as he jumped into the Alpina and blasted away from the villa.

Heading back towards Zurich, and from there to the Channel island of Sark.

Chapter 29

Wearers of the coveted winged dagger badge had their own unofficial version of the acronym 'SAS'. The second and third letters of which stood for 'Aggression' and 'Surprise'. The first stood for 'Speed', and thanks to that discipline Ben had spent the greater portion of his adult life getting the job done with no time to waste.

Exploiting the Alpina's performance capabilities to the full he flouted the Swiss highway speed limits to make it back to Zurich in an indecently short time, miraculously unhindered by the traffic police. By midday he was at the airport, returning the car with just a slight pang of regret and then racing to catch the Gatwick-bound flight that he'd booked en route. He was in London by 1.45 p.m. GMT, having gained an hour on his return trip from Europe, and landed just in time to dash across the terminals and jump on the small Aurigny twin-prop Dornier that would take him over the English Channel to Guernsey. On his arrival there, it was only a ten-minute hop over to St Peter's Port, where he was lucky enough to get straight on a ferry crossing to Sark.

It had been green lights all the way, but now the pace of Ben's hectic journey was about to slow down considerably.

Still travelling under the name Palmer, he stood on deck leaning against the railing, smoking and watching the tiny island grow gradually larger on the horizon. The sky was blue, the sun was warm and the sea was as calm and flat as a millpond. He had little idea what he might learn on arrival, if anything. He knew he'd be pretty much out of options if it led nowhere. But here he was. This was the only way to reach Sark, eight nautical miles from Guernsey. There were only a few passengers aboard, the vessel being a far cry from the big cross-Channel car ferries that regularly chugged up and down to the larger islands, and none of them looked like hired killers hunting the same quarry as he was. As Ingrid had said, the only motor vehicles allowed on Sark were a few farm tractors and the crane that was used for unloading boat cargo, and the island's roads were unsullied even by ambulances or fire engines. And so it was a very different and strange world on which Ben found himself disembarking that afternoon.

Apart from the pier itself at Maseline Harbour, there was no visible sign of human habitation, giving the strangest impression of landing on a totally deserted and somewhat forbidding island. Some of the passengers looked a little bemused by the tractor and trailer whose function was to cart arrivals up the steep hill from the port. 'All aboard the toast rack,' the driver called out jokingly to his passengers. Ben, preferring to walk it rather than be jostled about on the rattling trailer and suck tractor fumes all the way up the hill, just smiled and waved him off. He slung his bag over his shoulder, fired up another Gauloise and set off up the slope in the warmth of the sun.

The climb took him up to the village and a street called the Avenue. A horse and cart clip-clopped by as he walked along. It was as though he'd stepped through some kind of magic portal or fallen down a wormhole through space and time to land in a bygone century. But he wasn't here to marvel at the strangeness of his new environment. He intended to start searching for his target without delay – which, on an island covering less than two square miles in area, shouldn't prove too hard. If the bad guys had already got to Rudi Bergenroth, they were even better connected and organised than Ben would have given them credit for.

Where to start looking? He gazed around the village square. There was a pub and a guest house, a post office, a tea room, a small estate agent's office and a shop on the corner offering bicycle rental, along with a few old stone residential houses with shuttered windows. He'd been toying with the idea of conducting his search by simply going from door to door as he'd thought about doing in Liechtenstein, working by a process of elimination until the man in Ingrid's holiday snap happened to answer his knock. But now he was here, he was beginning to think that even on a minute island of no more than four or five hundred inhabitants, that could take a long time. Not to mention the possibility that Bergenroth might get wind of a stranger looking for him and do another runner. There were bound to be any number of boats handy in which he could make his escape.

No, Ben decided, this situation called for another approach. Thinking back to the photo, he remembered the name of the farmhouse where Ingrid and her man had stayed during their visit here. Sark must get its fair share of tourists but this was May, still relatively low season. Back home in Galway, Ben had met a few families who kept returning to rent the same holiday properties year after year. What if, in realising his dream of revisiting Sark, Bergenroth had done the same?

In which case, Ben was thinking, what had worked well for him in Liechtenstein might work here too. He crossed the square to the estate agent's office, went in and asked the pleasant young woman there (bearing no resemblance whatever to Fräulein Stumpf) about the possibility of taking out a rental lease on Beauvoir House for a week or two.

'One of our most popular properties,' the young woman told him with a smile. She spoke with a touch of French accent, and the name badge on her cardigan said JEANNE. 'I know it's been available again lately, but just let me check . . . Oh no,' she said, looking through her records, 'I'm afraid Beauvoir House has been taken until the thirtieth. Sorry to disappoint you. You just missed it by a few days.'

Which seemed to tally with the timing of Rudi Bergenroth's sudden departure from Liechtenstein. 'That's a shame,' Ben said, feigning disappointment. 'A friend of mine stayed there a year or two ago and raved about it. Said the view was amazing. I wouldn't mind exploring that part of the island anyway. How would I get there?'

Jeanne laughed. 'Why, the same way you get about anywhere else on Sark. On foot. Or you might be able to hire a horse and buggy to take you. Alternatively you could cycle there. Try Mr Brown's bike rental shop on the corner.'

'I'll do that,' Ben said.

A few minutes later, furnished with a ten-speed Dawes touring bike and directions to get to Beauvoir House, he mounted the saddle and rode off.

Bicycling along twisty little roads empty of traffic and totally unadapted to the modern age of motorised transport might have seemed more of a culture shock to the typical visitor to Sark than to someone used to living on the rugged, unpopulated west coast of Ireland, but all the same that odd feeling of having time-travelled back to the last century was still with him as he made his way across the island. What was mostly on his mind, though, was the prospect of meeting the elusive Rudi Bergenroth. Ben didn't suppose the man would take too kindly to being found. Like Tony Kitson, he was most likely to assume that Ben meant him harm. Even if cold-hearted assassins didn't generally turn up at your door unarmed and on a pushbike, he might have some persuading to do.

Beauvoir House was situated on a narrow lane just a few minutes' ride up the coast from the village, perched high over the rocks and the rolling surf below. As he pedalled around the bend in the lane Ben instantly recognised the place from the photograph in Ingrid's kitchen. He dismounted, leaned his bike against a drystone wall and walked up to the house. There seemed little point in sneaking around the place looking for a covert way inside, given that his appearance couldn't have come as much more of a surprise as it was. Deciding on a direct strategy, he knocked at the front door, then took a step back as he heard the sound of movement inside, and prepared to come face to face with Rudi Bergenroth.

Chapter 30

The door slowly, tentatively creaked open a few inches. Ben braced himself for what was about to happen. But then he did a double-take and stared. Because instead of being confronted with the lean, grizzled, middle-aged Austrian he'd seen in Ingrid's photo, the smooth, apple-cheeked face that peeked out of the gap in the doorway at chest height was that of a young boy of about eleven or twelve.

For a second the two of them just stood there blinking at one another. Then Ben said, not knowing what else to say, 'Oh, hello. What's your name?'

The boy frowned up at him without replying, then turned back inside the hallway and bawled, 'MU-UUM! THERE'S A FUNNY MAN AT THE DOOR!' A moment later the door opened wider and the boy's mother appeared, a sandy-haired woman in her mid-thirties. 'Go and help your dad,' she told the boy, and he ran past her into the house. She looked uncertainly at Ben, then gave a thin smile and said with her hands on her hips, 'Hi, can I help you?'

'My apologies,' he said. 'I must have come to the wrong place. Have a great day.'

He got back on the bike and set off the way he'd come, feeling foolish and disheartened. Here he was, an experienced professional tracker of abduction victims and missing people, blundering about like an idiot with nothing to go on but mistaken assumptions. Maybe this was going to be harder than he'd thought.

It was nearing 5 p.m. by the time he returned to the village, back at square one with no real idea where to go next. It was clear to him that some more creative tactics were called for.

A lot of tourists must pick the island of Sark as a holiday destination, but what kind of people were they? He reasoned that the majority by far would be families, like the folks currently staying at Beauvoir House, or couples like Rudi Bergenroth and Ingrid who'd visited last September. Perhaps not so many would be single men; and perhaps more unusual still would be a single man from further afield, such as a foreign European country. Which meant that the sudden and unexpected arrival of a lone traveller from the German-speaking regions wouldn't go unnoticed in a tiny, isolated provincial community where everyone must know everyone else, especially at low season when fewer tourists would be landing here.

Ben knew he couldn't very well start accosting local residents in the street to ask them if they'd seen a foreigner going around the island. And it wasn't as though Bergenroth would be attracting attention to himself by running about in Lederhosen, singing Austrian yodelling songs and eating Bratwurst in public. But village gossip was what it was, as Ben had learned first-hand from the rumours he'd occasionally heard about himself in his little corner of rural Galway. Anytime someone out of the ordinary came to live in a place, there was bound to be talk. Plenty of it.

Ben needed to access the inside track on the gossip mill somehow. The question was, how to get them talking to him? He racked his brain for a while before the idea flashed into his head: maybe the best way to find out the local chit-chat about a foreigner in a small community was to act as if you were a foreigner yourself. It seemed a convoluted piece of logic. Perhaps it was an unlikely sort of plan. But there was only one way to find out if it could work.

It was getting late in the afternoon, but the little tea room in the village square was still serving, and Ben decided that was as good a place as any to put his idea to the test. A little bell tinkled as he pushed through the door. Like everything else on this island, it felt like stepping into the past. A few locals were seated at tables, finishing their afternoon tea before the place closed up for the evening. A mousy-haired woman in an apron was working behind the counter. A glass cabinet next to her was filled with the remnants of the day's selection of pastries, scones and cupcakes. He walked up to her with the most charming smile he could muster, and putting on a clipped, formal-sounding German accent that sounded preposterously exaggerated to his ears, asked if it was not too late to enjoy a pot of tea and perhaps sample one of these here little cakes? Pointing to the glass cabinet.

'Those – are – *scones*,' she replied, speaking artificially slowly and loudly, the way you do when explaining something to a foreigner.

'Ah,' he said. 'I see. *Gut, gut. Wunderbar*. Then I will have two, please. Perhaps with some of the jam?'

Going over to a vacant table while she prepared his order, Ben was aware of a very elderly and well-dressed man, seated with his wife at another table, shooting hostile looks his way. Getting attention already. He pretended not to notice, sat down, and soon the smiling mousy-haired lady brought him his tea and scones, with a pot of jam and some of those little individual pats of butter on a tray. '*Vielen dank, gnädiges Frau,*' he thanked her graciously. '*Das sieht lecker aus.* It looks delicious.'

'I'm damned if I'm going to sit here listening to any more of this,' the old man at the other table grumbled in disgust to his wife. 'I'm off home. You finish your tea, Ethel. I'll see you back at the house.' He pushed himself upright and headed for the doorway, walking stooped. He paused on his way out to shoot another furious glower at Ben, and muttered darkly under his breath, 'Bloody Jerries are invading us all over again,' before he stalked out of the tea room.

Ben acted nonchalant and went on drinking his tea. It was a minute or so before the elderly woman, Ethel, now sitting alone and looking quite restless, stood up and came stiffly over to Ben's table. 'Pardon me for interrupting,' she said, leaning close and speaking *sotto voce*, 'but I must apologise for my husband's behaviour just now. I do hope you weren't too offended.'

'Not in the least. But *ich verstehe nicht* ... I do not understand. He is not liking ze Germans?' Ben asked, feigning innocence.

'You see, Harry was a small boy during the occupation of the Channel Islands, during the war.' She explained that her husband had never forgiven Ben's countrymen for their June 1940 bombing of St Peter's Port Harbour on Guernsey, killing thirty-three people, one of whom had been his beloved uncle Peter, a local fisherman. 'Still, it's all in the past now, isn't it,' she said benevolently. 'But some people hold on to grudges, and I'm afraid Harry's one of them. I'm Ethel, by the way. Ethel Dandridge.'

'Stefan Nachtnebel. It is very nice to meet you, Ethel. There are no hard feelings, I can assure you,' Ben replied. He was worried about letting the accent slip. 'I did not understand what he meant by an invasion, though.'

'Oh, you're not the only German visitor on the island. Another gentleman arrived here to stay not so long ago. Now Harry will be perfectly convinced that where there are two, there'll soon be three, and then the advance party will quickly grow into a whole attack force. He'll be ready with his wild-fowling gun, just in case.' Ethel's kindly face wrinkled into a grin.

Ben smiled back. 'Then perhaps I should warn my compatriot that we are in danger of being found out and repelled back into ze sea. Where might I find him?'

She gave him a conspiratorial look. 'There are very few secrets here on Sark, so that's an easy one. I heard that the gentleman took the old Adonis Cottage. Mrs Dingle in the post office told me he's visited the island before, on holiday, and loves it here. Mr Burgermeister, I think he's called. Took the cottage for an indefinite period, apparently. And he even paid cash for three months' rent in advance, and told Jeanne Martinot at the estate agents that he wouldn't be needing the cleaners sent in every week and would look after the place himself. A very quiet living gentleman, it seems, and so well educated. Or that's what I've heard.'

The gossip machine really had gone into overdrive concerning Herr Burgermeister. Ben said, 'Adonis Cottage, a curious name, *nein*?'

'It's called that because it stands on the cliff overlooking Adonis Pool, a tidal pool right on the southwesternmost tip of Little Sark, where some of the more adventurous islanders like to go swimming in the warmer months.'

'I see. And how might I get to this scenic spot? I have a bicycle.'

'You'll have to go over La Coupée. That's the causeway between the main island and Little Sark, to the south. Look out for cross winds. Then just keep going until you reach the south edge of the island, and you'll be there. You can't miss the cottage. It's the only one on that whole stretch of cliffs.'

'Thank you so much,' Ben said, with a polite bow of the head. 'I may take advantage of your kind advice. And I will certainly enjoy visiting your beautiful island.'

Ethel wished him a pleasant stay, then hurried off to rejoin Harry, pausing for a quick chat with the tea room proprietor before she left.

Ben was impatient to leave, too, but didn't want to be seen to be rushing off too quickly. He finished up his tea and scones, paid his bill just as the tea room was about to close for the day, and set off once again on the Dawes ten-speed. This time he headed due south down the length of the island, pedalling hard with the sea breeze in his hair, relieved and even a little surprised that his little theatre act had paid off so well. The sun was beginning to dip over the sea, casting a vivid late afternoon hue over the landscape that brought out every rugged detail and seemed to amplify its greenness so that he could have easily believed he was back home in Ireland. He sped over the hundred yards of causeway joining the two parts of the island, a raised curving ridge just ten feet wide with vertiginous drops of more than 250 feet on each side and the waves breaking white on the rocks far below. Reaching Little Sark on its far side, he followed the winding lanes towards the south edge of the land.

And there, perched on the cliffs ahead, exactly where Ethel Dandridge had described it, was the cottage he was looking for. It was smaller and even simpler than Tony Kitson's little home in Yorkshire had been, with a single squat chimney at one end and a rough slate roof over whitewashed stone walls. It had no back door, and the tiniest of windows looking out across the sea. Somewhere across the flat blue-grey water was Jersey, and a long way beyond that the coastline of Brittany. A man come seeking refuge from danger couldn't have sought out a more secluded and lonely place to lie low.

Ben rested his bicycle in the long, coarse, waving grass, strode up to the cottage and rapped loudly on the door.

No response. Ben knocked again, more insistently. After a long pause, he thought he heard the sound of a cautious footstep coming from inside. There was the scrape of a bolt being drawn back, and then the door creaked open.

And this time it wasn't the rosy-cheeked face of a young boy staring at him in surprise from the doorway, but the lean, grizzled and unshaven features of a middle-aged man who bore a striking resemblance to the person in Ingrid's photograph.

Chapter 31

Rudi Bergenroth stood there gaping at Ben for maybe three quarters of a second before his expression of speechless surprise turned into a look of horror and he tried to slam the door shut. But by then Ben had already wedged it with his foot, blocking it from closing.

Bergenroth was much more of the inveterate bookish type than Tony Kitson had been. He didn't whip out a concealed weapon, and he didn't try to put up any kind of fight as Ben came pushing through the doorway. Wide-eyed with panic he backed away inside the cottage, holding up his palms in surrender and gasping, '*Nein, nein, bitte töte mich nicht!*' Please don't kill me! Funny how people reverted back to their native language in times of extreme terror. Stumbling backwards into an armchair, he tripped and fell into it.

Ben closed the door and stood over him. Bergenroth was so terrified he looked as if he was about to pass out. 'Relax, Rudi, I'm not going to touch you. I'm here because of your late friend Hugh Mortimer.'

'W-who are you?' Bergenroth gibbered.

'Just someone who got mixed up in this by chance. My name's Ben Hope.'

'How-how did you . . .?'

'Find you? It wasn't all that hard, Rudi. I paid a visit to Ingrid in Liechtenstein.'

'You didn't . . . you didn't . . .'

'No, I didn't. Put that idea out of your head,' Ben told him. 'Apart from weeping into her vodka and tonic over a broken heart, Ingrid's fine, safe and well. And I'd like her to stay that way. I'd even like you to stay that way, too. But there are killers out there doing bad things to innocent people, and unless they're stopped, both you and Ingrid are going to be in danger for as long as it takes for them to catch up with you. So unless you want something nasty to happen to your lady friend, and unless you want to spend the rest of your life looking over your shoulder, what you need to do is settle down, stay in that chair and give me the information I need. All right?'

Bergenroth shook his head in bewilderment and stammered, 'W-what information are you talking about?'

'To fill in the gaps of what I already know. For starters you might want to tell me what the connection was between you and Hugh Mortimer. What the two of you have been getting up to with your secret codes and ciphers. And why any of this historical stuff about those damned princes in the Tower and Richard III and Perkin bloody Warbeck still matters so much that people can get hurt and killed over it.'

'You are not a historian.'

'Really? You can tell?'

'How much did Hugh explain to you already?'

'Nothing,' Ben said. 'He came to me for protection, and soon afterwards he was dead. How did you know?'

'From a general email announcement by the Richard III Society,' Bergenroth replied sadly. 'I would never have learned of it otherwise.'

'Lucky,' Ben said. 'Not everyone else has been. Like Hugh's friend Tony Kitson, for instance.'

Bergenroth frowned. 'Kitson . . . Hugh mentioned his name to me. One of the English Ricardians. You mean . . .'

'He's dead. A bullet in the liver will have that effect on people.'

'*Ach.*' Bergenroth passed his hand over his eyes and gave a shudder, as though he could feel the gunshot ripping through his own organs.

'You're the only person left alive who can help me now, Rudi. You know who sent Hugh those threatening letters. You know who did this. The people you're running from are the same people who killed Hugh and blew up my friend. So talk to me. Help me to help you. That's the only way you can make this end.'

Bergenroth looked at him. The fear showed deep in his eyes. 'How *does* it end? I have asked myself that question a thousand times.'

'It ends with them going away,' Ben said. 'Gone, finished, dead and buried. You can't make that happen. But I'm here now.'

'B-but how can you do this, on your own?'

Ben replied, 'You leave that part to me, Rudi. It's what I do. Then once I'm finished, you can go back to your life. Someone's waiting for you there.'

'Ingrid,' Bergenroth groaned. '*Meine liebe* Ingrid. Do you think I wanted to break her heart? I love her. After what happened to Hugh I was so frightened that if they caught up with me there, she might get hurt.'

'You were right to be afraid,' Ben said. 'But running doesn't guarantee her safety. They're out there hunting for you. At best I might be just two or three steps ahead of them. I don't need to tell you what happens if they find her. They won't kill her right away. Maybe they'll just cut off a few fingers or put her eye out to make her tell them what she knows.'

Bergenroth looked aghast. 'Oh, please do not say that, I cannot bear to hear it!'

'You want her to be safe, you need to help me. Start talking, and make it fast. The clock is ticking and I'm not in the mood for another long history lesson.'

Bergenroth nodded in resignation, looking suddenly drained and exhausted. 'All right. I will explain everything. Yes, it is true, Hugh Mortimer and I were working on something together. Yes, I know who is behind this, who murdered him and why. And yes, it all revolves around the history. But if I just tell you the name of the man responsible, why should you believe me? I could be a crazy person making the whole story up. You need to understand how this all came about. And I need you to believe I am not crazy.'

Next to the fireplace was a small table where Bergenroth had been sitting drinking cocoa and reading a newspaper when his unexpected visitor had arrived. Ben pulled a chair away from the table, planted it opposite the armchair and sat down backwards in it, leaning his arms on the backrest and looking intently at the Austrian.

'Then convince me,' he said.

Chapter 32

'If you are already familiar with the story of the princes, then I presume I don't need to begin at the beginning. But where do I start? There is so much information to relate.'

'Start where Tony Kitson left off. He was telling me about Hugh Mortimer's claimed blood relation to Perkin Warbeck when we got interrupted.'

Bergenroth asked, 'How much exactly did you learn about that?'

'Only that Hugh believed he was descended from him,' Ben replied, 'and that there was a collection of old coins and other items that supposedly proved the connection. That's as far as we got, but I think it's at the heart of all this.'

'It is,' Bergenroth said, nodding. He reflected for a moment, then asked, 'Had Hugh told Kitson about the medallion?'

This was the first Ben had heard of a medallion. He shook his head. 'If he had, Tony would have mentioned it to me.'

'Ah. Without the medallion you cannot possibly understand. It is the key to everything.'

'Then you'd better tell me about it.'

The fear had left Bergenroth's eyes now, replaced by a look of intensity. 'Its story dates back to that critical time in British history. It was a small silver pendant that had been specially made for Elizabeth of York, when she was a girl.'

'Elizabeth of York, the princes' elder sister?'

'Yes. The medallion was very beautifully made, with a cast unicorn motif on one side and her name engraved on the other. She used to wear it all the time. Now, when the younger of her two brothers, Richard, was only a small boy he so admired it that his sister gave it to him as a gift. As she had done before him, he wore it constantly. He was still wearing it when he and his elder brother, Edward, were taken from the Tower of London following Edward's failed ascendance to the throne. Sometime after that, the two boys left England. Elizabeth would not see the medallion again for a long time, until the year 1497.'

That date sounded familiar to Ben, from Kitson's account and from Mortimer's notes. He said, 'The year Perkin Warbeck was arrested.'

'Correct again. You see, it is little known that, upon Warbeck's return to London as King Henry's prisoner, Elizabeth came face to face with this man who claimed to be the rightful heir to the throne. The moment she met him, even after all those years, she recognised him as her brother.'

'I'm surprised her husband would have let her see him,' Ben said. 'Taking a bit of a risk, wasn't he? He must've expected that she'd know who he really was.'

'He did not let her,' Bergenroth replied. 'It is a historical fact that he strictly forbade any such meeting, and I think that is what must have aroused her suspicions. Why was the king so insistent on her not being allowed to see this man's face? What was he trying to conceal from her? But she was not without her own power and influence, and she was able to arrange a secret meeting. Sadly, we have no way of knowing for how long they spoke, or what was said between them, or even whether their encounter was completely private. But we do know, from a particular historical source, that there was no doubt at all in Elizabeth's mind that this Warbeck was indeed her brother. He is said to have had some unusual facial features – the eyes were slightly different, and there was some scarring around one. He was quite distinctive in appearance.'

'And I'm guessing he was wearing the medallion, too,' Ben said. 'The same one she'd given him when he was little.'

Bergenroth nodded. 'As if any more proof were needed to support her conviction. But of course there was no way she could tell any of this to her husband, the king. She could have been accused of treason and executed along with the "Pretender". It was quite a predicament. The poor woman must have been going crazy, with literally nobody around her she could confide in. In her desperation she sent a coded letter to her aunt, Margaret the Duchess of Burgundy, telling her that she believed beyond any doubt that this young man was exactly who he claimed to be, her brother Richard. As evidence she included a drawing of the medallion that she had done from memory. But, as she went on to write in her letter, her hands were tied.'

'So it's thanks to this letter that we know the meeting took place. You say it was written in code?'

'Obviously, this was intended to protect her secret from being discovered by the king's far-reaching spy network. In the event, of course, like Elizabeth the Duchess could do nothing to save Warbeck from his eventual fate. As for the encrypted letter itself, it disappeared and did not resurface until centuries later. That was when my ancestor, Gustav Bergenroth, came across it hidden inside an old book in a library in Antwerp.'

'And deciphered it?'

'Yes, being the brilliant code-breaker that he was. It was a startling discovery, because that letter was the final proof of Perkin Warbeck's true identity.'

'From what Ingrid told me, you've inherited his interest in ciphers and codes yourself.'

'Indeed. I became fascinated with the science of cryptology as a young man. It has been a passion for much of my life.'

'And I'm guessing that you have the letter now?'

Bergenroth nodded. 'It is one of the few things that came down to me from my ancestor. I have studied it in great detail and checked the deciphered code many times, and have no doubt whatsoever that it is genuine.'

'All right,' Ben said. 'So let's say that Perkin really was who he claimed to be, Richard the surviving prince. But I still don't get the connection to Hugh Mortimer.'

'I will come to that,' Bergenroth assured him. 'Now, after Warbeck's execution, the silver unicorn medallion was passed into the possession of one "Richard Perkins". An alias, as it happens. Are you aware of who that was?'

Ben remembered what Kitson had told him about the secret child that Warbeck and his wife Catherine Gordon had managed to produce while he was under house arrest. 'He was Warbeck's son.'

'And from there onwards, the medallion remained in the family's possession until, many years later, the genealogy having branched out to the Mortimer line, it came to Hugh himself as part of a collection of artefacts, including some original Warbeck coins minted at the time of his attempt on the throne.'

'The same medallion?' Ben asked. 'How can we know that for sure?'

'Because I have seen both and I can tell you that they are the same. You asked me what my connection was with Hugh. Let me tell you the story of how he and I first met. Two years ago I travelled to London to attend a large gathering of the Richard III Society, at which he was also present. It was a chance meeting, but an incredible one. After the first day's lectures were over, we and a few of the other delegates were sitting outside having a drink in the sunshine. It was a warm summer's afternoon, we were all relaxed, and Hugh had taken off his tie and unbuttoned his shirt. That was when I saw, to my amazement, what he was wearing around his neck.'

'No prizes for guessing,' Ben said.

'He wore it every day, in honour of the man he firmly believed to be his ancestor. There was no question it was identical to the one Queen consort Elizabeth sketched in her coded letter. What are you doing?'

'Making a phone call,' Ben said, whipping out his phone. A thought had come to him while Bergenroth was talking. He'd been inclined to throw away Lance Mortimer's business card at the time – but now he was glad he'd hung on to the phone number, because it was going to enable him to check if what the Austrian was telling him was true.

Lance answered his mobile on the third ring, sounding keen and eager and probably thinking this was a client booking a golf lesson. His enthusiasm waned somewhat when Ben, putting a finger to his lips and shooting Bergenroth a warning glance to stay quiet, introduced himself as Paul Harris.

'Oh yeah, I remember you,' Lance said diffidently. 'What are you calling for?'

Ben wasn't going to bother asking him about the police investigation, since he knew that would be going nowhere. 'I hoped you could help me with something. The first time we spoke, on the phone, you told me that when you had to go and identify Hugh's body, something was different about him. Something missing, you said. Have you been able to remember what it might have been?'

'That's a bloody bizarre sort of question,' Lance replied irritably. 'Why the hell would you be asking?'

'Think carefully, Lance. Was it something he might normally have been wearing? Like a piece of jewellery?'

That seemed to jolt Lance's memory. 'His little pendant thingy,' he blurted out, suddenly remembering. 'Yes, that's what it was. Of course! I was so upset at the time that I didn't think.'

'By a pendant thingy, do you mean a silver medallion with a unicorn on one side and a woman's name engraved on the other?' Ben asked.

'It was just a trinket that belonged to some dead relative or other. Hugh always wore it around his neck, for sentimental reasons, I suppose. But then when I went to identify him it wasn't there any more. What does it mean? Did he lose it in the lake? Did someone nick it? Was it valuable? And how the hell did you know about it, anyh—?'

Ben cut him off short, ended the call without another word and put his phone away. 'That was Hugh's brother. He's just corroborated what you said.'

'So I gathered,' Bergenroth said, raising an eyebrow. 'You are not very trusting, are you, Mr *Harris*? Do you believe me now?'

237

'Not taking anything on trust is the reason I'm still alive,' Ben replied. 'All right, let's recap. Hugh had the silver unicorn, and after he was killed it was gone. But it still doesn't mean anything. Any opportunistic killer might have taken it because they thought it was valuable. Lance was actually right about that. Or else it might not have been taken at all. Like he said, maybe it came loose in the struggle and is lying in the mud at the bottom of the lake as we speak.'

Bergenroth smiled for the first time. 'I'm afraid you are not seeing the deeper significance of all this. The medallion itself is only secondary here. Do you not understand what the deeper implications are for history?'

'Then why don't you enlighten me?'

'It is really very simple,' Bergenroth replied. 'Let me put it in a nutshell, as you British say. If indeed Hugh Mortimer was genuinely descended – as I believe he was – from the royal pretender who called himself Perkin Warbeck, then it means that the Plantagenet line never ended. Which in turn means that, in effect, the whole Tudor royal bloodline was illegitimate.'

Chapter 33

Ben stared at him. This was it, the punch line, the end point of all the historical intrigue that he'd delved into first with Tony Kitson, then with Rudi Bergenroth. The conclusion seemed so obvious now, and yet he hadn't seen it coming.

Bergenroth read his stunned expression and nodded. 'That is right. I repeat, their entire claim to the throne of England was a fraud, a deception. We can now ascertain beyond any doubt that Henry Tudor himself seized the throne illegally and suppressed the rightful claim of the true heir. This means that none of his Tudor descendants had the slightest legal right to be on the throne or declare themselves kings or queens of England. The evidence proves that they were usurpers, and that their entire dynasty should never have existed.'

Ben said nothing.

Bergenroth went on, 'Needless to say, this is a revelation of huge importance. It is hard to conceive of an alternative version of British history, or world history for that matter, without a King Henry VIII there to split England away from Catholicism and establish the Anglican Church, or a Queen Elizabeth I to prevent the invasion of the British Isles by Spain, colonise North America and make England a world power, laying the foundations for the future global expansion of the British Empire. For better or worse, the influence of the Tudor kings and queens completely shaped the destiny of modern Britain. Who can imagine the course that history might have taken without them?'

It took Ben a few more moments to get his thoughts straight. 'Then . . . what about the modern British royal family? Does this make them all usurpers too?'

Could it be true? Suddenly, he was seeing some enormous conspiracy looming up in front of him like a giant shadow. If this was what Hugh Mortimer had been into, claiming royal descent and threatening to tear down the whole establishment . . . it was mind-boggling.

But Bergenroth quickly dissolved that idea. 'That would have been something, *ja*?' he chuckled. 'But no, the modern royals, the House of Windsor, originate from a whole different line. The Tudor dynasty ended in 1603, when Queen Elizabeth I died childless and the throne was passed over to the Scottish Stuarts, unifying England and Scotland. In fact the "House of Windsor" itself was a fabrication. It was founded in 1917 by King George V, when the name Windsor was adopted as a political ploy to divert attention away from the royal family's German roots at a time when Britain and Germany were at war. Their real family name is Wettin and they belong to the Saxe-Coburg-Gotha dynasty, dating back to the Prussian Duke Ernest I in the early nineteenth century. One might argue that the so-called House of Windsor are no more British than I am. But whatever they may be, in no way are they directly related to the House of Tudor, other than by various secondary connections through marriage, the inevitable result of the widespread interbreeding among European royal dynasties that was intended to keep power in the family, so to speak. In this instance, you might say that their mongrel bloodline is as much their strength as it is their weakness.'

'Right,' Ben said, shown up for his ignorance. The massive conspiracy theory faded from his imagination as quickly as it had appeared. Thinking out loud he muttered, 'Then it must be something else. Who could be so threatened by the revelations of this Tudor deception that they would plant car bombs and dismember, drown and shoot innocent people?'

Bergenroth seemed to read Ben's thoughts. 'I believe it is not so much a matter of trying to conceal the fraud itself,' he said. 'Too much time has passed, and the historical strands are too densely interwoven and complex for the majority of people to unravel. Nobody stands to be toppled from any position of power by the secret.' He paused. 'But on a more practical level, there are financial interests involved that could most certainly be problematic for certain people.'

Ben looked at him. 'You said you know who did this.'

'But before I tell you, there is still a little more background to explain. You see, the Perkin Warbeck coins and the medallion were not all that Hugh inherited. Among the items that came down to him through the family line were some documents dating back to that time, among them the historic deeds to a fine English estate called Hartington Abbey.'

'Hartington Abbey?' Ben recalled Tony Kitson having mentioned some papers, though he'd been vague about what they were. Then he remembered something else Kitson had said, about the property that Warbeck's wealthy noble father-in-law had given as a present to the newlyweds.

'Yes, Hugh came to believe that he had a claim to its ownership, based on his descent from Perkin Warbeck. The abbey and its lands had been gifted to Perkin and his wife Catherine based on the assumption that he was really the heir to the throne of England. If that turned out to be incorrect, then Perkin would not be entitled to it. All that was missing from the equation is the final proof of his legitimacy.'

'The medallion.'

Bergenroth said, 'More specifically, the fact that Perkin was wearing it on that occasion when he was briefly reunited with his sister, Elizabeth of York, now King Henry's queen. And likewise, based on her coded letter to the Duchess of Burgundy, the same proof that would verify Perkin's claim to the throne also supported Hugh's ancestral claim to the ownership of Hartington Abbey. Which, as you might imagine, had fallen into Tudor hands following Perkin's execution in 1499.'

'So when you and Hugh met up, that's when the pieces all came together,' Ben said.

'Exactly. Hugh had the deeds and the medallion, and I had the deciphered letter to prove that the pretender Perkin Warbeck was in fact the rightful King Richard IV of England.'

And now it all came down to a property claim. That was what this whole thing had been about, all along. Land. Estate. Money. A great deal of money. Hadn't that always been the first and best reason for killing people, all through the ages?

Ben said, 'I'm guessing that Hartington Abbey is still standing.'

'Oh *ja*, very much so. Earlier on in the fifteenth century it had been just one of the many properties that Lady Catherine's father, the Earl of Huntly, owned in Scotland. But the Anglo-Scottish border remained ever-changeable during that period, due to the ongoing wars between the two countries. The town of Berwick-upon-Tweed, once part of the ancient Kingdom of Northumbria, changed hands over a dozen times before it was finally retaken for the last time by the English in 1482. And so Hartington Abbey, situated just a few miles from Berwick, has officially been located in England ever since. It fell into disrepair during the sixteenth century but was later restored, and in the early 1700s it flourished and grew into the fine manor estate that it is today. The current owner is one Lord Jasper Lockwood, a direct descendant of the powerful noble family to whom Henry VII passed the abbey soon after his coronation. An extremely wealthy man, with many powerful connections.'

'And so did Hugh make a legal challenge to the ownership of the estate?'

'That was his intention,' Bergenroth replied. 'And he was on the verge of doing so. But being the cautious man that he was, even after all the painstaking research he had carried out over the years he had been holding back from making his move until he could be completely sure of his ground. The last thing he would have wanted was to find himself embroiled in a lengthy court battle, which might have ended in failure and made him look like a fool – or even worse, liable for legal costs and damages. He and I spent a great many hours on the phone together, going through the historical evidence, to make absolutely sure that his claim was well founded before he could take it to a lawyer. In the event, he never got that far.'

'Then someone must have found out what he was up to,' Ben said.

'Somehow, yes,' Bergenroth replied with a frown. 'Is it possible that they could have been listening in to our phone conversations? Did Hugh somehow let it slip to them what his intentions were? I find that hard to believe. But I suppose we will never know.'

'You said this Lockwood has powerful connections.'

'Powerful, and dangerous. When the first threatening letter arrived, Hugh dismissed it as a joke. But soon afterwards came another, and another, and we began to realise that the threat was a serious one. Jasper Lockwood evidently wasn't about to cede his territory without a fight. But still Hugh wouldn't back down.'

'Of course not,' Ben said. 'Not where money was concerned.'

Bergenroth shook his head. 'You misunderstand his motives. Hugh's ambition was not to possess Hartington Abbey so that he could set himself up as Lord of the Manor and live in splendour. Instead, he planned on turning the place into a museum and heritage centre dedicated to the history and legacy of his Plantagenet ancestors. We would have been partners in the project.'

'Still, even those kinds of modest ambitions can get you killed,' Ben said. 'Especially when some rich guy stands to lose millions over them. And it looks like you picked the wrong rich guy to mess with.'

'I wish I had never become involved in any of it, but how was I to know? Now you understand why I was too terrified even to call Ingrid on the phone after I left Liechtenstein, to tell her I was all right and that I still love her. These people must have ears and eyes everywhere. What you tell me about this poor man Tony Kitson proves it even more clearly. And your friend they hurt. Blown up, you said. It is all so terrible. What am I going to do? How can I trust what you say, that you can put an end to this situation?'

Ben was no longer listening. He stood up and went to the window, looked out at the sunset sky and the darkening sea, and felt the power of the rage slowly burning inside him.

He had what he'd come here for. A name.

And that name was Jasper Lockwood.

Chapter 34

Northumbria, England

At the same moment, some four hundred miles north of the Island of Sark, another man was standing at another window, gazing pensively out at a different view.

Seen from the height of his oak-panelled study at the top of the east tower of Hartington Abbey, the estate's rolling acres seemed to stretch to infinity. The tiered formal gardens surrounding the medieval stately home had taken centuries to cultivate to their present state of many-coloured perfection. Beyond those lay the orchard from which the abbey's own cider was produced, and the grazing meadows where the rare and beautiful Hartington wild cattle roamed free. Beyond that again lay the green expanses of yew, silver birch and spruce forest, against the distant backdrop of rugged hills that were home to herds of red deer, soaring ospreys and even the occasionally-sighted golden eagle. It was much the same view, virtually unchanged apart from the introduction of a few more recent estate cottages, lodges, private roads and walking trails, that his ancestors had been looking out at, all these generations dating back more than five hundred years.

But not for very much longer, because the centuries-old era of the Lockwoods at Hartington Abbey would soon be coming to an end. And for Jasper Lockwood, the present Lord of the Manor, that change couldn't come soon enough.

The reality was that Jasper's family seat had never held much attraction for him, and less and less so as the years went by. He'd been based down in London for the whole of his professional career and seldom ventured back up north. Since inheriting the estate and title upon his father's death and then taking early retirement five years ago at the age of fifty-six he'd somewhat resentfully divided his time between here and the other places he'd much rather be, like his luxury bachelor pad in Mayfair or the secluded privacy of his beach-front villa in the Seychelles. Hartington Abbey meant precious little to him, nor did he give much of a damn about the traditions and legacy of the illustrious family name – unlike his father, the previous Lord Lockwood, who couldn't shut up about it after a few glasses of port.

The only slight pang of regret Jasper was likely to feel over getting rid of the place would be the loss of what little kudos was to be derived from getting to call himself 'Lord of the Manor', a privilege that dated back to ancient law. But what did he care? Money was the only thing that really mattered to him.

Money, money, money. As dearly as he loved the stuff – craved it, adored it, fairly worshipped it even – the unfortunate reality was that in contrast to those past Lockwoods who had turned the estate into a thriving enterprise and built the considerable family fortune on its back, the world of commerce and finance had never been Jasper's strong suit. The career at which he'd excelled for nearly thirty years, rising close to the top of the ladder, had called for a very different set of skills. On his retirement, mistakenly fancying himself as a high-flier, he'd blundered into a series of very ill-advised business investments and ventures that one after the other had gone horribly wrong, burned most of the Lockwood fortune to the ground and left him in dire need of cash.

To make matters even worse, at the same time he was discovering that the responsibilities of running a large estate were a much greater challenge than he'd bargained for. The thought of all those lost millions and the steady stream of more and more money into a black hole made his stomach ache. His one and only solace was the prospect of regaining it all, and quite a bit more besides, from the impending sale of Hartington Abbey.

At this moment, as he stood gazing out of the study window with his desk behind him, Jasper was impatiently waiting for a phone call from his buyer. Or, more correctly, from his buyer's lawyer, seeing as the buyer himself was far too great and important a figure to be lowering himself by dealing with such mundane matters directly. What a prick, Lockwood thought to himself. But a prick with money. Already a billionaire three times over by the age of thirty-two, and ready to write a very large cheque in return for becoming the new Lord of Hartington Abbey and the proprietor of one of the most historic stately estates in northern England.

Soon, Jasper promised himself. Soon all these worries and problems would be at an end and he'd be able to bugger off away from this country, putting all his troubles behind him for ever. And good riddance to the late lamented Hugh Mortimer, who'd been such a thorn in his side and caused so much stress and aggravation.

Hugh Mortimer. Just the sound of the name made Jasper want to spit. Until not so long ago, he'd quite forgotten that the man even existed. They hadn't been in touch since their days at Cambridge, way back in the mid-sixties. The two of them had attended different colleges – Jasper at Downing reading Law, Hugh studying Medieval History at Trinity – and it was unlikely they would have ever even met, if they hadn't happened to both be members of the university's English longbow club. The keen archers would meet every Tuesday afternoon at St John's College playing fields, for practice and tournaments. Jasper and Hugh were both fiercely competitive young men, by far the best archers in the club. However it was Hugh Mortimer who had the edge, nearly always beating Jasper to the trophy.

To describe the pair as bitter rivals would have been an understatement. As intensely as Jasper had learned to despise Hugh Mortimer back in those days, it was actually Hugh who felt the stronger animosity. The reason for his negative feelings hadn't had to do with archery. Rather, they had come about ever since Jasper had revealed, in casual conversation, the name of the Lockwood family estate in Northumberland. By sheer coincidence, it turned out that the young Hugh Mortimer's fascination with all things to do with medieval England had led him to believe that Hartington Abbey had historically belonged to his own family, who had been cheated and robbed of its ownership back in the fifteenth century.

Poor deluded Hugh. He'd been completely obsessed with it, even compulsively wearing that old silver medallion that he maintained backed up his claim. Jasper, of course, had dismissed the whole notion as completely absurd. Hartington had belonged to the Lockwoods for so long that nobody could credibly challenge their right to it. And yet Hugh just wouldn't leave it alone, picking arguments about the matter whenever they met. The dispute would always follow the same tired old lines. 'You're living in my house,' Hugh would say tauntingly. 'One day you and your rotten family will have to pack your bags and leave, and it'll be mine. Just you wait and see.'

'I pity you,' Jasper would sneer back at him. 'You're mentally quite unhinged, you know.'

'We'll see who's right,' Hugh would reply. 'Just wait until I can prove it in court. Then you'll be out, Lockwood.'

The last argument between them had also been the last time they'd met, at the end of Cambridge Easter Term in June 1966. Jasper had returned home to spend the summer at Hartington, then taken a year out to travel around Europe before taking up a job in the Home Office. The following year, 1968, he'd applied for a post with the British Security Service, MI5, marking the start of a long and highly successful career in the secretive, murky world of intelligence.

With the passing of the years, the memory of crazy Hugh Mortimer faded from Jasper's mind. He had plenty of other things to worry about as he gradually climbed up the echelons of MI5. His first-class Cambridge law degree enabled him to study for a Masters in Criminology even while he was holding down his full-time job as an intelligence analyst. From there he was promoted to a senior position with MI5's Protective Security Advice Team, where he stayed for eight years before moving to International Counter-terrorism. By his mid-fifties he'd worked his way up to Assistant Head of that division, with maximum security clearance and a great deal of power and responsibility.

A very high salary, too, with a pension to match after taking his early retirement – but somehow whatever he earned was never enough to keep him in his glory. He simply loved the nice things in life too much – expensive wine, classy watches, exclusive restaurants, luxury travel and fancy cars, not to mention the succession of fancy women who wouldn't have looked twice at a paunchy, balding and markedly unattractive little man like him if not for the jewels and high living they enjoyed at his expense.

That endless appetite for more was what would plunge him into near-ruin when the chickens of his bad investments soon came home to roost and he was additionally faced with a vast repair bill when a section of the abbey's ancient roof timbers was found to be dangerously worm-eaten and close to collapse. Reeling from another financial punch in the guts, Jasper had put Hartington Abbey on the market the very same day the roof restoration was completed. The Maserati and the vintage Bentley had already gone, along with his place in Mayfair and the beautiful ocean-going catamaran moored on the south coast. The stately home was one of the last assets he possessed. Unless the right buyer came along very soon, his prospects would be looking grim indeed.

Mercifully, it hadn't been long before his saviour appeared, in the form of a lesser but nonetheless extraordinarily wealthy young Saudi prince by the name of Hassan Bin Ibrahim Al Sharif. The prince was an Anglophile who had studied economics at Oxford and planned to expand his domestic business enterprises overseas into the British property market. Being also a great lover of finely-bred horses, his dream was to develop a large part of the grounds into an equestrian sports venue second to none, while the house would be converted into a lavish hotel and conference centre. Jasper raised no objections to the plans, especially when he saw the eye-popping sum of fifty million pounds that the prince was willing to offer. Al Sharif could blast the whole damned estate into a crater in the ground for all Jasper cared, once the money was safely in the bank. Enough beautiful cash to not only rescue him from the imminent threat of bankruptcy that had been hanging over him, but to set him up in fine style for the rest of his life.

And so the negotiations began, with Jasper wasting no time trying to push the price up even higher. The prince was in no great hurry and seemed to have little interest in haggling over the cost, as though ten million here or there were of no consequence to him. Which they probably weren't, Jasper thought. Within a month, they were very close to settling on an agreed deal for sixty million pounds.

It looked as if Jasper's financial worries were over. Then one night, out of the blue and just as the negotiations over the sale of Hartington Abbey seemed to be progressing smoothly towards their highly satisfactory conclusion, *it* happened.

Chapter 35

Jasper had been sitting up late that evening, alone in the comfort of Hartington Abbey's grand library, reading an engaging novel with a glass of brandy at his side, when the unexpected phone call came.

'Lockwood,' he replied tersely, not happy to be interrupted at this uncivilised hour. 'Who's this?'

The voice on the end of the line sounded slightly slurred, as though the caller had been drinking. It also sounded strangely familiar.

'Good evening, your Lordship. Remember me? I'm the fellow who's going to take away your big fine house, just like I always used to tell you.'

'*Mortimer?*' Jasper exploded. He could barely believe his ears. How long had it been? What on earth could the idiot possibly want, calling him after all these years?

'Thought old Hugh had gone away, did you?' slurred the voice. 'Well, no such luck, dear boy. I'm still very much in the picture. And you'll soon be hearing a lot more from me, because the time has finally come.'

'What the hell are you talking about? You're insane. And you're drunk.'

'Oh, I've had a few, I'll admit. Why not? I'm celebrating the fact that at long last, after waiting all this time, I have the evidence I needed to prove that what you thought was yours is really mine. So get ready, because it'll soon be time for you to start packing to leave, just like I promised you in our Cambridge days. And there's not a damn thing you can do about it.'

Jasper scowled at the phone. 'Evidence? What evidence? There is none, except for the ravings of your twisted imagination. You'll get nothing from me, Mortimer. I can assure you of that.'

'Oh, yes I will,' jeered the drunken voice. 'And just you try and stop me, *Lord* Lockwood! Ha ha ha!'

'Get off the phone, you bloody lunatic,' Lockwood thundered at him, 'and don't you ever call this number again, is that clear?' He slammed down the receiver, went to storm away, then as an afterthought unplugged the phone connection from the wall. At least there was no way that madman could pester him on his mobile.

Jasper went back to his book and his brandy and tried to forget what he'd just heard, but something about the phone call had deeply troubled him. Hugh Mortimer might be crazy, but even Jasper had to admit that his old rival was anything but stupid, and the things he was saying now were totally consistent with what he'd been saying forty years ago. As wild as it sounded, what if there really was some sort of foundation to this claim of his?

At any other time, Jasper might not have paid it any notice. But his affairs were so desperately precarious, and so very much depended on this property deal going through, that Mortimer's renewed threat had got right under his skin, making him feel vulnerable and agitated. After a sleepless night he'd got straight on the phone early next morning to a former connection from his intelligence days, a man he

253

knew by the name of Dexter Chance, though he also operated under a variety of other identities.

Thanks to the often murky world in which MI5 dwelled, during his years as a senior agent Jasper had come into contact with more than a few of those strange and shadowy figures whose covert existence crossed the line into some very dark and dirty areas indeed, which included assassinations, abductions and other illegal acts secretly carried out at the behest of the agency. Chance was one of those. With his gawky looks and thick-lensed spectacles he might not fit the stereotypical image of the master spook, but he was a skilful and cunning operator with just the kind of ambiguous morals and quasi-criminal connections that could now come in extremely useful for Jasper in his hour of need. As a man of secrets Chance could also be trusted to keep his mouth shut, like the men who worked for him. As long as the price was right, he'd do whatever was required, ask no questions and leave nothing behind that could be traced to himself or his employers. Jasper might be fast running out of cash but he still had plenty enough to retain their expert services and cover all the necessary travel and equipment expenses.

Phone taps and covert surveillance were the stock-in-trade of folks like Chance and his associates, and it had taken them very little time to put eyes and ears on the unsuspecting Professor Hugh Mortimer at his Yorkshire residence. Short of a dedicated spy satellite, they soon had everything in place to observe every detail of his movements and listen to every word he said, as closely as if he'd been a key terror suspect.

What Jasper now learned from the intercepted conversations between Mortimer's home and a man called Rudi Bergenroth in Liechtenstein only confirmed his paranoid suspicions raised by the phone call. There was talk of historical property deeds, and of proof of genealogical lineage, and all kinds of details that sounded worryingly plausible. Especially alarming was the mention of a silver pendant or medallion (and of course Jasper remembered all too well what that was referring to) that could be used as evidence not only to trace Mortimer's family tree back to Tudor times, but to corroborate his claim to Hartington Abbey. It seemed that back during the late fifteenth century, the estate had been illegally grabbed from its rightful owner, who had been hanged for treason after owning the property for a very brief time and never actually lived there, as far as anyone could tell. But if that previous owner turned out to have had descendants, and if those descendants could prove they belonged to that bloodline . . .

In short, all of this spelled serious trouble for Jasper and threatened to undermine the property deal he was depending on so heavily to save his skin. If his buyer got wind of a potential contested claim of ownership, it could be nothing short of disastrous. Even if Mortimer's claim was baloney, a legal dispute – even worse, a court case – could hold up the much-needed sale indefinitely or even derail it altogether. What if the prince lost patience and went elsewhere? Jasper was very unlikely to find such a good deal again. Or any, for that matter, if there was any truth to Mortimer's claim.

Try and stop me, Hugh had taunted him on the phone. Unfortunately for the professor, Jasper was left with little choice but to do just that.

Initially he'd thought simple intimidation might work, by means of those silly letters that Jasper had personally pieced together out of newspaper clippings and sent from random post boxes across England, having to travel miles for the purpose. But when the phone taps revealed that Mortimer and Bergenroth were continuing their correspondence unabated, Jasper knew he was going to have to take things to the next level, and fast.

All that took was another call to Dexter Chance, who was already in position with his men and awaiting further instructions. They'd been observing Mortimer's outings on the lake and the idea of staging a boat accident was an obvious choice for agents in their line of work. They weren't exactly new to this kind of dirty work. Once their orders were received they'd carried out the job quickly, efficiently and in a way that averted any suspicion of foul play.

That should have been the end of it. Jasper felt no moral qualms over what he'd done. And he'd have been able to rest easy, if it hadn't been for the involvement of this man called Hope.

It was Chance who'd first spotted him in Dublin, the day that Mortimer had flown to Ireland for their meeting at the hotel. The instant they'd intercepted Mortimer's phone call to the man the previous day, they'd been scrambling to find out who he was. Lockwood's old MI5 counter-terrorism connections had come in useful once more; a discreet call to a former underling informed him that this Benedict Hope had the kind of top-secret military record that could only belong to an ex-Special Forces operative. The more Jasper learned about Hope's past and current activities, the more worried he became. In the wake of the failed threatening letters, he could think of only one reason why the professor would have a meeting with someone like Hope: to hire him for protection.

Won't do you much good, Jasper had thought to himself. He wasn't about to let anyone get in the way of his plans. Not Mortimer, not this man Bergenroth, not even Mortimer's associate Tony Kitson with whom he'd been in contact. They were all targets.

As for Hope himself, they'd no idea what sensitive information Mortimer might have passed to him at their meeting, and Jasper wasn't inclined to give it the benefit of the doubt. The car bomb had been intended to take Hope off the table for precaution's sake. Thanks to Chance's mistiming, however, it had failed in its objective and only made matters worse. Hope was now a problem that just refused to go away, despite everything that Jasper and his motley crew of hired killers could throw at him.

Cut to the present, and Jasper was caught up in a race against time. In his desperation he could only pray that his precious deal didn't collapse before Hope was taken out of the equation once and for all. The only problem at this point was that the bastard seemed to have dropped off the radar, last seen in Yorkshire when they'd eliminated Mortimer's associate Kitson in a messy operation that had very nearly ended in total failure. In its aftermath Jasper had had to double Dexter Chance's money to persuade the man to stay on, especially after he'd collected several shotgun pellets in his left buttock during the fight. At this moment Chance was in Manchester, doing the rounds of his seedy connections and dredging up the last few individuals he could find who were prepared to take on such dangerous work.

Meanwhile Jasper was hanging on to the possibility that Hope might have been injured in the exchange of fire and had gone to ground, perhaps dead in a ditch somewhere.

But a horribly unnerving voice in the back of his mind kept telling him that he should be so lucky. If they could just get the property sale done and dusted in time, he was home free. He'd have the money wired to a Grand Cayman bank, jump on the first plane to the Seychelles and be laughing in his hammock under the palm trees before you could say Jack Robinson.

Jasper turned away from the study window and stared heavily at the inert, silent phone on his desk.

'Come on, ring, you bastard.'

Chapter 36

Saudi Arabia

By the standards of many of the Saudi royal family's numerous billionaire members, Prince Hassan Bin Ibrahim Al Sharif's palace in Riyadh would have been considered a modest little bachelor pad. Its externally minimalist design of sandstone and marble belied an interior filled with breathtakingly lavish splendour that made the palaces of Versailles and Buckingham look like shepherd's huts by comparison, while its mere twenty-acre grounds comprised a helipad and hangars for the prince's four helicopters, ornamental gardens modelled on those at his father's eighteenth-century French château, luxury guest accommodation for up to forty people, three separate swimming pools and a polo field with adjoining stabling and paddocks for the prince's collection of much-pampered Arabian horses.

It was on that polo field, mounted astride his favourite of those horses, that Prince Hassan was at this moment charging to victory in the final chukka of a closely-contested tournament between his own private team and some visiting contenders captained by his older cousin, Prince Salman bin Faisal. The thundering of hooves, the enthusiastic cheers of the crowd and the *crack* of the struck ball echoed around the field under the burning afternoon sun. Today's match was only a friendly contest, but Hassan was far too competitive and aggressive a sportsman to play with anything less than a life-or-death attitude, the same approach he invariably took to all he did. Whether it was polo, tennis, golf or business, simply being the best wasn't good enough – he had to be *perfect* at it, and to lose was the ultimate shame.

Needless to say, Prince Hassan was his team's Number 1 offensive position, being the fastest rider and the most accurate hitter with an excellent seven-goal handicap that made him one of Saudi's top players. Standing up in the saddle with the warm wind on his face and the magnificent powerhouse of his pearl-white Arabian stallion Jabbar surging across the field at full pelt under him, muscles rippling and mane flying, Hassan broke the opposition's line with ferocious aplomb, wielding his polo stick like a scimitar in a spectacular off-side swing that struck the ball hard and true from the forty-yard line to score the decisive goal of the match just seconds before the final horn sounded to end play.

The thrill of winning was what Prince Hassan lived for, turning his blood to wine as he wheeled Jabbar around with his stick raised in triumph and a beaming grin on his face. He jumped down from the saddle, patted his noble steed and turned to receive the congratulations of his teammates. 'Better luck next time, cousin,' he said to the disappointed Prince Salman.

Still flushed with victory and drinking up the admiring looks he was receiving from all quarters, the prince handed Jabbar back to his handlers to have his leg and tail wraps removed and be dried off before returning to his stall, which was larger and more comfortable than the homes of most average Saudi citizens.

After doing his rounds, downing a few glasses of non-alcoholic champagne, shaking hands and being patted on the back (by those of sufficiently elevated social rank to dare touch a prince in so familiar a manner), Hassan broke away from the crowd and headed off alone through the grounds. But before he returned to the coolness and tranquillity of his palace he made a quick detour to pay a visit to Ayesha. She was his beloved pet Bengal tigress, who spent her time padding among the rocks and specially imported Asiatic Gulmohar trees of her large fenced enclosure, swishing her stripy tail, snarling at nothing in particular and enjoying her daily twenty pounds of camel and goat meat.

Hassan opened the gate and stepped confidently into the enclosure. 'Ayesha, my beautiful,' he said tenderly, running his fingers through her coarse fur as she came up to rub herself against him and lick his hand, her great flat head near chest height to him and her eyes closed in bliss. 'Are you contented? Are you hungry?'

The huge cat could have turned from affectionate to ferocious in the blink of an eye and eviscerated him with those huge teeth and razor-sharp claws, but Hassan was quite unafraid and even admired her for it, seeing something of his own nature in such a dangerous and unpredictable creature. He'd brought her up from a cub and was one of the very few people she tolerated entering her domain. Just last month, she'd killed and partially eaten one of the keepers, but it was the stupid fool's own fault for disturbing her during mealtime. 'You should have seen me just now,' he said, petting her fondly. 'It was another fine victory.'

Leaving Ayesha with a quartered goat carcass to gnaw on, the prince returned to the private haven of his personal quarters within the palace. His master suite covered over four thousand square feet and had two bathrooms, though he only ever used one for himself and never entertained women in his rooms. He had no wives or current romantic attachments, much preferring his own company to that of any female. After his long, cool shower he spent a few moments admiring his lithe, muscular and perfectly-toned physique in the bathroom mirror. Then he put on a silk robe and walked through into his palatial ultra-modern living-room, large enough to hold a party for up to a hundred guests if he so chose – but strangely for a man who enjoyed the adulation of his inferiors, he disliked the frivolity of socialising. Adjoining the living-room was a full-sized cinema, complete with red velvet-covered walls and a twelve-metre screen, in which the prince enjoyed watching action and adventure movies (he loved Bruce Willis but his favourites were early James Bond films, and among the many cars he owned was the actual Aston Martin DB5 Connery had driven in *Goldfinger*, snapped up at auction for a piffling $4.6 million). Next door to the cinema was his personal bodybuilding and fitness gym where he spent two hours each day lifting weights, and the vast dining room where he ate his solitary meals every night, simple and frugal dishes of grilled lamb or chicken.

On one wall of the living-room hung a large gilt-framed oil portrait of his multi-multi-billionaire father, whose own much larger and more opulent palace was located not far away in Riyadh, though these days he spent most of his time at the château in France, or one or other of his castles in Scotland. On the opposite wall was the photo portrait of Akeem, which Hassan now paused to look at, as he often did.

His elder brother had been the apple of their father's eye, always the favourite son, until his untimely death in a powerboat accident in Monte Carlo two years previously. Ever since the tragedy, it had been Hassan's personal mission to prove to his father that he, the younger son, was every bit as worthy as his late brother was, and undeserving of the hothead image with which he felt he'd been unfairly branded by the family. It was true that in his younger years he'd often acted impetuously, and that he still tended towards arrogance, impatience and the petulant behaviour of someone too used to always getting what he wanted. But now he was over thirty he was slowly coming to embrace more mature ways, though no less driven to rise swiftly to the top of everything he undertook. That was the reason why Hassan had lately decided to branch out on a new property venture of his own, to show that he, too, could excel at business. He was determined to turn his Hartington Abbey project into every bit as much of a success as his father's own lucrative acquisitions across the world.

Hassan poured himself a glass of fresh orange juice – he never broke the strict Saudi code prohibiting alcohol, even when nobody was watching – and stepped out of the French window. From his balcony he had a view over the palace gardens and the bustling city beyond. Men with machine guns and Doberman Pinschers patrolled the perimeter at all times, and the security-conscious prince never left the compound without his bodyguards.

As he gazed at the view his mind turned back to the Hartington Abbey purchase negotiations. For some time now he'd been perplexed by how long they were taking, as though some unknown factor had come into the picture to delay their progress. A keen reader of human behaviour, he had sensed a certain reluctance on the part of the seller and wondered whether the Englishman might be having second thoughts. Surely it couldn't be over the offer price, which Hassan had thought was extremely generous. Then what? He couldn't understand it. And it annoyed him when he couldn't understand things.

And so, after pondering the problem for a short while, Hassan had decided to find out what was going on. His method of doing so wasn't by any means unusual for him. Whenever he conducted any sort of business, either buying or selling, it was his standard policy to put his spies to work. The more he could find out about the other party, he reasoned, the more insight he gained into who he was dealing with, and the better placed he was to anticipate whether they might try to double-deal or cheat him in any way. He thought of this simply as putting out feelers, and as far as he was concerned, the end justified the means. He was therefore quite happy to sanction the use of phone taps, surveillance teams, room bugs and hidden cameras, and of course he had the unlimited financial means to make such things possible.

One of his bodyguards had a brother called Farouk, who had worked as a special agent for the Saudi General Intelligence Directorate until Hassan had employed him as his own private chief of spies. Farouk was in charge of a hand-picked team of loyal men, each an expert at espionage and counter-espionage in his own right, whom he could deploy anywhere in the world at a moment's notice. The team had travelled to England aboard Hassan's personal Boeing 747, where they had set about learning everything possible about this Lord Jasper Lockwood. They had had little difficulty penetrating his home, from which he'd been absent at the time, and placing hidden microphones enabling

264

them to eavesdrop on his mobile phone conversations in addition to those on his tapped landline. And what they'd soon found out was very interesting.

It had come as no great surprise to Hassan to discover that Lockwood was in serious financial trouble. He had already intuited that the man was probably deep in debt and therefore desperate to make as much as he could on the sale. Hassan had therefore come to suspect that the reason for the delays was that Lockwood was stalling him while trying to get a better deal elsewhere. That was very disappointing. Hassan did not like to be disappointed.

But what the prince's spy team revealed next was completely unexpected. It seemed that Lord Lockwood's problems were more than just financial, and that he was prepared to go to some quite remarkable lengths to resolve them. From their initial covert base in Northumberland Farouk and his men had followed the detective trail to a lakeside property in Yorkshire, and very soon afterwards from there to the unlikely location of a tiny fishing village on the west coast of Ireland. The findings they'd reported back to their employer, with photographic and video evidence sent via encrypted email, were nothing short of fascinating.

Farouk's hidden observers had watched from nearby as a team of operatives carried out the murder, by drowning, of the same man whose phone line Lockwood had had under surveillance for some time. In quick succession they'd witnessed the scene of a car bomb attack in which a young woman had been critically injured. They had ascertained that both incidents were the work of the same men, led by a shady, quasi-official former British intelligence operative called Dexter Chance who was working for Lockwood. The information gleaned from their audio surveillance of Hartington Abbey made it clear why.

For a few days Hassan had been mulling over what to do with all this knowledge. Then late yesterday evening he'd received Farouk's latest update, now reporting from another location in the north of England where it seemed that Lord Lockwood's troubles had recently taken another, even more dramatic, turn. This time Farouk and his men had followed Lockwood's hit team to a remote cottage near the city of York, where they'd launched an attack on what should have been an easy target for such a superior, heavily armed force. Instead, it had turned into a bloody rout and a near-total loss for Lockwood's hired guns. It was clear that a new player had now entered the game, an opponent who was more than a match for the English lord's firepower. Lockwood had had a good run until now, but his luck had changed and he'd suddenly found himself seriously out of his depth dealing with this man whose name, according to the intelligence reports provided by Farouk, was Ben Hope.

Their research into the identity and background of this man Hope was even more intriguing. The files on him were extremely hard to access, but Farouk's connections within Saudi Intelligence and the infinite financial resources at their disposal made for a powerful combination. There was little they couldn't find out about anyone they chose. Full name Benedict Hope. Nationality British, mother Irish, both parents deceased. Ex-military with thirteen years' service with 22 Special Air Service, retired with the rank of major. Currently working as a freelance operative and believed to be residing in the Republic of Ireland, address unknown.

At which point, having been mulling over it all morning, Prince Hassan had formed an idea in his head and decided it was time he made direct contact with Jasper Lockwood. There'd been no time before the polo match to make any arrangements. He walked back into the living-room and picked up a phone. The person he called was one of the many lackeys whose job it was to be constantly on standby awaiting their master's instructions and then carry them out to the letter.

The prince told him: 'Get the Boeing ready for first thing tomorrow morning. We're going to England.'

Chapter 37

Signs for Sheffield flashed by as the Suzuki Grand Vitara raced up the M1 motorway, its wipers beating against the rainstorm lashing down from the dark clouds. Lord Jasper Lockwood gripped the wheel tightly and kept his foot down hard on the gas in his rush to get home to Hartington Abbey as fast as his wheels could carry him.

Unable to bear the stress of hanging around at home waiting for the phone to ring, Jasper had been off to London to spend a day and a night with a woman of his acquaintance. The lovely Greta – in actual fact no longer quite so lovely these days as in her prime – was the widow of one of his former MI5 agents. Their on-off fairly casual relationship dated back years to when her husband had still been alive, and they'd managed to keep it secret even afterwards. Greta was a brassy, cold-hearted bitch who hardly bothered to hide her contempt for him now that most of his money was gone, but was happy to do her bit to milk him for the few pennies that were left. Jasper had often felt like dumping her in the past, but she still offered some kind of solace and also happened to live in a very comfortable penthouse flat in Belgravia where he felt safe and protected.

Now that his luxury cars were all sold off, he was using the old Japanese four-wheel-drive that was kept as a runabout on the estate, and made him blend more anonymously into the traffic. He was fairly certain that nobody was following him, though his constant preoccupation with Ben Hope had grown into a state of nervous paranoia that had him flinching at shadows. He'd barely been able to relax even in the presence of the lovely Greta.

Where had that bastard Hope disappeared to? No trace of him since the Kitson incident. And with Dexter Chance still in Manchester recruiting new henchmen Jasper was alone, vulnerable and terrified that Hope could suddenly turn up at any moment.

Jasper had been threading his way northwards through the London traffic that morning, in no particular hurry to get back to Northumberland, when his mobile had started ringing. The call had been automatically redirected from his home phone. The foreign-sounding voice on the other end had informed him that some unexpected visitors were en route to Hartington Abbey from Saudi Arabia. One of these visitors was none other than the illustrious Prince Hassan Bin Ibrahim Al Sharif himself. The royal jet was due to land at Edinburgh Airport that afternoon, whereupon the prince and his entourage would be whisked the fifty or so miles to Berwick-upon-Tweed by limousine. Needless to say, the caller added solemnly, this visit was a very great honour for which the appropriate welcome arrangements must be made.

In that magic moment all Jasper's worries had been washed away. He could hardly contain his excitement. This surely had to be it, the payoff he'd been waiting and praying for! A visit from the prince could only mean one thing. Jasper knew how these Arabs loved to flaunt their spending power by throwing paper money around, and sixty million was nothing to a man of such ridiculous wealth. Visions of suitcases stuffed with banknotes swam tantalisingly in front of Jasper's eyes, making him so breathless with anticipation that he'd eventually had to pull into the Watford Gap services to get himself together and wait for the palpitations to subside. Then he'd sped off again, caning the Grand Vitara mercilessly northwards up the motorway.

It was a six-hour drive from London, about as much time as he calculated it would take a private jet to fly all the way from Saudi Arabia. At last, just after three in the afternoon, Jasper skidded to a halt in the gravel courtyard of Hartington Abbey, saw to his exhausted relief that his visitors hadn't yet arrived, and ran inside the house to start making preparations. Never had he so regretted having dispensed with the services of his butler and maids, now having to do everything himself. Deciding that he'd greet the visitors in the great library, he feverishly got to work setting out chairs, his best crystal glassware and whatever snacks and dainties he could find in the abbey kitchen. He'd been scuttling down to the cellar for bottles of champagne when he suddenly remembered that, of course, anything alcoholic was strictly off-limits for the Saudis. He'd have to make do with carafes of iced, lemoned mineral water, in the hope that such humble offerings would satisfy his Highness. What a bunch of bloody killjoys those Arabs were.

Once that was all taken care of to the best of his ability, he'd had a bare twenty minutes to pace up and down, wringing his hands and trying to control his nerves, before the sound of tyres crunching on the gravel made him dash to the oriel window overlooking the courtyard. With a leap of his heart, he saw the procession of gleaming black limousines pulling up outside.

Jasper needed all his willpower to remain composed as he went out to meet his exalted visitor. The cars parked in an orderly line, with the longest and plushest of the limousines in the middle and the others flanking left and right, from which stepped a dozen serious and tough-looking men in dark suits, dark glasses and shiny black shoes. The prince's personal security detail made the likes of Dexter Chance and his men look like third-rate club bouncers by comparison. And such was the VIP ranking of their principal that the strict UK firearms regulations had been relaxed to allow the bodyguards to carry an assortment of automatic weapons as black and shiny as their shoes. Jasper was deeply impressed by such a display of diplomatic clout, worthy of a visiting world leader.

The last car doors to open were those of the prince's own limousine. Out he got, tall, athletic, offensively young and handsome and extremely elegant in his flowing white thobe and kaffiyeh. His eyes were dark and intelligent and his black beard so perfectly trim and neat that it appeared painted on. With the ethereal grace of his station he stepped from the car and waited for Jasper to hurry over to greet him.

'Your Highness, it's an honour to receive you at my humble home,' Jasper said obsequiously, repeating the lines he'd been rehearsing for the last three hours. He tried not to stare at the limousines, wondering which one might contain those blessed suitcases of cash inside.

'Not too humble, I hope,' the prince replied in his perfect English, with a flashing white smile. 'Considering the asking price.' He turned to his men, who allowed themselves a discreet ripple of laughter at his joke. 'These are my bodyguards,' Hassan said to Jasper. 'I trust their presence does not alarm you? A man of my eminence cannot leave home without them.'

'Not in the least, your Highness. Please, please come inside. I hope you'll find everything to your liking.'

Five of the bodyguards accompanied the prince inside the main building, while the rest remained planted outside like sentries, scanning the grounds through their dark glasses as though they expected assassins to burst out of the rose bushes at any moment.

'No servants?' the prince commented as they stepped through the grand entrance hall with its vaulted ceiling and magnificent carved panelling.

'This happens to be their day off,' Jasper replied carelessly, the big magnanimous Lord of the Manor looking out for the little people's welfare. 'This way, please.' As he led his guests towards the great library he noticed that one of the bodyguards was carrying an attaché case. Was there money inside? he wondered. How much cash could you fit into a case that size? Unable to repress his curiosity he dared ask, 'To what do I owe the unexpected pleasure of your Highness's visit?'

'Merely a social call,' Hassan replied modestly. 'As I am shortly to become the new owner of this property, it seemed only right that I should come to view it sooner or later. What I have seen so far meets with my expectations.'

Relief and joy flowed through Jasper's veins like warm honey at those words. 'I'm delighted to hear that your Highness is still keen on going ahead.'

'Oh, very much so. And please, let us dispense with the formalities. You may address me as Prince Hassan.'

They were seated inside the grandeur of the old library, with the prince at the head of the long table looking approvingly around him as Jasper poured the drinks for him and his silent men. Then the business talk began.

It wasn't quite what Jasper had expected.

'As I was saying, Lord Lockwood,' the prince said, smiling, 'I am still very much looking forward to completing the purchase of this delightful little house. But I must confess to having my doubts of late as to whether you were still in the market to sell.'

'I've been having a few minor problems,' Lockwood confessed, as nonchalantly as possible but deeply uncomfortable having this conversation in front of the bodyguards. 'Nothing I can't fix.'

The prince laughed. 'Oh yes, I know all about your problems.'

Lockwood stared at him with a glass of lemoned water halfway to his lips. 'You do?'

'Indeed. I have made it my business to find out,' the prince said, abruptly dropping the smile and his eyes hardening. 'And I know exactly what has been going on. It is clear that you have been stalling me, and why.'

'B-b-but . . . I . . .'

The prince raised a slim, perfectly manicured hand. 'Silence, please. Now you must understand that *nobody* stalls Prince Hassan Bin Ibrahim Al Sharif. I do not consider such deceptive strategies acceptable in business negotiations. In light of this insult, I have therefore felt obliged to reconsider our deal and make you a revised offer.'

'W-what kind of revised offer?' Jasper stammered.

'The terms of the deal remain exactly as before,' the prince told him, 'except for the purchase price. Which I am reducing to five million pounds sterling. I trust this is acceptable to you.'

For a few stunned moments Jasper thought he must have misheard. The Arab hadn't said he was reducing it *by* five million. That would have been bad enough. It was reducing *to*. He blinked and felt colour rising in his cheeks. 'Well, as a matter of fact, no, it's not acceptable. It's not acceptable at all. It's fifty-five million short of what we agreed.'

'Indeed it is,' the prince replied. 'But as with all negotiations, nothing is settled until the deal is signed.'

'What the hell makes you think I would give it away at that price?' Jasper blustered. 'I might as well let you have it for nothing!'

'Why, how kind,' the prince said graciously. 'Thank you. I accept.'

'It was only a figure of speech, for God's sake!'

'Ah, I see. You were making a joke. I, however, am not joking. And indeed, Lord Lockwood, you should be thankful I chose to reduce my offer by a *mere* fifty-five million. I am in a generous mood, and I will not tolerate any further abuse of my generosity. Which is how I would interpret any attempt on your part to negotiate the price even just a penny higher. Am I making myself understood?'

'It's outrageous!' Jasper shouted, thumping on the table. The bodyguards gazed coldly at him. 'It's robbery, pure and simple. I'd have to be mad to accept!'

Prince Hassan smiled. 'Do you enjoy watching movies, Lord Lockwood? I do. I watch a great many of them. And there is one in particular I would like you to see.'

'Movies? What on earth are you talking about?'

The prince snapped his fingers, and the bodyguard with the attaché case immediately picked it up and set it flat on the table, popped the catches and raised the lid. What it contained wasn't money. Instead, he took out a small portable DVD player and a shiny plastic disc jewel case. He carefully removed a recordable DVD-R with no label from the case and inserted it into the player, then angled the device around so that Jasper could see the screen.

'What is this?' Jasper demanded.

'Watch,' said the prince.

Chapter 38

Jasper stared numbly at the small screen, unsure whether this was really happening or he was having some horrible waking nightmare. All eyes around the table were on him, watching his expression as the DVD began to play.

The first piece of footage looked oddly familiar to him, because it was almost exactly the same as the video clip he'd received from Dexter Chance after the killing of Hugh Mortimer. *Almost* the same. In this version, the events had been filmed from a different angle and slightly further away up the shore of the private lake.

As far as Jasper had been aware until this moment, only Dexter Chance's men had been positioned on the far side of the lake to watch and record the work of the frogmen. Now he realised with a shock that there must have been a second observation team. And not his.

Jasper's mouth dropped open and all the colour drained from his face as he sat watching the replay of Hugh Mortimer's last moments on this earth. The solitary figure in the boat, surrounded by still, flat water that suddenly churned into foam as the two divers burst from the surface either side. Grabbing the edges of the hull and rocking it violently, so that the man in the boat toppled into the water. The three figures disappearing under the surface, bubbles rising. Then some time later, the two divers leaving the empty boat drifting on the water as they made their way towards the shore.

'W-where did you get this?' Jasper said weakly. He already knew the answer.

'Keep watching, please,' the prince replied.

The next piece of footage showed a dark, rainy scene, somewhere very different. Houses packed close together either side of a narrow village street. People gathered on the rain-slicked pavement, some pointing, some staring, some covering their faces in horror. Flashing blue lights filling the night sky, and the red-orange glow from the burning car down the street. Paramedics loading a stretchered figure into the back of an ambulance. Police officers swarming everywhere as firemen put out the blaze.

'What a shame not to have seen the explosion itself,' Prince Hassan said. 'Still, it is as exciting as an action film, do you not agree? I half-expected Bruce Willis to appear. But of course that could not be. Because this happened in real life. The bomb planted by your employee, Dexter Chance.'

Jasper flinched at the mention of the name. He shoved the DVD player away from him. 'What? Who? Don't be absurd. I don't know anyone called Chance. This has nothing whatsoever to do with me.'

'No?'

'Absolutely not,' Jasper protested. 'Who was that poor bugger in the boat? What's that car on fire? What the fucking hell is this about? We're supposed to be doing a business deal.'

'My, my. With such fine acting skills, you could have starred in a movie of your own. But wait, there is more.'

277

Now the screen cut to a clip of the blazing wreck of Tony Kitson's cottage, videoed on a mobile phone camera. This was one piece of footage Jasper had never seen until now, and he gaped at it in disbelief.

'Your opponent is a clean worker,' the prince said. 'Only minutes earlier, the scene appeared like a battlefield, something from a war film with bodies lying everywhere. Do you enjoy war films, Jasper? I do, very much. *The Dirty Dozen* is a great favourite of mine. Lee Marvin and Charles Bronson.'

'Opponent? What opponent? I have no idea what you're talking about.' But Jasper knew just how lame and unconvincing his denials were sounding.

'Next on this disc is some audio material I would like you to listen to,' the prince said. 'Perhaps this will clarify your mind.'

The sound clips were just short segments edited from hours of phone-tap recordings. First Jasper heard the voices of Hugh Mortimer and his associate Rudi Bergenroth in Liechtenstein. After twenty seconds it switched to a different segment, and Jasper recognised the sound of his own voice giving instructions to Dexter Chance. 'That's a mobile phone conversation!' he blurted. 'You must have planted mikes in my house!'

'Ah, so it seems your memory has returned,' said Prince Hassan with a smile. 'Abdullah, you may turn off the machine. I think our friend has seen and heard enough.'

'So it's a shakedown,' Jasper fumed. 'I agree to let you have my property for this daylight robbery price, or else you'll hand this evidence over to the authorities and land me in prison for the rest of my life. Is that right?'

The prince looked shocked. 'Please, Lord Lockwood. Surely you would not take me for a common blackmailer? That would be most hurtful.'

'Oh, really, that's not what this is about?'

'Not at all. I am a businessman. It goes without saying that I would capitalise on the situation to tilt the deal in my own favour. Who can blame me for that? But I am also a human being, and not without sympathy for your predicament. Please trust that I haven't come to threaten you. I would like to help you.'

'So you'd rob me blind, but then you want to help me?'

Prince Hassan sighed. 'If only you had come to me sooner with this problem. We could have worked together to find a far more effective solution than to let your gang of incompetents make such a mess of everything and cause a poor innocent woman to be maimed for life. Now you face far bigger problems that could have been avoided. The most pressing of which is the threat posed to you by this man Benedict Hope.'

Jasper was amazed at the range and depth of the prince's research. 'You know about Hope?'

'I told you, I know everything. Now, it appears to me that he has little personal interest in the man you drowned. But when you hurt the woman, it became a different story. You goaded the tiger, my friend. That was a very foolish thing to do.'

'It wasn't meant to happen that way,' Jasper protested.

'I am sure it was not. However, this is the inevitable outcome when one entrusts important tasks to amateurs. The results speak for themselves, and will continue to do so for as long as you insist on employing such men. However many you send against Hope, you will get back only corpses.'

'I told you it wasn't anything I couldn't handle,' Jasper replied angrily. 'I'll send more.'

'But you have no more to send,' Prince Hassan said. 'None you could find at such short notice, and certainly none whom you could trust. All that remains to you is your operative Dexter Chance, the lone survivor of your last attempt, who has proved to be nothing but a liability to you. Your resources are running out. You have so little money left that you have even had to sell your possessions and lay off your house staff.'

Jasper boggled. They'd known this all along.

The prince continued, 'Hardly a strong position to be in, you must agree. To make matters worse, at this moment you have absolutely no idea where this man Hope is. He seems to have entirely disappeared.'

'All right, all right! You've got me. I admit I couldn't have screwed this up worse if I'd tried to. I'm broke, I'm out of options, there's some kind of ninja warrior out there on the loose who's wiped out virtually all my men and next he'll be coming for me. My only consolation is that he doesn't know my name or where to find me. Meanwhile you've got me by the balls and fifty-five million quid that was coming to me has gone up in smoke. Well played. Congratulations.'

'Allah looks favourably upon a man who admits his mistakes. I like you, Jasper – I may call you Jasper? And as you have so generously agreed to my revised deal terms, I would like to do you a favour in return. I think you will find that it suits both our purposes.'

Jasper was highly wary of any favour the prince might want to do him. 'I don't suppose I have much choice, do I? So what do you have in mind?'

'I am someone who always has the best of everything,' Prince Hassan said. 'I do not say that to boast. It is just who I am. Nor am I the kind of man who would have panicked and rushed into hiring a gang of idiots to solve my problems. On the contrary, just as everything I do is perfectly planned and flawlessly executed, the people I choose to carry out my orders are experts and professionals second to none. They do not fail. And so, the favour I propose to offer you is that my men will eliminate this new enemy you have brought against yourself.'

Jasper brightened. This was a much better offer than he'd feared. 'You're saying you'll take out Hope for me?'

'That is precisely what I propose. He may pose a challenging target, but he is one man operating alone. We can crush him, and we will, to enable us to close this deal. Which, as I say, serves both our interests, by simultaneously allowing me to proceed with my goals for Hartington Abbey, and allowing you to remain still a reasonably wealthy man. More importantly, a free man who will not have to spend the rest of his days living in fear of retribution.'

'I suppose that makes sense,' Jasper said grudgingly, still thinking of his lost millions and his much - diminished prospects for the future.

'However,' the prince added, 'I believe it would be a grievous error of judgement to simply kill this man Hope out of hand, the moment we catch him.'

'It would? Why?'

'Come come, a man with your intelligence background should be able to see exactly why. As you have conceded, since the latest encounter between him and your men, Hope is suddenly absent from the picture. The question is, where has he gone? I suggest the answer is that he has gone in search of the other player in this game, the sleeping partner. The co-conspirator.'

'Bergenroth?'

'We should not forget his involvement in this, my friend. Because even though he is in no position to make an ownership claim on this property on behalf of his late associate, we have to assume he is in possession of all the same information Mortimer was. Therefore, if my guess is correct and Hope has managed to trace his whereabouts, we can be confident that Hope, too, is now privy to the same knowledge.'

'I hadn't forgotten him,' Jasper said irritably. 'And Hope won't have found him, either. Two of Chance's contacts in Germany drove over to Liechtenstein to check the last known address we were able to trace, from his phone records. He'd moved on. There's no way—'

'No way that Hope could not have outwitted them and managed to follow Bergenroth's trail? How sure can you be of that, Jasper? Given Chance's track record to date, are you not placing a little too much faith in the abilities of his associates?'

Jasper's blood ran a little colder as sudden doubt gripped him and an unnerving possibility came into his mind. 'But that would mean . . .'

The prince nodded. 'That, contrary to what you thought, it is perfectly possible that Hope does indeed know the identity of the man who maimed his woman, inadvertently or otherwise, and hence knows where to find you. It might be reasonable to assume he is on his way here as we speak. It could even be that he has already reached you, and is at this very moment lurking somewhere within the grounds, watching and waiting for the right moment to strike. Men like him are trained in the art of stealth warfare, and they are deadly efficient. You are not as safe as you think you are, my friend.'

'Then what the hell can be done about it?' Jasper asked, flustered.

The prince replied, 'When a man-eating tiger begins to prey upon the villagers, there is only one way to catch him. It is a job for a professional hunter. You may have been a fine spymaster in your day, but I regret to say that when it comes to this kind of work you are but a dilettante. Farouk here' – pointing at the bodyguard to his right – 'is the man you need to catch your tiger.'

'But he works for you,' Jasper said, confused. 'In Saudi Arabia.'

'I have decided to remain in Britain for a few days,' the prince told him. 'I like Scotland very much, and so I will be staying at the State Apartments in the Palace of Holyroodhouse in Edinburgh. Modest accommodation for a man of my tastes, but tolerable enough for a short visit. Farouk will stay here, as part of your protection detail.'

'And I'm supposed to stay hidden and twiddle my thumbs with nothing to do until this is over, is that right?'

The prince smiled. 'My dear fellow, yours is the most important role to play.'

'And what might that be?' Jasper shot back resentfully.

'Why, Jasper, you are the bait. The tethered goat that will draw the beast into the trap.'

Chapter 39

Not even the most attentive eyes would have been able to pick out the figure of the man watching Hartington Abbey from afar. He was hunkered down prone among the bushes at the edge of the forest, beyond the outer fringes of the estate grounds where the land rose up to meet the treeline. His outline was camouflaged by foliage and he had barely moved at all for hours, lying there so utterly still and silent that he was undetected by the rabbits foraging about the slope and even a wandering deer that had ventured from the woods earlier that day. The lie of the land gave him a fine vantage point from which to observe the house and grounds through the high-magnification Swarovski spotting scope mounted on its low tripod among the long grass.

Ben had been here for one and a half days, taking his time, patiently reconnoitring his target and working out his best strategy. His fastest means of travelling to Hartington Abbey had been by air from Guernsey to London, with a stop-off to equip himself with some things he needed, and then from London to Edinburgh, leaving him with just a short drive down the east coast and back over the border into northern England. The Citroën seven-seater he'd rented at Edinburgh Airport, under the guise of Mike Palmer, was hidden a long way off, where it couldn't be found. Nobody had seen him make his way on foot to his destination. Nobody knew he was here.

This kind of work was exactly what the SAS had trained Ben for, though he'd been a natural at it even before the military instructors had begun to shape his skills. When staked out around an enemy camp or suspected terrorist base he and his troopers might often have had to remain in position for days on end, totally unseen but missing nothing. On his arrival at Hartington Abbey he'd waited for evening to fall and then used the cover of darkness, wearing his newly-acquired night-vision goggles, to scout out three separate observation posts in different areas of the higher ground overlooking the property, with invisible paths connecting them.

Each of his hidden OPs gave him a separate perspective on Jasper Lockwood's little kingdom, from which different angles he could piece together a complete picture of the layout. From the gatehouse on the road, which lay far off to the south side beyond the estate buildings, a long driveway passed through an avenue of ancient oak trees and under a high stone arch into the main courtyard. The grand entrance to the main abbey building was another great arch, above it the intricate oriel window of what Ben, drawing on his theological studies from long ago, guessed would have been the abbot's living quarters. Adjacent to the main building was a large stone guest house with tall gothic windows and another tower at one end. He was no architect but he would have said it dated back to around the mid-fifteenth century. Other buildings stood among the gardens, like the great thatched tithe barn no doubt built originally to store the abbey's livestock, as well as the share of their crops that the peasant farmers would have been required to donate to the church each year. In another, now mostly ruined, adjoining building, the medieval monks would have spent their simple, silent lives in prayer and worship.

Lockwood's old family residence wasn't in the same league of grandeur as some historic English buildings Ben had seen, like Belmont Abbey in Herefordshire, where monks still followed the sixth-century Rule of Saint Benedict. But it was still pretty damned impressive, with its great archways and castellated towers intact and standing after all these centuries and so many wars and rebellions that had seen much of England's heritage architecture reduced to rubble. No wonder Hugh Mortimer had had such designs on the place, Ben thought. And no wonder its present occupant would go to such lengths to prevent anyone from taking it from him.

Ben was interested in more than just the architecture. Working in shifts from one observation point to another he'd been able to form a three-dimensional map of entrances and exits, main doors and side doors, and a rough sense of the internal layout. He spent hours watching the windows for any glimpse of the person he'd come here to find. The one image of Lord Jasper Lockwood he'd been able to find online showed a small, disagreeable-looking man with a paunch and not much hair on top. This was the man who had ordered the car bombing that cost Aurora her leg, her future, her life's dream. Ben had memorised his face and would know him anywhere.

But for most of that day and a half, the only living soul Ben had seen down there apart from the crows that perched on the roofs, towers and chimney stacks was what appeared to be the sole staff member on the whole Hartington Abbey estate. He was a bent, white-haired old guy who was clearly employed to attend to the gardens but who did nothing much except tinker about in a potting shed. Ben found that very strange. Where were the admin and domestic personnel that must surely be needed to run a concern of this size? Where were the security people at the gatehouse? More importantly, where the hell was Lord Jasper Lockwood? There was no movement to be seen in any of the windows. Nobody emerged from the main building or the adjoining guest house. If Lockwood was at home, then he was either asleep or dead. If he was away, then Ben would wait for his return. He had no problem keeping up his hidden observation posts for as long as it took.

Which, as it turned out, wasn't too long. Just after three that afternoon, the glint of sunlight on an approaching vehicle way down by the gatehouse made Ben train his spotting scope to see a four-wheel-drive SUV roll in through the main gates, come speeding up through the aisle of oak trees, pass under the arch and drive around the buildings to pull up in the courtyard outside the grand entrance.

As Ben watched, the driver's door swung open and the car's solitary occupant jumped out and hurried towards the main building. Ben turned the scope's magnification up full to get a better look at him before he disappeared inside. A man in a beige jacket, not big, not tall. He was bareheaded and didn't seem to have a lot of hair on top. The way he moved suggested a middle-aged man a little stiff from a long drive, his step hurried and agitated as though he was anxious about something. Ben's OP was too far away to be able to make out his features clearly, but he was certain of the identity of who he was seeing.

Lord Lockwood, where have you been hiding?

Ben decided to give the man a few minutes to get settled before paying him his surprise visit. He counted slowly to three hundred. Then packed up his spotting scope and tripod, hid his bag under the bushes, and began making his stealthy, invisible way down towards the estate. It would take him about ten minutes to cut across the orchards and grazing meadows where wild cattle wandered idly in the sunshine, a little longer to make his way through the formal gardens and then the more exposed ground between those and the buildings. He'd already selected the little side door, half hidden amidst the ivy at the foot of the east tower, through which he planned on making his entrance.

The elderly gardener was still fiddling about in his potting shed. Closer up, he looked as though he'd probably worked here at the estate since about 1942. Ben slipped past him and stalked through the gardens, moving from ornamental shrub to planter, from gazebo to statue plinth. Drawing closer and closer to the house. Lockwood had been inside for almost twenty minutes. Enough time for him to kick off his shoes, visit the bathroom, pour himself a drink, flop into a soft chair and relax a little. Which was how Ben wanted him to be when he sprung his surprise.

But now it was Ben's turn to be taken by surprise. And if he hadn't waited for just those few short minutes before making his way to the house, he'd have been caught right out in the open and in trouble. Because suddenly he was no longer the only visitor arriving at Hartington Abbey that afternoon.

With almost no warning, a line of gleaming black limousines came speeding into the grounds, tyres crunching over the gravel, and pulled up in formation in the courtyard. Ben was already beating a tactical retreat through the gardens to avoid being seen. He made it to a low wall and ducked quickly behind it, peering over the top as the car doors opened and tough-looking men in dark glasses and dark suits stepped out and assembled in the courtyard. Serious faces and automatic weapons told him these weren't a bunch of neighbours dropping by for a cup of tea. They were a well-organised and highly professional security detail, but whose? From their olive-skinned complexions and jet black hair they could have been Lebanese or Syrians, Libyans or Iraqis or from just about anywhere in North Africa or the Middle East.

Now Ben had well and truly missed his chance of catching Jasper Lockwood alone. The Lord of the Manor emerged from the main building to greet his guests and stood smiling anxiously under the abbot's archway. A moment later, the rear passenger door of the most stretched out and opulent limo was opened and out stepped a strikingly handsome and elegant man in his thirties, whose dress instantly told Ben that the visitors to Hartington Abbey weren't Syrians or Libyans, but Arabs. He was wearing the flowing white robes and red chequered headgear of a high-up Saudi digni-tary, maybe even a prince judging by the deference of his entourage. Wondering what the hell was going on, Ben watched as Lockwood stepped across to greet the principal guest. They shook hands and spoke for a few moments, then disappeared inside accompanied by a group of armed body-guards while the rest remained outside.

Ben couldn't help wondering what a Saudi royal – if indeed that was who Lockwood's surprise visitor was – could be doing here at Hartington Abbey. It must have to do with money, that was for sure. He could be making some kind of investment in the place, perhaps some development project that Lockwood needed co-financing for. Or maybe the prince was buying it. A property of this scale and historical interest had to be worth a pretty penny. Perhaps that would explain why Hugh Mortimer's purported ownership claim could have been such a particular threat to Jasper Lockwood, coming at a highly inconvenient time when he was looking at making a killing on it.

But those weren't the main thoughts running through Ben's mind at this moment. With the place suddenly swarming with armed men, something told him that the wisest course of action was to pull back to his safe ground without getting caught. He slipped away from behind the wall and made his exit, keeping his head ducked low, darting from cover to cover the way he'd come. This time he very nearly got himself seen by the old gardener, who'd emerged from the potting shed and was setting about starting up a lawnmower, apparently oblivious of the contingent of gun-toting Arabs who'd just invaded the grounds. Maybe this was an everyday occurrence at Hartington Abbey, although Ben somehow doubted it.

Twenty minutes later, back at the edge of the forest and stretched out once more in the long grass with his eye to his spotting scope, he counted eight guards outside the house. Plus five inside, plus their principal, made fourteen. All he could do now was wait and see what happened next. He bided his time, eating a little from his store of provisions and drinking a little water from the two-litre bottle he'd brought. He resisted the urge to smoke, even though there was nobody close enough to smell it. Now and then he checked the scope, but nothing was happening down there. The eight guards in the courtyard mostly remained planted like sentries, taking occasional turns to patrol and circle the house.

An hour passed before he saw any more significant movement. At last, the door of the main entrance opened and the man in the white robes appeared together with Lockwood and the same number of guards who'd accompanied them inside. It looked as if they were leaving. Lockwood and the robed man shook hands again, before the latter got into his limo and one of the guards closed the door. Then the thirteen guards all climbed into their cars, and one by one they rolled away, reforming the same stately procession they'd arrived in. Lockwood watched them go, then returned inside the house. Even from this distance, he looked satisfied with himself, no longer agitated and nervous like before.

Fourteen had arrived. Fourteen had left. Now that whatever business they'd had was done with, the Lord of the Manor was alone again.

And the moment had come for Ben to move back in and conduct some business of his own.

Chapter 40

This time, as he drew closer to the buildings, there were no unexpected arrivals. No squads of armed men patrolling the grounds. Nothing stirred behind the leaded gothic windows of the abbey or the adjacent guest house. No sign of any movement anywhere at all, and nobody to stop him as he crossed the courtyard to the main building.

Ben reached the little iron-studded oak door at the foot of the east tower and wasn't surprised to find it locked. But the original medieval deadbolt that would almost certainly have been impossible to get past had long since been replaced by a more modern Yale lock which, using the little collection of picks he carried in his wallet, he was able to defeat in less than a minute. The door creaked open and he ducked quickly through into the tower. From the low doorway, worn stone spiral steps led him up the inside of the round tower walls until another heavy oak door, this one unlocked, opened into some kind of anteroom to what would have been the abbot's quarters in medieval times. The ceiling was high and vaulted, with elaborate motifs and heads like those of gargoyles carved into the beams. Milky rays of light filtered through narrow arched windows.

What a place to live.

And what a place to die in.

Ben pushed on through the labyrinthine passages and found himself in a part of the building that had been restyled two or three centuries ago, a warren of dim empty rooms, many of them clearly unused since a long time ago, with sad, cold fireplaces, dusty paintings and white drapes over the furnishings, giving the place a ghostly, abandoned air. It would have been easy to believe the abbey was deserted, if he hadn't known Lockwood was in here somewhere.

Deeper inside the building he found a suite of rooms that showed signs of recent habitation. The furniture was undraped, a man's jacket hung over the back of a chair and a copy of a classic car magazine lay on a coffee table. On a fine antique sideboard stood a display of trophies, newly polished and gleaming in the light from a window. They reminded Ben of the archery trophies he'd seen in Hugh Mortimer's home, and in fact they weren't so very different. Among the shiny cups was a small bronze statue of a pistol shooter, aiming his weapon one-handed in the classic target stance. The competition trophies were all engraved with Jasper Lockwood's name and dated back to the eighties and nineties. His Lordship evidently hadn't lost the target sports bug from his old archery days, graduating to more advanced weaponry in later years.

The thought of pistols was a reminder to Ben of how naked he felt without one, alone in enemy territory. Then again, he told himself, he didn't need a gun to deal with the likes of Jasper Lockwood. He moved on with his search of the house. Stalking along corridors, moving in total silence, checking every door. Still no living trace of the man.

Then Ben froze in mid-step. He'd heard something. He stood immobile, holding his breath, straining to hear it again.

The noise had come from behind a door just ahead. The creak of a floorboard, as if someone within the room had sensed his approach and shifted furtively away from the door.

There it was again, the same soft tread. No question about it. Someone was in that room. Someone who knew Ben was there, and didn't want to be found.

And that someone must be Jasper Lockwood.

Ben stepped towards the door and gripped the carved wooden knob. He counted to three, tensed and ready for whatever he might find the other side of the door. He was fully prepared to come face to face with a loaded shotgun. It wouldn't be the first time. He knew what to do. He quietly turned the knob and eased the door open. Just a narrow crack at first, then a little wider, pressing his foot against the bottom of the door in case Lockwood tried to slam it shut.

There was no resistance against the door. No further sound or movement from inside. Had he imagined it? He didn't think so.

Ben swung the door wide open and stepped quickly through it, glancing around him. No shotgun pointing in his face. No Jasper Lockwood on the other end of it. The room seemed to be empty. The bright sunlight filtering in was tinged golden red by the ivy that grew thick around the tall, narrow bay windows. On the inside, the windows had cushioned seats and were flanked by long, heavy drape curtains. In the middle of the room a table was surrounded by chairs. The tall carved fireplace reached almost to the ceiling.

That was when the door slammed shut behind him. And that was when Ben realised that the room wasn't empty after all. The man who'd been hiding behind the door looked similar to the other three who suddenly emerged from behind the window curtains. Dark suits. Black hair and olive skin. Broad shoulders and tight waists and serious, hard expressions.

It was a trap. And the creaking floorboard had been a deliberate lure. In the fraction of a second that Ben had to understand what had happened, he knew he'd been tricked. They must have guessed he was watching the house. Using the distraction of the limousine convoy arriving at the main entrance, they'd sneaked more men in from the opposite side. When the fourteen had left, those extra men had stayed behind. It was a classic piece of deception and he'd walked right into the ambush.

The guy who'd been hiding behind the door came at him from behind and tried to pin his arms behind his back as the other three all rushed him from the front. Ben rocked back hard against the one behind him, throwing all his weight against him and crashing him into the wall and driving the wind out of his lungs, then smashing the back of his head against the guy's face. Simultaneously he was lifting both feet off the ground and driving them with all his force into the chest of the nearest guy charging him from the front. The oncomer was knocked off balance, staggered backwards into his comrade coming up behind him, and they both fell. Then Ben freed himself from the slackened grip of the one behind him, slamming a hard elbow into his throat before spinning back around to plant a closed fist right into the middle of the fourth guy's face.

The fight had started well. The attackers might have had the advantage of surprise but Ben had them on aggression and speed. For a second, all four of his attackers were sprawled on the floor. Without hesitation Ben closed in on the nearest and delivered a brutal groin kick that brought out a screech of agony and made the guy snap into a foetal position. He wouldn't be getting up again for a while. But it wasn't over yet, because the other three were already springing back onto their feet. Ben snatched up one of the chairs from around the table and broke it into splinters over the nearest one's head. The guy went down with a grunt of pain, but in the instant the chair was swinging towards him one of his companions had managed to rush into the gap in Ben's defences and took him down with a lashing kick to his side.

Ben hit the ground rolling. He ignored the flash of pain that lanced through his lower spine. Saw the sole of the shiny black leather shoe coming for his face, caught it in mid-air before it made contact and used the leverage of the guy's foot to twist his lower leg viciously sideways. A crackle of popping cartilage sounded from the guy's knee and a howl burst from his mouth. Still clutching his trapped foot Ben surged back upright and drove him hopping and helpless into the fireplace. He crumpled against the grate and Ben waded in with two savage kicks to his face and throat that put him out of action.

Two down, two to go. The remaining pair were still in the fight, eyeing him warily, looking for the next opening to attack. Ben circled around with his back towards the window, framing himself against the bright sunlight to disorientate them. He said, 'Come on, then. Let's finish it.'

But then the room door burst back open and three more of the same black-haired, olive-skinned, broad-shouldered men in dark suits stepped in.

Chapter 41

Ben didn't move. The three men stepped up to join their comrades. Now the odds had gone back up to one against five. They took off their jackets, rolled up their sleeves and clenched their fists.

No guns or knives. That meant they were intent on taking him prisoner. It also suggested to Ben that they'd been doing enough homework about him to be concerned that he might have been able to capture a weapon from one of them in the struggle and use it against the rest. They'd been perfectly right to worry about that. These guys weren't stupid.

As for why they needed to take him alive, that was an interesting question. But Ben had no intention of hanging around here to learn the answer. Snatching up a piece of the broken chair from the floor he swung it hard against the window behind him and shattered the glass. Then, before anyone could stop him, he leaped up onto the window seat and dived out of the jagged hole in the pane.

Jumping out of a high window to evade getting beaten to a pulp by multiple attackers, it was a question of weighing up one risk against another. Ben could only hazard a guess that the thick ivy around the windows would be growing all up the wall and strong enough to take his weight. If he turned out to be wrong, he was in for a long drop to the courtyard below.

It was a lucky guess. Gripping the rough ivy in both fists he felt it sag away from the stonework, but it held. This was the second time in the last few days that he'd been forced to escape from a window this way, He scrambled down the ivy like an abseiler with his feet planted against the wall. A face appeared through the broken window above him, peered down for an instant and then withdrew. Someone yelled, 'Don't let him get away!' in Arabic, a language in which Ben had become fluent in his SAS days. But he wasn't about to oblige them, if he could help it. The plan to get Lockwood was aborted. His only goal now was to get to safety, regroup, re-evaluate and then reattack.

Ten feet above the ground he let go of the ivy and jumped the rest of the way, landed as he'd been taught in parachute training and instantly sprang back up to his feet and broke into a sprint away from the building. There was no way of knowing how many more men had been lying in wait for him, or how long it would be before they came after him.

Not long.

He'd crossed the courtyard and was tearing across the lawn when he heard the yell in Arabic, 'There he is!' He threw a glance back over his shoulder without slowing down and saw five men chasing him.

Ben ran faster. He hurdled the low wall he'd hidden behind earlier, when the limos turned up. Sprinted along the length of an ornamental hedge and across another stretch of lawn and reached the side wall of the great thatched tithe barn. He paused there to catch his breath and peered around the edge of the barn to see his pursuers coming after him. They'd be here in a matter of moments. His mind worked fast. There wasn't much chance that he could make it all the way back to his refuge on the high ground without them following him. His best option was to try to hide, wait for them to move elsewhere and then slip away unnoticed.

The old tithe barn had two enormous wooden sliding doors held by a padlocked chain, and a smaller man-sized entrance inset to one side. It wasn't locked. Ben ducked through it, found a rusty bolt on the inside and slid it home. With any luck the Arabs would just keep moving on.

It was dark inside the barn, just a few shards of dusty light shining through the cracks between the wooden planking and an ancient ventilation vent high up in the roof. A faint earthy smell emanated from the compacted dirt floor. Long gone were the days when the huge space would have been filled with bushels of corn and barley and sacks of turnips and cabbages and other produce forcibly wrested by way of taxes from the local peasant farmers. In modern times all it contained were a few rustic hand tools stacked in one corner, some fencing materials piled up in another, and a collection of motorised grounds maintenance equipment: ride-on mowers, leaf blowers, an all-terrain buggy hitched up to a trailer. Ben investigated the buggy, thinking of its use as a getaway vehicle. There was no key in the ignition, but there might be a way to get it started.

Too late. They'd caught up with him. And his bluff had failed, because they knew he was here inside the barn. The chain holding the sliding doors rattled, followed by a loud thudding against the smaller inset door. Arabic voices outside; then a crunching splintering rending crack as the bolt tore away from the frame and the door crashed half off its hinges and they came piling through.

Only two of the five had been among the number who'd set on him inside the house, one with a bloody nose and the other a swelling eye. The other three were fresh. As they all came rushing headlong into the barn, Ben quickly turned to the stack of tools in the corner, spotted a four-pronged steel garden fork with a sturdy wooden shaft, snatched it up and turned it on them like a weapon. One came at him; Ben jabbed the fork at his face and forced him back; but then the other four, undeterred, flew at him all at once, and in the rush he got swept off his feet with multiple heavy blows landing on him from all sides. There was a screech as he managed to plant the fork through someone's foot, pinning it to the dirt floor. Then another loud grunt of pain as he slammed a fist into a jaw and felt something give with a crunch. He lashed out left and right, back on his feet now and fighting like a wild man. But he'd lost his defensive weapon and he was being backed into a corner from which there was no escape.

Then there was another shout from the doorway, and more men came charging inside the barn. At that moment, the outcome was sealed.

Ben had been in a lot of fistfights in his life, sometimes against crazy odds. And he'd won many more than he'd lost. But not even a skilled unarmed combat expert like him could successfully see off so many determined opponents all at once. A stunning blow to the side of the head put him off balance. Then a vicious kick that he didn't see coming sent him back to the ground, and they closed in on him, pummelling him so fast that he was at serious risk of being overwhelmed. He fought back as hard as he could and got a few good blows in, broke someone's wrist and someone else's nose.

But it was hopeless, and he knew it. His vision dissolved into a white starburst as another punch caught him square.

He tried to hit back, but someone was clamping his arms so that he couldn't move. One of the injured, streaming blood all down his face, screamed, 'Kill the pig!' 'No,' said another voice, 'we have our orders.'

After a few more blows, he wasn't fighting back any more. They flipped him over on his face in the dirt, bound his wrists behind his back with plastic cable ties and fastened his ankles and knees together so that he couldn't have stood up even if he'd been conscious enough to make the effort. The men grabbed him by the arms, hefted him out of the barn and started dragging him back towards the abbey.

Chapter 42

Consciousness returned slowly and in layers, like awakening from a drugged sleep. With it came the memory of the battering he'd received, along with the pain that filled every part of his body. Lastly came the dawning realisation that he couldn't move, because he was tied securely to a chair. One length of thick rope was wrapped around his chest and another fastened his legs in place. His wrists and ankles were bound with plastic cable ties that had been pulled so tight they were cutting into his flesh. He blinked to focus his blurred, hazy vision and gazed around him. The room was large and high-ceilinged, its walls lined from top to bottom with bookcases. Everything seemed to be swirling.

Ben wasn't alone in the library. Three men in dark suits stood around him like prison guards. Two more were minding the doorway. They stepped aside as the door opened and another man entered the room.

Lord Jasper Lockwood couldn't suppress the wide grin that spread over his face at the sight of his bound, helpless and bloodied captive. He walked across the shiny wooden floor and stood gazing at Ben, savouring the moment. 'Well, well, look what we have here. If it isn't the chap who's been causing me all this trouble. Not looking quite so formidable now, are we, *Major* Hope? Or may I call you Benedict?'

Ben said nothing.

'I'd just as soon instruct these gentlemen to put a bullet in your head,' Lockwood went on. 'I'm sure my man Dexter would love to oblige, once he gets here. Or better still, I'd be only too happy to do it myself. It's been too long since I last pulled a trigger. But perhaps we needn't resort to such extreme measures. I understand that you're in possession of certain information. I invite you to share it with me. If you cooperate, we might be able to avoid any more unpleasantness.'

Ben remained silent. He'd been through this kind of thing before. The SAS took a pretty rough approach to interroga-tion resistance training, which for practical reasons they liked to make as realistic as possible. Being rigorously knocked around, tied to a chair and threatened with various forms of severe violence if you refused to answer questions was all part of the routine. One peep to your interrogators, and you failed the test. Ben had never failed in the past, and he had no intention of failing this time either.

'It's really very simple,' Lockwood said with a conde-scending smile. 'You can make this easy on yourself. All I want to know from you is where Rudi Bergenroth is hiding. I don't even expect you to reveal to me what he knows, because I already have that information. Just his current whereabouts will suffice. Then once we've verified that the information is correct, all this will be over very quickly.'

Which Ben didn't interpret to mean they would let him go. That was where the bullet-in-the-head part would come into play.

'Now do bear in mind,' Lockwood continued, still smiling, 'that it would be very foolish of you to try to protect Bergenroth by lying to us. We simply wouldn't tolerate dishonesty. Likewise, it would be equally unproductive to refuse to speak to us at all, which would only result in our having to resort to more stringent means of persuasion. My associates are very adept at extracting the truth out of people. Their methods aren't particularly gentle. You wouldn't like that to happen, would you?'

Ben stayed quiet.

'You've only got yourself to blame, you know,' Lockwood said, plainly enjoying the moment. 'Just like that idiot Mortimer. I did all I could to warn him off before things had to go to the next level, but did he listen? And you're just as stubborn as he was, aren't you? When my man Chance blew up that silly bitch of a floozy of yours, you could have done the smart thing and backed off. But oh, no, you decided to keep coming after me. And now look where it's got you. Some people just have no sense.'

Ben still said nothing, but the fire that flashed in his eyes at the mention of Aurora said plenty. Lockwood flinched visibly and his smile melted into a sneer. He stepped back. 'All right, Hope, play it any way you like. You asked for it. Farouk, please show our guest that we mean business.'

The man called Farouk had been standing in the background, watching impassively. Now he came forward and stood over Ben. He slowly removed his suit jacket, folded it neatly and handed it to one of his colleagues. Then he took his time unbuttoning his shirt cuffs and rolling the crisp white sleeves up to the elbow. His dark, implacable eyes gazed into Ben's. He braced his feet a little apart. Drew back a clenched fist, rotating at the waist. Then drove the fist hard into the side of Ben's face.

Ben anticipated the impact and rocked his head back to absorb the worst of the blow. It didn't make a lot of difference. The white flash of pain dissolved into little spangling starbursts that blotted out his vision. He shook his head to clear them away. Whatever these men did to him, he wouldn't give them a thing.

Jasper Lockwood seemed to be enjoying the show. 'Hit him again,' he ordered Farouk.

Farouk did as he was told. Another hard blow, another flash of pain. More stars. Ben's head lolled forward with his chin on his chest. He closed his eyes.

'And again,' Jasper said, rubbing his hands together with something like glee. 'Harder this time. Smash his teeth. Break his nose. He'll talk to us. Oh yes, he'll talk to us all right. You wait until we get started with the pliers and the blowtorch.'

Farouk lowered his bloody fist and shook his head. 'Enough. There will be no more punishment for the moment.'

'But I order it!' Jasper snapped at him.

Farouk replied calmly, 'I take orders only from my master, not from you. When my master returns, he will tell us the correct way to proceed.'

Jasper pulled a face. 'Fine, then call him.'

'My master is not to be disturbed.'

'Oh, I see,' Jasper said in sarcastically flowery tones. 'Then when might we expect him to grace us with his presence once more, so that we can continue our business?'

'I have already spoken with him,' replied Farouk. 'He informs me that he will be here early tomorrow.'

'So we just have to sit around waiting until then, do we?'

'My master will not be rushed,' Farouk said, with a raised eyebrow and a warning note in his voice.

Jasper was fuming, but as he glanced around the room at the serious faces of the men it was clear he knew he was powerless over them. 'Very well,' he said, trying to seem unbothered by it. 'Then we'll just have to keep this piece of scum prisoner overnight. Plenty of places we can lock him up. Follow me. And for God's sake don't let blood drip all over the Persian rug.'

The prince's men unfastened the ropes holding their prisoner to the chair. He was drifting in and out of consciousness. With his wrists and ankles still bound tightly together Farouk and three others half-carried, half-dragged him out of the library. Jasper led the way to the abbey's inner courtyard, stopping by a utility room to pick up two long steel torches and a ring of old iron keys that hung on a hook. Then he showed the men through the arches of a medieval cloister and to an ancient oak door inset into the thick stone wall. He unlocked it and showed the men down an echoing stairway to a cellar. It was an ancient barrel-vaulted space that lay deep below the abbey and probably predated it, barred with another heavy oak door. It was so dark down there, with no electric light, that they needed to use the torches to guide their way. Jasper unlocked the cellar door. 'Chuck him in there,' he said, handing Farouk the keys. 'There's no way he can escape.'

'This is not our job,' Farouk objected.

'It's your master who's keeping us all waiting,' Jasper replied acidly. 'So until he returns, Hope is your responsibility. Which means you get to play jailer for a while. All right, boys?'

'That one is a real *ibn al kalb*,' one of the men muttered resentfully in Arabic as Jasper left them to their work. 'Quiet,' Farouk snapped. They dragged the prisoner into the dark, dank cellar and dumped him on the stone floor.

'I think he's dead,' said one, shining his torch down at the inert body.

Farouk shook his head. 'He is alive, for the moment. But soon he might wish he wasn't. Untie his hands and feet.'

'Are you sure?' said another.

'He will not fight,' Farouk said. 'A man knows when he is beaten.'

The ties binding Ben's wrists and ankles were cut with a sharp knife. He lay still on the hard, cold floor. 'Leave him for now,' Farouk ordered them. 'We will return later with some food and water.'

Ben only dimly heard the cellar door slam shut, the scrape of the key in the lock and the echo of their retreating foot-steps in the stairway. Then there was silence. His eyes fluttered open, saw nothing but pitch darkness. He knew he was badly hurt, but felt strangely disassociated from his body. He closed his eyes again and drifted back into unconsciousness.

Chapter 43

Wakefulness came and went. Time dragged on. His captors had taken away his watch along with the rest of his things, and so he had no way of knowing how many hours had gone by before he felt fully alert again. It was only when he tried to move that the pain flooded through his body, making him gasp. He lay there in the darkness, checking himself all over for damage.

He expected to find plenty, and he did. Somewhere under the swelling cuts and bruises under his face was a sharper pain that told him his cheekbone might be broken. Nothing else seemed to be fractured, but he couldn't move his left arm properly and he was pretty sure the shoulder was dislocated. The nausea and dizziness made him think he'd likely sustained a mild concussion, too.

Nothing much he could do about the cheekbone or the concussion. But his shoulder was another matter. He couldn't leave it the way it was. The slightest rotation of the joint in any plane made something grate in there and caused a jolt of fresh agony so intense that he thought he was going to pass out. Gritting his teeth, he managed to rock up to his knees. He had a good idea what to do, because he'd done it before. And he knew from that past experience that this was going to hurt. In fact it was going to hurt like hell. But at least the pain told him he was still alive.

Bent over on his knees on the hard, cold floor, he let his breathing become deep and slow and tried to let his muscles relax until he was in something like a meditative state. He'd once known an Indian Yogi, a tiny, fragile old man with a long white beard, who could bring his heartbeat down to thirty a minute, just by mind control alone. The best Ben had ever managed was about forty-five. He waited until the tension had gone out of his body and the pain seemed remote and distant. His heart gradually settled. Slower. Slower. Fifty-five beats a minute. Fifty. He felt serene, almost dreamy.

Now for the bad bit. If he did it wrong, he could end up with all kinds of tissue damage and make things a lot worse – or he might trap a nerve, which would cause the pain to ramp up tenfold and completely cripple him. If he did it right, he'd still suffer about the worst agony imaginable, but only for a few moments.

Here we go, he thought. Inch by inch, he raised the bad arm until it was bent over his head. His fingers reached downwards, past his ear towards the corner of his jawbone and the side of his neck. The grating and burning inside the shoulder joint were unbearable, but he bore them anyway. *Just another inch*, he told himself as he extended his trembling fingers towards the opposite shoulder. Then with his other hand he rammed the heel of his palm hard against his raised elbow, pushing it upwards and inwards at just the right angle.

Now came the excruciating wash of agony as the dislocated joint popped back into place with an audible *crunch*. He stifled the cry that wanted to burst from his lips. The darkness seemed to swirl around him, and he fought hard to resist the faintness that threatened to swallow him up into a black hole. The sweat poured down his face, stinging the cuts. He breathed hard until the pain began to subside. Then, very tentatively, he tried moving his left arm again, and found that he could. The pain was still there, but much duller now. His range of motion was restored.

Job done. He nodded to himself in grim satisfaction. Maybe not quite fighting fit, but at least he was reasonably functional again. That was all that really mattered to him.

As he sat there in the dark waiting for the pain to ease away more fully, he focused on the thoughts swirling through his mind. Who was the 'master' the guard called Farouk had been talking about? Ben thought it had to be the man in the white robes who'd come to visit Lockwood earlier. He'd looked like a prince, and everyone seemed to treat him like one. Ben half-remembered them saying that the master would be returning to the abbey tomorrow. In the morning? Afternoon? Either way, Ben knew he couldn't be here when that happened. He had to get out of this place.

Slowly, blindly, still nauseous and dizzy, he explored his dark prison. The cellar was twenty paces in length and ten paces in width. There were no windows, because it was deep underground. Just the one door, securely locked from the outside with no keyhole on the inside, making it impossible to pick. When he stood at his full height and reached up with his better arm he could feel that the cellar ceiling was concave like the inside of a barrel. Built for strength by the medieval masons who'd known how to create structures to last a thousand years.

As he ran his fingers along the craggy curve of the ceiling he felt something cold and metallic protruding from the stonework, and realised that it was an ancient hook. At one time, many centuries ago, they must have used this cellar for hanging the venison, pheasant, hare and other game destined for the abbot's table.

Groping around in the blackness Ben found more meat-hooks set into the stone arch. A whole row of them, set about arm's width apart. Thinking about their historical purpose made him think of how hungry he was. That in turn made him think of his jailers. Were they happy to let him starve down here with no food or water? Judging by the way they'd been so careful not to kill him earlier, he didn't think so. They needed him alive, for now. Which meant they needed him healthy, fed and watered for his big day tomorrow, when the prince came back and his interrogation would begin for real, ending with him either tortured to death or his brains blown out.

He put that idea out of his mind. Knowing that sooner or later, perhaps sooner, the guards would return with food and water for him. That was an interesting thought.

He felt around the cellar floor for loose pieces of rock or stone block that might serve as a crude impact weapon when the chance came. There was nothing but dust and grit and rat droppings. Then he turned his attention back towards the meat-hooks overhead. He reached up with both arms, wincing at the pain in his left shoulder, gripped a cold metal hook in each hand and tested them with his weight, raising his feet off the floor and letting himself dangle. No problems there. They were so strongly fixed into the stone that he could have dangled a piano from each one. When he raised himself higher up by the hooks until his head touched the ceiling, he found that there was some kind of stone ledge above the barrel-vaulted curve of the roof supports.

Now that interesting thought in his mind was slowly developing into something fuller, and the aches and pains in his body, the dizziness and the nausea were easier to ignore. With a grunt of effort he hauled himself right up, got a purchase on the stone ledge and found that it was wide enough for him to scramble on top of it and wedge himself in, with just enough headroom to crouch hunkered down on his knees and elbows.

He clambered up onto the ledge and got himself into position. It wasn't exactly comfortable but he felt better up here, poised in his little secret nook eight feet above the floor. Alone and alert in the darkness. Back in his element. He might be injured, but an injured predator could be even more dangerous.

Like a hungry leopard perched in a tree.

Waiting.

Chapter 44

Late that evening, some of the men were sitting around the table in the brightly lit abbey kitchen playing cards while others lounged in a servants' recreation room nearby, watching an explosive action thriller on TV. At this moment, nobody knew or much cared where Lord Lockwood had taken himself off to. He'd last been seen stumping off upstairs to his private quarters, muttering discontentedly to himself. They'd been glad to see the back of him for a while.

While the others were relaxing, Farouk had got on the phone once more to his master in Edinburgh, to update him on the latest developments and confirm that he would be arriving at Hartington Abbey first thing in the morning with the rest of his entourage.

When the call was over, Farouk rejoined the men in the kitchen. He looked at his watch and said, 'Time to check on the prisoner. Tareq, Musa, take water and something to eat down to the cellar. We have to keep him well until morning.'

Armed with a long metal torch, the ring of keys and a tray loaded with a jug of water, some crusts of dry bread and a banana from the kitchen, Tareq and Musa dutifully headed back outside and through the shadowy cloister to the cellar door. Tareq unlocked the outer door by torchlight while Musa held the tray. Then the pair descended the stairway, their steps echoing in the narrow passage. They listened at the inner door, heard nothing, exchanged shrugs and opened it up and stepped inside. Tareq shone the torch beam towards the area of bare stone floor where they'd left the prisoner lying motionless, seemingly dead. He wasn't there any longer. The torch beam swept around the room, searching for where the prisoner had moved to. He couldn't go far in such a small space.

But there seemed to be no sign of him. 'He's gone,' Musa said in a low voice filled with fear. Having to face Farouk's rage if something had gone wrong would be bad enough. The prince's wrath would be far more severe.

'It's impossible,' Tareq replied, shining the torch here and there and barely able to believe his own eyes. 'He couldn't have escaped. The door was locked. There are no windows. He must be in here somewh—'

There was no sound, no warning. The next thing Musa and Tareq knew, a dark shadow seemed to detach itself from the arched cellar ceiling above their heads, dropped down and flattened them both to the floor. The tray fell with a crash and the water jug burst apart. The heavy steel torch that Tareq had been shining around the cellar clattered over the flagstones. Then the light flashed in a wild arc as the torch was snatched up and came lashing down, first at Tareq's head and then at Musa's, in two fast and savage blows aimed with enough skull-crushing force to incapacitate or kill.

It was all over in an instant. The men had never stood a chance.

Ben stood over the inert bodies with the torch in his hand. As brief as the violence had been, the effort had left him gasping and dizzy and unsteady on his feet. The nausea of his concussion had come flooding back with a vengeance and his shoulder had started throbbing again. He dropped down on his knees next to the two motionless shapes on the floor. Checked their pulses. Neither was dead. He could easily and quickly have finished them off if he'd so chosen, but he lacked both the energy and the heart. Instead he dug through their pockets for the ring of keys, found it, staggered to his feet and over to the cellar door.

When he'd locked the men inside, he flung the keys into a dark, dusty corner and began making his way up the steps. Reaching the top he pushed through the outer door and stood there leaning against a cloister arch, sucking in gasps of the cool night air and waiting until he got his breath back again. His vision still wasn't quite right. He rubbed his eyes, and flinched at the sharp stab of pain from his damaged cheekbone. He knew he was in no kind of condition to go hunting for Jasper Lockwood now. To even attempt to take on the armed heavies protecting him would be suicide. No, his only option was to escape to safety, try to fix himself up and recuperate as quickly as possible, then return to finish what he'd started. Or die trying.

For the moment, he had to try to remember the way they'd brought him here earlier, bound and half unconscious. Though he'd been playing deader than he really was, his memory was fogged and it was a mental struggle to retrace his steps. He kept hold of the torch, to use as a weapon if necessary, but he didn't dare to turn it on in case one of his enemies spotted the light. From the cloister he groped his way to the inner courtyard, then found a little flagstone path through a garden that skirted the side of the abbey and led him back to the main courtyard. He was on more familiar ground here, and there was enough starlight to see by. His main worry now wasn't being unable to orientate himself out of here, but whether he could make it any distance through the grounds before he collapsed.

But he did make it, and he didn't collapse. Not yet. One step at a time, willing himself to keep moving as he threaded his uneven way through the darkness towards the edge of the abbey gardens and beyond. The wild cattle had settled for the night. At last he reached the edge of the slope that led towards the trees. Just another burst of energy and he'd be in the safety of the forest.

He paused a few moments, resting in a nook among the bushes. Looking up he picked out the seven bright stars of Ursa Major, the constellation of the Plough. From there he could trace a line across to Polaris, which gave him the sky clock he'd been trained to read in the military when all other technology failed.

The sky clock told him that it was somewhere around 3 a.m. The position of Polaris also gave him a bearing for where he'd hidden his rental car, a good mile and a half away on a small lane the other side of the forest. He wasn't sure if he could make it that far on foot, in his condition. The pain racking his whole body seemed to grow more crippling with every step. And besides, his captors had taken his car key along with his watch and wallet. He worried that in his present state, his mind might be too foggy to be capable of breaking past the vehicle's security system and hotwiring the ignition.

All things considered, he decided that rather than try to return to the car he should aim to cut through the trees to the thickest part of the forest, make himself a hidden camp there and hole up for as long as necessary before he felt ready to move on again. He lacked a knife or any other tool for cutting twigs and branches or excavating a basic shelter, but he could rely on his survival skills to go to ground like a hunted animal and be unfindable by the enemy.

All these things he knew he'd have to get done soon, before Lockwood's thugs discovered his escape and came looking for him. And before his own dwindling energy levels ran down to nothing and he was incapable of going another step. Reluctantly dragging himself away from his nook among the bushes he started up the slope towards the forest treeline. He was absolutely determined to make it. But he knew he was in trouble. A wounded soldier stranded in hostile territory, alone and unsupported with all the odds stacked against him. At tough times like these, the motivational lines by James Elroy Flecker that were carved on the memorial clock tower at the SAS's old HQ in Hereford always came back into his mind.

We are the Pilgrims, Master: we shall go
Always a little further: it may be
Beyond that last blue mountain barred
with snow,
Across that angry or that glimmering
sea

Always a little further. Always . . . a little . . . further. On and on he went. He reached the treeline and slipped through the shadows of the forest. He felt safer here, and confident that he could evade all but the most skilled and relentless pursuers. But at the same time, he could feel his strength ebbing with every plodding step.

Still, he wouldn't give up, not even when every cell in his body was screaming at him that he needed rest. He kept putting one foot in front of the other. Thorny bushes ripped at his legs and twigs lashed his face. He stumbled over fallen logs and into ruts filled with mud. Sometimes he kept going even when the rest of his body and mind had gone to sleep.

Deep in the thick woods, the tree canopy prevented him from telling the time from his constellation and now he'd completely lost his bearings. The forest seemed to go on and on for ever. Everything seemed to be spinning. He stumbled and fell, and lay there in the dirt and the dead leaves and moss for a while, trying to will himself to get back on his feet. Twisting his head, he thought he could see an odd sort of light flickering through the trees from further up ahead. And straining his ears, he thought he could hear something, too: the sound of voices.

But it was all so distant, as though it belonged to another reality. In this reality he was sinking, sinking, his eyes were closing and his body was being drawn down into a soft dark abyss.

Then he was gone, drifting deep into unconsciousness.

He didn't know how much time had passed before his eyes fluttered back open again. He was lying on his back on the soft, spongy forest floor, looking straight up at the night sky through a circle of treetops. But somewhere close by stood another circle, made up of the silhouettes of strange dark figures that had gathered around where he lay and were peering down at him. The soft glow of flickering firelight behind them seemed closer now.

For a confused, disorientated instant he thought the figures were more of his enemies, come to recapture him and take him back to the abbey to be tortured and killed. He started trying to struggle to his feet. But then a strong hand firmly but gently pushed him back down, and a deep gruff voice said, 'Take it easy now, buddy. You're in a bad way.'

Ben lay back. The sharp throbbing in his head and face felt as though someone was whacking him with a peen hammer at every heartbeat. He managed to groan, 'Who are you?'

The gruff voice spoke again. It replied, 'We're angels.'

Chapter 45

At that late hour of the night, the gang had been winding down from a bout of serious partying in their favourite secluded woodland spot when one of them quite accidentally came across the man's body among the bushes. The discovery had been made by a young bike club devotee called Darren Dixon, though he'd much rather have been known by a tough-sounding nickname such as Mad Dog or Butch or Grinder, like some of his more senior and higher-ranking peers. Darren was just nineteen and what was officially termed a Hang-around, the lowest-ranking of his order with a long road ahead of him before he could graduate to the level of a Prospect, and then finally the fully-patched lifelong chapter member he dreamed of becoming.

Along with his lack of a club patch, Darren also didn't have quite the tolerance for alcohol of some of the older men he idolised, like Sprocket, Taz and Izzy. who could each down an entire bottle of Wild Turkey or Rebel Yell in a single session and still be able to ride their bikes in a straight line. After several too many shots of the hard stuff that night, Darren had wandered away from the camp fire to relieve himself (and maybe throw up) at a discreet distance. But then, half-blind inebriated as he was, he'd lost his way and ended up stumbling about among the trees. Then he'd tripped over something that wasn't a tree root or a rock hidden among the dead leaves, and gone sprawling in the dirt.

As he scrambled drunkenly to his feet Darren felt around for the much-prized knuckle duster that had fallen from the pocket of his denim cut-off, and instead found what felt very much to him like a human hand on the ground. Which freaked him out somewhat at first, until he found that the hand was attached to an arm, and the arm to a body. Thrilled at having come across an actual real-life corpse, he suddenly found his bearings and became instantly sober enough to stumble back to the camp fire and alert the others to his cool discovery.

'Shit, guys, come and see! There's a fuckin' stiff in the woods!'

Sprocket, Izzy and Taz had wandered over to check out the dead guy, accompanied by their fellow full members Weezer and Nikko and a couple of the Prospects, Sven and Ox, the latter nursing a bandaged hand from his earlier scuffle with another called Little Mick. Sprocket's girlfriend Rusty, whose real name was Deb and who was training to be a nurse when she wasn't being an outlaw biker chick and pillion seat decoration, followed out of curiosity. Rusty couldn't personally be admitted to the gang, females being denied membership as a rule, but as an honorary tag-along and unofficial medical officer, she was much respected by the rest.

'This guy ain't dead,' Sprocket said thoughtfully, after nudging the corpse with the toe of his boot and seeing it stir slightly.

'What you reckon he's doing out here on his own?' asked Sven.

'Fucker could be an undercover pig,' rumbled Ox. 'Come to fuckin' spy on us.' This was a potential concern, since their chapter had had its fair share of troubles with the police and they were always on the lookout for snitches and narks and the like. One of the primary tenets of their organisation was ACAB: All Cops Are Bastards. Needless to say, nobody who had ever served in the law enforcement line or judiciary system, in any shape or form whatsoever, could be remotely eligible for membership. In the gang's world, such individuals were universally regarded as the lowest form of subhuman scum.

'Nah, I don't think so,' said Taz, bending down to examine the apparently still-living stranger more closely by the flame of his lighter. 'This guy's had the shit kicked out of him. Looks like he's pretty badly banged up.'

They were debating what to do with him when the stranger's eyes fluttered open and he tried to get up. 'Who are you?' he managed to ask.

'We're Angels,' Sprocket said. Then the stranger passed out again.

'We've got to get him back to the camp,' Rusty said. 'Let me take a look at him. We can't let the poor sod go and croak on us.'

Once they'd determined as best they could that the injured man could be safely transported, the Angels carried him back to their camp where they built the dying fire back up to a bright blaze and laid him carefully down in its light and warmth. Their tents were rigged up in a circle at a distance from the camp fire, each one with a motorcycle parked up beside it. Darren's little Yamaha was the sole non-Harley, only tolerated because the kid was working hard to save up for his first proper man's machine.

The stranger from the woods wasn't the only casualty on whom Rusty had had to ply her medical skills that night. The gang's parties tended to be somewhat riotous, and it wasn't unusual for fights to break out. This one had kicked off when Little Mick had drunkenly stumbled into Ox's custom Fat Boy and knocked it off its sidestand, damaging a mirror and scratching some of the chrome. With a howl of anguish, Ox had lumbered over to pick up his beloved mount, then charged Little Mick like an enraged bear and swung one of those ham-sized fists at him. But being much quicker and less sozzled than the big guy, Little Mick managed to duck the blow; whereupon Ox's fist connected with a solid tree trunk and broke three knuckles. Rusty had patched him up with painkillers and a bandage from her first-aid kit. Now she attended to the stranger's cuts and bruises, a couple of which she thought might need stitches. And that cheekbone didn't look too good, either. Taking advantage of his unconscious state to tentatively probe the injury, she could be all but certain nothing was broken in there. It was a wonder that his nose was still intact, too, after the pasting he'd taken. Somewhere under all those bruises he wasn't half bad-looking, she thought to herself.

It was while she was dabbing antiseptic on his wounds that the stranger woke up again. 'Where am I?' he muttered.

'You're safe here with us,' grumbled their leader, who was sitting by the fire puffing on the stub of a fat cigar and watching his girlfriend at work. 'But more to the point, *who* are you?'

'My name's Ben,' Ben replied. 'Ben Hope.'

'Lucky we found you, mate. Lucky for you, that is.' The biker held out a brawny, oil-stained hand that was mostly blue with tattoo ink and had half an index finger missing. He was maybe eight years older than Ben, with thick wiry hair just beginning to silver. His eyes were slitted, sharp and strikingly blue, and he gave off the supremely confident aura of someone who'd been through a lot and could handle himself well. 'Name's Sprocket. This ugly bunch of misfits are Izzy, Taz, Ox, Mack, Nikko, Sven, Weezer and Smokey. And this lovely lady who's patching you back together again is Rusty.'

'Fix you up good as new, mate,' said Smokey, nodding affectionately Rusty's way.

'Sorted me out more than once,' Nikko concurred.

'And me,' said Izzy. 'Like when I done my knee in comin' off the Wide Glide at ninety. Couldn't exactly call a fuckin' ambulance, could I? Seeing what I was carrying in my saddle-bags at the time,' he added with a sly smile.

With names like that Ben thought the gang sounded like a sixties' pop group, but he was grateful to them for having rescued him. Rusty looked sweet and pretty despite a few too many piercings, though the men were a grungy lot with their long unkempt hair, grizzled beards, enough inkwork between them to have kept a backstreet tattoo artist in work for a year, gruff flinty expressions and scuffed metal-studded leathers covered in patches and badges. It wasn't until he saw the jacket hanging from the handlebar of a nearby motorcycle, with its winged skull logo across the back and the legendary name emblazoned underneath, that he understood what they'd meant by 'Angels'. He'd heard of local British chapters of the famous American biker club, but never met any of the real deal before.

'So what's the prognosis, darlin'?' Sprocket asked Rusty with a nod to their patient.

'He's been in the wars, all right,' she replied. 'But I reckon it looks worse than it is. I don't think your cheekbone is broken,' she told Ben. 'I'm pretty sure you've got some minor concussion, though.' She asked him a few pertinent questions about headaches and blurred vision, dizziness and nausea and a few other telltale symptoms, and peered closely into his pupils. 'I'll pop a couple of stitches into that cut on your cheek. The rest of it should heal up okay on its own.'

Sprocket said, 'Sounds like you'll live, buddy.'

'I'll bet it hurts like a bugger, though,' chuckled Izzy. 'Here, get some of this down yer neck.' He passed Ben a whisky bottle, one of the few lying around that weren't empty. Managing to sit a little more upright, Ben put the bottle to his lips and took a long gulp. The others looked on approvingly.

'Have some of this as well,' Nikko said, handing Ben a joint so large it resembled something like a carrot. 'Pep you up a bit.'

Ben wasn't into recreational drugs, never had been, but he figured that anything that could help with the pain and dizziness could only be beneficial. He took a few puffs of the joint and felt a little better already. How long the effect might last, he couldn't say. But whatever weird chemistry was happening inside his brain as a result, it seemed to be helping.

'So what were you doing out here in the woods?' Taz asked, still a little suspicious of the stranger. 'And how'd you get all punched up anyway?'

'You on the lam, mate?' asked Mack. Judging by the wolfish grins around the camp fire, it seemed as if the idea of his being some kind of wanted desperado on the run appealed to the Angels quite a bit.

Ben could see no reason to hide the truth from them. And so, as the whisky and whatever concoction was in that joint began to take more of an effect on him and the pain gradually faded into the background, he recounted the whole story.

Chapter 46

Or, at any rate, he told them enough to cover all the main points. He somehow didn't think that the Northumberland chapter of the infamous Hell's Angels Motorcycle Club would be too interested in learning about political plots and skul-duggery five centuries old, historic rivalries over the throne of England or the legitimacy or otherwise of the entire Tudor dynasty. Boiling it down to the basics he began by explaining, 'Down there in the valley, there's a big old house. The guy who lives in it is a lord.'

It was clear that Ben's new companions weren't too impressed by Jasper Lockwood's social status. 'Arsehole,' Nikko spat. 'Like all of them.'

'I know the place,' Sprocket said. 'Ridden by there a few times. Heard some posh bloke lived there. So this Lord Whatever, you and he have some kind of disagreement?'

'You might say that,' Ben replied.

'What'd the prick do?' Taz asked. 'Set his fuckin' bailiffs on you for poaching rabbits on his land?'

'Been there, done that,' said Ox.

'Not exactly,' Ben said. 'He had his thugs put a bomb in a car with an innocent woman inside, blew her up and maimed her for life.'

Which seriously displeased the Angels, because even though theirs was a men-only organisation, their code of honour regarding the treatment of women was unambiguous and strictly upheld. It didn't seem to surprise them too much that a Lord of the Manor could be capable of such things.

'Was she killed?' asked Rusty, frowning deeply.

'Just her career,' Ben replied. 'And her future. And her whole life's dream, everything she'd worked for. You won't get to Covent Garden on just one leg. But other people got it worse.'

'Sounds like there's a lot more to this story. Why don't you go back to the beginning and tell us the whole thing?' said Sprocket, who Ben was starting to understand was the keenest intellect of the gang. But the others were a surprisingly insightful and quick-witted bunch too. As enthralled as they were disgusted by his account, they peppered him with questions from all angles as he laid it out for them.

'So this professor bloke, what'd he want you for?'

'For protection,' Ben said. 'Except I didn't realise it at the time.'

'Yeah, but why you?'

'Because of what I used to do for a living.'

'A living,' Ox laughed. 'I used to have one of them, too.'

'So what was that, mate?' Izzy asked more seriously.

'You weren't a copper, were you?' Nikko wanted to know, with a look of deep suspicion.

'No, I wasn't a copper.'

'Then what were you?'

He had no real option but to tell them. Given their fairly obvious anti-establishment leanings, Ben wasn't sure how they'd react to his having spent a long time in the military. He needn't have worried, because it turned out that both Mack and Weezer had served in the British army for a while. 'I was a corporal, Yorkshire Regiment,' Weezer said proudly. 'You?'

'Major,' Ben replied. '22 Special Air Service.'

Ox guffawed, 'Fuck off. Don't give us that bollocks.'

Ben shrugged. 'I don't need you to believe me.'

But as the bikers grew more convinced that he was telling the truth, they were awed to be in the presence of a bona fide SAS guy. Ben soon understood why they resonated so much with the achievement of getting into the most legendary Special Forces unit in the world. As Sprocket explained, the challenge of being accepted into their noto-riously exclusive club represented the perfect parallel to the journey of a fledgling SAS hopeful. It could take years and years to graduate through their ranks from being a lowly hangout member – 'like young Darren here,' he said, pointing at the blushing nineteen-year-old – to being welcomed in as a full member entitled to proudly wear the patch, with all the honours and privileges that came with it. The winged dagger badge proudly worn by those who made it into the SAS was no different, as far as they were concerned.

'Cut a long story short,' said Taz, before Ben could get any deeper into his story. 'This lord bloke—'

'Lockwood. Jasper Lockwood.'

'Right. This Lockwood arsehole fucked you over and hurt your woman.'

'She's not exactly my woman,' Ben said.

'But he fucked her up good and proper and you're pretty pissed off about it, yeah? That's what this is all about.'

'That, and the two innocent men they murdered. One of them was a soldier, too, back in the day. They shot him in the guts. I watched him die. The first one, they drowned. And they'll keep doing it.'

Sprocket nodded pensively. 'That's bad. But nobody does this evil shit for no reason, unless they're a fuckin' psychopath. This guy Lockwood, what's he after?'

'The usual,' Ben said. 'It all comes down to money. Protecting what he has. And wanting more.'

'Tell us something new,' said Sven.

Sprocket said, 'All right, I think we get the picture. Question is, brother, what are you gonna do about it?'

'First I'm going to finish getting stitched back together by the lovely Rusty here,' Ben said.

'You bet, sweetie,' Rusty said with an alluring smile.

'Next I'm going to drink some more of that whisky, and smoke some more of this.' He held up the half-finished joint. It seemed to be having an amazing effect on him, better than any painkiller. 'Whatever the hell this is.'

'Good old-fashioned weed,' said Nikko. 'Laced with a little crystal methamphetamine. It's my own personal recipe. Does it for me.'

Now Ben understood why he'd started feeling so much better so quickly after virtually his first puff of the stuff. Methamphetamine had been used widely in warfare for many decades after its invention by a German chemist in the late 1800s. In World War II the British authorities called it Benzedrine and issued it by the truckload to infantry, tank crews and RAF bomber pilots to increase mental alertness, boost morale and eliminate fatigue, pain, hunger and the brain-frazzling effects of living constantly in the shadow of violent bloody sudden death. Military commanders like Field Marshal Montgomery had praised its ability to make soldiers fight harder and for longer. The US Army loved it too, while the Nazi Wehrmacht called it Pervitin and even spiked chocolate with it. Japanese Kamikazes dosed themselves heavily before their final missions, to make them feel invulnerable. At least those guys hadn't needed to worry about the drug's powerful addictive qualities.

'Whatever gets the job done,' Weezer laughed.

'I get the feeling that's not all you're planning on doing, mate,' Sprocket said to Ben, eyeing him keenly in the light of the flickering camp fire.

'You're right,' Ben replied. 'When I've done all that, I'm going straight back down the hillside to Lockwood's place. I'm going to grab him by the hair and drag him out of the house kicking and screaming. Then I'm going to put a bullet right here between his two eyes.' He tapped the centre of his forehead with his index finger.

He'd said it with such cold deliberation, such a look of absolute sincerity, that the bikers knew he meant every word. The older men, Sprocket, Izzy and Taz, pursed their lips and looked thoughtful. After a moment's awestruck silence Nikko and a few others burst into huge grins. 'Seriously? Fuckin' excellent!'

'Count me in,' said Smokey. 'Oh, man. This I've got to see.'

'And me,' Nikko echoed.

'I'd give my bike to be there,' Mack mused.

'Careful,' Weezer said. 'I think he means it.'

Sprocket cut them off short with an authoritative wave of his four-fingered hand. 'Nobody's in until I say they're in.'

The Angels' camp fire was dying. Rusty picked up some more pieces of dead wood and tossed them on, sending up a little shower of embers like fireflies. There was a silence. Sprocket tossed his stogie into the flames and then lit up a

330

fresh cigar. He turned to Ben. 'You're talking about some heavy shit here, my friend. How serious are you about this?'

'As serious as it gets,' Ben replied.

'That's what I thought. You look it. So what's the deal? This guy Lockwood, is he alone down there or does he have help?'

'When I left the place he had about eight men with him,' Ben said. 'But more were on the way. They could be arriving come daylight. Doesn't leave much time to get in there sooner, so they'll have to be dealt with too.'

'How many more?' Sprocket asked.

'By my count, about another thirteen,' Ben said. 'Not counting their leader.'

Sprocket nodded. 'More than twenty men altogether.'

'Enough to keep me busy.'

'Are they armed?'

'To the eyeballs,' Ben said. 'These aren't the same bunch Lockwood was using before. They're in a different class. Professionals.'

'And what about you?'

'I'm a professional too,' Ben said.

'But you're not armed. Not that I can see.'

'I'll figure that one out as I go along.'

Sprocket nodded again. 'All right. So let's say you do. Then what? You reckon you're just going to walk in there and take on all these people by yourself?'

'It's how I do things,' Ben said. 'I work alone these days.'

'Ain't been working out too well for you lately though, has it?' Sprocket chuckled, pointing at Ben's battered face. 'Looks like these boys gave more than you bargained for.'

'I wasn't expecting them,' Ben replied. 'This time, they won't be expecting me.'

'I don't know,' Sprocket said doubtfully. 'Seems to me like you could do with some backup from the iron horse cavalry, my friend.'

Ben shook his head. 'I'm not asking for anyone's help. I won't be responsible for what might happen down there.'

'I know you wouldn't ask,' Sprocket said with a dry smile. 'I can see that's not your style, and I'm cool with it. But what if someone was to offer their support?'

Ben looked at him. 'Why would you do that?'

'Because some stuck-up piece of shit who thinks he can go rolling over people just because he's got the power and wealth,' Sprocket said, 'well, that's the kind of bastard we really don't take too kindly to. Is it, boys?'

'Amen,' said Izzy.

'He needs his arse kicked,' said Weezer.

'Big time,' Smokey agreed.

'I appreciate the offer,' Ben said. 'It's a generous one. But with respect, like I said, these men are professionals. I know you pride yourselves on being tough—'

'But we're just a bunch of hairy bikers, is that right?' Izzy finished for him, scowling.

'Don't misunderestimate the Angels, man,' warned Taz. The others said nothing, but didn't look happy.

Ben could see that he'd offended them. 'I wouldn't like anyone else to get hurt, that's all.'

'Relax, boys,' Rusty said. 'He didn't mean anything by it.'

Sprocket had a look that told Ben he was working over an idea in his mind. He said, 'Remember what Iz was saying before, about coming off his Wide Glide?'

Ben nodded. 'At ninety. That's an experience.'

'And how he needed fixing up kind of discreet, like, because of what he was carrying in his saddlebags?'

Ben said, 'I remember.'

'Thing is, see,' Sprocket told him, 'we do a bit of trade on the side. It's how we make a lot of our cash. Not that we can make a fortune out of it. But as long as it pays for our petrol and a few treats on top, we're happy.'

'I thought maybe it had something to do with the meth-laced weed,' Ben said.

Sprocket made the same kind of sly smile that Izzy had made before. 'That, and other things. Show him, Iz.'

With a grin, Izzy got up and walked back through the circle of tents to where his Harley stood gleaming dully in the firelight. He walked with a slight limp. Probably the result of that high-speed crash, though he could have come off a lot worse. The motorcycle was heavily customised and fitted with big black leather saddlebags, Pony Express style, draped over the rear mudguard where the pillion seat should be. Izzy bent down to unbuckle the straps of one of the saddle-bags, opened it, and pulled out the item that was carefully hidden inside, wrapped in an oily rag. An item that would have earned him at least five years in prison if he was caught in possession of it. But then, Ben figured that was the outlaw ethos of the gang. To not give a shit. And to not get caught.

Izzy stumped back over carrying the item, and handed it to Ben. It was a shotgun, but not the kind that Ben had been used to handling in combat. This one had started life, prob-ably quite a few decades ago, as a bog-standard, plain-Jane double-barrelled twelve bore, the kind of basic utilitarian device that could once be found propped up next to the door of every farm cottage in rural Britain, for protecting livestock from foxes and bringing in the odd rabbit or pigeon to stick into a pie. But somewhere in its history, someone had taken a saw to both ends and turned it into the shortest scatter-gun Ben had ever seen. The barrels were cut off flush with the wooden fore-end and were only about nine inches long. At the other end, most of the stock had been cut away, leaving just the pistol grip. The result was a weapon you could easily tuck inside a coat pocket or even stick into your belt, like a pirate's pistol of old. It had twin hammers that had to be manually cocked, and no kind of safety catch. Two triggers set one behind the other, the front for the right barrel and the rear for the left. Simple, solid engineering that would last centuries. Not an accurate piece by any means. You wouldn't go hunting with it. But as a crude across-the-room combat blaster the sawn-off would be hard to beat.

'I won't even ask you where you got this thing,' Ben said, turning it over in his hands. He cracked open the breech and peered through the empty chambers at the fire. The twin bores were smooth and polished.

'We have our resources,' Sprocket replied enigmatically. 'And our clientele. We don't sell to no fuckin' villains or armed robbers, no one like that, only to our fellow brethren who're in need of something to protect themselves. But business is getting harder and the supply's getting tighter all the time. Bastard government have got us all wrapped up in this country.'

'Take me to America, man,' muttered Ox, shaking his head wistfully. 'Daytona, Florida. That's where I want to be.'

'Got a full belt of ammo for her in my other saddlebag,' Izzy said, pointing at the gun. 'Twenty-five rounds, three-inch magnum loads. Enough power to knock down a fuckin' brick wall with.'

'Are you offering to sell this to me?' Ben asked.

'She's not for sale. She's mine. What I call my peace of mind gun.'

'We've all got them,' Taz interjected. 'Everyone except the prospects and the hang-arounds, that is.'

'I got a pocket knife, and my knuckles,' Darren piped up. Weezer cuffed him affectionately over the back of the head.

'Not trying to sell you anything, mate,' Sprocket told Ben. 'But we're happy to let you make use of it, if it'd help.'

'It'd help,' Ben said. 'That's for sure.'

'You need some wheels too,' said Ox. 'I can't ride with this busted hand. Borrow my Fat Boy if you want it.'

'Ox can ride pillion with me,' said Weezer.

Ben was astounded by their generosity. 'I have a car, but it's parked a long way off.'

Izzy grinned. 'Bollocks to that. Why go around in a four-wheeled cage when you can ride free?'

'You *can* ride a bike, can't you?' Nikko asked.

'I can ride,' Ben said.

'Besides, you'll be rolling along with us,' Sprocket said. 'We can't show ourselves up, can we?'

'I'll borrow the gun,' Ben told them. 'I'll even borrow the bike. But I'm not borrowing manpower. I told you, I don't want the responsibility.'

But the suddenly hardened, fierce and scowling expressions around the camp fire told him he'd offended them again. Maybe not a wise move to make.

'We take responsibility for ourselves,' Sprocket said. 'Nobody fuckin' tells us what to do. And we've decided we want to help. So you just try and stop us.'

Chapter 47

Musa and Tareq had been gone almost an hour before anybody realised there was a problem. Farouk and three others grabbed their weapons and more torches and hurried down to the cellar. Everything seemed normal from outside the locked door. But then one of the men happened by chance to shine his light on the ring of keys lying in a dusty corner, and they realised what must have happened.

'Open it! Quickly!' Farouk ordered them, fearing the worst. And his fears were soon proven true, when the cellar door swung open and their torch beams landed on the inert bodies of their two associates. The prisoner had gone.

Musa and Tareq weren't dead, but they were both comatose from their head injuries and in need of a hospital. Right now, that was Farouk's bottom priority. If they didn't recapture the fugitive before his Highness arrived early in the morning, there would be hell to pay. Farouk reasoned that Hope wasn't in any condition himself to have gone very far. Then again, the man wasn't so badly hurt that he couldn't take out two strong, fit opponents. Catching him again, and doing so without killing him, wasn't going to be easy.

Farouk quickly got things organised. The limp, unresponsive Musa and Tareq were carried from the cellar and laid on couches in the servants' recreation room, while six men armed themselves with machine pistols, walkie-talkies and all the spare ammunition they could carry, and set off in the four-wheel-drive estate buggy. The manhunt would begin with a sweep of the abbey grounds and then widen out to the surrounding countryside. Farouk could only pray they found him quickly.

It wasn't long before Lord Lockwood, disturbed from his night's rest by all the commotion, hurried downstairs in his silk dressing gown to be told the news of Hope's escape. His reaction was predictable.

'WHAT! HOW IS IT POSSIBLE THAT YOU COULD FUCK THAT UP?'

'We untied him,' Farouk admitted. 'I did not believe he could get away. It was a mistake.' It was the nearest that the tough, capable Arab could come to being sheepish, but even so he wasn't going to let himself be humiliated by this belligerent little man. 'Hope will soon be back in our hands,' he asserted with a lot of outward confidence. 'There is nothing to worry about.'

But as the night wore on, Farouk was beginning to look less confident. The search party were radioing back every thirty minutes to report their total lack of success. They'd checked every corner of the estate as best they could and were now beginning a sweep of the higher ground and the woodland beyond. But it would take many more men to be able to comb so much ground effectively. Even then, it could take days. And Hope would be getting further away with every passing minute, in any given direction.

As the first light of dawn approached and still no trace of him, Farouk knew it was futile. But he didn't dare to alert his Highness. 'Keep trying!' he yelled into his radio.

Meanwhile, Jasper Lockwood had returned to his own lavish suite of rooms, but he hadn't gone back to bed. And in fact he'd done very little sleeping that night, because his mind was buzzing too much to relax. He'd been brooding all day and all night about the way Prince Hassan was treating him. How dare this spoilt rich brat force his arm like this, conning him out of fifty-five million pounds with blackmail and threats?

'No bloody raghead is going to dictate terms to me,' he muttered under his breath, over and over again. 'Who does that jumped-up shit think he is?' Now as he restlessly paced up and down, pausing occasionally to look out at the gradually lightening sky, the scheme that had been slowly forming in his head began to take shape. And if His Royal Highness thought he was the only one who could manipulate the situation to his advantage, he was about to get the lesson of his life.

While Jasper had been furiously racking his brains all these hours in search of some devious, complicated Machiavellian strategy to tilt the balance back in his favour, it had suddenly hit him that the best solution to his problems didn't have to be complicated at all. In fact, its genius lay in its sheer simplicity. The Arabs thought they were taking charge of the situation by eliminating Ben Hope? Well then, fine, Jasper thought. Let them. He had every confidence that they'd soon find the bastard hiding in some outbuilding on the estate, and bring him back to finish what they'd started.

The next part would come as a total shock to Hassan. Once Hope was out of the picture and they knew where Rudi Bergenroth was hiding, Jasper's plan was to turn the tables on the prince and retrieve the incriminating evidence he was blackmailing him with. Bergenroth would be dealt with in due course, but those bits of video footage and phone tap audio were much more of an immediate concern. Needless to say, there was no way on earth that Hassan would voluntarily hand them over. He would have to be persuaded. And Jasper believed he had the means to do that.

The habit of secretly bugging his own meetings was one that Lord Lockwood had acquired in his MI5 days. It provided him with a transcript of conversations that he could later replay and analyse at his leisure, working out the angles, reading between the lines and helping him detect deceptions and double games. In the wilderness of mirrors that was the intelligence world, where nobody could be trusted and nothing was ever as it seemed, you soon learned to trick the tricksters and bluff the bluffers. More often than not it had proved unnecessarily overcautious, but on other occasions it had served him well, when certain individuals tried to be too clever for their own good or attempted to get one over on him. It also came in useful as a means of entrapment, when people said things that could be used against them later.

Jasper couldn't have anticipated the trap Hassan had sprung on him. If anything, he'd recorded their conversation only out of long-established routine, or perhaps so that he could later gloat over the wonderful moment when a happy deal was struck. That wasn't to be, of course. But unbeknownst to the prince, every word of their discussion was stored on a hard drive, and it meant that Jasper now had some evidence of his own that he could use as he saw fit. The audio recording was clear evidence of Hassan's guilt in any number of crimes, including conspiracy to murder, that not even the richest and most powerful people on earth could afford to have made public. Even though the prince was guilty of far less actual wrongdoing than Jasper was, his fall from grace would be much further and more spectacular.

In return for not disclosing his own evidence, Jasper would require Hassan to meet two basic conditions: firstly, that he immediately drop his own blackmail attempt and hand over all existing copies of the incriminating video footage and phone tap recordings; and secondly, that he agree to revert the Hartington Abbey sale price back to the original sixty million.

Blackmailing the blackmailers was a dangerous game. For Jasper to actually make use of his illicit recording would be to blow himself up along with his enemy. However, the prince couldn't be certain he was bluffing. How did Hassan know his opponent wasn't really crazy enough to press the nuclear button?

Then again, Jasper knew there was still a strong possibility that Hassan would refuse his terms. If it came to that, there would remain only one option. Jasper hadn't yet lost quite all his faith in the abilities of Dexter Chance and the new recruits he'd been gathering. To pull off that last-ditch measure would require a surprise attack, overwhelming the Arabs with maximum force. Chance's instructions would be clear and simple: kill 'em all, except their leader the prince, who'd be easily distinguishable from the others in his white robe and silly headgear.

What happened next would be a bloodbath. But it was the only way Jasper could get out of the mess he was in. With all his bodyguards lying dead around him, if his Highness wanted to negotiate for his own life to be spared it would cost him a billion dollars, wired to the offshore bank account of Jasper's choosing, in addition to surrendering the evidence. And if he still refused . . . well, that would be that.

It was a wild and desperate plan, the biggest gamble of Jasper's life, and maybe the last. But Hassan had left him no choice.

Just after dawn, he sneaked down a backstair and outside to a small walled garden area where none of the prince's hidden microphones could listen in. Taking out a burner phone, he dialled Dexter Chance's number. Chance picked up immediately. Jasper spoke quietly behind a cupped hand, glancing nervously at the abbey windows in case someone might be watching.

'It's me. Are you still in Manchester?'

'I was just about to call you, boss. Why are you whispering?'

'Never mind that,' Jasper hissed irritably. 'Tell me how you're doing over there.'

Chance replied, 'Doing well, boss. Recruited another good bloke last night. Roddy McIver, ex-military copper. That makes eleven so far.'

Jasper thought that twelve men, including Chance, should just about cover it. As long as they were well enough armed. 'What about equipment?'

'Enough to fight the next couple of world wars with, boss. But I used up all the money you gave me. These things don't come cheap.'

'That won't be a problem,' Jasper assured him. 'Now listen. There's been a development and I need you here as soon as possible. How soon can you get everyone together?'

'I can be with you in a couple of hours,' Chance said. 'What kind of development, may I ask?'

'The kind that calls for decisive action and is worth a considerable extra cash bonus, for all twelve of you. How does that sound?'

'Sounds like music to my ears,' Chance said. 'And the guys won't be unhappy either. How much are we talking about?'

'A hundred grand for each of them, and double that for you,' Jasper said, through gritted teeth. If things didn't go well, there was no way he could afford that much. But then, if things didn't go well, there might be nobody left alive to pay.

Chance made an appreciative little grunt. 'For that kind of money, they'll do anything you ask.'

'I should bloody hope so. Now, here's what I want you to do. When you get here, it's imperative that you don't use the main gate and don't come up to the house. Got it?'

'Got it, boss.'

'You'll need to be discreet. *Nobody* must see you arrive. Enter the grounds via the south entrance—'

'The disused gate right on the far side of the estate?'

'That's the one. It's padlocked, so bring bolt cutters. Text me on arrival, using the codeword "EAGLE". Then make your way to the old fisherman's cottage in the trees by the river. You know where it is.'

'Copy that.'

'Then once you're in, be ready and on standby for my signal. If the operation is a go I will call you on this number. The instant you receive that call, you will proceed immediately with the instructions I'm about to give you. You do *not* make the slightest move unless I call. Understood?'

'Understood, boss. No move unless.'

'Good. Now listen to these instructions very carefully because you're only going to hear them once.' Jasper spelled out his orders, specifying exactly who was to be eliminated and, more importantly, who wasn't. It wasn't rocket science, but when he'd finished he made Chance repeat the whole thing twice nonetheless so there could be no possible doubt or misunderstanding. 'This will need to go like clockwork, Chance. There will be zero room for error. Do all your men understand what's required of them?'

'Absolutely, boss. You can count on us.'

When the call was over, Jasper put away his phone and sneaked back inside the abbey. In his quarters he rubbed his hands and grinned to himself as he strutted excitedly up and down. 'Shoe's on the other foot now, Your Royal Highness. Now you're about to find out what happens to people who screw around with Jasper Lockwood!'

Chapter 48

After a frugal 6 a.m. breakfast of dates, bread, cheese and raw camel milk, the latter specially flown in fresh just for Prince Hassan, the limousine convoy departed from the Palace of Holyroodhouse and sped southwards towards the Anglo-Scottish border.

Jasper Lockwood was slurping his morning coffee and chewing on a piece of lukewarm toast when the procession of gleaming black cars swept through the gates of Hartington Abbey and came rolling into the main courtyard. Farouk and his companions had spent the last hour milling nervously about in anticipation of the prince's return. The injured Musa and Tareq were slowly showing signs of recovery, though they'd be out of action for weeks. The search party who'd been out all night had only just returned, empty-handed, glum-faced and exhausted.

Shortly before dawn the searchers had come across the remains of a camp fire in a clearing deep in the forest, the embers still warm to the touch, and some flattened undergrowth that appeared as if some tents had been pitched there. Fresh tyre marks in the dirt suggested a group of people on motorcycles had spent the night in this part of the forest and struck their camp at first light. The searchers concluded that these must be nomadic vagrants, the UK equivalent of the roving Dom communities of their native

344

country. Or perhaps this was just another example of the moral degeneracy of the British nation, some criminal gang using the forest as an illicit meeting place to deal narcotics or partake in other nefarious activities. Such things were of course virtually unknown in Saudi Arabia, where drug dealers were automatically put to death, no exceptions. But whoever had been camping in the forest that night, the searchers thought it unlikely that the fugitive would have ventured anywhere near them. Everything they knew about him pointed to the fact that he was a lone wolf. Where he'd gone, and if he'd slunk off to die or to recover, was anybody's guess.

Jasper was mildly upset by their failure to recapture Hope, but it said something about the scale of his current gamble that at this moment the prospect of a vengeful ex-SAS professional killer roving the countryside wasn't his primary concern. Some two hours after dawn, he'd received the coded text message 'EAGLE', telling him that Dexter Chance and his new recruits were now in place at their hidden location on the estate. Their presence nearby made him feel much better and gave him the confidence boost he needed to implement the next part of his plan.

Watching from a window, Jasper saw the elegant white-robed figure of Prince Hassan Bin Ibrahim Al Sharif step out of his limousine, surrounded by the same thirteen heavily-armed men who'd accompanied him to Edinburgh. Farouk went out to meet his master, shoulders slumped and head bowed in shame, ready to face all kinds of wrath and punishment. This should be fun to see, Jasper thought to himself with a smirk. Maybe the prince would grab a machine pistol from the nearest bodyguard and personally execute Farouk right there on the spot for neglect of duty, or else have him flogged to death or impaled on a spiked railing. That was the kind of thing these bloody barbarians did to one another in their own country, after all. But to Jasper's disappointment, after listening calmly to his servant's admission of failure, the prince reached out benevolently, placed his hands on Farouk's shoulders and embraced him in a gesture of forgiveness that looked almost brotherly.

The prince seemed to be in a congenial mood this morning. *Let's see how that camel shagger takes what I've got to tell him*, Jasper thought. He gulped down the dregs of his coffee, gathered his courage and stepped out into the sunshine.

Hassan greeted him with a friendly smile. 'Ah, Jasper, I trust you had a pleasant night?'

'Why, of course,' Jasper replied tersely. 'After your men made it so nice and easy for Hope to escape from his cell. Knowing that I was in danger of being murdered in my bed at any moment. Just what I need to help me sleep like a baby.'

'Farouk has explained to me what happened. It was an honest mistake for which I have forgiven him.'

'Oh, how jolly nice.'

'It is of no great concern. I do not believe Hope will be back, having received a taste of what would happen to him if he dared try again. In any case, Jasper, the sooner we can conclude our business, the sooner you will be able to disappear to your newfound haven of safety, where Hope will never find you. Speaking of business, let us waste no more time. I have pressing engagements to attend to back in Riyadh.'

The prince turned and snapped his fingers at a couple of the men standing by his limousine with their weapons dangling from their shoulders. At his signal they opened the boot of the car, reached inside the cavernous space and lifted out five identical Italian designer leather travel bags, each stuffed full and bulging. Despite himself Jasper's heart quickened at the sight of them, but he kept his expression stern.

'I believe in getting things done quickly,' the prince said. 'You may count your money if you wish, but it has already been triple checked to the last penny. All five million of it. Then it is just a matter of signing some papers, and we are done.'

This was it. The moment of truth. Grab the money and run, or make his stand and roll the dice. Which was it to be? For the briefest moment, Jasper teetered on a knife-edge. But then he thought again about the humiliating treatment he'd received at the hands of this cocky young upstart, and he made his decision.

'I'm afraid it may not be quite as simple as that,' he said stiffly.

The prince smiled, somewhat disconcertingly as though he could read Jasper's thoughts. 'No?'

Jasper shook his head. He was committed now, come what may. 'No. We need to talk, but not here. Please come inside.'

Hassan motioned to Farouk and three of the other bodyguards, who grabbed the bags. With his men in tow he followed his host back to the grand library, where they took their places around the table as before. The bodyguards set the bags down on its gleaming surface.

'What I have to say won't take long,' Jasper informed his Highness.

'Is there a problem?' the prince asked pleasantly.

'For you there is,' Jasper replied. 'Not for me.'

'I am most intrigued to hear more.'

'You will. But before we begin, perhaps you should ask your minders to wait outside.'

'Why would I feel that to be necessary?'

'Because,' Jasper told him coldly, 'I intend to speak frankly to you, and you may prefer that this discussion remain strictly between ourselves.'

The prince shook his head. 'I trust these men with my life. I have no secrets from them and it is my wish that they be present.'

'As you please.' Jasper cleared his throat. 'Well, your Highness, it's like this. I regret to tell you that, after reconsideration, I've decided that your proposal is not acceptable to me. Nor do I intend to bow down to blackmail and extortion. So I'd be grateful if you would return the so-called evidence in your possession. It won't do you any good to hold on to it.'

Hassan looked completely impassive as he digested Jasper's words. 'I see.'

'That's not all,' Jasper said. 'Furthermore, I also refuse to sell you Hartington Abbey at such a paltry fraction of its value.' He pointed at the cash-filled bags. 'This isn't what we agreed. The price was sixty million, and that's what I expect to be paid. Which means there are fifty-five bags missing from this table.'

'Those are very bold words, my friend.'

'That's how it is,' Jasper said. He kept his eyes fixed on the prince and tried very hard to ignore the hostile glares of the large, tough bodyguards.

'And if I happen to disagree?' Hassan asked.

Jasper said, 'Then I'll make public the fact that you, sir, a member of the esteemed Saudi royal family, are in fact

348

nothing better than a fraudster and a criminal. You will be shamed and discredited, and your reputation will never recover. I'll see to it that the whole world learns what you tried to do.'

'Interesting. And on what proof do you propose to expose my transgressions? Surely you would not be so low as to make secret recordings of your business negotiations, Jasper?'

Jasper ignored the question. 'You have been warned. Do yourself a favour and heed it.'

The prince stared at him. Then the faintly amused smile that had been hovering at the corners of his mouth slowly expanded into a broad white grin and his eyes twinkled. Then he rocked back his head and began to laugh, softly at first, but soon building into a great booming explosion of mirth that resonated all around the library. The bodyguards looked incredulously at their prince, then at one another, and then their severe faces melted into expressions of absolute hilarity and they all burst out in a simultaneous chorus of hoots and guffaws, clutching at their sides, tears rolling down their cheeks as though they'd just been told the funniest joke in the world.

Jasper sat there tight-lipped and felt all the colour drain from his face. He pushed his chair away from the table and got to his feet. 'So it's like that, is it?' he said in a strangled voice. 'Very well, gentlemen. So be it. Would you please excuse me for a moment?'

As he left the room he was shaking so badly with rage that he could barely hide the wobble in his step. He closed the door behind him with as much composure as he could, then strode quickly down the passage to a small cloakroom toilet. Locking himself in, he leaned against the wall and breathed deeply a few times to settle his anger, but it didn't help much. Those bastards! *Bastards!* Well they'd asked for it. He sat on the toilet seat, tore out his phone with a trembling hand and started prodding buttons.

Chance's voice came on the line. 'We're here, boss. On standby and ready to rock, just like you ordered.'

'You know what to do,' Jasper barked at him. 'Do it! Do it right now!'

Chance sounded only too happy to oblige. 'Roger that. On our way.'

Jasper put away his phone and took another deep breath. There was no going back now. He felt reasonably safe locked in here, and had no intention of coming out again until the shooting was over. He closed his eyes and waited for the fireworks to begin.

But then, as the Lord of the Manor sat there huddled on the toilet, the strangest thing happened. Because no more than four or five seconds could have gone by before the sound reached his ears of all hell breaking loose outside. The morning air was suddenly split by the crash of gunfire and the sound of breaking glass and a chaos of yelling voices, accompanied by a gigantic rumbling that rattled the ancient windows of the abbey and seemed to shake the ground.

Jasper's eyes snapped back open. His heart and mind started racing in confusion. What was going on? Some devastating earthquake, striking here in the north of England of all places? No, it sounded more like an artillery barrage, a tank invasion. Like a war breaking out. Or perhaps something on a slightly smaller scale. But that didn't make sense.

How could it be happening so soon? Chance and his men couldn't possibly have got here so quickly from the fisherman's cottage.

And so if it wasn't Chance and his men, then what the hell was it?

Chapter 49

The motorcycle gang often camped out in the same spot, deep in the privacy of the forest where they could hide away from the rest of the world and be themselves, and the track through the trees to their favourite clearing was worn smooth by the passage of large, heavy two-wheelers not at all suited to offroad riding. The track emerged onto a minor road that descended from the tall craggy hills to the east and wound gently downward in snaking curves through the Northumbria countryside for three or so miles, where it skirted the edge of the Hartington Abbey estate and passed by the main gates on its way towards the town of Berwick-upon-Tweed.

It was off to the side of that little-used hill road, in a secluded layby with a sweeping view of the abbey and its estate below, that Ben and his newfound allies had spent the early part of that morning in observation and planning, having struck camp before dawn. The pain of Ben's cuts and bruises was still hovering in the background, but thanks to the lasting effects of Nikko's miracle concoction they were no more than a minor discomfort, while the nausea and dizziness that had completely crippled him last night seemed to have vanished altogether. Ben wouldn't have wanted to make a habit of using this stuff routinely, but as a quick-fix field medicine it still came in just as handy as it had for the combatants of World War II. Rusty had done a nice job of stitching up his cheek, promising him, 'Don't you worry, my flower, you'll soon be back to your old lovely self.' She'd also insisted on checking his other bodily wounds in case of serious internal damage, as far as could be judged by a combination of visual scrutiny and careful prodding around. Ben hated being fussed over but Rusty possessed a kind of matronly authority that couldn't be resisted. She'd let out a low whistle when he removed his shirt, and not just in appreciation of his athletic, well-toned physique. The bikers all had their share of scars from motorcycle crashes, broken-bottle bar fights and bare-knuckle dust-ups with other gangs, but nothing to rival the collection of battle mementos Ben had accrued over the years.

'Jesus, you've been through it all right,' Rusty murmured. 'Where'd you get this one?' Pointing at the crooked white line that scored the right side of his ribcage.

'Afghanistan,' Ben said casually. 'Just a bullet graze.'

'And this one?'

'From a gentleman with an AK-47 in Zaire. I didn't quite get out of the way of his bayonet quick enough.'

'What about that one there?'

Ben peered down at it. 'You know, I really don't remember where I got that.'

'Well, Mr War Hero, I think you've come off pretty lightly this time around. You can put your shirt back on.'

At this moment the lovely heroic flower was lying prone on his belly like a sniper in the long grass at the side of the road, the perfect vantage point from which he could watch the main gate and buildings of Hartington Abbey far below. This observation point was a few hundred feet more elevated than the slope from which Ben had been watching yesterday, and offered a broader if more distant view. Sprocket was crouched in the bushes to one side of him, Taz to the other, both scanning the lie of the land with their keen narrowed eyes. The rest of the bikers waited nearby. Nearly two dozen of them in total, loitering impatiently by their parked machines, some of them making last-minute mechanical adjustments, others checking their weapons. It was a beautiful sunny morning with the promise of a fine day ahead. Quite what it might bring, Ben couldn't say. He'd shared out the last of his Gauloises with the gang and he, Taz and Sprocket were quietly smoking as they observed the target. The minutes crept by. Ben had a pretty good idea of what he expected to happen before too long.

He was right. A few minutes before seven, a faraway moving object caught the sunlight. A car, several miles off, approaching from the north. It was travelling fast, going at least eighty miles an hour. No, Ben told himself, not one car but several.

Sprocket's sharp eye had picked them out, too. 'Incoming,' he muttered. 'Just like you said, mate. Looks like the reinforcements have arrived.'

Ben sighed to himself. It had been a tough decision to hold back and wait for them to turn up. If he'd made his move earlier he might have been able to attack Lockwood's position when it was still at its weakest – but not without the risk of Lockwood's associates landing right on top of him at the least opportune moment. This way, at least, he could rely on the enemy being all in one place when he launched his attack. That was what he'd based his plan on.

Now all he could hope for was that it would work.

As they watched, the procession of black cars made its rapid progress towards Hartington Abbey and grew steadily more visible. A couple of luxury saloons leading the convoy and a couple more at the rear, with the stretch limousine sandwiched in the middle. Within a few minutes they reached the abbey, swept in through the main gates and up the long driveway, through the avenue of trees. They passed under the great arch into the abbey's courtyard and rolled to a halt in the same orderly formation as before, with the limo at the centre. From this distance they looked like tiny black ants, and the figures that emerged from them were barely visible specks. All but one of the specks were black too. The white speck that appeared from the largest car, Ben knew, was none other than his Eminence, the master, or the prince, or whoever or whatever the hell he was. To Ben, the only thing that mattered about the guy was the fact that he was protected by a detail of armed bodyguards who were all that stood in the way of his own desire to get to Jasper Lockwood.

Two more tiny figures emerged from the abbey. Much too far away to be sure, but Ben's intuition told him that one of them was Lord Lockwood himself, come to greet his returning visitor. For a few moments there seemed to be some discussion going on. Then the white speck and several of the others disappeared inside the building.

Now the enemy were all gathered together in one place, with no idea of what was about to hit them. It was time.

'All right, folks,' Ben said, springing to his feet and turning to his companions. 'Everyone clear on what they need to do?'

Nods and mutterings of assent from the gang. The plan of attack that Ben had come up with that morning was a simple one. He could be certain that since his escape the men would have been scouring the grounds, and probably the woods as well. Hence, it was no longer an option for him to return the way he'd come. He had to find another way in – and what better way than straight through the front door? Meanwhile, to penetrate the enemy's defences required the use of diversion tactics. That was where the Angels came in, and Ben knew he could count on them to make the diversion as spectacular and explosive as possible.

'I want to hit them so hard and fast that it'll make their head spin,' he'd explained to Sprocket. 'There are too many of them, and too well-armed, to take on in a head-to-head fight, so instead we'll have to confuse the hell out of them and divide their forces. For that I need all the noise, thunder, mayhem and bloody chaos you can stir up. You think we can manage that?'

'Noise and thunder is what we do best,' the gang leader replied with a wicked smile. 'Trust me, they'll think a fuckin' hurricane landed on their heads.'

It had taken a while for the two of them, equally strong-willed and tough-minded men used to being in command, to thrash out the particulars of the attack plan. Finally they'd settled on a compromise strategy that was acceptable to both, and they'd gone through every detail with the others until Ben was satisfied each gang member fully understood their role.

'I'm ready,' Izzy said. 'Me too,' said Smokey. 'Go for it, man,' agreed Nikko. Sven was hopping with anticipation and Weezer was so pepped up he could barely speak at all.

'Then let's roll,' Ben said.

He felt clear-headed, energised and perfectly calm, the way he'd always felt in the lead-up to battle. He walked over to the motorcycle he'd been allowed to use, which for the Angels was a serious honour to bestow on a stranger. Swinging a leg over the Harley's low seat, he took hold of its wide handlebars and hefted its weight off its sidestand. In the saddlebag behind his left hip was the sawn-off shotgun Izzy had loaned him, along with the coiled ammo belt. He pulled out the belt and buckled it around his shoulder like a bandolier. Then took out the shotgun, cracked it open, drew two cartridges from their belt loops and slid them into the chambers. He thrust the gun back into the bag, ready to be drawn left-handed while his right hand worked the throttle. Those Angels who had similar weapons did the same.

Ben thumbed the starter and the V-twin motor thundered into life between his knees and blasted out through the gleaming chrome exhausts. The rest of the Angels mounted their machines. No helmets, because helmets were for wimps – or for those roads where the hated cops could be expected to be around. Most of the gang were riding solo. Ox had been relegated to Weezer's pillion seat as arranged, because of his damaged hand. Rusty was perched in her usual place behind Sprocket with her back against the tall sissy bar and her arms looped around her man's middle. Darren, the young gang hang-around who'd found Ben in the woods, hopped up onto the back of Izzy's heavily modi-fied chopper. Being light and nimble and able to move fast, he'd been chosen to play a key part in Ben's plan and he couldn't stop grinning with pride.

One by one the motorcycles erupted into life, until their combined noise filled the morning air like the roar of a Harrier fighter jet taking off. The revving of two dozen big-twin engines and the bellow of open pipes sounded like the prelude to a war. And maybe that was what it was, though it was like none that Ben had ever fought in before. Crude old obsolete weapons in place of the latest military ordnance. Studded and patched black leather instead of tactical assault gear. The charge of the heavy brigade, rolling down on Jasper Lockwood's fortress like some kind of rebel guerrilla army, a two-wheeled fighter squadron riding to death or glory.

The Angels sped off down the hillside in a spread-out V formation that took up the whole road. Sprocket led the way, with Ben in second place behind him and the rest following as they rumbled through the curves. Down the hillside they went, maintaining their close formation at speeds of over eighty miles an hour. The tension was building fast as the gates of Hartington Abbey drew closer. Taz gave Ben a thumbs-up and a huge grin. On the final approach Ben twisted his throttle and the powerful machine surged ahead into the lead position, as they'd planned. Then he'd reached the gates and was easing off the throttle and leading the way through.

This was it now. They accelerated hard along the tree-lined avenue towards the big archway. Ben reached behind him and drew the sawn-off shotgun left-handed from its saddlebag. He thumbed back one hammer, then the other. Knowing that his comrades behind him were doing the same.

Under the archway they roared, the thunder of their motors echoing off the stonework. Running past the abbey buildings with the main courtyard dead ahead, Ben could see the line of black cars parked outside. The guards had taken up their positions like yesterday. As the din of the approaching motorcycles reached their ears they were turning round in surprise, some of them reaching for their weapons while others just stood and stared.

Ben charged into the courtyard, heading straight for them. The rest of the squadron was right behind. One of the guards leaped out of the way to avoid being run down by a tide of heavy machinery.

And then the mayhem began.

Chapter 50

'We ride in among them and open fire as we go,' Ben had said to Sprocket on the hillside that morning. 'We cause as much destruction as possible, but we're not going to shoot anyone. Clear?'

'What kind of half-arsed battle is that?' Sprocket had asked, frowning.

'One where I'm not responsible for any of you guys committing murder,' Ben had replied. 'Because that's something you don't want to live with, trust me, and neither do I. One loop of the courtyard, then we turn around and we ride out just as fast as we can and get the hell out of there. Or you do.'

'What about you?'

'I have a job to do. But don't worry. If I'm right about what will happen next, you folks will have plenty to keep you busy.'

And now they were in the thick of it, Ben had to trust that the Angels would stick to the plan. As the bikes came storming into the courtyard he levelled his weapon towards the stretch limo and squeezed off his forward trigger. The massive boom of the right barrel discharging its load was half drowned out by the din of engines. The gun recoiled heavily in his hand and the side windows of the limousine disintegrated into a million fragments of tinted glass.

Ben canted his motorcycle around in a tight curve, scraping the edge of one footboard along the ground. He pointed the gun at another of the black cars and tugged the rear trigger. The same kick and boom, the same heavy payload slamming into the bodywork of the vehicle as its gleaming front wing was turned into a buckled tin colander, the tyre burst into rubber shreds and the car sank down at one corner.

Now his gun was empty, he braked to a halt in the middle of the courtyard, ejected his spent rounds, plucked two more cartridges from his bandolier and stuffed them into the smoking chambers. All around him, the blast of gunfire was mingling with the thunderous roar of two dozen Harley-Davidsons as the bikers unleashed their destruction on the cars, the abbey windows and anything else that wasn't alive. Pure chaos, total sensory overload, every bit as stunning and paralysing for the enemy as Ben could have wished. The bodyguards might have been well trained to handle most kinds of surprise threats against their principal, but this kind of absolute bedlam, appearing out of nowhere and exploding so suddenly and violently on all sides around them, was well beyond the scope of what they were expecting. Those who hadn't run for cover among the buildings or were ducked down between their cars were confusedly managing to get off the odd shot or two, but their aims were wild, their focus was scattered and all they succeeded in doing was to break a few more windows and crater the walls of the abbey buildings.

Ben gunned his throttle and took off again, crumpling more car bodywork like a tin can and blowing out a head-light with his third shot as he went. So far so good, but now it was time to get out of here fast before one of the bikers caught a bullet. They'd already risked far too much. Catching sight of Sprocket and Rusty in the middle of the melee he signalled to them to move off. Sprocket raised a thumb in acknowledgement, veered his bike around and roared off in the direction of the archway. Ben was right behind him, and the rest of the machines fell into line and followed. One of the guards jumped out from behind a stone pillar and rattled off three shots that passed dangerously close to Ben's ear, the third one ricocheting with a howl off his handlebar and taking his mirror with it. Ben swung the shotgun towards him as he thundered past and squeezed off his fourth shot, blowing a chunk out of the medieval masonry and sending the man scurrying back under cover.

Maximum mayhem, zero casualties on either side. It wasn't Ben's usual style of warfare, but Phase One of his plan had gone well. Now was the moment to implement Phase Two, and hope that worked even better.

This was where young Darren's speed and agility was to come into play. As the escaping motorcycles sped away from the abbey and made their break for the main gates, Ben skidded his machine to a halt on the driveway. Izzy's chopper drew up level. With a backward glance to make sure they weren't seen, Ben quickly dismounted, still clutching his weapon. Next came the thrilling moment Darren had been waiting for to prove his worth to the gang. Springing like a monkey from the pillion seat of Izzy's chopper he took Ben's place on Ox's bike, revved it up wildly and took off again with the rear wheel churning up the driveway and Izzy following close behind as the Angels went storming out of the gates and accelerated off up the road.

Ben slipped out of sight behind the trees that lined the driveway. Now he was about to find out whether Phase Two of his plan was going to work. In the abbey courtyard the guards were like a stirred-up hornets' nest, running this way and that in an uproar, yelling in Arabic, staring and pointing up the driveway in the direction of the fleeing motorcycles. One was jabbering on a radio, and though Ben was too far away to hear what he was saying he guessed the man was in communication with his master. Lockwood and his associates inside the building must be as bewildered by what had just happened as the guards on the outside.

Seconds later, it seemed that the guard with the radio had received his orders, because then the men did just what Ben had been hoping they'd do. Guns in hands, several of them piled into the cars that weren't too damaged to be unusable, fired up their engines and gave chase to the attackers.

Hidden from view by the foliage of the trees, Ben smiled to himself as the cars came streaking past one after the other and went screeching out of the gates in pursuit of the Angels. The motorcycle gang had at least a quarter-mile head start on them, and their thunder was fading into the distance. There was no way the cars, badly peppered with buckshot, critical internal components damaged and with half their tyres blown out, would be able to catch them on these twisty roads. Sprocket and the others knew the area well and they'd lead them a merry dance for miles.

The diversion had worked perfectly. Now the enemy forces were significantly thinned out and the abbey was far less well defended. Only a handful of remaining guards were visible in the courtyard and they were too preoccupied with the aftermath of the attack to be even remotely aware of Ben's presence. He fed two more rounds into the chambers of his weapon and moved off unseen through the trees, making his stealthy way back towards the buildings. His goal was to reach the tower through which he'd entered yesterday, with a decent chance that he'd find the door at its foot still unlocked. Then he'd retrace his path through the warren of passages and sniff out wherever Jasper Lockwood was hiding.

Ben threaded his way from cover to cover until he'd reached the last hedge behind which he could screen himself from view. To reach the tower from here meant having to cross twenty yards of open ground, where he'd be totally exposed for a few risky seconds. He paused and peered out from behind the hedge, waiting for the moment when he could be certain nobody was looking his way. From his hidden position he could see five guards hanging agitatedly around the main entrance. He couldn't tell if any of them were among the ones he'd encountered last time. Five modern automatic weapons against his antiquated two-shot hand cannon. Not the worst odds he'd ever faced in his life, but not the best either. If he was lucky he might be able to make the dash across the open ground without being spotted. If he wasn't lucky, he might have to engage them. And then, there was no way of knowing how many more could be lurking around the corner of the building, beyond his line of sight.

He thought, *Fuck it.* Counted One . . . Two . . .

But he never counted Three. Because just as he was gathering his energy to burst out from cover and make the sprint across to the tower, the sound of gunfire erupted again from within the courtyard.

Chapter 51

The unknown gunmen had appeared as if out of nowhere. Whoever they were, Ben knew right away that they didn't belong to the same retinue of guards. Instead of dark suits their clothing was casual. They weren't of Middle Eastern appearance. But most tellingly of all, they were clearly trying to kill them. And they were no less heavily armed than their opponents.

Within moments a wild skirmish had started up in the courtyard. From his concealed position Ben saw four, five, six of the newcomers flitting among the buildings, exchanging volleys of shots with the Arabs. One of the guards went down; then another; then one of the mystery attackers was pinned down in the nook of an archway by a sustained burst of fire that chewed away part of the stonework before it got him. There was a scream and flecks of red appeared on the arch, and the guy slumped lifelessly to the ground.

Now the skirmish was escalating into a full-on gun battle as more of the dark-suited Arabs appeared from the buildings, to be met by more of their assailants. Ben couldn't see clearly what was happening, or how many there were, and he was too stunned to even count.

Then he saw something that stunned him even more. Because one of the attackers was a face he recognised. A brief glimpse, even from this distance, was all Ben needed to know he'd seen the man before. And he knew exactly when. The first time had been on the busy street outside the Merrion hotel in Dublin. The last time had been in a remote field in Yorkshire. Then he'd been wearing a ski mask, but not now. He was the tall guy with the thick glasses and the widow's peak. The hired killer who'd murdered Tony Kitson and most likely been involved in Hugh Mortimer's death too. The man who'd planted the bomb that had maimed Aurora.

The mist of Ben's confusion suddenly vanished and he understood what he was seeing here. For whatever reason, Jasper Lockwood was trying to take out the Arabs. Some kind of internecine conflict was happening between them.

As he watched, he saw two more guards go down, followed by another of Lockwood's thugs. The guy with the widow's peak rattled off a burst of gunfire at an unseen target and then disappeared between the buildings. Ben was gripped by a violent urge to go after him, and it took an equally violent effort to resist it. Perhaps he'd be able to catch up with the guy later, if the Arabs didn't get him first. But for the moment it was Jasper Lockwood, the man behind it all, who had to take priority.

One of the dead guards had managed to stagger a few paces before he collapsed in a twisted bloody heap, and was lying next to his fallen weapon about thirty yards from where Ben was hiding. Ben broke from cover, dashed across to the body, snatched up his gun and then ran back, keeping close to the wall as far as the tower. The door at its foot was still unlocked, as he'd hoped it would be.

Ben slipped inside the tower and paused at the bottom of the spiral steps to check his captured weapon. It was the compact version of the Heckler & Koch G36 battle rifle, shiny and new as befitted a bodyguard to a visiting foreign VIP of special eminence. It still had about half the contents of its thirty-round magazine. A weapon he'd spent a lot of time training with in the past. It felt comfortable and familiar, almost as natural to him as an extension of his own body. 'That'll do,' he muttered to himself. He ditched Izzy's sawn-off and the cartridge belt at the foot of the stairway and headed quickly up the spiral steps. The wall of the round tower was three feet thick, solid stone, but he could still hear the sporadic bursts of gunfire from outside. Let them wipe each other out, he thought grimly. It would save him the trouble of having to do it himself.

Reaching the head of the stairway he retraced the same route as before, through the vaulted chambers that had housed the medieval abbot and deeper into the more modernised parts of the building. If Lockwood and his white-robed visitor had been having a business meeting, he might find them together. Which meant he'd also find the visitor's armed protectors. He was glad of the fifteen rounds in his weapon's magazine. He might need every last one of them.

As he'd done the day before he moved fast through the winding passageways, checking room after room and finding them all empty. A doorway brought him to a T and he took the left turn, which led him to another, broader stairway heading back down to the ground floor, into another older part of the building where the floors were uneven and the patina of the ages was everywhere to see. It was all nooks and alcoves, archways and stained glass, tapestries and dark wood panelling. For a moment he worried about getting lost in the labyrinth; but then he entered another passage and the faint memory came into his mind that this was the same way they'd brought him after his capture in the tithe barn. A little further along was the door of the book-filled room where he'd been tied in the chair and endured his interrogation.

He paused close to the wall by the library doorway, listening hard for sounds of anyone inside. Nothing. But his sixth sense was whispering to him again. He quietly, carefully reached out and twisted the carved wooden door knob. The door was locked.

And then he wheeled violently away from the doorway as a storm of fully-automatic gunfire ripped through the solid oak from inside the library and peppered the plaster-work of the opposite wall.

Looked like his sixth sense had been right once again.

Ben braced his feet wide into a combat stance, loosed a couple of return bursts back through the shredded door and heard a cry from inside. Then another burst into the lock, sparks and splinters flying. He crashed the door open with a hefty kick. Swivelling his weapon side to side, ready to shoot whatever he saw in there facing him.

Ben took in the scene. Four men inside the room. He guessed they'd locked themselves in when all the gunfire had started up outside. One of them was the bodyguard who'd come up to the door, sensing Ben's approach. He was lying dead in a blood pool that was spreading over the polished wood floor. The other side of a long table, with his back to the library bookcases, was the tall elegant black-bearded man in the white robe. On the table in front of him were five large holdalls, full and bulging. One had its zipper pulled slightly open and the stacks of fresh banknotes were visible inside. To the left and right of the man in white were three more guys in the same dark suits, all armed. The two on the right, Ben hadn't seen before. The guy on the left was the one he remembered as Farouk, the man who'd done all the beating up on him when he was tied to the chair.

Ben figured that getting beaten up now and then was all part of his job. But he still didn't appreciate it much, and so he shot Farouk next. A burst to the upper chest and Farouk crumpled without a sound and tumbled back against the bookcase behind him. One of the men to the right fired and the bullet tore through the side of Ben's jacket and slammed into the wood panelling by the door. Ben nailed him in the H&K's sights, felt the gun vibrate against his shoulder, heard the percussive rattle, saw the guy go down. The other one tried to duck down below the table, so that he could shoot from low down and cut Ben's legs out from under him. Sneaky. Ben stitched a ragged line of bullets into the tabletop. The assault rifle's 5.56mm bottleneck rounds ripped through the gleaming wood and punched into the guy's body before he could get off a shot.

Three seconds, three more combatants down. The man in the white robe was staring at Ben with wide eyes and holding up his empty palms, saying, 'No, no, no!'

Ben wasn't going to open fire on an unarmed man. He lowered his weapon. A thin wisp of smoke trickled from the end of its barrel. He said, 'Who are you?'

The man in the white robe quickly regained his composure when he saw he wasn't about to be cut down like his men. 'I am Prince Hassan Bin Ibrahim Al Sharif. And you must be Major Benedict Hope. It seems you are every bit the warrior they say you are. Am I to understand that you are not going to shoot me now?'

'Not as long as you keep your hands in the air where I can see them,' Ben told him. 'I'm here for Lockwood. Where is he?'

'Right behind you,' said a voice from the doorway.

Chapter 52

Ben turned, but he didn't turn quickly enough. The report of the 9mm pistol sounded like a soft pop after the deafening high-velocity rifle fire. Its bullet drilled through the right sleeve of Ben's jacket and he felt the cold shock of the injury. His fingers involuntarily let go of the rifle. It clattered to the floor and he clamped his hand to his arm and saw the blood oozing from between his fingers. He felt no pain, just tingling and numbness. The pain would hit later. If he lived that long.

Lord Jasper Lockwood was standing in the library doorway. He wasn't alone there, because standing next to him was the person who'd just shot Ben. It was the guy with the glasses and the widow's peak. The hired killer. The car bomber. The Glock pistol in his right hand was pointing at Ben's chest.

Now Ben was thinking maybe he should have shot him earlier, after all. But then he realised that someone else had done it for him, only not as efficiently as he would have. The bomber was bleeding, and worse than Ben was, from a wound in his side and another in his left shoulder. He was swaying a little on his feet and the muzzle of the Glock was wavering from side to side. That was the only reason why he'd failed to put a fatal shot into Ben at this close range.

Jasper Lockwood had no weapon. He pointed at Ben and the prince and yelled, 'Kill them both, Chance!'

So now the bomber had a name at last, Ben thought. Chance blinked and tried to steady his aim at Ben's chest. This time, he looked as if he could make his bullet count. His finger tightened on the trigger.

By Ben's reckoning, if he was going to die anyway, then he'd die fighting. He wasn't going to be able to snatch his fallen weapon off the floor in time, let alone make effective use of it with only one good arm. Instead he launched himself at Chance with all the power and speed he could summon up, making a lunge at Chance's gun hand in a desperate attempt to deflect its aim. He managed to grab the man's wrist and wrench it upwards and to the side.

Chance fought back. He might be badly hurt himself, but he was still strong and his fear made him determined. Ben's own strength and determination were fuelled by his hatred of this man who'd hurt Aurora. In his mind's eye all he could see was the explosion lighting up that rainy night street in Roundstone, County Galway. He wasn't going to back down. He was going to put an end to this man, even if it spelled the end of his own life too.

The struggle only lasted seconds before the pistol went off. But by then it was pointing up at the ceiling and its bullet smacked harmlessly into an oak beam. Ben kept a death grip on Chance's wrist, like holding a tiger by the tail. No telling how many more rounds might be in its magazine. Next his knee was driving hard into the pit of the man's stomach. Chance doubled up with a grunt of pain and his thick glasses went flying. Ben crashed him against the wall and delivered another knee strike to the groin. Chance cried out and lost his grip on his Glock, which spun to the floor and slid across the shiny boards to Jasper Lockwood's feet.

Out of the corner of his eye, Ben saw Lockwood going for the weapon. His thoughts flashed back to those pistol shooting trophies he'd found upstairs. And it wouldn't take an accomplished marksman to pump him full of bullets at this range. Ben let go of Chance, got to the fallen pistol just as Lockwood's hand was lunging down towards it, and swept it clattering across the floorboards with a kick.

Now Chance was coming at him again, half blind without his glasses but possessed with wild rage. Ben whirled back round to meet his attack, twisting at the knees and waist and focusing all his power and momentum into a savage strike that delivered the bent point of his left elbow with maximum force into Chance's throat, crushing his windpipe and stopping his attack in its tracks.

It was a killer blow, inflicted with cold, pure and calculated intent. Chance staggered back, clutching at his throat, eyes popping, gasping for air with a terrible wheezing sound. He wouldn't survive long, as oxygen starvation began to shut down his brain and organs. But Ben didn't like to watch an enemy die a slow, tortured death. Not even this enemy. So he wrapped his left arm around Chance's neck, twisted his head this way and that, felt the resistance point in his upper spine and gave it a final hard wrench that broke his neck with a sound like snapping a dry branch.

Chance slumped dead to the floor.

Jasper Lockwood stood staring in horror at the body, then at the fallen pistol, then at Ben. Then he bolted for the open door. But not quickly enough, because before he could reach it Ben had grabbed him by his shirt collar and yanked him one-handed back off his feet. Lockwood tumbled to the floor with a terrified squawk. Ben pinned him with a knee to the

373

chest and hit him twice in the face with his left fist, knocking him half senseless.

Lockwood's shirt collar was torn and several buttons had been ripped loose to reveal something small and bright that was hanging from his neck by a slim chain. Ben grabbed it and snapped the chain free. It was a silver medallion, the size of a coin. One face of the medallion was embossed with the motif of a rearing unicorn. On the other, in flowery elliptical script that was only slightly faded and smoothed with time, was engraved the name *Elizabeth*.

Ben recalled what Rudi Bergenroth had told him. The Elizabeth in question was Elizabeth of York, who had received the pendant as a gift as a small girl, later to pass it to her little brother Richard, whom she wouldn't see again for many years before he returned in the ill-fated guise of Perkin Warbeck. The same medallion whose sight had convinced her of the royal pretender's real identity. The same one that had come down the line to Hugh Mortimer and been worn by him for decades, until his murderer had claimed it for himself as a trophy.

Lockwood groaned, stirred and tried to get up. Ben punched him again, harder, and he slumped back to the floor unconscious.

Prince Hassan Bin Ibrahim Al Sharif had picked up the fallen Glock pistol. He held it up to show Ben, then pointed at the dead man on the floor. 'His name was Dexter Chance,' he said. 'A former intelligence operative. He was employed to perform dirty jobs for our friend here. But I think you knew that, Major Hope. In any case, I thank you for saving my life. He would have killed us both if you had not stopped him.' He tossed Ben the pistol.

Ben caught it with his left hand. He nodded towards the cash-stuffed travel bags on the table. 'Looks like your business deal is dead in the water, though. I can't see these negotiations going any further.'

'No matter,' Hassan said. 'Europe is full of historic properties for sale. I will soon find another investment for my five million pounds, and much more. But you are shot, my friend,' he added, eyeing the blood that was dripping from Ben's wounded arm.

'I've had worse,' Ben replied. He pulled off his jacket, peeled back the blood-soaked sleeve of his shirt and saw that the bullet had gone cleanly right through the fleshy part of his upper arm, leaving only a small exit hole. Thank God for 9mm full-metal-jackets that penetrated deep through tissue and didn't expand into little lead mushrooms carving out massive bottle-shaped wound channels.

That was when he realised that the shooting outside had fallen silent sometime within the last few minutes. Whatever had happened out there, it was over. The prince looked around him at the dead bodies of his own men, Farouk and the two others. If their deaths upset him much, he didn't show it. He pointed at the limp, unconscious Jasper Lockwood and asked, 'What do you propose to do with this son of a dog?'

Ben was pondering that question himself when he heard a new sound break the silence from outside. The rumbling thunder of big motorcycles gathering in the courtyard.

'It seems that your associates have returned,' the prince said.

Chapter 53

Ben stuffed Chance's Glock in his belt and tucked his right hand into his pocket. The numbness in his wounded arm was beginning to give way to pain now, and it would get much worse. He wanted to go and meet the Angels but there was no way he was leaving Lord Lockwood in here unsupervised. Ben grabbed him by the scruff of the neck and dragged him one-handed out of the library, along the passage to the entrance hall and then out through the arched doorway to the courtyard where Sprocket and the others were sitting astride their machines. Dead bodies lay strewn everywhere. Some in dark suits, others belonging to Dexter Chance's crew.

Taz made a low whistle. 'Fuck me, this place is a sodding butcher's yard.'

'You okay, pal?' Sprocket asked Ben wryly.

'I did what I came here to do,' Ben replied. 'Or almost.' He let go of Lockwood's shirt and his Lordship slumped on the entrance steps. He was slowly coming round again, moaning softly and clutching his head.

'Is that the guy?' Sprocket asked.

'This is him.'

Nikko said, 'Thought you might need a hand back here, but it looks like you've got things under control.'

'Mostly under control,' added Rusty, seeing Ben's bloody arm.

'It's only a scratch,' Ben said.

'Another one for your collection.'

Ben said to Nikko, 'I'll take another puff of that magic stuff of yours, though.' His arm was beginning to throb badly now, and the rest of his aches and pains were returning after his fight with Chance.

'No problemo,' replied Nikko. 'Don't go getting yourself hooked on it, though, mate.'

'Maybe you should take a break from getting beaten up, shot and stabbed all the time,' Rusty advised.

'Funny,' Ben said. 'I was thinking the same thing myself.'

To the Angels' surprise, the white-robed and turbaned figure of Prince Hassan appeared from the abbey entrance and stood beside Ben on the steps, looking impassively at the bodies lying about in the courtyard. 'Where are the rest of my men?'

'We gave them the slip a few miles back down the road,' Sprocket replied. 'I expect they'll drag their sorry arses back here eventually, if they haven't got lost in the country lanes.'

'And if their cars make it this far,' Weezer laughed.

'So are you going to shoot him, or what?' Taz said, pointing at Lockwood. 'That's what you said you were going to do.'

Lockwood suddenly appeared to come back to life at the sound of Taz's words. 'I didn't do anything!' he protested, trying to struggle to his feet. Blood dribbled from his cut lip where Ben had hit him. 'Please don't hurt me! It's all just a terrible misunderstanding!'

'Yeah, go tell that to the poor girl you blew up,' Rusty yelled at him. She looked ready to grab Sprocket's shotgun and finish him off herself.

'Be quiet.' Ben grabbed Lockwood and shoved him down again.

'I'll give you anything to let me go,' Lockwood pleaded, clasping his hands together and looking imploringly at Ben. 'Anything! Name your price!'

'Do not believe his lies,' said Hassan. 'He no longer has two pennies to his name.'

'There's five million pounds in cash sitting on the table in that library,' Lockwood went on desperately. 'Take it!'

Hassan chuckled. 'Unfortunately, his Lordship seems to forget that money is not his either. He refused the sale.'

'My estate, then' Lockwood bleated. 'It's everything I own and it's worth millions. It's yours if you let me go.'

'Looks like a big maintenance hassle to me,' Ben told him. 'I'm not in the market anyhow.'

The approaching sound of engines, and of pattering tyres and metallic grinding and clanking, made them all look round. 'Uh-oh,' said Weezer. 'The boys are back. And they've got to be seriously pissed off.'

One by one the black cars came limping back through the tree-lined avenue and rolled into the courtyard. Two of them were running on flats and another had a bumper hanging off and smoke pouring from under its bonnet. Only one had its windscreen still intact. The buckled, holed doors creaked open and the men piled out with their guns raised, ready to take their furious revenge on the attackers who'd humiliated them. The bikers reached for their own weapons and for a few tense moments it looked as though the battle was about to kick off all over again. Then Prince Hassan stepped forward with his hand raised, commanding his guards to stand down. 'Put your weapons away at once. If any of you so much as fires a single shot I will have his eyes gouged out and his body impaled and burned alive.'

'I think he means it,' Smokey said.

'Nice boss to work for,' Sprocket muttered.

'Reminds me of why I never wanted a real job,' said Nikko.

Hassan turned to Ben. 'My business here is now concluded and it will soon be time for me to return home. But before I go, two remaining matters must be settled. First, in my country, a man of honour must always repay his debts. Having saved my life and earned my everlasting gratitude you must now tell me what it is I can do for you in return.'

'I don't want your eternal gratitude,' Ben told him. 'But I'll settle for what's in those bags you brought with you.'

Hassan broke into a beaming grin and he laughed out loud. 'First a skilled warrior, now an adept businessman. Very well. The money is of little consequence. It is yours to do with as you see fit.'

'And the other matter?'

Hassan's smile dropped and his face became hard. He pointed at Lockwood. 'My second wish is that you allow me to deal with this unworthy filth in my own way.'

'By gouging out his eyes and impaling and burning him alive, too?'

'First he wasted my time and attempted to cheat me, then I believe that he plotted with his men to assassinate me. Such insolence and disrespect are not acceptable. He must be severely punished.'

Lockwood's face turned white and he started trying to crawl away. 'No! No! Hope, do something. You can't leave

379

me in their hands like this. They'll take me apart. It's not human!'

'You'd know all about showing compassion to your fellow men, Jasper,' Ben said. 'But don't worry. I have a few scruples left.'

Hassan wasn't happy. 'The code is a simple one. He would have seen me dead. He must die.'

'You have your code, I have mine,' Ben told him. 'And I don't allow prisoners to be executed in cold blood.'

'Then how do you propose to resolve this situation? Surely you cannot mean to let him go? You, of all people, having seen the suffering and harm this mangy dog is capable of inflicting? This I cannot believe.'

'Yeah, man,' said Taz. 'You said you had a job to do. You told us you were gonna drag this fucker out of his house kicking and screaming and put a bullet between his two eyes. Your own words.'

'And I was looking forward to it,' added Weezer.

'I know that's what I said,' Ben agreed.

The whole time they were talking, Lockwood was keeping up a constant background chatter by pleading more and more desperately, on his knees abjectly begging for his life. Ben looked at him and felt something like pity for the wretched man. But in the unlikely event of there being one thing that a Saudi prince and a Hell's Angel could ever agree upon in this world, this was it. You couldn't just let a character like Jasper Lockwood get away with murder. The moment he thought he was off the hook he'd be laughing at you behind your back and all too happy to start getting up to his old tricks again. Plus you'd never be safe from his vindictive ways. Lockwood was like a disease infestation, a pestilence, that would keep returning, unless it was totally and permanently stamped out.

'Then how *are* you gonna deal with it, bro?' Sprocket asked, with one eyebrow raised and a half-smile on his face.

Ben was silent for a few moments, then made his decision.

Chapter 54

'We'll settle it like people did in the olden days,' he said.

'Olden, like medieval times?' Rusty asked. 'Picked the right place for it. You fellas going to have a jousting match or something?'

'On bikes?' said Darren. 'That'd be awesome.'

'Ain't using mine, I can tell you,' huffed Ox.

'Not that olden,' Ben said. He turned to Lockwood. 'I saw your pistol target shooting trophies, Jasper. Seems you're a pretty decent shot. How about I let you have a sporting chance? Winner walks away.'

In a heartbeat, Lockwood's expression of abject terror gave way to one of doubt and confusion. Then the tiniest ray of hope appeared in his eyes as Ben's proposition sank in and he was able to see a faint chance of actually getting out of this alive. 'How does that work exactly?' he asked in a voice full of distrust, like someone offered a bargain that was too good to be true.

'One shot each,' Ben said. 'At twenty-four paces.'

'You're bleeding mad!' Weezer burst out.

A tiny smile appeared at the corners of Lockwood's mouth. His eyes flicked up and down at Ben's injured arm and it was obvious what he was thinking. 'A duel.'

'You're a man who appreciates history,' Ben said. 'Think of it as keeping the old traditions alive. I'd have proposed we shoot with longbows, but I only have one arm.'

'Winner walks away?' Lockwood asked suspiciously.

Ben nodded.

'How can I trust you?'

'Because you have my word,' Ben said. 'You kill me, and I guarantee you won't be touched. Hassan?'

The prince frowned. 'I am not in favour of this foolish idea. But if that is your wish, I will consider myself duty bound to honour it. If he wins, my men will not harm him. That is my command.'

'Sprocket?'

Sprocket shrugged. 'Whatever you say, man. I think you're off your rocker, but it's not our fight. You go down, nice knowing you and we'll be on our way. That's a promise.'

And Sprocket's promise was good enough for Ben, any day.

Weezer was shaking his head in disbelief. Izzy wasn't so sure either. 'Why are you doing this?'

Ben replied, 'Because I'm crazy and I don't give a shit. And because I'm not a cold-blooded murderer like his Lordship here.'

'I have a pistol,' said one of the Saudis. He drew a shiny black Walther 9mm from his concealed holster and offered it to them.

'And here's Chance's,' Ben said, taking the Glock from his belt. 'Are you ready, Jasper? Then let's do it. Right here, right now.'

The Angels dismounted from their bikes and gathered to one side of the courtyard, along with Prince Hassan and what was left of his men. One of the guards briskly, expertly emptied out the chambers and magazines of both handguns and reloaded them each with a single round. One shot each, like in the olden times of flintlock or percussion duellers. He held them out butt-first, the Glock in his right hand and the Walther in his left.

Ben said, 'Jasper, choose your weapon.'

Lockwood's colour had returned, along with a lot of his confidence. He clearly believed he stood a good chance of winning this. He considered his choice of pistols, then opted for the one on the right. Chance's Glock.

Which left Ben with the Walther. It felt big and clumsy in his left hand. He'd never been quite as proficient shooting southpaw, and his left shoulder was aching from yesterday's rough treatment. But he would make the best of what he had, like always.

The rules of the duel were just like in historic times. The combatants would stand back to back, then on the signal each of them would take a dozen steps forward. When they were twenty-four paces apart, each would turn to face the another, raise his weapon one-handed as in a formal target competition, take aim and fire his single shot. The witnesses were to ensure that all proprieties were strictly observed. If neither duellist was fatally injured, the contest would end in an honourable draw and both parties were free to walk away.

Prince Hassan seemed to be relishing the event. The Angels looked tense. Rusty stood at Sprocket's side, biting her lip and shooting Ben an anxious look that said, *Are you really sure you want to do this?* Ben caught her eye, and smiled at her.

Noon was approaching. The sun was high in the sky, shining warmly down on the courtyard of Hartington Abbey. The combatants moved into the middle of the wide open space where they'd have all the room they needed, no dead bodies in the way, and the buildings either side offered a safe backstop for any missed shots.

Ben and Lord Lockwood stood back to back with their weapons at the ready. 'You're a dead man, Hope,' Jasper said in a low, gloating voice, as if he was already the victor. Ben said nothing.

It was time.

Chapter 55

At Prince Hassan's signal, the two men began to pace forward. Eyes front, no looking back until it was time to turn and face each other. Ben felt serene. The pain of his wound seemed to fade into the background. He was barely even aware of the many eyes watching. All that existed was the pure intensity of the moment.

Three slow, steady paces. The soles of his boots crunched on the fine gravel of the abbey's courtyard. The sun felt so pleasant and warm. He reflected on his life, the people he'd known. Those he'd loved and lost in the past; those others he'd leave behind if he died here today.

Five paces.

Maybe it *was* crazy, he thought. But he felt he was doing the right thing. He hadn't had a bad run of it, these past thirty-odd years. He'd crammed a lot into the short time he'd been alive. Seen and done so many things, saved a lot of lives and achieved more than he'd ever dreamed was possible. And so dying like this was okay, if that was to be.

Six paces. The ancient stone buildings opposite him crept slowly closer, step by step. In this strangely prolonged moment Ben was able to take the time to admire the beauty of the abbey's medieval architecture and think about all the people who'd lived and died here through history, what it must have been like for them all those centuries ago. He thought about the newlyweds Perkin Warbeck and his wife Catherine Gordon, and the life they might have had together in this beautiful place if things hadn't gone the way they had.

All mostly forgotten now, swallowed up in the mists of time. In a few hundred years from now, his duel with Lord Jasper Lockwood would have faded into history too, gradually lost from memory. Totally insignificant. As if it had never happened.

Seven paces. Eight.

And then Ben heard someone let out an angry yell, followed a fraction of a second later by the crack of the pistol shot behind him.

Ben stopped pacing. He didn't turn around. He closed his eyes and stood there breathing slowly. Scanning himself mentally from head to toe, waiting for the icy cold feeling of shock that told him he was shot and about to fall dead on the ground.

But no. He was alive, and still with only one bullet hole in him. Lockwood had cheated the rules of the contest and turned and fired early. It was as if the temptation had been just too much for him. His one chance to do it right, to act honourably and with courage, and he'd screwed it up. And in his haste to shoot his opponent in the back, he'd fluffed his aim, jerked the trigger and missed.

Ben slowly turned around to face him. Jasper Lockwood stood there only sixteen paces away, his empty weapon dangling at his side, his face as white as a ghost's. The Angels were all shouting at him.

Ben shook his head at them, and they stopped shouting. A hushed silence fell over the abbey courtyard.

Ben raised his weapon. He let the sights square up on his target. His face was completely expressionless and impassive, as though it was a tree or a fencepost he was taking aim at, and not a living human.

'You can't do this to me!' yelled Jasper Lockwood. 'I won't allow it, do you hear?'

Ben took his time aiming. He slowly sucked in a deep breath, then let half of it out to steady himself as perfectly still as possible for the shot. One bullet. No second chances. *Make it count.*

Lockwood stood there staring at him. His face had turned from white to red. Then he let out a strangled wail, threw down his gun and fell to his knees and started scrambling away in desperation towards the cover of the parked motorcycles.

Sprocket, Taz and two of the prince's men broke away from the crowd and hurried after him. Ben lowered his pistol as they ran across his field of fire. They grabbed the whimpering Lockwood, dragged him roughly to his feet, frogmarched him back into the middle of the courtyard and planted him back in the same spot from which he'd broken and run. 'Don't you dare move,' Sprocket warned him. 'Or I'll shoot you myself.'

Ben waited until the others had moved away to safety. Then he raised his pistol again.

'It's not fair!' Lockwood screamed, gesticulating widely with his arms. 'None of this is fair! I won't—'

But whatever it was that he wouldn't, nobody would ever know. He was still in indignant mid-sentence when the flat report of Ben's pistol split the air. The bullet crossed the space of sixteen paces in a fraction of a second, hit Lord Lockwood squarely between his two eyes and blew out the back of his skull.

Lockwood stood there for a moment, as though suspended from invisible wires. He blinked. Swayed on his feet. Then his knees buckled under him and he went straight down like a demolished factory tower collapsing into its own footprint.

Ben said, 'That one's for Aurora.'

The Angels came forward and stood around Lockwood's body, prodding him with their feet as though they needed to make sure he was really dead. They needn't have bothered checking.

The prince's men exchanged grins and high-fives. Hassan himself was laughing with delight as he came striding over to congratulate the victor. 'Oh, that was something truly special. I would gladly have paid double the money for such a show. Better than any Bruce Willis movie I have ever seen.'

Ben threw down his empty pistol. His arm had started hurting again, worse than before. He felt sick and depressed and very, very weary.

'I would gladly shake your hand, my friend,' the prince said. 'Perhaps next time, when you are recovered. Then you must come and work for me. I need men like you.'

'It was interesting meeting you, Hassan,' Ben told him. 'But it would be better we don't meet again.'

The young Saudi royal was still laughing as he climbed into his bullet-riddled limousine and drove off with his remaining men, including the half-dead Musa and Tareq, who had had to be carried to their car. Once they were all gone, it was just Ben and the Angels and a lot of dead bodies that were going to be someone else's problem to dispose of. If they could even identify most of them.

'You've got to let me look at that arm,' said Rusty, coming over to where Ben had sat slumped on a low wall.

'It's nothing,' he muttered. Now that it was over, he felt too deflated and exhausted to really care that much. Like a man in a trance he watched the blood drip from his fingers to the ground in fat little red spots.

'Nothing my arse,' she retorted. 'You need looking after.'

'Reckon it's about time we made tracks, people,' Sprocket said, with a glance back towards the road. 'Before the pigs turn up and call in their troops. There's gonna be a few questions about what happened here today.'

'Something I need to do first,' Ben said. 'Give me a hand, will you? I'm a little unsteady on my feet.'

Sprocket and Izzy took his arms and helped him back into the abbey's grand library. The two Angels were getting pretty used to seeing dead bodies by now, and barely gave the corpses of Dexter Chance, Farouk and the other two guards a second glance as they stepped over to the table where the leather bags were still sitting untouched.

The sight of just one cash-stuffed holdall would have been enough to blow Izzy and Sprocket's minds. Five of them together, each equally bulging with stacks of pristine banknotes, all fifties, had a mesmeric effect and they stood staring as though it were something out of a dream.

Five bags, five million. It didn't take much effort to do the mental arithmetic. 'I appreciate your help, guys,' Ben told them. 'And so this is for you.' He shunted one of the heavy bags across the table.

'You're kidding, right?' Izzy gasped.

'That's a lot of money, bro,' said Sprocket. 'More than I've ever seen before, that's for damn sure.'

'Should help keep you on the road a while longer,' Ben replied. 'And you won't need to take risks selling drugs and guns any more.'

'What about the rest of it?' Izzy asked, pointing at the other four bags. Ben looked at him and could see he was being sincere. In Ben's weakened state just the two of them, let alone the whole gang, could have jumped him and taken all five million for themselves. That was, if they'd been a dishonourable bunch of renegades with no moral code. But that wasn't who they were.

'It's not for me,' Ben said. 'It's for a friend.'

Chapter 56

Sprocket and Rusty's home, five miles the other side of Berwick-upon-Tweed, was a static caravan in a field they rented from a farmer. It wasn't very large and it certainly wasn't very opulent, but it was well-kept, cosy and comfortable and it was Ben's refuge for the next four days while he recuperated from his injuries. Rusty fussed over him day and night, and plied his gunshot wound with home-prepared herbal poultices that she insisted were much better for him than whatever pharmaceutical drugs she might have been able to pilfer from the local hospital where she was doing her trainee nurse internship. Ben was in capable hands, and he felt better each passing day. Rusty fed him like a fighting-cock and obligingly went shopping for new clothes to replace the bloodied items that she burned in a brazier. Only his boots and jacket survived.

There was no TV or radio in the static caravan, and it was only through Rusty's daily reports that Ben received any news of the incident at Hartington Abbey. The authorities were completely at a loss to explain what on earth could have led to the deaths of Lord Lockwood and all the other victims of what appeared to be some kind of feud between criminal gangs. The police were still trying to identify many of the dead. The only witness they'd so far managed to find was an elderly gardener who lived on the estate. He claimed to have been fast asleep while the drama unfolded, and had only discovered the bodies afterwards. No suspects had as yet been named and the investigation was expected to be ongoing for quite some time.

On the fourth day Ben felt strong enough to venture outside and help Sprocket with the motorcycle rebuild project he'd been working on in his shed. The bike was a 1949 Harley Panhead that Sprocket was lovingly restoring to its former glory. 'Got some extra cash for spare parts now,' he joked.

'You earned it,' Ben said.

The next day, Ben bade goodbye to his friends and called a taxi to take him and his four heavy leather bags to the railway station. 'You stay out of trouble, now,' he told Rusty as she hugged him tight.

'Look who's bloody talking,' she laughed.

Sprocket and Ben bumped fists. 'Ride safe, brother,' the Angel said. 'Maybe see you on the road.'

'You never know,' Ben replied.

On the train to Edinburgh, in a quiet smoking carriage with the four holdalls piled on the seat next to him along with his green bag he'd retrieved from Lockwood's study, he called Rudi Bergenroth.

The Austrian sounded deeply relieved to hear from him. '*Ja, ja*, I'm still here on Sark. I've been waiting for you to call me. And so,' he added apprehensively, 'what has happened?'

'It's over, Rudi. I'll spare you the details, but let's just say that our business has been taken care of. Nobody's coming after you any more. You and Ingrid are safe now. Free to get on with your life.'

'*Ach, mein Lieber, das ist fantastisch!* What time is it? I must start packing my things! I will be on the very next ferry off this island and running back to Liechtenstein as fast as I can to be with her again.' Bergenroth paused as a thought came to him. 'And what about Harting— that is to say, what about the place?'

'Fallen vacant, now that its former owner is out of the picture. Which I suppose technically leaves the way open for Lance to make his claim as next of kin. That is, if he had any idea about any of this. Whatever, I'm afraid that's the end of any plans you and Hugh might have had for a historical heritage centre.'

'Oh, it is no longer important to me. All that matters is that we are safe now.'

'One thing you might want as a keepsake,' Ben said. 'Hugh's medallion.'

'Elizabeth's unicorn? You have it?'

'It's of no use to me. I still have Ingrid's address. I'm in-between places right now but when I get to my next stop I'll stick it in the post. Sound good?'

'To have the medallion worn by Perkin Warbeck . . . oh, that would be too much. How can I thank you? I owe you so much, including my life.'

'No need to thank me. Just say hello to Ingrid for me. And be happy.'

Ben's next call was to his own home number in Ireland.

'Winnie, it's me.'

'Ben!' her voice exploded in his ear. 'Oh, I was so worried. Are you all right? Where have you been? Are you coming home?'

'I'll tell you all about it,' he promised, knowing he wouldn't. 'But never mind me. I was calling about something else. Where is she?'

Chapter 57

Ben checked his scribbled note of the address and said to the taxi driver, 'This is it.'

The road through the village was too narrow to have pavements and kerbs. The cabbie pulled his Ford Mondeo up outside the house. It had been a long drive from Southampton Airport, and that was where Ben would be heading straight back once he was done here. 'Keep the meter running. Can you give me a hand with the bags?'

'No problem, Guv,' the driver said.

It was a sunny late afternoon deep in the leafy Hampshire countryside. Birds were chirping overhead and bumblebees hummed about the borders and flower beds of the pretty little hamlet of Blissley Green, close to the edge of the New Forest. The driver popped his boot lid, hefted himself out of his seat, waddled around to the back and grabbed a bag handle in each hand. 'Blimey,' he said, as he'd said at the airport. 'What've you got in here, lead ingots?'

'Four million in cash,' Ben replied.

The driver laughed. 'That's a good one. Four million in cash. Ha ha!'

'I won't be long,' Ben said.

It was a modest little brick house, with a white picket fence and a small, nicely-tended garden with a water feature that tinkled and sparkled in the sunshine. He went to light a Gauloise, then thought better of it and put his pack away. The curly wrought-iron gate creaked on its hinges as he opened it. His right arm was still quite tender and he winced as he picked up the first pair of heavy bags and carried them through the gate and up the short path. When all four bags were outside the front door he collected himself, took a long deep breath and rang the bell.

The woman who answered the door was in her late forties or early fifties, with reddish bobbed hair and the strained, tired expression of someone who'd been through a lot of recent stress and unhappiness. Ben immediately saw the resemblance to her elder sister, as well as to her daughter. She looked so oddly familiar that he almost felt as though he knew her. As far as she was concerned, though, this man who'd turned up at her door unannounced was a total stranger. The woman smiled politely, despite her confusion, and asked, 'Can I help you?'

'I'm sorry to disturb you,' he said. 'My name is Ben. I'm a friend of your sister Winnie. She told me Aurora had come back here to stay with you. I'm here to pay her a visit, if she'll see me.'

The woman drew in a sharp breath, realising now who he must be. 'Oh. I wasn't expecting—'

'Is she at home?'

'Yes, yes, she's here,' her mother replied, a little flustered. 'I, er, do please come inside. You can leave your bags in the hallway. Gosh, they do look heavy. Her room's upstairs. Hold on a minute while I let her know you're here.'

The little house was light and airy inside, and smelled of fresh flowers and home cooking. The sound of a TV football game was coming from somewhere downstairs.

Ben had never felt so nervous in his life. He'd been dreading this moment. He hovered uncertainly in the hallway while the woman hurried up the stairs. From around the bend in the landing he heard the turn of a handle and the creak of a door and her voice saying, 'Darling, there's a visitor here to see you.' There was a certain pregnant tone to the way she said it. Then the door closed for a few moments and he heard some more muffled conversation that he couldn't make out.

The woman was smiling when she came back downstairs. 'Please go on up, Ben. Can I offer you a cup of tea and a slice of cake?'

'That's very kind, but no thanks.'

Ben trod up the stairs. Chintzy wallpaper, salmon pink carpet. Around the bend in the landing he saw the bedroom door ahead, slightly ajar. He paused outside it and tried to remember the words he'd been rehearsing in his mind. His heart was thumping. He almost turned back at that point.

Fuck it. He took another deep breath and pushed the door open and stepped into the room.

'Hello, Ben,' Aurora said.

The room was decorated like a teenage girl's, unaltered in the years since she'd left home to chase her dreams and build the career that would never be. She was sitting half up on her bed, in the same position he'd last seen her when she was in the hospital. Not so very many days ago, but so much had happened in the interim that it seemed like months had gone by. Then, she'd been wearing a patient's gown and a surgical cap. Now she was in jeans and a bright green sweatshirt and her hair was freshly washed and hung over her shoulders, trimmed a little shorter where it had been scorched in the blast. The burn marks on her face were healing well. She looked as beautiful as she'd ever looked. His eye ran down and stopped at the pinned-back empty leg of her jeans, and he swallowed.

'Hello, Aurora.'

'I didn't think I'd ever see you again,' she said.

'Here I am,' he replied. All the meaningful things he'd been wanting to say seemed to have completely deserted him, and his words sounded painfully lame and inarticulate.

'What brings you here? Happened to be passing by?'

'Not exactly.'

'Come and sit by me,' she said, the same way she'd done in the hospital. He shuffled closer to the bed and sat down. She reached out and took his hand. She peered at him. 'What happened to you? You've been in an accident or something. And you're all pale. Are you in pain?'

'I'm fine.'

'You went after them, didn't you? The people who did it?'

He shrugged and made no reply.

'I wish you hadn't. You promised me you'd stay safe.'

He'd never made that promise. 'It needed to be done,' he said after a beat. 'It's over now.' Except how could it ever be over for her, now that her life would never be the same again? The moment he'd said it, his own words made him feel sick.

'I'm glad you're all right, Ben.'

'How is it?' he asked, daring to look again at the empty place where her leg should have been.

'Oh, you know. A nurse comes every day and changes my dressing, checks me over. I'm not supposed to wear jeans but they make me feel more normal.'

'Winnie told me you live here now.'

'For a while, anyhow. Until I get back on my—' She stopped. 'They'll be happy to look after me here for ever, if I want. But sooner or later I need to pick up the pieces and get back to having some kind of life. I'm already getting about better than I was at the start.' She motioned at the pair of crutches that leaned in the corner near the bed.

He paused. 'Listen. I—'

'What, Ben?'

'I brought you something.'

'Flowers?'

He should have thought of that. 'No, I didn't know what kind to get.'

'Let me guess. Another get well card.' The little dressing table across the bedroom was covered in them.

'Not that either.'

'Am I supposed to guess?' she asked, smiling. 'Show me. Where is it?'

'I left it in the hallway downstairs,' he said. 'It's for your future, Aurora. I know it can never make up for . . .' His throat suddenly tightened up and he couldn't say any more.

'You mean you haven't brought me a new leg?' she said. 'Damn, how disappointing.'

'No, but you can use it to get one. Dr Moore told me about the Waters and Mallory clinic in London. And that's just the beginning. You can have anything you need. To help make things normal again. Like they would have been.'

She looked strangely at him. 'Ben, what are you talking about?'

'There's something you said to me, back in Ireland,' he said. 'About how if things didn't quite go the way you wanted them to with your career, you'd like to open your own ballet school. Is that still something you'd like to do?'

'Oh absolutely,' she laughed. 'On three floors, with practice studios and its own little theatre and all the best dance teachers, attracting the most talented youngsters from all over the world. Just as soon as I can raise the millions that'd cost.'

'Then do it,' he said. 'Do it tomorrow. Start looking for the right property and make this happen.'

'How?' she asked. Her smile had gone and she was staring intently at him. 'How can I do that, Ben?'

'Because you can,' he said. 'You can do anything you want.'

She seemed to understand, but she didn't stop staring at him so hard that her eyes seemed to bore straight through him. 'What did you bring me, Ben?'

'It was all I could do,' he said. 'I wish it could have been so much more.'

'There are other things I could have wanted,' she said in a quieter voice, squeezing his hand. 'Things I've been praying for night after night.'

'What things?'

'Like the thing that just walked in my door. I've pictured it so many times. And here you are.'

There was a long silence between them.

He shook his head. 'I'm not good for people, Aurora.'

'Don't say that. You can't blame yourself for what happened to me. It was just what it was. Wrong place, wrong time.'

'The wrong place was being with me,' he said. 'I'm bad to be around. People get hurt because of me.'

'But that can change,' she said. 'It's not who you really are.'

He looked at her. 'Can it change? Sometimes I think it never will.'

'Then what?' she asked.

'I just go my own way,' he said. 'Like it's always been.'

'Like you're about to do now, I suppose?'

He nodded. 'I have a taxi waiting outside. I only came by to deliver your present.'

'And say goodbye.'

'Yes. And say goodbye.'

'Can I kiss you? Just the once?'

They kissed. Then he squeezed her hand one last time, stood up and left the room. He didn't want her to see the tears in his eyes. He walked down the stairs, past the four bulging bags in the hallway whose contents he hoped could bring her at least some kind of happiness. Headed out of the door and down the path towards the waiting taxi.

EPILOGUE

At dawn the next morning he was back on his beach in Ireland, sitting on the flat rock looking out at the waves rolling in. He sat like that for a long time, smoking his cigarette and listening to the crash and roar of the Atlantic surf, and thought about all the things that had happened in his life, and how things felt different now. Maybe that was something Aurora had taught him to feel.

And maybe that wasn't such a bad thing.

But nothing could change who he was. He knew that. This was the road he would walk alone, taking him wherever it happened to take him. There would always be another distress call from someone in need of his help. And he would always be there to answer it.

Ben flicked away the stub of his Gauloise and watched it fizz in the rock pool by his feet. Then he stood and started walking back up the shingle beach towards the house. Far overhead a solitary gull floated on the wind, and the rising sun felt warm on his face.

He was home again, until the next time.

AUTHOR'S NOTE

It's often said that truth can be stranger than fiction, and that's certainly the case with the incredible real-life saga of King Richard III, the so-called Pretender 'Perkin Warbeck' and the still unresolved murder mystery surrounding the fate of the missing princes. Of course, for there to be a proper murder mystery, there needs to have been an actual murder committed . . . and if you've read the book you already know that the popular version of the story, derived mainly from William Shakespeare's stylised portrayal of Richard as the ultimate wicked uncle, may well be a long way from the truth of the matter.

Back in 2005 when this novel is set, not even Ben Hope himself could have predicted that just seven years later, in September 2012, thanks to the efforts of real-life heroine Philippa Langley and the Richard III Society, the long lost remains of the king would be rediscovered in Leicester where they had lain buried for centuries under what latterly became a council car park. More recently another unexpected and historically significant event took place, coincidentally as I was nearing completion of this novel: after nearly a hundred years of campaigning by the Richard III Society, new signage at the Tower of London now acknowledges that there is no evidence that Richard had the princes murdered, stating simply that 'We may never know what happened'.

Well, now maybe we do!

For the most part, in writing this novel I stuck as accurately as possible to the verifiable facts. However, eagle-eyed history buffs will have noticed that in a few places I've interwoven some fictitious details for the purposes of the story. One of these is the silver unicorn medallion purportedly worn by Elizabeth, future Queen consort of Henry VII, and later by Perkin Warbeck. That's a product of my own imagination, as is the meeting between her and Perkin, for which there's no historical evidence (though who knows?). The code-breaker Gustav Bergenroth really did exist, but again there's no evidence that he ever decoded a secret letter from Elizabeth proving Perkin's real identity. That, too, was my own addition, so you won't find it in any history books!

There are a couple of other areas where I need to confess to having played a little fast and loose with the historical account: firstly, while it's true that the Earl of Huntly did for a while look favourably on the marriage between Perkin Warbeck and his daughter Lady Catherine Gordon, his wedding gift to them of 'Hartington Abbey' near Berwick-upon-Tweed is my own invention. And last but not least, there's no real evidence at all that the short-lived union between Perkin and Catherine ever resulted in the birth of a secret child. That is also fiction – at least, as far as we know. Such things have been known to happen . . .

For readers interested in learning more about this truly fascinating area of history, I'd strongly encourage joining the Richard III Society, which will open up an Aladdin's cave of information and help support the great work they do. (I'm only sorry that I killed off poor Tony Kitson, who was doing such a fine job of running their York branch.) Also check out Philippa Langley's Missing Princes Project, by visiting the link below. On the book front, *The Survival of the Princes in the Tower* by Matthew Lewis is an excellent source of information and will fill in the many, many gaps and omissions inevitably left by a novel like this one. Additional highly recommended reading includes *The Maligned King* by Annette Carson and *The Mythology of the Princes in the Tower* by the late John Ashdown-Hill.

I hope you enjoyed reading *The Tudor Deception* as much as I enjoyed writing it. Look out for more Ben Hope adventures in the future!

Links:
Richard III Society: www.richardiii.net
The Missing Princes Project: https://revealingrichardiii.com/langley.html